PRAISE FOR

The Silk House

'Buckle up for a spine-tingling story . . . Kayte Nunn deftly switches
between two timelines, weaving her ingenious plot. Beautifully
written with heart-stopping pacing'
The Australian Women's Weekly

'The story carries all the elements of a classic gothic tale . . .
that comes with a thrilling twist in the final pages'
Daily Telegraph

'This spellbinding story intertwines three strong, fearless women in
the pursuit of fulfilling their dreams'
Family Circle

'The ghostly stories of three women who had all spent time at a
mysterious boarding school are beautifully woven together in this
time-hopping and spellbinding tale. An exceptional gothic mystery'
Woman's Day

'From the first page, *The Silk House* seems to cast a spell of
its own . . . an unnerving ghost story and a delight to read'
Weekly Times

'The stories of three fascinating women weave seamlessly together
in this atmospheric book set against the sumptuous backdrop of the
eighteenth-century silk trade. The titular Silk House is at once eerie
and evocative as it leaves its mark on its inhabitants – and as its
influence transcends time to create a mystery that is so compelling
I found myself racing towards the final pages. Utterly spellbinding'
NATASHA LESTER

'*The Silk House* is an elegantly woven ghost story that both chills and delights. I was torn between racing through the chapters as the story unfolded, and holding back to savour the beauty of the prose. Set in an old house that is a character in itself, this evocative tale of mystery and secrets continued to haunt me long after I turned the last page'

JOANNA NELL

'A haunting, atmospheric novel that is near-impossible to put down'

SALLY HEPWORTH

'Kayte Nunn has the gift of creating characters, stories and settings that become as cherished as old friends. Her awareness of humans and their intricacies make her stories relatable. In *The Silk House* she transports us to a fascinating time and place, in the late eighteenth century, and seamlessly brings us back to the present day. This book is the best kind of escapism: thoughtful, colourful and meaningful'

SOPHIE GREEN

PRAISE FOR

The Forgotten Letters of Esther Durrant

'If you enjoyed *City of Girls* by Elizabeth Gilbert, read Kayte Nunn'

The Washington Post

'Nunn's US debut is an engaging, dual-period narrative tracing Esther's journey towards healing and wholeness as well as Rachel's attempts to move beyond her wanderlust and unwillingness to commit to a home, job or relationship. The ending highlights the enduring power of love and forgiveness'

Booklist

'Vivid descriptions highlight intertwining plot lines that seamlessly build to a satisfying climax. For fans of authors such as Lauren Willig and Kate Morton'
Library Journal

PRAISE FOR

The Botanist's Daughter

'Two incredibly likeable, headstrong heroines . . . watching them flourish is captivating. With these dynamic women at the helm, Kayte weaves a clever tale of plant treachery involving exotic and perilous encounters in Chile, plus lashings of gentle romance. Compelling storytelling'
The Australian Women's Weekly

'The riveting story of two women, divided by a century in time, but united by their quest to discover a rare and dangerous flower said to have the power to heal as well as kill. Fast-moving and full of surprises, *The Botanist's Daughter* brings the exotic world of 19th-century Chile thrillingly to life'
KATE FORSYTH

'The whole book is a delight . . . Perfect reading whilst sipping a g & t in a beautiful garden somewhere in the sun'
ROSANNA LEY

'I loved *The Botanist's Daughter*. I was transported to the 1880s and Chile, to contemporary Sydney and Kew. A gripping, warm-hearted read'
JOY RHOADES

The LAST REUNION

The LAST REUNION

KAYTE NUNN

hachette
AUSTRALIA

hachette
AUSTRALIA

Published in Australia and New Zealand in 2021
by Hachette Australia
(an imprint of Hachette Australia Pty Limited)
Level 17, 207 Kent Street, Sydney NSW 2000
www.hachette.com.au

10 9 8 7 6 5 4 3 2 1

NATIONAL
LIBRARY
OF AUSTRALIA
A catalogue record for this
book is available from the
National Library of Australia

ISBN: 978 0 7336 4538 9 (paperback)

Cover design by Christabella Designs
Cover images courtesy of Shutterstock
Author photo by Jane Earle
Typeset in 12.2/18.2 pt Minion Pro by Bookhouse, Sydney
Printed and bound in Australia by McPherson's Printing Group

For Bettina, Penny, Rhonnie and Sue: for your friendship, your kindness, your strength and your vulnerability.

'But when the blast of war blows in our ears,
Then imitate the action of the tiger;
Stiffen the sinews, summon up the blood,
Disguise fair nature with hard-favour'd rage.'

HENRY V, WILLIAM SHAKESPEARE

Author's note

The Burma Campaign of the Second World War has often been referred to as 'The Forgotten War'. The women of the Women's Auxiliary Service – WAS(B) – were recruited from England, India and Australia, and served alongside the soldiers, enduring the same arduous conditions and often operating under enemy fire. They were the closest to the frontline of any servicewomen in the entire war; many were mentioned in dispatches for their bravery and several were decorated at the end of hostilities. According to General Sir William Slim, Commander of the British 14th Army in Burma, these women showed 'the highest standard of devotion and courage'; while, as stated by Admiral of the Fleet, First Earl Mountbatten of Burma, 'living and working in the more uncomfortable conditions [yet] were able to do much to alleviate the hardships of the campaign'.

Yet few have ever heard of them, and almost all of them are now gone from this world. They are the forgotten women of the forgotten war.

ONE

✦

Oxford, 1976

It was the work of a moment; a tiny revenge for a much graver crime. She had never stolen so much as a packet of sweets before. She did not, as a rule, lie, cheat or steal. But this was different.

She wiped a film of sweat from the back of her neck, lifting the damp strands of hair in an effort to cool herself. Her cotton sundress – madras, designed for an Indian climate – clung to her legs, and a blister had formed on her heel from the strap of her sandals. She'd experienced this kind of heat before, had almost forgotten how it sapped the spirits, how it became an act of will to carry on regardless.

She barely noticed the thin strips of grass that had bleached to the colour of bone alongside the pavement, the wilted flowerbeds and the leaves hanging limply from the trees. The summer had sweltered on for forty days without rain. Things were so dire that the government had appointed a Minister for Drought. It was unheard of. Unprecedented. Records had tumbled.

She walked alone, her mind occupied with other matters, on her way to Beaumont Street. In her handbag was the newspaper clipping that had enticed her into the city on such an insufferable August afternoon.

She'd parked her car – a new Rover that purred like a kitten and was a dream to drive – along the wide boulevard of St Giles', a few minutes' walk from the museum. The city was subdued, students and dons long departed, their staircases silent, pigeonholes empty of the swathe of flyers and notes that cluttered them during term time. Tourists punted on the Cherwell with varying degrees of skill, or stopped for a beer in perhaps the Eagle and Child, The Bear or, if they could find it, The Turf. It was too hot to do anything but cool off with liquid of one kind or another.

Reaching the entrance to the Ashmolean, she glanced up at the tall classical columns and slipped gratefully into its frigid embrace. Nodding to the attendant, she cast about, looking for a sign. Her eyes locked on a stand that pointed to the exhibition. *Little Treasures. Netsuke from the Edo period.*

Her heart stuttered for a moment and her breath came in little puffs. 'Are you all right, madam?' the attendant asked as she leaned against the desk to steady herself.

'Yes, yes,' she said, in a voice that didn't sound like hers. 'Quite all right, thank you. The heat, you know.'

The attendant smiled. 'Nice to be in here, then.'

She straightened up, flashed a weak smile in return, then clutched her handbag to her side and walked towards the sign. It stood at the start of a long corridor, and she began to walk faster, the soles of her sandals clicking loudly on the hard floor. She soon came to a halt at a doorway. The room beyond contained glass display cases dotted at intervals along its edges, with a large rectangular case occupying the centre.

She was the only person there.

Moving forward, she started at the left-hand side, scanning each of the cases, the tiny sculptures, searching for the one, the inch-high ivory that she knew as intimately as the freckles on her own skin: the ink-stained carved detail, the tiny flap behind the ear, the winking jet eyes.

She passed a carved cherry-wood snail, an octopus hiding its face behind twisted tentacles, a wide-eyed goldfish, two milky quails with tiny amber stones for eyes perched on a bed of millet, a wasp settled on a half-eaten pear carved from bamboo, a frog peering out from inside a sycamore key . . .

All remarkable in their own right, but not the one she sought.

Then, suddenly, there it was.

The fox-girl. Cleverly lit from underneath so that it seemed to glow of its own accord, luminous against the coal-black backdrop.

She held her breath and peered into the case, examining the tiny form for clues. There . . . there was the infinitesimal scratch on the right cheek, the worn skirt where a thumb must have rubbed it a thousand times over.

As she leaned against the glass, its bevelled edge slipped on the wooden case beneath and she sprang back as if it had given her an electric shock. She glanced around, but the room was still empty. Silent.

From then on, until she left the museum a few short minutes later, she felt as though she had stepped outside of herself, as though it were someone else's index finger that pushed the glass once more, as it moved half an inch across the felt, grated slightly on the wood.

It was the work of a moment to lift the glass with the tips of her lacquered nails and slide her other hand underneath, feeling the ivory ridges against her skin.

She took seven in all: the octopus, the birds, a curled-up cat licking its paw, an ivory camellia, a tiny dragon and of course, the fox-girl. She wanted to make it look like a common-or-garden theft, that no one piece was more important than another.

She dropped six of them into her open handbag, but she couldn't let go of the fox-girl, curling her fingers tightly around it, her hand a fist, the netsuke's edges hard against her palm. The sweat had dried on the back of her neck and she shivered, as though the earlier heat had been hours rather than minutes ago.

Using her nails again, she pulled the glass back into place and turned to leave, her heart thrumming like a tabla. As if in a dream, she floated past the attendant and emerged into the light where the day hit her with the force of a firecracker, its white heat blinding.

She'd walked two hundred yards along St Giles' before she let herself breathe out, half-expecting to hear sirens at any moment, to feel a firm hand clap on her shoulder.

Ignoring the curious stares as she entered the front bar of the Eagle and Child, she ordered a half-pint of shandy, drinking it almost straight down and then asking for another.

~

Two days later, there it was, on page four of *The Times*, in a narrow column, below the fold.

Stolen: seven rare and valuable netsuke

On 20 August, from the Ashmolean Museum, Oxford. Douglas Pullman, curator of Asian artefacts at the museum, believes professionals carried out the theft of the Japanese netsuke, as it went undetected for several hours and the locked display case was undamaged.

She made a slight scoffing sound in the back of her throat. The case hadn't been locked. She read on:

Among them was the famed 'fox-girl', dating from the eighteenth century. A reward of twenty thousand pounds is offered for information leading to their recovery. 'Collectively, the current worth of these netsuke can be estimated to be in the region of one hundred and fifty thousand pounds,' said Mr Pullman. 'However, they are well documented, so will prove difficult to sell, unless the thieves have found a buyer with no scruples as to owning them. It is likely these pieces will stay hidden from sight for quite some time.'

The woman refolded the newspaper, placed it on the table in front of her and began to spread marmalade on her toast, a quiet smile tugging at her lips.

TWO

✥

London, 1999

'Behind every successful woman . . .'

Olivia struggled through the door to the office, furling her sodden umbrella, and winced at the stream of water that was rapidly soaking the expensive carpet, darkening the plush dove grey.

. . . is an unappreciated, unpaid assistant who works her butt off for little reward.

'. . . stands a man. Sulking,' she said instead, finishing the sentence for her boss.

'Oh jolly good,' said Elaine. 'You've hit the nail on the head.'

Olivia held her tongue, allowing Elaine to gloat, and to explain. She'd lay bets the bonhomie wouldn't last past lunchtime, but nevertheless she was curious about the cause.

'The sale,' Elaine said, a note of impatience creeping into her voice. 'Last night at Bonham's. Smashed the reserve on the lacquerware; the *inro* did particularly well. It's one in the eye for Martinson.' She leaned so far back on her swivel chair that Olivia was worried she might catapult through the window behind her, but Elaine stopped herself just before the point of no return.

'I suppose it is,' said Olivia.

Jeffrey Martinson was Elaine's arch-rival. The only other London-based independent dealer in Asian art, and although on the several occasions Olivia had met him she had found him perfectly pleasant, a frosty encounter between her boss and Jeffrey had shown her that he and Elaine could barely stand to be in the same room.

She'd only just started the job and had been full of excitement at attending her first London sale. As they walked into the room, Martinson had held the door open for them, greeting Elaine warmly. Olivia had been taken aback to see her boss sweep through the doors with not a word of acknowledgment, leaving Olivia trailing in her wake.

'Oh, don't mind her, darling,' he whispered to her. 'She's hated me since I supposedly poached one of her best clients. Of course I did no such thing.'

'Somehow that doesn't surprise me,' said Olivia dryly, putting a hand to her mouth as if she'd said more than she should have.

Martinson rewarded her with a knowing smile as he smoothed back his already immaculately pomaded hair and adjusted the lapels of his jacket.

Elaine hadn't exactly said as much, but Olivia was aware that it wouldn't help her career prospects if she were seen to fraternise with the enemy, however cordial he might be. After that, whenever she attended a sale, she made sure not to be seen talking to Martinson, in Elaine's presence at least, though he always gave her an acknowledging nod or subtle wave.

Elaine kept a tight control of the activities, proceeds and staff of her eponymous company, Cholmondeley's (pronounced 'Chumley' in that peculiar, posh English way of eliminating entire syllables from certain words), guarding her clients fiercely and keeping potential vendors even closer. It was undoubtedly the reason she had been so successful, building up the two-and-a-half-person agency (in addition to Elaine and Olivia, Reg the accountant came in one day a week) over nearly three decades until it was one of the country's most respected, albeit one of the smallest. 'Niche. Boutique. Expert and absolutely discreet,' Elaine had said when she interviewed Olivia.

'Anyway, you're late.' Olivia was jerked back to the present as Elaine narrowed her eyes accusingly.

'*Religieuse*?' Olivia offered, swallowing a tickle in her throat and hoping to placate her boss with her favourite pastry. 'They're from that place you like. The new one near Sloane Square. *Le Merveilleux*.' She'd been delayed not only by the detour to the patisserie but, more importantly, by a phone call from Brand's, an art-detection agency that had contacted her – in the strictest confidence – shortly after she joined Cholmondeley's. She knew better than to mention the latter reason. 'It's bucketing down outside, so I can't vouch for the state of them.'

'You'll make me fat,' Elaine replied, before relenting. 'Oh, go on then. Put it on a plate, won't you? A coffee wouldn't go amiss either. *Cafetière*, not that instant muck.'

Olivia, who by this time had unbuttoned her coat and hung it on the hat stand by the door, walked the four steps to the tiny kitchenette and flicked on the kettle, pulling a tissue from a box on the side as her nose began to run. She blew noisily and hoped she wasn't coming down with something; she couldn't afford to be sick.

The offices were the ground floor of a tiny mews house – originally built as stables – in Belgravia. When Olivia first saw it, she had sighed and gone quite limp at the perfection of the cobbled lane, the white-painted square window frames and the pretty window boxes overflowing with pink geraniums. It was everything she'd imagined a hidden corner of London might be, dreaming about it from her girlhood bedroom on the other side of the world.

Three months of tedious day-to-day tasks, of working two jobs (the other at a bar in the evenings and at weekends that actually paid her rent) and of not putting her education – a degree in art history and a Masters in Asian art – to full use hadn't tarnished the shine of living in the city. 'It's an internship,' Elaine had said, as if that excused the requirement to offer a salary. 'With a view to a permanent role, if things work out.' It was a vague promise, but Olivia remained hopeful. She ignored the occasional flicker of guilt at the retainer she received from Brand's. The art-detection agency had suggested what they referred to obliquely as an 'arrangement'. They paid her a trifling amount, but it helped with the rent on her dingy South London bedsit. All they asked was that she keep her eyes open and if she came across a hint of anything dodgy, to pass on the information. She was morally opposed to stolen art, so it made for an easy decision; and besides, a girl had to do what she could to get by.

Occasionally Elaine allowed her to handle the rare, precious artefacts. As she stroked shiny lacquer undimmed by the centuries, or polished a piece of carved jade, she liked to imagine their creator, working away in a small, cluttered workshop, hopeful that someone might find their art beautiful and desirable, oblivious to the fact that they would one day command stratospheric prices across the world, that they might be fought over at auction, stolen from galleries and private collections, or disappear in the chaos of war and unrest.

Elaine gave Olivia the title of assistant, though they both knew that she was over-qualified for the job. What it actually boiled down to was general dogsbody: maker of hot drinks, opener of letters, licker of stamps, occasional organiser of Elaine's personal life, and – Olivia's pet hate – filer of every document that came into the office, of which there were far too many. She probably could have secured a more senior position at another dealer, though it was a small industry and there weren't many specialists, even in London. But Cholmondeley's was one of the best, particularly when it came to Asian art, and she'd bargained with herself that the experience would be invaluable even if the pay was, for the time being, non-existent.

Olivia had stopped at the patisserie aiming to sweeten Elaine up before she raised the subject of a three-month review. She delivered the cream and choux pastry – not dissimilar in shape to Elaine's well-upholstered frame – on a Meissen plate, setting down a matching cup and saucer. She inched aside a raft of papers to make space on Elaine's desk, the surface of which always looked as though a hurricane had swept through in the night. She had made the mistake of tidying the wide expanse of mahogany only once; not something she would repeat. 'Now I can't find a bloody thing,' Elaine had fumed at the time and Olivia feared she might dismiss her on the spot.

She stood back now and was on the point of opening her mouth to ask the question she had been silently practising on the way into work, but the phone trilled and she was left gawping like a goldfish. Elaine glared at the handset in front of her and reached for the pastry. 'Get that, will you, please?'

Olivia retreated to the front office and picked up her extension. 'It's Mr Berkeley, about last night's sale,' she called out, after placing him on hold.

Elaine waved to her to put it through and Olivia could see her lean back on her chair once again, settling in for a congratulatory chat with one of her most lucrative clients.

Olivia went to her desk and turned on her computer. A filing tray on her desk almost overflowed with paperwork and she promised herself – again – that today would be the day she tackled it. The filing was stored at the back of the office in an airless, windowless box room that smelled of dust and old books. Twelve filing cabinets left scarcely enough space to open the drawers. It wasn't a pleasant place.

Olivia had just bitten into a Rich Tea when the phone rang again; a red light indicated that Elaine was still on one of the other lines. 'Good morning, Cholmondeley's,' she said, her voice muffled by a mouthful of crumbs.

'What's that? I say, do speak up!' said an imperious-sounding woman's voice on the other end.

'Sorry,' Olivia said, swallowing hurriedly. 'This is Cholmondeley's. How may I help you?'

'Elaine. Is she there?' The accent was as crisp and precise as a blade.

'I'm sorry, Elaine's in a meeting.' Elaine's preferred line. 'May I take a message?'

'Oh drat. Ouch. Get down, will you?'

'I'm sorry?'

'I'm sitting with a lapful of puppies.' A series of yips and whines echoed down the line. 'Bette had her litter overnight. Five of the blessed whelps. Took me quite by surprise.'

The woman's tone was neither pleased nor annoyed, and Olivia wasn't sure whether to offer congratulations or commiserations.

'You're new, aren't you? Australian?' the voice prompted.

'Er, yes . . .'

The woman rattled on. 'Charming accent. You sound just like an old friend of mine. Now, where was I? Oh yes. Listen, dear, tell Elaine that Beatrix has decided to sell. The netsuke. Including—' There was a rustle and another series of yips, a muffled curse as the woman dropped the phone. 'The fox-girl,' she added, *sotto voce*.

A piece of biscuit caught in Olivia's throat and she had to hold the phone away from her mouth as she coughed to dislodge it. Despite the heat pumping out from the radiator, a chill ran through her, giving her goose bumps beneath her sweater.

Had she heard correctly?

'I say, are you there?'

Olivia gathered her wits. 'Yes, Mrs . . .'

'Pelham. Beatrix Pelham.' The woman spelled it out as Olivia wrote it down on a sticky note. 'Elaine has my number.'

There was a click as the woman hung up and Olivia was left staring at the words she'd written.

The fox-girl. Possibly the rarest netsuke ever carved. Certainly the most valuable. Olivia clearly remembered the day she first saw a netsuke; she was a teenager, and they featured in the pages of an old book her father had owned on Japanese art. He'd pointed out the fox-girl as one of his favourites. Made from creamy ivory stained with ink, it depicted the figure of a girl wrapped in a cape, the hood of which had fallen down to reveal the face of a fox. As she studied it, her father told her the story of the *kitsune* of Japanese mythology, a wise old fox that was said to be able to assume the form of a beautiful girl who would seduce a man before eating his liver or heart. She had been immediately fascinated by the rather gruesome legend; looking back, it had been partly responsible for propelling her towards studying Asian art for her Master's.

Later, as a first-year student, Olivia had come across a grainy black-and-white photograph of the fox-girl, taken sometime in the seventies when it was loaned as part of an exhibition at the Ashmolean in Oxford. It was, like all netsuke, small enough to fit in the palm and carved 'in the round', in three dimensions. Attributed to master carver Gechu, who was thought to have lived in Osaka, and fashioned in the late eighteenth or early nineteenth century.

The Rolex watch of its time.

Late one sultry summer afternoon a thief or thieves had forced open the locks on one of the glass cases where the fox-girl, and several other rare and valuable netsuke, were displayed and made off with them before an alarm could be raised, so the newspapers stated.

The fox-girl had not been seen since, though rumours of its whereabouts had swirled for decades. Reports had occasionally surfaced of sightings in private collections as far flung as Tokyo, New York, even here in London, but each time they had turned out to be false, generally inferior reproduction copies, or netsuke in a similar style but lacking the delicacy and finesse of the original.

She'd been intrigued to learn that netsuke, the toggles traditionally used by Japanese men to secure small containers to their *obi* (the wide sash that wrapped around their kimonos), had become, by the twentieth century, highly collectable artefacts. Generally no bigger than a couple of inches, they were often exquisite three-dimensional reproductions of fruits, animals, mythical creatures, even gods, and could be carved from cherry wood, ivory or even nuts. 'They feature two carved channels or holes by which the *inro* (container) cord is secured,' her father had explained. 'The *netsukishi*'s skill at placing these is almost as important as their mastery of form.'

As she thought about the fox-girl, her hand strayed to the thin leather cord of her necklace through which was fastened the one netsuke she owned. It wasn't a pretty creature, featuring the trunk and tusks of an elephant, the eyes of a rhinoceros and the tail of a cow, but it was a *baku* – a chimera said to swallow bad dreams. It had been a graduation gift from her parents and she had worn it like a talisman ever since.

She glanced down at the note again, tore it from her pad and went into Elaine's office. Her boss was still on the phone, her chair now turned to face the window and her back to Olivia. She stuck the note where Elaine would be most likely to see it, on top of a pile of other notes, some of which were so old they featured the sun-faded, curving script of Olivia's predecessor.

Instead of returning to her desk, she picked up the overflowing basket of paperwork and walked down the corridor. If Elaine should ask, she would have a cast-iron reason for being in the filing room.

When she was there, she dumped the basket on top of one of the cabinets and went to the drawer marked N–Q then riffled through its contents until she found the file marked 'Pelham'. The initials 'MOB' were cryptically scrawled in pencil on the top.

She found a space on the floor to sit, drew up her knees and leaned against one of the cabinets before opening the file. She could feel herself holding her breath as she began to scan the contents, searching for any mention of the fox-girl. Could the secret of its whereabouts, unseen for twenty-odd years, rest somewhere within these dusty manila covers?

THREE

⚜

Calcutta, 1944

Beatrix Fitzgibbon leaned towards the mirror of the powder room at The Calcutta Club, dabbed at a smudge of lipstick, smoothed an errant curl into place and frowned at her reflection. Cool aquamarine eyes looked back at her, set below straight brows and a wide, high forehead. Her hair, once ginger but now – thank heavens – a dark fox-red, kinked at the slightest humidity, but her skin was fair and clear. (Mother swore by Pond's Cold Cream and insisted on a parasol if going outdoors, for they both tended to freckle.) She had inherited her father's determined chin, and although it looked better on her twin brother, Archie, than it did on her, she wasn't one to dwell on such matters.

This was the third such luncheon she had attended in the past month; each time with the same women, the same conversations, the same gossip. The tedium was enough to make her yawn, though of course she'd been brought up not to do such a thing in polite company. With each day – and each social obligation – that passed she longed to do something more useful with her time, especially since her brother had gone off to war the year before.

'Oh, there you are.' A blast of noise and a fug of heat invaded the room, followed by the whiff of perfume – Schiaparelli's Shocking she hazarded, smelling cloves, cinnamon and jasmine – and cigarette smoke.

Plum Vellacourt, the emptiest head of the lot of them. Loud, frivolous and flighty, shallower than a goldfish pond and with a tendency to chase anything in a uniform. Stories circulated of her out late at night in neighbourhoods no self-respecting Englishwoman should be, and she always looked as if she were having far too much fun while others shouldered the whole business of being at war. Although mostly irritated by her, Bea was sometimes filled with envy that Plum could take life so lightly, as if it were all a game and they were, of course, on the winning side. Her own approach to things was far more serious, especially since Archie had left and brought the possibility of loss much closer to home.

Bea dried her hands on a towel and made to leave.

'Have you heard? I'm joining up!' Plum danced around the room, shimmying her hips to an imaginary band and gleefully saluting herself in the mirror.

'I'm sorry?' Bea asked, thinking immediately of her brother, how jaunty he had been when he first appeared in his uniform. It had been weeks since his last letter, and though she'd pored over the words, she'd been unable to get a proper sense of his new life. Like most men, he rarely expressed his emotions, especially on paper.

'Joining up,' Plum repeated. 'A few of us are. Bubbles Morgan-Jones, Lydia, Marie . . . There's a woman, Captain Nin Taylor, running an outfit called the Wasbies. According to Lydia they're the closest to the frontline any women can get.' She hiccoughed gently, grabbing the basin nearest to her for support. Bea had heard stories of terrible rationing back home in England, but at The Calcutta Club the champagne continued to flow unchecked.

She arched an eyebrow and met Plum's china-doll gaze in the mirror, quelling the flicker of jealousy that her words had ignited at the mention of joining the war. 'The Wasbies? What precisely do they do?'

'Canteens, I think. Or something like that. Sounds like it'll be a lark. Get me out of Calcutta, anyway. I'm going for an interview in the morning, but I've heard they'll take almost anyone who's fit enough. How about you, Bea?' Plum looked at her from beneath thickly fringed eyelashes. 'Fancy it? Or would your mother rather keep at least one of you by her side?' The corners of her mouth turned down and her blue eyes filled with false sympathy. Bea bristled, as she so often did whenever Plum spoke to her in that faintly patronising tone. The woman had an uncanny knack of rubbing her up the wrong way and it took all of her good manners not to bite back with a stinging retort, though there were plenty that could have formed on her lips if she'd allowed them.

'I'd better go and finish my drink,' Plum trilled, tossing her blonde hair and seemingly unperturbed by Bea's lack of response. 'After tomorrow, who knows when there'll be another?'

Bea could swear the young woman's restless energy still hung in the powder-room air after she left. Certainly her perfume did. She glanced at her watch. Mother was waiting for her at a table on the other side of the door, most likely pulling on her lace gloves in anticipation of leaving the club. Bea collected the handbag she'd left next to the basin, sighed and returned to the luncheon.

The bombing of Calcutta had stopped last year, once the Japanese had diverted their fighters elsewhere and the blackout had been lifted, though barrage balloons still hung in the skies over the city to deter any further attacks. They had removed the brown paper covering their windows, and Bea no longer woke in the morning wondering which of the city's buildings might have been reduced to rubble, the stone colonnades sheared off, roofs at incongruous angles.

During the bombing, many locals had fled the city, and fewer hawkers – selling fruit and vegetables, bread and even toffee – called at their door. For the Fitzgibbons and others like them, however, life had returned to a kind of normal, though Bea knew well enough that they were largely removed from the harsh realities of war. While the threat of imminent danger had worn off, so too had the feeling of at least being a part of things, in the midst of it all, if not actively fighting then at least bravely enduring.

Bea had resigned herself to sitting out the war contributing nothing more than rolling bandages with her mother and – with precious little enthusiasm, it must be said – attending secretarial college, while her father and brother served in the British Indian Army. It was hard to be apart from Archie especially, and so many passages of his occasional letters were blacked out by the censor that very little was left to glean from them, and she had to rely on her imagination to fill the gaps.

She often thought of the day he left, creases still in his uniform trousers, hair clipped so short it left a white stripe on the back of his neck. The proud look on their parents' faces. The sickness in her own heart that was part envy, part fear for his safety, which she did her best to cover up with a brave smile.

'Don't look so glum, Beebee,' he'd chided, for he had seen straight through her. 'I'll be back before you know it, safe and sound and just the same as always.'

She'd nearly lost her cool then, begged him not to leave her, but of course she couldn't. He'd pulled on a lock of her hair and crushed her with a bear hug, lifting her off her feet and making her squeal. If only she could feel his arms around her again now.

'Oh darling, there you are.' Her mother beamed as Bea returned to the table. 'Ready?'

As they were leaving, Plum and Lydia approached, arms curved lightly about each other's waists, foreheads almost touching as they shared a private joke.

'Oh, Mrs Fitzgibbon,' said Plum, still giggling. 'I was just telling Bea the exciting news.'

'What's that, my dear?'

'We're signing up. It's the chance to do our bit at last. It sounds completely thrilling: we'll be driving trucks of supplies out to the men in the thick of the action. We're going along to the Army HQ tomorrow to meet Mrs – sorry, Captain – Taylor. See if she'll have us.'

'Good for you both,' Bea's mother replied staunchly. 'Of course they will, two fine young women. They'd be mad not to take you.'

'Do you wish Bea might go too?' Lydia asked.

'I confess this is the first I've heard of it, so you've not given me much time to form an opinion.' She smiled indulgently at the two young women. 'In any case, I suppose that is largely up to her.'

Bea shrugged. 'Really, I . . .' she stuttered. 'I thought you needed me here, Mother.'

'Come on, Bea, it'll be *such* fun if we all go,' Lydia pleaded.

'I'm really not sure . . .' The prospect of spending any more time with Plum and Lydia than she already had to didn't hold much appeal. There was the chance, though, however slight, that it might take her closer to wherever Archie was stationed. Besides, she was itching to do something more useful than pack surgical dressings. She couldn't bring herself to admit to the two of them that she was interested.

'I can manage perfectly well by myself, you know, if that's what you're worried about,' her mother said later, as they walked home. In the distance, Bea watched three or four young boys with kites. They coated the strings with powdered glass, and the game was to cut down their rivals until only the victor's kite remained. They ran and shouted, oblivious to everything but waging their own battles in the sky. Everyone wanted to fight, it seemed.

'With Father, Archie and me gone, you'd be left on your own. In all good conscience, I couldn't do that, Mother,' Bea insisted.

'Nonsense, darling. I have my friends. I'm an Army wife, don't forget; I'm quite used to being on my own. And Jeet can always move into one of the rooms off the kitchen. I'll be fine.'

Bea bit back a grin at the idea of their houseboy, Jeet – sixty if he was a day, reaching Bea's shoulder and weighing, she guessed, less than seven stone dripping wet – taking on an intruder. 'But it might be dangerous,' she said, though in truth she was more excited than scared by the prospect.

'Oh, poppycock! I very much doubt the British Army would send women into the heat of battle.'

'You've given it some thought, then,' Bea replied, a note of amusement in her voice.

'Don't tell me you haven't,' she said, resting a hand on her daughter's shoulder. 'You've been away with the fairies since we left the club. I *do* notice things. I know it wasn't exactly your first choice to be stuck at home with me.'

Bea registered her mother's encouraging expression and decided in that moment to put herself forward. If Archie could do it, why couldn't she? For one thing, it meant she wouldn't have to return to secretarial college. The thought of not having to spend another day learning shorthand brought an involuntary grin to her face.

Not for a second did she entertain a concern that they might not want her. Bea had been wanted all her life: doted on by her *amah*, cherished by her parents (though they did send her back to England to boarding school from the age of seven until she was eighteen; the one cloud on the otherwise sunny horizon of her childhood), spoiled by her numerous aunts and uncles, teased by her adoring brother.

Head girl, hockey captain and a whizz at tennis, badminton, croquet and any number of card games. Accomplished horsewoman. When she paused to think of herself – which was not often, for she was not the type given to deep introspection – it was as a jolly good sort, a sensible girl who could cope in a crisis, could be relied on in a pinch, rarely flustered. She said as much to Captain Taylor when she met her at the barracks the next day, trying not to feel as though she was boasting. She omitted to mention that she wasn't much of a cook, for there was no sense in focusing on the negatives.

There had been a line of women waiting to be interviewed when she arrived on the dot of nine. Her starched, striped cotton frock, which had seemed so fresh when she'd put it on an hour or so before, had already wilted in the muggy heat that enveloped the city. Monsoons were expected at any moment, and the sky had begun to darken, the air growing heavy. She spotted Plum and Lydia ahead of her, but she skulked at the back of the queue. She didn't want to be seen by them, at least not until she found out more about this madcap idea.

'Miss Fitzgibbon.' Captain Taylor's smile did not reach her eyes, which remained a cool, appraising grey. 'Captain of the First Eleven,' she said, reading from Bea's hastily filled-in application form. 'I take it you are still fit?'

Bea nodded. 'I ride as often as I can.'

'Good, good. You'll need plenty of stamina. It's not exactly going to be a picnic, you know.' She stared hard, as if taking Bea's measure. 'We need the right sort of woman.'

Bea had never wanted to be the right sort of woman more than she did in that moment. 'If you please, ma'am . . .'

Captain Taylor's gimlet gaze momentarily softened. Bea had taken note when one of the soldiers addressed her as such and had followed suit.

'I'm not afraid of mucking in,' she said confidently. 'Or roughing it. I've often camped with my brother in the school holidays, that sort of thing.' She tried not to wince at how lame that sounded, for tramping in the Lake District hardly compared to forcing one's way through thick jungle, under enemy fire, did it?

Captain Taylor didn't seem to have noticed. 'A brother?'

'Twin, ma'am. He's serving, though I'm not allowed to know where.'

Archie was an officer in the Signals – she hadn't the faintest idea of his current whereabouts, though privately she suspected he might be in Burma. It was a large part of why she'd decided to join up, for she missed him like only one half of a whole could.

Not that they'd always got along. In fact, her early childhood had mostly been spent in an effort to keep up with him, of suffering the consequences of a series of pranks at her expense, with the corresponding scars to prove it. Remembering, she absentmindedly rubbed the divot on her elbow. They'd been out riding, hacking through the countryside in the gold-tipped light of late afternoon, not far from their grandparents' house in Kent, when they came upon a beech hedge blocking their path. Bea slowed her pony to a walk and sidled alongside it, looking for a way through. 'Don't be a chicken,' Archie called from a way behind her. 'Domino will get over that easily.'

The sun disappeared behind a cloud and as the light changed Bea felt a moment of doubt descend. 'No thanks,' she said, gripping the reins and pulling her horse around and back in the direction they had come. 'It's getting late anyway.'

Archie ignored her and raced his horse towards the hedge, jumping up and over with a careless grace, landing neatly on the other side. 'Easy-peasy,' he called out to her, his voice travelling towards her on the breeze.

Bea was a better rider than her twin, but her mount was smaller and she'd never jumped her over anything nearly so big. However, if Archie had done it, then she didn't allow herself the option of not following his lead. With a mix of annoyance and trepidation, she swung Domino around and away to give herself enough of a run-up, then kicked her into a canter, doing her best to judge the distance to the hedge.

Her heart lifted into her throat and she hung on with all her might as the mare gathered herself and made a heroic effort to clear the hedge. They sailed over, clipping the top of it and landing heavily on the other side. Domino stumbled, but caught herself as Bea fell forward onto the horse's neck.

'I can't believe you made me do that,' she puffed, pulling up beside Archie, annoyed and pleased with herself all at the same time.

'Told you, you could,' he grinned back.

The damage to her elbow came later on that ride, as she misjudged a tree branch and it scratched a great chunk out of her, but she always associated the scar with that heart-stopping moment of flight.

'Quite. Quite.' Captain Taylor's voice broke through her thoughts. 'You'll be used to the rough and tumble of male company then. Know how to handle yourself.'

Bea nodded.

'You are very young. But most of you boarding-school girls are used to putting up with a bit of hardship. Resourceful too.'

'And resilient, ma'am,' Bea ventured.

Captain Taylor pursed her lips, as if unsure whether or not to believe Bea. 'Higher School Certificate?' she asked, her pencil moving down the form.

'With distinction,' said Bea. She couldn't keep herself from boasting. 'Top of the year in maths.'

'Excellent. We need someone in each team with a head for numbers.' Captain Taylor toyed with her pencil.

'I don't suppose you can drive a truck?'

Bea shook her head.

'Oh well, not to worry; there'll be others who can, and there'll be training too. You'll need to pass a medical, and have a few jabs. But all of that being well, we'd be very glad of you.' She marked the bottom of the form with a neat signature and handed it to her. 'See the sergeant on the way out. He'll point you in the direction of the MO.'

'MO?'

'Medical officer.' She looked up from her desk and waved Bea out. 'Send in the next one, won't you?'

The entire interview had taken no more than fifteen minutes.

Half an hour later, Bea emerged from the barracks with a sore upper arm from the various immunisations they'd given her – yellow fever as well as smallpox – and clutching a handful of forms that confirmed her as formally enlisted in the Women's Auxiliary Service (Burma), and a large canvas kitbag, which together with a tin trunk she was to use to pack her essentials. The line of women outside Captain Taylor's office had, if anything, grown longer.

'It won't all be difficult,' Captain Taylor had added before Bea left her office. 'Part of the job is keeping the men's morale up, and there'll be dances and whatnot that I am sure you will enjoy.'

Bea's enthusiasm faltered for the first time. She hadn't intended joining the Army so she could Palais Glide her way through the war, but before she could raise an objection, Captain Taylor had handed her the enlistment papers.

Bea was to take the train to Guwahati and then on by road to Shillong, a hill station in Assam to the north-east where the Wasbies were headquartered. Beyond that, she hadn't the faintest idea what she had let herself in for.

Shaking off the feeling of having jumped straight off a cliff, she broke into as decorous a run as she could manage, heading for home before the rain began to sluice down. Would Plum and the others be on the platform the next morning? Perhaps – and this was a far more appealing prospect – she might even come across Archie again somewhere out there.

FOUR

❧❖❧

London, 1999

'I'm afraid you will have to go.'

Olivia nearly spilled the cup of coffee she was holding. She'd emerged from the file room after about twenty minutes, figuring if she was gone for longer, Elaine might miss her and start to bellow. The Pelham file had contained faded carbon copies of correspondence between Sir William Pelham and Elaine, going back some thirty years. It appeared Cholmondeley's had acted for Sir William off and on, acquiring a number of pieces from the Han and Song periods for him. More recently, Elaine had sold several Qing Dynasty porcelains, on behalf of Mrs Pelham. Over the years, there had been half a dozen previous netsuke purchases – all animals – on behalf of the Pelhams, which told Olivia they had once been collectors.

When she got back to her desk she had run a search on anything related to the fox-girl, not expecting to find much. The first couple of sites didn't tell her anything she didn't already know; even *Asian Art Monthly* had only a brief paragraph mentioning the theft. Then she went to the Ashmolean site. When it eventually loaded, she found a photograph of the netsuke and a link to another site, and as she clicked on that it came up with a plain screen on which were the words: 'Reward offered. Twenty thousand pounds for information leading to the return of the fox-girl.'

She stifled a gasp and scanned the rest of the page. There wasn't much. A phone number, no name. That was it, nothing more.

Twenty thousand pounds.

It was a lot of money in the 1970s; still was, to her anyway.

She didn't know yet if Beatrix Pelham really did have the original, the stolen one. It could just as easily be one of the fakes that were known to exist.

'Olivia, are you listening to me?'

'I'm sorry? Go?' She imagined for a single, heart-stopping moment that Elaine was dismissing her. 'Go where?'

'To Pelham House, of course. To appraise the fox-girl. And at once. I can't risk Beatrix changing her mind. Write up a condition report as well.' Elaine studied her, as if deciding whether or not she could trust Olivia with the responsibility. 'It's in Wiltshire. You'll need to take the train from Paddington. Pewsey's the nearest station. Here—' She held out a piece of paper on which Olivia could see a two-line address scrawled, together with a fifty-pound note. 'See if there's a train this afternoon. This should more than cover the fare, and a taxi once you get there.'

'But it's three days before Christmas.'

'Exactly,' said Elaine, tapping her pen on a notepad impatiently. 'Even more reason why we should get a move on. Can't risk anyone talking her out of it over the holiday. And anyway, I'm off to the Canaries tomorrow and can't possibly get down there myself; there's simply too much to do here. Don't bother to come in on Christmas Eve. I shan't be here in any case.' She smiled at Olivia as if she'd done her the most enormous favour (something that should have set off an alarm then and there, for Elaine rarely smiled), then looked back towards her office and the chaos on her desk. 'Now, do be certain to stay on the right side of her, she's a mad old bag . . .'

MOB. The meaning of the cryptic letters on the front of the file suddenly became clear. As did the reason Elaine was so keen to hand the job over to Olivia.

'But if she decides she likes you she'll be as sweet as pie. I hope you like dogs. The old woman's completely bonkers about them.' She pursed her lips in distaste.

Olivia nodded. 'But *the* fox-girl? Really?'

Elaine gave her a conspiratorial look. 'I've had a feeling for *years* that they've been hiding something. And it sort of makes sense. Her husband was the type.'

'The type?'

'The kind of man who *wants*. Wants to possess things. Believe me, I've met enough of them over the years. Some of my best clients, in fact. They assembled a collection of several dozen netsuke, though I've no idea how they came to have the fox-girl. It certainly wasn't through me. You'll need to make sure

30

Beatrix can demonstrate provenance. If she doesn't have that; it's game over.'

They both knew there were ways of selling things on the quiet, but certainly Elaine hadn't given any hint that she was likely to get involved in such a practice or didn't trust Olivia enough to let her in on it.

'Of course.' Olivia had plenty more questions, including what had happened to Sir William, but Elaine issued a barrage of further instructions, hustling her out of the office before she had a chance to enquire further. 'And if she does have provenance, don't come back without a commitment to Cholmondeley's,' were her final words.

Olivia dodged the station crowds, narrowly avoiding a clash with a tired-looking woman wielding an armful of bulging shopping bags. The concourse was thronged with people, most of whom seemed to be heading off early on their Christmas break and were lugging suitcases and backpacks of all shapes and sizes, adding to the chaotic, end-of-term feel. Olivia still couldn't get her head around the fact that it was the festive season, despite the carols playing over the tannoy and the tinsel decorating the windows of the shops. It was a long way from her experience of Christmas at home, which revolved around seafood and sunshine somewhere on the coast with her parents, aunt and uncle, and assorted cousins. Early-morning swims, sultry afternoons of board games and naps, and a stack of well-thumbed paperbacks were the order of the day. Shoes – apart from an old pair of thongs – were entirely superfluous. Just thinking about it made her homesick.

She planned to get the 12.30 service, hoping to return on the 6.30, the last of the day. It was about an hour and a half to Pewsey, and then, according to Elaine, about ten miles to Pelham House.

Olivia's nose was still running and the earlier tickle in her throat had ratcheted to sandpaper level, so she bought cough lollies along with a packet of sandwiches from a kiosk in the cavernous arrivals and departures hall, then turned to check the huge, flickering departures board to see what platform she needed.

She was out cold almost before the train pulled out of the station, her head lolling back on the headrest. What felt like only moments later, she was woken by the insistent musical ringtone of her phone. She gazed at it blearily, not registering that her thigh was resting up against that of the man sitting next to her. Embarrassed, she hastily moved it away and answered the call.

'Liv?'

It was Rob, the co-owner of Blinder, the bar where she worked in the evenings.

'Yes?'

'Hiya love. Giving you a bell to let you know that we're offering you a lovely break over Christmas,' he said, in a tone that sounded falsely upbeat. 'What with all this end-of-the-world, millennium palaver, we're cutting back on staff.'

She didn't believe it for a minute; she knew that she was being blamed for getting one of their best customers off-side. She'd slapped the man's hands away after he'd brushed up against her one too many times, hissing that if he so much as breathed near her again she'd kick his balls into next Tuesday. She'd worked in enough pubs as a student to have come across men like him before and had learned that the only way to deal with them was never to show weakness or fear.

She ended the call and groaned out loud before erupting into a sneeze, causing several of the carriage's other passengers to look up from their newspapers and books and at least one of them to tut disapprovingly. The sandpaper in her throat had now ramped up to razor-blade level and she rummaged in her handbag for a cherry lozenge, popping it in her mouth and settling back into the seat.

Try as she might she couldn't go back to sleep again, and instead gazed blankly out of the window. Sooty back ends of buildings had given way to grey–green sweeping hillsides cut occasionally by the winding ribbon of a road. Telegraph poles flew by, spindles etched black against the cloud, and the train chuntered and juddered in a soothing rhythm. It was only early afternoon, but the winter darkness wasn't far away. She felt a sharp pang as she imagined what her family would be doing, halfway across the world. Sand beneath their toes, ocean dips, fresh mangoes and thick slices of wood-fired bread for breakfast, evening drinks beaded with condensation, buckets of prawns and lemon-spiked mayonnaise, salty skin and suntans . . . tears pricked at her eyelids. She must be coming down with something, for she didn't normally feel quite so sorry for herself.

Distraction arrived in the shape of the ticket collector, who clipped her day return and informed her that Pewsey was the next stop.

She shivered as she alighted from the train, the wind whipping her long hair about her face, gusting up her trouser legs and sending piles of leaves scurrying in circles about her ankles. She left the platform and looked hopefully about for a sign of a taxi, but there was none to be had.

'You look a bit lost, love.' A man in an official-looking dark uniform and peaked cap spoke to her kindly.

'Do you know where I can find a taxi? I need to get to Pelham House.'

'Aye.' He started to say more, looked as if he were about to warn her of something, but stopped abruptly and pointed to the waiting room. 'There's a phone over there. Number's on the panel next to it.'

Nodding her thanks, Olivia found the number, booked a cab and went to wait outside the station. If anything it felt colder here than in London, and she shivered, pulling her coat tighter about her body and stamping the feeling back into her feet.

The sky held the promise of rain, possibly snow. She'd heard a forecast earlier that morning warning of freezing overnight temperatures and discussing the likelihood of a white Christmas. Betting agencies were even offering odds on it, which had amused her. She sneezed again, and felt her eyes water, her nose run.

A brown sedan pulled up to the kerb and the driver rolled down his window and peered across at her. 'Taxi for Goddard?'

Olivia nodded and opened the rear door.

'Pelham House, you said?' he asked when she had clipped on her seatbelt.

'That's right. Is it far?'

''Bout twenty minutes. Just outside Winterslow.'

He didn't offer any further information, and Olivia was glad not to have to make small talk. The car hurtled along increasingly narrow lanes, finally turning into one so constricted, the weeds growing on either side brushed against the car doors and she held her breath that they wouldn't meet anything coming in the opposite direction. It was the first time she'd ventured into the countryside since arriving in England and she was unnerved by these tracks originally made for a horse and cart, and which would have travelled considerably slower than they were.

Olivia closed her eyes briefly, hearing the soporific swish of the windscreen wipers as the taxi rumbled along.

Minutes later, she shot forward in her seat as the car came to an abrupt halt, skidding in front of a pair of rusted, curlicued iron gates. They were bordered on both sides by a high stone wall that stretched into dense woodland. The left gate stood slightly ajar from its twin, and Olivia could just make out tussocks of thin grass growing across the bottom. It didn't look as though it had been opened – or closed – in a very long while.

It had begun to rain, and the drops quickly changed to sleet.

'Here you are, love. That'll be ten quid.'

'But where's the house?' Olivia peered doubtfully through the window.

The taxi driver looked at her as if she were simple. 'Through there, about half a mile.'

'You can't take me any closer?'

He shook his head regretfully. 'That's as far as I can go.'

She grumbled under her breath as she handed over the money and gathered her things, fishing her umbrella out of her bag and undoing the stud that secured it. As she stepped out of the taxi, the driver waved her off with a cheery, 'Give us a bell when you want picking up, love. Good luck; she's a contrary one, that's for sure.'

Olivia huddled under the umbrella and walked towards the gates, finding as she reached them that the gap was just wide enough for her – minus the open umbrella – to fit through. Getting soaked, she staggered slightly, feeling dizzy. Despite the cold, she was raging hot all over now, either sweat or rainwater was inching its way underneath her clothes and trickling down her back. Reminding herself sternly what she was there to accomplish, she continued on, dodging the puddles and holding the umbrella angled in front of her like a shield against the weather.

As she rounded a corner, the house appeared in front of her: a large, square, Georgian-era country residence set amid sprawling grounds. Simple, solid and built to endure for centuries. On a kinder day, she could imagine that it would be quite charming, but now it simply looked forbidding, the stone dark with rain and towering above her.

She reached the portico, noticing flaking paint on each of its fat round columns, and set her umbrella down before lifting the iron doorknocker.

She waited for what felt like an age, all the while growing colder and colder, but there was no answer. She knocked again. There didn't seem to be any lights on inside the house, and there was no way of seeing into the downstairs windows, for each had curtains drawn against them.

It was getting steadily, inexorably dark.

Refusing to give up, she tramped across the wet, overgrown, leaf-strewn lawns around to the back of the house, trying to ignore the damp soaking her boots. She found a back door, made from solid wood, with no way of peering inside, and knocked as loudly as she could manage, then stood back, her teeth chattering, grasping her elbows and clenching her jaw to try to quell the tremors.

As she was on the point of going back around to the front of the house again, the door opened and in the dim light, all she could see was the barrel of a shotgun, pointing directly at her.

Sweat broke out on her forehead as the gun swam in front of her eyes and she felt her knees crumple like soggy cardboard.

FIVE

Shillong, 1944

O ne by one, the women staggered out of the convoy of Jeeps and into the grounds of Cleve, the house that served as the Wasbie HQ in Shillong. They looked nothing like the neat and orderly troops they'd seen on the way into the town, but then they had no uniforms yet – the Army only kept stores for men.

Bea's trunk was fifteen pounds heavier than anyone else's, she reckoned, but at least she was able to lift it, which was more than Bubbles and Plum seemed capable of. Unlike the others, Bea had packed books instead of frocks and fripperies, unable to leave her favourites – *The Hobbit*, *Murder in the Cathedral*, *Robinson Crusoe*, *Swallows and Amazons*, *Kim* and *Gone with the Wind* – behind. In the frenzy of packing the night before she left, she had tossed out much of the clothing that her mother helpfully suggested she might need, and gathered up books instead. It had occurred to her that there would very likely be precious little in the way of reading material where they were headed, and that perhaps some of the other women and even the soldiers too might be grateful for something to take their minds off things.

She had also tucked away a handful of HB pencils, a sketchbook, a small palette of watercolours and a couple of sable brushes. Her mother had pressed on her another bag, which contained tins of boiled sweets (most of which had already been shared and consumed on the journey) and two bottles of Gordon's gin.

'Perhaps we should have brought some poison in case we fall into the hands of the Japanese,' one of the women had whispered as the train shuddered away from the station, a thought that killed Bea's appetite entirely. Plum and some of the others didn't seem to have heard, for they chattered away unconcerned, as if they were going on a jolly outing rather than off to war. Bea was quieter, apprehensive about what was to come. She'd read the British newspapers avidly while in Calcutta, and gleaned enough to know that it wasn't going to be anything like they had ever experienced. Her imagination had been working furiously ever since she'd joined up.

It was two days since leaving Calcutta and they were all tired and covered in grime from the journey. Few of the women had complained, though, even when they discovered that there were no lights in the train carriage and they had to spend the night in pitch darkness. Someone had brought a couple of candle ends and a box of matches, but these soon sputtered out and they were left unable to see even their hands held in front of their eyes. Bea was relieved to be in a carriage of women, for she didn't fancy fending off an exploratory hand in the middle of the night. Despite the dark and the swaying motion of the train, she hadn't got much sleep, the hard seat a poor substitute for a soft mattress.

Even Plum, who had greeted Bea on the platform in Calcutta with effusive hugs (Bea felt a twinge of remorse for her former negative thoughts) and then wittered on relentlessly until they reached Guwahati and transferred to the Jeeps, was now subdued. Bubbles, who with her heart-shaped face, breathy voice and mass of fair curls that perfectly embodied her name, was with them too. She'd arrived at the station late, almost as the train was leaving, in a fluster of bags and boxes. She had far more luggage than anyone else. Lydia hadn't made the cut; Plum had said something about her lack of physical fitness.

The final part of the trip had made all of them rather nauseous as they inched their way up narrow, winding roads with hairpin bends and stomach-lurching drops into the valley below. The only saving grace had been a distinct change in the weather; going from the heat and humidity of Calcutta to a cool mountain climate had been a pleasant relief. As they juddered their way along, Bea tried not to look down at the edge of the road as it sheered away into thin air. It was no small consolation when they finally arrived and she was able to plant her feet on solid ground again.

'Welcome to the Wasbies.' A motherly-looking woman with neatly curled brown hair and bright, merry eyes stood in front of them, beaming from ear to ear. She introduced herself as the Assistant Commandant – Mrs St John – and ushered them into the house. It was a long, low building with a tiled roof and was surrounded by numerous flowering shrubs – other, smaller bungalows were dotted about the smooth green lawns – and it seemed to Bea to resemble a rather fine guesthouse. It certainly looked like it was going to be more comfortable than she had expected. 'There's tea for you all and then later this afternoon we'll get you kitted out. In the meantime, I'd like you all to have a read of this—' Mrs St John began to hand out a number of printed booklets that had the words 'Conditions of Service' typed on the front. She then ushered them into a dining room, where an urn was steaming next to a tray of cut-up sponge cakes sandwiched with jam. Bea's stomach rumbled as she helped herself to a mug and poured in the milk.

'You're welcome to take it outside; the trees give a nice shade,' Mrs St John suggested.

'Here, it says that we get paid,' said Plum as they all sprawled on the grass with their tea a few minutes later.

'Well, what did you think?' smirked one of the other women who had travelled with them – Amelia, Bea recalled.

'I suppose I thought we were volunteers,' said Plum vaguely. 'Ooh, we get a rank and everything,' she added, ignoring the sniggers that came from some of the women. 'Does that mean we'll have to learn to salute?'

'Probably, Private Vellacourt,' said Bubbles, snapping to attention and almost giving herself a black eye in the process.

More laughter. 'That's the wrong arm, dummy,' said Amelia.

Bubbles' cheeks burned at her mistake. 'I'll get it right next time,' she said, under her breath.

'We get an allowance for uniform,' said Bea, studying the pamphlet.

'You will all be measured this afternoon,' said Mrs St John, who had stepped outside and picked up on their conversation. 'And you will need to label every item of uniform and equipment.'

'Sounds just like school,' said one of the women.

'Does anyone have any questions?'

'What about malaria?' Bea asked.

'Sensible question. You'll be issued with a supply of Mepacrine.'

'It's disgusting,' Bubbles whispered. 'Turns the whites of your eyes yellow.'

She was prevented from making further comments by a firm look from Mrs St John. 'As well as potassium permanganate for water purification, cuts and scrapes and even, if need be, for snake bite,' she continued.

'That's a little less like school,' Bubbles said, her eyes widening.

'You cut a cross – similar to the Union Jack – over the bite and then apply the potassium,' said Mrs St John.

The snickering ceased rather abruptly after that.

~

'God, I look like a stuffed partridge,' Bubbles exclaimed as she struggled to do up the belt around her jacket. Bea suppressed a grin; it *was* a little on the snug side.

'What will Charles say when he sees me like this?' Bubbles' fiancé had joined the Signals at the same time as Bea's brother, but not before placing a diamond the size of a robin's egg on her third finger and promising he'd be back as soon as the war was over.

'Do you think he will? See you like this, I mean?' Plum asked.

'Well, I hope he'll be proud of me when he does,' said Bubbles with a sniff. 'There's a chance we might be able to get leave together. I overheard Mrs St John saying that they do their best to coordinate it if you've a husband or fiancé who's also serving.'

'Been here five minutes and she's already talking about leave,' said Plum with a mean laugh.

'Don't listen to her,' said Bea. 'And I'm sure you'll get to see each other before long.' She didn't add that Archie hadn't been home since he signed up.

After tea, they had been shown to one of the bungalows and issued with borrowed uniforms to wear until theirs arrived. Bea had been dismayed to find that she was to bunk in with Bubbles and Plum but knew better than to make a fuss about it. It wouldn't be for long, just while they did their training, and then they would all be assigned to different canteens – or at least she hoped they would. She'd go round the twist if she had to put up with Plum's endless chatter for the duration of the war, and she was keen to meet new people, not be stuck with the same old faces from Calcutta.

One empty bed remained, but Plum had thrown her kitbag on it, commandeering it as her personal wardrobe. The bedclothes were barely visible beneath the flotsam of bright silk gowns, make-up, stockings and shoes.

Bea shrugged on a borrowed greatcoat that clearly had been tailored for someone far shorter and wider than she, for it fell to her shins and went around her almost twice. 'I think this must have belonged to a Gurkha,' she said ruefully, flapping the sleeves that stopped some way short of her wrists. 'Lucky you're shorter, Bubbles,' she said to the blonde woman who had put on her own greatcoat and was marching up and down as if on a parade ground.

They had also been issued with water bottles, a tin hat, mosquito nets, a torch, a tin mug, plate and cutlery, as well as a pair of gumboots and four khaki aprons apiece. They'd been told that a canvas bucket, camp bed and chair, collapsible washing stand, sheets and a pillow would be given to them when they were assigned to their canteens. They would wear khaki turbans to keep their hair out of the way when they were working, but would also receive a dress cap bearing a red square upon which a chinthe – the mythical lion often found guarding Buddhist temples – was embroidered in black: the WAS(B) emblem. Mrs St John had been wearing hers when she welcomed them and Bea thought it looked rather smart. As she arranged her own belongings neatly, she felt the first stirrings of pride at what she had so impulsively signed up for.

The three of them looked up at a brisk rat-a-tat to see a woman not much older than them standing in the doorway. Her chestnut hair was swept off her face by two hair combs, highlighting cheeks that dimpled when she spoke. She introduced herself as Sergeant Joy Hatfield – in a clipped South African accent – and though her expression was friendly, she didn't look especially joyful, particularly when she caught sight of the mess Plum had made. 'When you've finished unpacking, you're to muster at the front of the main house,' she said. 'We'll show you all of the ins and outs of the canteen and how to manage the stock. Sixteen hundred hours, and no later.'

'Sixteen what?' asked Plum when she had left.

'Four o'clock,' said Bea, resisting the urge to roll her eyes.

They filed outside at the appointed time, with Bubbles, who seemed to be continually running late, bringing up the rear. Bea was surprised to see that a group of about thirty women, most in civvies, with a handful of others in the khaki uniform she was getting used to seeing, was already assembled near the house. Joy stood at the front, an arm resting on the hood of a battered Chevy truck that had the words 'Mobile Canteen No. 3 WAS(B)' painted in large white letters on the side. Its tyres were almost bald and as Bea began to wonder how it would negotiate the treacherous mountain roads, two of the uniformed women began to open up the side of the truck, lifting hinged sides that swung out to form a canopy. 'This is where you'll serve from,' said Joy, indicating a counter inside the truck. 'Though when it gets busy, you can serve from the back as well. Come closer now, don't be shy.'

They all gathered around the truck, and Bea could see that the interior was lined from the floor to the roof with shelves on which sat hundreds of boxes marked with their contents: soap, cigarettes, hair oil, needles, shoe laces, razor blades, toothpaste, chocolate, buttons, Brylcreem, paper and pencils, along with what seemed like a million and one other sundries.

'You'll need to learn the prices of everything,' Joy added. 'In rupees. And brush up on your mental arithmetic. It can get rather busy when we pull in, and though you'll find the men generally form an orderly queue, you won't want to keep them waiting. How many of you understand Urdu or Hindustani?'

A few of the women raised their hands. Bea knew a smattering of words in both languages, picked up from Jeet and their other servants, but wasn't confident enough to admit to a sound understanding of either.

'Don't worry if you don't; you're all smart young women and you'll soon learn what you need. We also serve sandwiches and cakes, which are made before we leave, buns and fudge, fruit squash and so on, depending on what we can get.

'It's all common sense really,' said Joy. 'You'll be assigned to a canteen run by someone who knows what they're doing, and they'll show you the ropes. You'll pick it up quickly enough.'

She looked around at the expectant faces. 'One of the team will be responsible for keeping accurate accounts, with a daily tally of stores sold and monies received. Your team leader will also fill in the movement reports and submit them to HQ as required.'

Bea heard Plum groan before being shushed by Bubbles, who was standing directly behind her. 'Do take this seriously, Plum,' Bea said, exasperation getting the better of her.

Plum pouted prettily in response.

'The importance of your role in boosting morale cannot be underestimated,' said Mrs St John as she emerged into the sunlight, her eyes searching the women standing before her as if to impress this point upon them. 'The men need to see a friendly face, a cheerful smile,' she added. 'Some of them will have been in the jungle for weeks at a time, cut off from everything.'

Bea's thoughts flicked to her brother and his possible whereabouts, knowing that it was almost certain he was one of those isolated soldiers.

'You, too, might sometimes find yourselves only a few miles from the frontline; some of our canteens have had to operate within the sound of enemy gunfire, often evacuating at a moment's notice. You'll need to be able to follow orders, keep a cool head about you and not panic. And speaking of gunfire, you will all be taught how to handle a weapon, to fire a gun – accurately – though we hope you won't have cause to use one.' She gave them a wry smile. 'What, you thought you were coming just to cut up finger sandwiches?'

SIX

Pelham House, 1999

When Olivia came to her senses, she found herself in an impossibly high-ceilinged room, stretched out on a sofa. A thick pelt of dog hair covered the blanket that lay on top of her. It was probably musty, but her nostrils felt as if they had two rubber bungs inside them, so she couldn't smell a thing, which was likely a blessing. She sneezed. Wiggled her toes experimentally. Somewhere between the front door and this room she had lost her shoes. It was a minute or two before she recalled exactly where she was and what she was doing there. She remembered seeing the gun, but then . . . nothing.

Her eyes darted around the room. She appeared to be alone. Heat came from the belly of a huge fireplace, the flames fanned by a draught that rattled the windows in their frames. Her head pounded at the slightest movement, her mind thick as if stuffed with kapok, and her throat and her eyes scratched as though she'd recently waded through a dust storm. Her body ached all over and despite the warmth of the room she began to shiver underneath the blanket. Somewhere in the distance came the sound of china chinking and a dog's high-pitched yip, then silence.

'You poor thing.'

Olivia opened her eyes again to find an old woman bent over, staring down at her, her face only inches away. She blinked and saw a string of yellowing pearls, a pin-tucked blouse, a fraying pea-green cardigan and checked tweed trousers held up by a worn leather belt. She was very thin. Fine, fair skin crinkled around her eyes, stretched over sharp, high cheekbones and a strong jaw, before sagging from her neck like small dewlaps. Her hair was a shock of pure white that stood out like candy floss and looked as though it had last been cut by a pair of garden shears and was rarely tamed by a comb. The woman must have been quite lovely in her day, Olivia decided, for there was still a trace of fineness to her features and elegance in her stance. Her eyes were particularly arresting, the translucent colour of seawater, and Olivia found she could not look away from the veiled sadness she saw lurking there.

'Oh,' the woman said. 'What a young thing you are.' The woman – Beatrix Pelham, she presumed – put a cup and saucer on the table next to her. At twenty-seven, Olivia didn't count herself as especially young, but she supposed that to Beatrix she must seem so.

Paws clattered and slid over the parquet floor and Olivia felt a damp snout nuzzle her chin. 'Get down, Bertie,' Beatrix scolded, grabbing the dog's collar and holding him back.

Olivia cast about, remembering the gun, but Beatrix must have read her mind. 'Sorry for giving you such a fright, dear. I thought you were an intruder. I've been having a bit of bother, children from the village probably, daring each other to wind up an old woman because they've nothing better to do.' She paused, examining Olivia. 'You know, you really look rather dreadful. Prettiness notwithstanding, of course.'

Olivia blinked. She had never thought of herself as pretty, but she'd inherited her mother's tawny complexion and long, rod-straight, dark hair, which probably counted for something. It was all she could do to nod dumbly, though even that slight movement made her head swim.

'There's a chotapeg of whiskey there for you when you're up to it. Best cure for a cold there is.'

Olivia doubted that, but she could smell the sharpness of lemon, and something stronger, peat and oak. She fluttered her eyes, tried to swallow and then gave herself up to unconsciousness once more.

~

When she next woke, it was in another unfamiliar room. She had a vague memory of being helped up a long staircase and allowing her outer clothes to be removed. The curtains, which bore a faded pattern of toy soldiers and polka dots, were drawn. The embers of a fire glowed in the grate, and, looming in the dim light that it gave off, a small horse on wooden runners faced her from across the room. Its scratched, dappled rump and moth-eaten mane spoke of hours of mistreatment, though the look in its painted eyes was one of wild defiance rather than submission.

As the room came into greater focus, she noticed another bed, the twin to the one she lay in, with a matching sky-blue eiderdown and iron bedstead. The walls were papered in a tattered geometric pattern and there was a brownish stain in the corner, near the ceiling moulding. A faint smell of peppermints did little to ward off the odour of creeping damp.

On a set of shelves next to the fire was a balding teddy bear, a neat row of books, several battered board-game boxes and a large, white china rabbit with pink ears. Directly below was a three-storey wooden dolls' house, the front of which had been left slightly open, hinting at what might lie inside. Olivia stared at it, fascinated. It was a replica of Pelham House, right down to the terracotta chimneys. If she were to open it, would she find a nursery such as this inside? She felt as if she were a child again herself, tucked up under the blankets in a narrow single bed with a mattress that sagged into the bedsprings.

The rest of the house was eerily silent, and even the wind seemed to have ceased its incessant pummelling. It was still dark and Olivia had no idea how much time had elapsed since she had passed out on Beatrix Pelham's doorstep, nor how she could have ended up in this bedroom. Elaine, she knew, would be mortified by such behaviour; it was hardly professional. If the subdued glow from the fire was anything to go by, she'd been there for quite some time. She figured she had definitely missed the return train to London. She tried to be bothered by it, to figure out what to do next, but the bed was so warm and cosy and her eyes so scratchy and heavy, that it was easier to close them, to give in to the blanket of sleep that rolled heavily over her once more.

~

It was light now, and the mug of lemon and whiskey – she still had no idea what a 'chotapeg' was – had been replaced by a china cup and saucer containing a gently steaming, biscuit-coloured liquid.

'Earl Grey. Do you take sugar?'

Beatrix Pelham stood over her once again, a moth-eaten mustard–yellow cardigan having been swapped for the green one, her hair flattened on one side, standing up on the other.

'Er, no. Thank you.' Olivia sat up, noticing as she did so that she was dressed in an old-fashioned embroidered bed jacket, the satiny fabric slippery against her skin.

'How did I get here?'

'Why, I imagine you arrived by train, dear, didn't you?'

'No, I mean upstairs.'

'I helped you, of course. Practically had to carry you.'

Olivia wondered how she had managed it. Beatrix Pelham appeared hardly capable of getting herself upstairs, let alone a five-foot-six young woman, even one on the slight side.

Beatrix rearranged the pillows behind her and Olivia leaned back on them, gratefully accepting the cup.

'You *have* had a good sleep,' Beatrix said with satisfaction.

'Did I really . . .'

'You did. Slept the whole night. Half the morning too.'

'But my train?' Olivia began to pull the covers off.

'Afraid you've missed that. And by the looks of things, there won't be any running today. Not on the Great Western Line anyway.'

'Elaine . . .' Olivia narrowly avoided spilling tea into her saucer.

'No need to worry. I rang her earlier and explained that you'd been taken ill, and would be delayed for at least a day or so.'

'But there are only two days until Christmas. I'll have to be back before then.'

'She said not to worry and that she'd see you in January. Because of the weather she wanted to get to the airport before they started cancelling flights. Besides, you're not in a fit state to travel anywhere, and I told her as much. Anyway, it looks as though we're cut off.'

'Cut off?' Olivia's head was still thick and she began to feel uncomfortably hot. Sweat beaded her forehead.

Beatrix regarded her with an expression one might use on a feeble-minded friend, a mix of slight exasperation and pity. 'We've had nearly a foot of snow overnight, and it's still bucketing down. Haven't seen a winter like this since the big freeze of sixty-three.'

Olivia glanced towards the window, where the curtains had been drawn to reveal a blinding white landscape, the air swirling with fat flakes like one of her favourite childhood snow globes. As she craned her neck, she saw a thick layer resting up against the windowpane. Regardless of the snow, she was beginning to think Beatrix was anxious for her to stay. The woman certainly seemed pleased to have company in this big old house.

As she tried to decide what to do, Bertie padded in through the partly open door and hopped onto the end of the bed.

'Oh, get down, you silly old thing. This nice young lady doesn't want you bothering her.'

'No, really it's all right. I like dogs – he reminds me of one we had growing up.' She drained the cup and Beatrix reached for it.

'Just as long as he doesn't make a nuisance of himself. I think he's a bit put out that Bette and her puppies are getting all the fuss, aren't you, darling?' Beatrix ruffled the fur on the dog's neck and he rewarded her with an enthusiastic lick. 'I'll leave you to rest.'

Olivia watched Beatrix make her way to the door, walking with a slight limp, and felt surprise again that the woman had managed to get her up the stairs unassisted. Perhaps she was stronger than she looked.

'But . . .' Olivia protested. 'I really do have to get back to London.'

'Nonsense.' Beatrix paused in the doorway. 'We've already covered that. You're far too unwell to travel, and even if you were, the trains aren't running today, at least not according to the wireless. And I doubt they'd get something like that wrong.'

Olivia didn't have the strength to argue with her. Anyway, it wasn't as if there was anyone in London – with the exception of Elaine – to miss her. She'd been so busy working that she hadn't had time to make more than a few passing acquaintances. It struck her suddenly, sadly, that in a city of more than seven million people, she didn't have anyone she could call a friend.

~

When she woke again, the room was dimmer still. Bertie lay gently snoring at the end of the bed, his nose twitching at doggy dreams. She saw her bag on a table across the room and slipped out from under the quilt, shivering as the cold air hit her bare legs. Her head swam as she stood up, and she had to grasp the edge of the metal bedstead for a moment until it cleared. She shuffled over to her bag and rummaged through it until she found her phone. She pressed the ON button and waited for the tiny screen to light up.

Nothing.

The wretched thing had probably run out of battery. She'd lay bets that the old woman wouldn't have a charger. She threw the useless handset back into her bag and scuttled back to bed, burrowing under the bedclothes, her whole body shuddering with cold. Judging by the depth of snow now on the windowsill and the fact that fat flakes were still splattering against the windows, she rated the chances of the trains being back in service at less than likely.

She focused her thoughts on the reason she had come to meet Mrs Pelham. The fox-girl. Elaine had instructed Olivia not to return without the promise of it, and proof of provenance. Therefore, sick or not, Olivia had a job to do. Finding the fox-girl – the one that had gone missing in 1976 – would almost certainly put her career on the footing she wanted; she might even collect part of the reward, if it still stood. She smiled to herself, imagining the look on Elaine's face when she was able to show it to her. She was also curious to find out more about Mrs Pelham, this woman who was such a beguiling mix of old-school indomitable spirit and fragility.

As she was pondering her bizarre situation, the door opened and Beatrix bustled in carrying a tray covered with a cloth. 'Oh good,' she said, putting it on the bedside table. 'You've got a bit more colour in your cheeks. You were whiter than bone when I first laid eyes on you.'

Olivia's stomach gurgled in response to the rich aroma of chicken coming from the tray.

'Oh golly,' said Beatrix, hearing the sound. 'When did you last have anything to eat?'

Olivia's head was still so fuzzy, she couldn't quite remember. 'Yesterday?' she offered.

'Well this'll go down a treat. Soup and brown-bread soldiers. Nursery food. Gentle on the tummy. I hope you're not one of those dreadful vegetarians, or God help us a *vegan*.' She made it sound like a particularly nasty disease. 'Though heaven knows you're skinny enough to be one.'

Olivia smiled and shook her head.

'Anyway, there's nothing like chicken soup to make you feel better.' She laid a cool hand on Olivia's forehead and tutted to herself. 'You're as warm as toast.'

Tears pricked Olivia's eyes as an image appeared unbidden in her mind: being cared for by her mother when she was a child and sick, being given crackers smeared with butter and Vegemite while she was in bed and her mum not minding at all when she got crumbs all over the covers. 'That's really very kind of you. I don't want to put you to any trouble.'

'Nonsense. I haven't had anyone to cook for in years. Not since Willy – that's my second husband – popped his clogs. It's been me and the dogs for a long time now. Even the horses had to go; I couldn't manage them on my own. I think I was more upset to lose them than I was my husband, God rest his soul.' She gave a throaty cackle that was at such odds with her frail demeanour, it made Olivia jump.

'Have you always lived here?' she asked.

'Oh no. This was Grandfather's house. He left it to Mother – she was his only child – and then she left it to me. Willy and I moved in with her for a while, but then she lost her marbles and we had to put her into a home. The roof's now so full of holes it might as well be a sieve. Most of the paintings have gone to Elaine already. I'm down to my last few little treasures, and even they likely won't be enough.'

Ah. The fox-girl.

'I couldn't put it on the market, though,' Beatrix said, as if anticipating the question forming in Olivia's mind about selling the house. 'No. I'll see out my years here, one way or another, then my son can worry about what to do with the place. They'll have to take me out feet first. I'm too old to move again, did enough of that in my youth. I grew up in India; that was before the war, of course. There was a time when I vowed never to pack or unpack again . . .' Her eyes clouded and she drifted off, lost in memories. 'But then, there was a time when I vowed never to do lots of things, including getting married, and what do you know I did that, twice!' Beatrix gave another rasping bark of laughter. 'Tell God your plans and watch him laugh – isn't that what they say?'

'So I've heard.' Olivia grinned back at her, liking the old woman's spirit. Elaine had been wrong about her. She didn't seem at all mad.

Bertie, who'd woken up by now, sniffed at the tray of food and gave a small whine. 'Chicken necks for you in the kitchen, my darling boy,' Beatrix said, batting him off the bed and shooing him out of the room, limping a few paces behind.

The soup was delicious, savoury and comforting, soothing her tender throat. Olivia finished it in several hungry gulps, while her eyes travelled around the darkening room. The old toys and books made her wonder about Beatrix's son. He would likely be middle-aged by now – where was he, and why had he left his mother alone at Christmas? She doubted that these relics were his. The more she looked at them, she decided that they dated from earlier times, probably the first decades of the twentieth century if the dolls' house and the rocking horse were anything to go by.

Feeling a little better after her soup, Olivia climbed carefully out of bed. She walked over to the bookcase, seeing well-loved children's books: old editions of the Famous Five, several pony stories and a collection of adventures about a boy called Jennings. On the very top shelf was a collection of ten slim leather-bound volumes. As she slid each one out, she saw that they were stamped in gold – somewhat faded – on the front, starting at 1935 and going all the way to the middle of the following decade. They looked as though they'd not been moved for years, and as she opened the first one a musty smell tickled her nose and made her sneeze.

The name 'Beatrix Fitzgibbon' was inked on the first page in elegant, flowing copperplate. Olivia hesitated. Would she be intruding, eavesdropping on the private thoughts of a much younger woman? Curiosity got the better of her and she began to turn the pages: funny annotated drawings of people, watercolours of gardens, crudely drawn ponies, a game of croquet on a vibrant green lawn appeared before her. Then, red-brick buildings, hockey sticks and schoolgirls in uniform.

She gathered an armful and slid down onto the rug, piling the books beside her. As she slowly flipped the pages, she realised she was witnessing the story of a transformation from girlhood to womanhood at a time when the world was a simpler place, and of a developing artistic talent too.

It had been a long time since Olivia had picked up a paintbrush, something she had once loved to do, and as she traced her finger over one detailed sketch she felt a pang of regret at having stopped.

She tucked her feet under herself, barely feeling the cold now. She finished the first volume and reached for the second, and then the third, and fourth, and so on, seeing Beatrix's skill as a painter become more assured. There were sketches of a boy – Archie, according to the captions – who must have been around the same age as Beatrix, with a shock of carroty hair and drawn with either a scowl or a smile on his face; nothing in between. Then there were portraits of an Indian man wearing a saffron-coloured turban and white robes, a snake in one hand; the low façade of a bungalow surrounded by bright flowering trees; a woman in a sprigged muslin dress carrying a parasol, her hair caught up. Beatrix's mother perhaps? And was Archie her brother, a cousin? There was a tenderness in the sketches that spoke of a close relationship.

Two of the volumes were considerably more battered than the others, their leather bindings dirty, cracked and torn in places, the pages thicker and wrinkled, each one held together by a nearly perished elastic band. They appeared to have been carried through mud and rainstorms several times over. They even smelled different, of spices perhaps, though Olivia's nose was still partly blocked so she couldn't be entirely sure.

Here the watercolours were more subdued: khaki and sand, ochre and brown, olive and ebony. Pages and pages of pencil sketches and watercolours. Anglo-looking men in uniform, Indians, men with peaked caps and luxuriant moustaches, shirtless men lounging in camp chairs on a verandah, women in green bandanas and collared shirts, a watery downpour, tumble-down buildings, gorgeous ragged-haired dark-eyed children. The place names were unfamiliar: Shillong, Imphal, Dohazari. Olivia had no idea where they were from, but the foliage looked distinctly tropical, the occasional bright flower reminding her of those at home.

A few of the pages were scuffed, some sections had notes in scratchy pencil, others in faded ink. The penmanship was exquisite but its faded, looping script was almost impossible to decipher.

SEVEN

Shillong, 1944

'You can sleep when you're dead,' said Plum, throwing a towel at Bea's head.

Bea groaned and shaded her face with her arm. 'I didn't get a wink last night,' she complained as Plum and Bubbles got ready to go out. 'Nor the one before that.'

'You heard what Mrs St John said about morale,' said Bubbles as she shimmied her hips into a tight-fitting silk dress. 'It's expected that we'll go to the dances; help cheer up the troops. I hope Charles won't mind too much; of course, I wish it were his arms around me.'

So, dancing skills were in fact required. Bea sighed. 'I'm sure that's half the reason you signed up,' she said dismissively.

'Course it was,' laughed Plum, oblivious to Bea's sarcasm. 'God knows we've got to find some fun in this world. And we can wear mufti – not that ghastly uniform, not yet anyway.'

'I heard that when we do get kitted out, we'll have to wear it everywhere,' said Bubbles. 'Hey!' she cried as Plum pinched a stole and wrapped it around her shoulders. 'That's mine. Jolly well give it back.'

Plum shrugged and tossed it on the spare bed.

'Well, I don't know about the rest of you, but I'll be proud to wear mine,' said Bea. 'Proof that we're doing our bit.'

Bubbles finished doing up her dress, picked up a small hand mirror and applied a careful slick of scarlet lipstick with a practised hand. 'I'm sure that before long we'll be doing the more important, practical stuff,' she said, putting the lipstick down and fluffing her curls. 'But for now this is where we're needed.'

'It's freezing outside.'

'So? We've got coats, haven't we? Come on, Bea. It won't be the same without you. You'll enjoy yourself, I promise.'

It didn't seem as though they were any closer to the war, the real war, than when she'd been in Calcutta, but Bea got to her feet and pulled a crumpled gown off the end of her bed. 'Oh, all right then. But don't expect me to stay late,' she warned.

～

The officers' mess was a beacon of music and light, and Bea, Bubbles and Plum walked arm-in-arm (Bubbles, who wanted everyone to get along, had linked them together as soon as they set foot out of the door) towards it.

'You'll be outnumbered,' said one of the women slightly behind them. 'Expect there to be twenty of them to every one of us.'

'At least!' said another.

'Mind they don't get fresh.'

'And if you really don't want to dance with them, simply say you'd prefer not to. That usually works,' said Amelia.

'Stick together,' advised another. 'Safety in numbers.'

'Right-o,' said Bubbles, taking the words literally and pulling Bea and Plum closer. 'Best foot forward, hey?'

As they entered the Shillong Country Club, almost every head turned to watch them arrive. Bea pushed aside the feeling of being a specimen under a microscope, and took a slug of the gin-and-tonic that was handed to her as soon as they entered the room.

'Cin cin,' said Plum, raising her glass.

'Bottoms up,' added Bubbles.

'Down the hatch,' said another in their group.

Before long they were all, one by one, pulled onto the dance floor. The next three hours passed in a blur of feet and swirl of skirts as first one then another and another man claimed each of them, leading them in the jitterbug, the jive and swing. There was little likelihood of anyone being a wallflower. The soldiers' high spirits were infectious, cares forgotten if only for an evening, and even Bea found herself swept up in the energy of it all, though her feet were soon the worse for wear as the soldiers danced in their fighting boots and she had little but a pair of satin dancing pumps to protect her feet.

Taking a break between dances, Bea tried to quell her concern as she watched Plum flirt outrageously with a number of the officers, and worried that she might be leading them on. Nice Girls Didn't. That fact had been drummed into her since girlhood, and she worried that some of the women might give them all a bad name, that the soldiers might come to expect more from them than a willing dance partner and a cheerful smile. The men were mostly polite, but she could well imagine the danger of putting herself in a compromising position, unwittingly or not. Bubbles seemed able to keep them at bay while still laughing and joking. Bea heard her ask more than once about their sweethearts or sisters back home. Of course the diamond on Bubbles' finger served as a warning to those who might want to get too friendly.

'Well, aren't you a tall drink of water,' said one, his meaning clear.

'Loosen up, sister,' said another with a wink as he pulled Bea into a spin and nearly wrenched her arm from its socket. She hoped he was a better soldier than a dancer, for if not, she worried for his future. He offered her a stick of gum, which she declined with a brisk shake of her head.

'I think I've had enough now, thanks all the same,' she gasped, 'I fear my feet may not recover.' Though her toes were bruised by enthusiastic officers treading on them, she felt strangely exhilarated, if somewhat light-headed from the copious amounts of gin she'd drunk (partly in an effort to slake her thirst, partly in an attempt to relax). She noticed some of the soldiers standing at the bar amusing each other by throwing peanuts in the air and catching them in their mouths to loud whoops and cheers when they were successful. Looking at the scene, it was hard to believe that anyone present had a care in the world, that they did not stare death in the face day after day, night after night. Perhaps it was precisely because of this that they were so outwardly carefree.

Searching for somewhere to sit and rest for a moment, she found an empty chair at a table on the edge of the room. 'Is this taken?' she asked the young GI sitting nearby.

'Be my guest,' he replied, pulling it out for her.

'Not keen on dancing?' she asked as she settled herself, for she'd noticed that he hadn't moved from the table all evening.

She was puzzled by the pained look he gave her.

'Sweet baby Jesus,' said the soldier sitting opposite them. 'Are you kidding? Johnny lost both his legs three months back. He's still waiting to go home.'

Bea looked down, a deep blush of shame reaching her ears when she realised her mistake. Despite wishing the ground would swallow her whole, she opened her mouth to apologise, but the soldier stopped her with a hand. 'It's okay, ma'am. You weren't to know.'

Bea took a sip of her drink and tried desperately to think of something to say that wouldn't make the situation any worse.

'It's just swell to watch, you know?' he added kindly, putting her at ease after her thoughtless comment.

'I'm sorry . . .' she began.

'Don't worry about it, darlin'. It's kinda nice that you didn't notice; treated me like anyone else.'

She was saved from embarrassing herself even further by another soldier who came over to ask her to dance, and she gratefully took the hand he held out to her.

She tried to tell him her name, but the noise from the band had risen and they were in the thick of the dance floor.

'What's that?' he shouted, unable to hear her over the music.

'Never mind.' She concentrated on matching her steps to his.

After being thrown around like a cocktail shaker for a few numbers, she was ready to call it a night. 'We really must be going now,' she said, leaning into his ear so that he heard her this time. 'Lovely to meet you,' she added, seeing his bereft expression as she pointed to the door.

She cast about for Bubbles and Plum, catching sight of Plum's bright blue dress among the sober khaki-toned uniforms. She waved to get her attention as Bubbles and Amelia appeared at her side, their skirts still swinging from the movement of their final dance. 'I'm all in,' she said.

'Care to dance?' A tall, ruddy-faced officer approached. His accent was as soft as Irish mist, but the look in his eyes when Amelia politely declined was hard, his mouth puckered like a little boy being told he can't have a new bicycle for Christmas. 'How about you, then?' he asked Bea, who also shook her head.

'I'm exhausted, sorry.'

'Me too,' said Bubbles apologetically, 'I'm dead on my feet.'

He lifted his stubbled jaw and turned towards the bar.

'You're not leaving, are you?' asked Plum, who had extricated herself from the arms of a particularly handsome chap. 'The night's still young.' She looked hopefully from one to another, a moue of disappointment forming on her lips as she saw that they were serious. 'You girls go on, then. I'll stay until the others leave.'

'But we're almost the last ones here,' said Bea, exasperated.

'Nonsense, there's Barbara and oh, whatshername . . .' Plum gestured to the bar, where two of the women remained, surrounded by a knot of officers.

'I really think you should come with us,' said Bubbles.

'Who are you? My mother?'

Bubbles reddened. 'I'm only thinking of you,' she replied.

'Go on home, the three of you. I'll be perfectly fine,' Plum insisted, her eyes on the crowd as she tapped her feet in time to the music.

Bubbles stood there stubbornly.

'I promise I'll go when the others do.'

'Oh, leave her to it,' said Bea, losing patience and going to fetch her coat. 'So much for sticking together,' she muttered as they stumbled home. Her head, which had been buzzing from the sound of the band, was now pounding, pressure tight across her temples.

'I know Plum comes across as an empty-headed ninny,' said Bubbles, 'but she's a lot smarter than people give her credit for. She might surprise us all one day.'

'I doubt that,' said Bea darkly.

~

'We must be allowed to go further forward. That's what we're here for, after all.'

Bea was heading to the mess for breakfast the next morning when she passed a door, slightly ajar, to a room that she hadn't noticed before. The voice sounded firm but on the edge of exasperation. Slowing her steps, she paused to listen. There was only one voice – Mrs St John's, she now recognised – so she must be on the telephone.

'Our unit has its part to play, so let us do it. We are properly equipped and trained.' She paused briefly before adding, 'My girls are *not* a liability.'

Another beat of silence, then, 'Very well, I shall take the matter up with Lieutenant General Slim.'

Bea hurried along as soon as she heard the receiver being replaced. What was the penalty for eavesdropping? She wasn't sure she wanted to know.

She got to the mess and as she helped herself to a bowl of Corn Flakes she spotted two Wasbies in khaki uniform sitting a few feet away with their back to her.

'. . . my last canteen disbanded and a couple of the women went on leave.' As she spoke, Bea recognised Joy Hatfield's accent. 'I'm glad to be out of the last place – rumour was, it had been used as a brothel before we got there. We had to scrub it from top to bottom before we could move in.' She laughed lightly. Bea shuddered at the thought.

'Any news from Peter?' the other woman asked, serious now.

Joy shook her head. 'He still doesn't know I'm here – thinks I'm at home in Jo'burg with my parents. I haven't had the guts to write and tell him yet. Not after his last letter. He might decide I've gone completely barmy.'

'He really wants to call it off?'

Joy nodded, and Bea noticed her twist the gold band on her ring finger. 'I'm not even sure why I'm still wearing this, really.'

The other woman put an arm around her shoulder. 'This bloody war . . .'

'Anyway,' said Joy straightening up. 'Needs must.'

'How long are you here for?' asked the other.

'Not sure. I'm to help train up the new bods. There's been a bit of a recruitment drive, and they're flooding in now. Poor lambs won't know what's hit them.'

'Oh God, that reminds me. Did you hear the news?'

'What news?'

'About the *Khedive Ismail*.'

'No, what about it?'

'Sunk by a Japanese sub two weeks ago in the middle of the Indian Ocean. Barely any survivors. As well as nurses and FANYs, we think there might have been several Wasbies on board.'

'Oh no! Any idea who?'

Bea fumbled with her spoon and it clattered on the counter. The two women glanced behind them.

'Sorry, I didn't mean to interrupt,' she apologised.

'It's all right,' said Joy. 'And don't pay any attention to her. You'll all be fine.'

Bea didn't believe her for a moment, but resolved to keep her fears to herself. There was nothing to be gained in repeating the news about the sinking of the ship to the others.

~

When they left the main house after breakfast, Bea spied someone bending over the bonnet of a Jeep. She heard the clang of something metallic, followed by a string of choice swear-words. Bea stopped in her tracks. The voice was far higher pitched than she would have expected.

A moment later, the person straightened up and Bea realised that it was not a man as she had first thought, but in fact a woman. Her shoulder-length brown hair was pulled back at the sides of an oil-smudged face that was scattered with tiny freckles like a finch's egg. At least Bea thought they were freckles, but they could just as easily have been flecks of engine oil. She noticed that the woman's loose-fitting trousers were cinched at the waist by a wide belt and that she was also wearing practical-looking elastic-sided leather boots.

'Need a hand?' she asked, walking over to pick up the wrench that had been flung to the ground, Plum and Bubbles not far behind.

'Bloody oath,' the woman replied.

Bea handed her the wrench and introduced herself and then the others.

'Lucy Robertson,' the woman replied, the corners of her eyes creasing as she grinned at them all.

'Oh, an Aussie. What are you doing here?' Plum asked, tactlessly.

'The same as you I imagine,' Lucy replied, her voice pleasant.

'Don't mind her,' said Bea, frowning at Plum. 'She's got the sensitivity of a mosquito sometimes. Speaking of which—' She slapped at an insect that had landed on her arm, blood smearing her skin as she wiped it away.

'I lived in Hong Kong for a while when I was younger,' Lucy explained. 'And Japan before that. The advertisement in *The Age* said that the Army was looking for women with Far East experience, that they wanted those suited to a rough-and-ready life of adventure, and,' she looked at them with anticipation, 'that we'd be serving alongside the men on the frontline.'

Plum smirked and Bea and Bubbles both shot her a warning look.

'My brothers signed up to the Royal Australian Engineers,' Lucy added. 'I'd have given anything to have gone with them, reckon I have the stomach for it at least as much as they have.

But apparently it's a man's war, and I didn't have the aptitude for nursing.' She made a face at the thought.

'Why leave the safety of Australia?' Plum asked. 'Didn't you know that ships are being torpedoed left, right and centre?'

Bea started. Plum must have heard too.

'We all want to play our part,' said Lucy, wiping her hands on a rag that had been hanging from her pocket. 'And I know something about fixing trucks. Mum thinks I'm a sandwich short of a picnic, though.' She grinned again and even Plum smiled back.

'One of the men at the dance last night mentioned that it's heating up to the east, near Imphal,' said Bubbles. 'Wherever that is. And apparently Captain Taylor's had to evacuate several Wasbies from there.'

'I heard a rumour that there's going to be a push south, in Arakan, before the start of the monsoons. And they're sending canteens. They're so short-handed that some of us will be going too,' said Plum.

'We don't even know what we're doing,' wailed Bubbles. 'I thought we were going to get at least a couple of months of training.'

'If – and that's a big if – it's true, then they will surely match us with someone who is more experienced,' said Lucy calmly. 'And how hard can it be to serve tea and sell cigarettes? The Army is hardly going to put women directly in the line of fire. Who told you that, anyway?'

'I keep my ear to the ground,' said Plum.

Bea would lay bets that Plum had been chatting up the servicemen at the dance; the woman could get information from a granite statue, so a loose-lipped, loose-hipped soldier would pose no problem.

'Let's have a bit of shush now,' Bea said, hating how much she sounded like a bossy head girl, but continuing anyway. 'I don't know about the rest of you, but idle gossip and rumour only causes trouble.'

'Well, don't say you weren't warned,' said Plum.

~

Later that morning, they assembled at the front of the house once more – Plum arriving late from who-knew-where – as a convoy of Jeeps waited to take them to the hills beyond the town for target practice.

Bea was familiar with the sight of her father's service revolver, had watched him clean and oil it, but though he had explained its workings to Archie when he was still a boy, Bea had never been allowed anywhere near it. Guns, the unspoken message had been, were for men and boys, not the business of women and girls. She had never thought to mind before.

'Aim for the centre of the chest.' The sergeant – tall, and with a bristled moustache that reminded Bea of a toothbrush – pointed to his sternum. 'That way there's more chance of you hitting your target and doing the most damage.'

Plum yawned, as if it were all too tedious, and Bea had to nudge her with an elbow to get her to pay attention. She felt none too bright herself; the gin from the night before had left her feeling as dusty as the road they'd driven in on, and she had to screw up her eyes against the glare of the sunlight. The sergeant flicked a world-weary gaze towards them and Bea did her best not to look horrified at the prospect of shooting someone in the chest.

'You won't all be armed, but each mobile canteen will have a revolver or two, and everyone needs to know how to use it. This—' he said, holding up a gun for them all to see, 'is an Enfield number two.' He demonstrated the shooting stance, aiming towards the targets, old rice sacks that appeared to be filled with straw. 'Hold the gun with two hands, and keep your forearm in line with the barrel.'

'No limp wrists, duckies,' one of the women whispered, to a ripple of nervous laughter.

'Maintain a firm grip, keep your eyes open and don't hold your breath. Line up your sights and focus on the front sight, not the target.' He put the gun down and began to hand out pairs of earmuffs.

They took their turns to shoot, one by one, as everyone else stood at a safe distance and looked on. Only Lucy's shot hit the mark. ('Typical,' whispered Plum, earning herself a disapproving glare from Bea.) The sergeant stopped them and moved the target closer, until it was about fifteen feet away. 'Let's see how you get on now,' he said. This time, some of the women were more successful.

When it came to Bea's turn, she had to wipe her palms on her skirt, for they had become slick with sweat. 'Squeeze the trigger ever so gently while you maintain your focus on the sights,' he said. 'Lean slightly forward, not back.'

There was so much to remember. Bea's hands trembled slightly as she took aim. Even with the earmuffs, the sound of the gun firing made her jump and the recoil sent the gun jerking upwards, the bullet grazing the edge of the sack. 'Have another go,' the sergeant urged. 'Don't worry. Very few people get the hang of it first off.'

She did better with the next shot and the bullet entered the sack bang in the middle, sending a puff of chaff into the air. Bea felt a small thrill of satisfaction run through her and put the gun down with some reluctance.

'You'll be expected to attend target practice twice a week until you get your postings,' the sergeant said. 'Now, who's next?'

Plum slowly raised her hand.

Despite being given several more chances than the other women, Plum failed to hit a single target. After she'd finished, she put the gun down with a look of relief and walked back to where Bea and the others stood.

'I'm sure you'll get better with practice,' said Bubbles kindly.

'What are the chances we'll really need to use a gun, anyway?' Plum said, shrugging off her poor performance. 'We won't be anywhere near the Japs.'

'I wouldn't be too sure of that,' said Bea. 'Don't you think there's a reason they're teaching us how to shoot?'

❧❖❧

EIGHT

Pelham House, 1999

It was unlike any Christmas Olivia had celebrated in the past, but she did concede that it was at least more interesting than being on her own in her bedsit in London. She'd woken on the morning of Christmas Eve feeling much more like herself, and after Beatrix had brought in a tray containing a mug of tea, boiled eggs and toast, she decided it really was time she got up and out of bed.

She went downstairs with a new purpose. She was going to ask about the fox-girl, and then she was going to see about getting back to London.

'Oh no, no, no,' Beatrix said, tutting her disapproval when Olivia raised the subject of her return. 'You're stuck with me for a few more days, I'm afraid,' she said, sounding pleased at the prospect. 'Look—' She pointed to the window where the snow still lay, white and pristine.

Olivia shivered, despite the fact that she was wearing a thick Fair Isle sweater that Beatrix had left out, with the trousers she had arrived in. Even if there hadn't been any snow, she was starting to feel that this slightly dotty old woman had another agenda, that under no circumstances did she want Olivia to leave. Of course, Olivia could milk this a little, get into Beatrix's good books and learn the truth of the fox-girl. Brand's would certainly be interested to hear of its reappearance, as much as Elaine wanted to handle the sale. Olivia hadn't decided who to approach first. To be on the brink of solving a decades-old mystery was a thrilling prospect, whichever option she chose.

'But don't you have plans?' Olivia said. 'For Christmas, I mean?'

Beatrix looked up from where she was opening a slim pile of letters and greeting cards with a silver knife. 'Afraid not. My son, Thomas, lives in Singapore, and only ever comes back to England in the summertime. That's him up there.' She pointed to a dusty picture frame on the mantlepiece. 'Hates the cold, you see, and can't cope with this draughty old place.'

'But your friends? Won't they mind that you're on your own?'

Beatrix shook her head. 'There are a few in the village, but I'm not sure I'd call them friends. Acquaintances more like. And they've got their own families to go to.' She busied herself by neatly arranging her letters in size order.

With sudden insight, Olivia realised that Beatrix was even lonelier than she was, though she would probably be the last to admit it.

'But what about you? I do apologise that the weather has put the kibosh on your plans.'

'Actually, I was supposed to be working,' Olivia replied.

'Over the holiday? Is Elaine that much of a slave driver?'

'No, I have another job, in a bar. Or at least I did. But apparently I'm not needed anymore.' She was going to leave it there, but Beatrix's slightly raised eyebrow prompted a further confession. She sighed. 'I told a customer where to shove it. I was sick of him thinking he could touch me whenever and wherever he liked.'

Beatrix looked startled for a moment, then appeared to gather herself. 'Good for you for standing up to him. Shame about the job, though. But clearly it wasn't your fault.'

'That's not how my boss saw it, unfortunately.'

'I can well imagine – some things never change, do they?' Bea regarded her with a thoughtful expression.

'And I haven't really been in London long enough to make any real friends,' Olivia added in a quiet voice.

'Well, then,' Beatrix said brightly. 'We find ourselves alone, together. Goodness, there's a lot of post here – that'll teach me to let it pile up. What with Bette and her puppies, I haven't got around to it. It's nearly always bills, in any case.' Her expression became perplexed as she turned to the final white envelope, flipping it over to read the return address.

The stamp bore a picture of a team of men in a rowing boat, a bit like the surf lifesaving boats at home, coasting over a large wave and the word 'Eire' above it.

'Ireland,' Olivia said seeing it.

'Well, I'll be buggered,' Beatrix said, not taking her eyes from the scrawl on the back. 'Haven't heard from her in eons. Wonder what she wants after all this time?'

Olivia waited politely, not wanting to intrude, but still with the netsuke very much on her mind. She was on the point of raising that very subject when Beatrix used the letter opener to slit the envelope and pulled out a stiff rectangle of white card. 'Not Christmas greetings, then,' the old woman muttered.

Olivia could just make out a few lines of black copperplate centred on the card.

'That's certainly unexpected,' Beatrix said, sounding puzzled. 'An invitation to the fifty-fifth reunion of Number Fifty-Five canteen. And a New Year's dance. In a bloody castle!'

'A castle? Sounds exciting.'

Beatrix grunted noncommittally.

'What was Number Fifty-Five canteen?' Olivia asked, her curiosity piqued.

Beatrix paused for a moment before elaborating. 'Burma. Nineteen forty-five. Well, strictly speaking, we were formed in nineteen forty-four, so the beginning of this year would have been the fifty-fifth anniversary. But Plum never did have a good head for numbers.' She tutted, shaking her head as if she were a schoolteacher disappointed in a pupil's test result.

'During the war?' Olivia asked.

'Yes, darling. We made tea and sandwiches for the troops – char and wads, they called them – and jollied them along while they slogged it out in the jungle, that sort of thing. We were known as the "Wasbies". Soldiers used to pin welcome notices to trees, asking us to call in, if you can believe that. They were always frightfully grateful to see us.'

Olivia didn't think she'd ever been called 'darling' before, not by her parents or a boyfriend (though there hadn't been many of those, especially in the last few years), and she felt an unexpected burst of affection for Bea. 'I'm afraid I've never heard of them.'

'Yes, well, you and a great many others. We were the only women to serve actually on the frontline – closer than even the nurses.' Beatrix lifted her chin. 'No one, with the exception of Mrs Taylor, really thought we would cope for long,' she said, her eyes taking on a faraway look. 'They didn't think we'd survive in the jungle alongside the men – but we went and did it anyway. Proved them wrong.'

'Mrs Taylor?'

'Our Chief Commandant. Wonderful woman.'

Olivia was on the point of asking her another question, but Beatrix continued in a more brusque tone. 'Anyway, it was a very long time ago.' She slid the invitation back into its envelope. 'We were all such chums at the time, like sisters even; well, most of us anyway. Though Plum and I did fall out at the end. Which makes this invitation all the more surprising.'

'Who were they?' Olivia asked, suddenly curious.

Beatrix sighed, as if dredging up old memories was an unpleasant task. 'Joy Hatfield – she was supposed to be in charge of us, but she never made it feel like that. Then there was Bubbles Morgan-Jones, Plum Vellacourt and Lucy Robertson. We'd all spent time before the war in the Far East, and most of us spoke a little bit of Urdu or Hindustani, which came in handy.' She paused, and looked with a smile to Olivia. 'You remind me of Lucy a little, actually, and not just because of the accent, though she was Australian too. Wonderful girl, I often wished I could be like her when I grew up. Always cheerful, whizz of a mechanic, held her drink like no one I've ever met since. Came from somewhere called Abermain. Wine country, I think. She went back there for a while at least, but who knows after that? I couldn't have coped without them at the time, especially Lucy. But of course we lost touch, as one does.' She hesitated, her hands fluttering the envelope nervously. 'I can't believe Plum thinks she can gather us all together, and that she wants me there too.'

'All I really know about Burma is the railway, the POWs,' said Olivia. 'We studied it at school.' She had read the accounts of some of the survivors, knew a little of the inhumane conditions, the disease, the pitiful survival rate. There'd been plenty of Australian soldiers captured alongside the British.

'Yes, well, let me tell you, it was worse than you can probably even imagine. My brother was one of them.'

'Oh my goodness, I'm so sorry.' Olivia's hands flew to her mouth. 'Did he . . .'

Beatrix appeared not to have heard her, and was busily gathering the discarded envelopes into a pile. She tossed all but one onto the fire, where they blazed briefly before fluttering ashes up the chimney. She tucked the remaining envelope, the one containing the invitation, behind a candlestick on top of the mantlepiece. 'Met my first husband there, too,' she said, her eyes softening as she reminisced. 'And they taught us how to handle a gun. We had to sleep with a revolver under our pillows at one point.' She paused, a mischievous expression lighting up her face. 'Don't tell anyone, but I've still got mine upstairs.'

Having first met Beatrix toting a shotgun, Olivia could well believe it.

'Did you know we had a cigarette ration of fifty a week? Not to mention the booze . . . Of course, I smoked and drank like a demon back then. We all did. Complete dipsomaniacs, the lot of us; it was the only way to get through it, to switch off after all we'd seen. In some ways it was the time of my life, but war changes people, you know . . .' Her eyes narrowed and she got up to leave the room. 'Now, I think there's a pheasant in the freezer; shot it myself. A pie might be festive, don't you think?' She paused in the doorway. 'We're a bit short on fresh vegetables, though, but I expect we'll muddle through. It'll make a change to have someone to cook for. It's usually just me.' She gave Olivia a stoic grin.

'Mrs Pelham? Beatrix?' Olivia decided to get to the point, intriguing though the snippets of her past were. 'You know why I'm here, don't you? The netsuke – the fox-girl in particular.'

'Oh yes, darling – and that's a rather unusual example you've got there yourself. A *baku*, isn't it?'

Olivia touched her fingers to her neck. 'It's only really got sentimental value.'

'Quite. So does the fox-girl. Though others might beg to differ.' A guilty expression washed over the old woman's lined features. 'I might have been a bit premature in calling Elaine. Before, when we had all that rain, before it turned to snow . . . well, the water pouring through some of the upstairs bedrooms was so bad that I was almost at my wits' end. Then Bette had her puppies and I wasn't sure I could do it all anymore; couldn't see a way out. I think I rather panicked.'

From what she'd seen, Olivia didn't think that Beatrix was a person who panicked easily. In fact, if she had to hazard a guess, she would say that there was a thread of steely determination running through the woman, fragile though she might appear on the surface. 'I understand how hard it is to let go of things that you love,' she said gently. 'Especially if they have meaning attached to them. And I'm not here to persuade you to do something you don't want to.' The last statement wasn't entirely truthful, but she knew well enough when to tread softly. 'But I'd love to see it anyway,' she continued, choosing her words carefully. 'I've always been fascinated by netsuke: I love that so much effort went into making a very utilitarian object beautiful, something that would charm and delight the wearer. That they exist so long after the craftsmen are nothing but dust. And that there are still those who appreciate such small things.' It was perhaps the first time she had given voice to her belief that the mundane should still be beautiful.

Beatrix gave her a sideways look, as if weighing up Olivia's sincerity.

'My first husband had a thing for Oriental art, and animals.' She sighed, as though the memory were still fresh in her mind. A muscle ticked in her jaw and she appeared to come to a decision. 'Very well, then. I'll get it out – and the others – and you can at least take a look.'

Olivia relaxed. She had achieved her first objective, but a subtle approach was still needed, for she could sense Beatrix's stubbornness. She would have to curb her natural impatience. Softly, softly was the way to get the woman to trust her. 'Lovely. Now, is there anything I can help with?'

'No darling, don't you worry. I'm going to do a bit of pottering. You still look a little peaky; why don't you go to the small sitting room, there's a fire in there. I've put Bette in there too, and her pups. It's along the hall, second on your left.'

Olivia took her time finding the sitting room, easing open doors as she came to them and peering into shadowy rooms, curious as to what the house contained. The first two offered nothing more than a few items of dustsheet-covered furniture, but the third door led to a familiar room, where Olivia had first woken up in, two days earlier. It was several degrees warmer than the rest of the house and she felt her fingers and toes – despite the fact that she'd layered two pairs of the Argyle socks that Beatrix had also lent her – begin to defrost. A high-pitched whimper came from an old wine crate – *Saint-Émilion*, the print on the side read – lined with a garish crocheted blanket, and she went over to investigate.

They were tiny, eyes still sealed shut, mouths blindly searching for their mother's teats. With their chocolate and cream coats and oversized, soft pink noses they looked more guinea pig than canine, but Olivia knew that once they opened their eyes they would be much more attractive.

She didn't go too close, for fear of upsetting Bette, though she seemed oblivious to Olivia's presence, completely exhausted by new motherhood.

There was an old wing-backed chair pulled close to the fire, with a matching footstool. The stuffing was coming out of both of them, but a tartan rug covered the worst of the rips, and Olivia sank down into it.

The walls were largely bare, with several tell-tale rectangles where, Olivia presumed, paintings must have once hung. It was a well-proportioned room, with high ceilings and large, square-paned windows that overlooked the snow-covered lawn, but the interiors were time-worn, with peeling wallpaper, faded rugs and scarred antique furniture. The curtains were threadbare, their flowered pattern lighter at the edges where the sun had caught them over the years. An air of genteel shabbiness, rather like that of its owner, prevailed.

Olivia checked her watch. Ten-thirty. No one in London would be missing her, though her family in Australia might be wondering why they hadn't heard from her.

The fire crackled, the puppies snuffled and whimpered, and outside it continued to snow, a winter wonderland straight from one of the handful of Christmas cards propped on the mantlepiece. Olivia felt as if she had stepped out of her old life and was cocooned in another world altogether. She'd had so little time off in the past three months and she was still feeling rather wobbly, so it wasn't too much of a hardship to while away several hours gazing out at the wintry scene.

~

Dinner that night was in the kitchen, where a cream-coloured Aga stood in what was once a large inglenook fireplace. 'Fingers crossed there's enough oil to last the winter,' Beatrix said as she noticed Olivia staring at it. She had wrapped a tea towel around her waist and her hair was wilder than ever. Olivia guessed that her budget and inclination didn't run to a weekly wash and set. The knees of her tweed trousers bagged and the edges of her jumper were frayed; the backs of her slippers were broken and had definitely seen better days. Olivia looked down at the jumper Beatrix had lent her – it was perhaps a newer one, with only a tiny darn at the wrist.

Beatrix pulled a pie dish from the oven and set it on a board. Next to it was a bowl of green peas glossed with butter, and a bottle of wine, the cork already pulled. 'The last of Willy's cellar, *quelle dommage*. I'm sure I don't appreciate it quite as much as he did, but it's a decent drop nonetheless. There are some glasses in the cupboard there, make yourself useful and pour for us, won't you, darling?'

Olivia leaped up from her seat, happy to be able to help. As she poured the wine, she saw the invitation that Beatrix had opened that morning had been taken out of its envelope and now sat on the table. She read the date: 31 December 1999. New Year's Eve. The biggest night of the century. Then she saw the address: Beatrix had been right, it was to be held in a castle.

'I don't expect she's worried about the millennium bug, knowing Plum,' said Beatrix, seeing Olivia's glance. 'We all thought the world was going to end once, with Hiroshima. This Y2K nonsense seems insignificant in the grand scheme of things.'

'Are you thinking of going?' Olivia handed her a glass and picked up the invitation. 'What a way to see out the twentieth century – in a castle in Ireland.'

'Actually it's a manor house, but no less impressive, so I understand. Besides, Plum always did like to put on airs,' she sniffed. 'It was built in the nineteenth century, I think, so not exactly ancient, not in castle terms anyway.'

'She's offering to put you up,' said Olivia, reading the note scrawled in the corner.

'The last thing I'd want to do is stay there.' A shadow passed over Beatrix's face and for a moment she looked every one of her seventy-odd years.

'But these women were your friends, and you've not seen them for so long. Aren't you curious?' Beatrix was uncharacteristically hesitant, and Olivia suddenly felt she might have overstepped the mark.

'A little, I suppose,' Beatrix said finally, before taking a slug of wine. 'But I haven't left Winterslow in forever. I don't really go anywhere anymore; one of the few benefits of getting to my age is that I don't have to do anything I don't want to.' She put the glass down and began to rummage in a drawer, finally pulling out a vicious-looking bone-handled knife.

'But isn't this a bit different?' Olivia asked gently.

'Pfft.' Beatrix pursed her lips and puffed out her cheeks as she cut into the pie, releasing whorls of steam. 'I suppose.'

Olivia took a sip of her wine, and then another. It was smoky, savoury and fruity, and she sent a silent thank-you to the late Willy Pelham. 'Tell me some more about Burma,' she said, her mind darting back to the sketchbooks she had found in the children's bedroom. 'It sounds fascinating.'

Beatrix laughed throatily. 'Dirty, hot and smelly, more like. I'll tell you one thing: I've never worked so hard in my damn life. Eighteen hours a day sometimes. Trying to sleep with the sound of gunfire echoing all around us. Stepping over the bodies of dead Japs. Up at four in the morning to meet a train, burning our hands on the tea urns, fighting off the mosquitoes as the sun went down. Blisters . . . oh the blisters from opening can after can of food. Soya links and Spam.' She made a face. 'Making do with whatever was dropped by parachute – parajutes they were called, made from hessian when the parachute silk ran out. We did have a fairly good Christmas there I seem to remember, despite the circumstances – turkey, mince pies, the lot. Butchered my first pig,' she said proudly. 'Stared at almost certain death,' she added.

'I suppose anything that came after that would have seemed trivial,' said Olivia, captivated by Beatrix's words and the idea of an experience so far from anything she had ever come across.

'In some ways. But of course we couldn't wait for the war to be over. It was pretty bloody. Seems like another lifetime now.' Beatrix placed a plate heaped with pie and peas in front of Olivia. 'Hope you're hungry.'

'It looks delicious, thank you.' Olivia picked up her cutlery, then paused. 'Will you tell me more about your friends? About Lucy?'

'Well, as I said, she was Australian, and much bolder and more sure of herself than I was,' she half-smiled. 'She was very good at fixing things. Kind, too. Very kind to me, actually.' Beatrix's eyes clouded over and she blinked several times. 'There was one time . . .' She perked up. 'We came back to find a panther curled up on the verandah. Black as the ace of spades, he was. Gorgeous creature, but terrifying all the same. Lucy suggested we might have it as a pet – as if!' She laughed. 'We had to get the sappers to fire at it to chase it away, but we wouldn't let them actually harm it.'

Olivia wolfed down a mouthful of pie. Australia had its share of deadly wildlife, crocs and snakes, but encountering a panther in front of your house was something else entirely.

'Another time there was a large banded snake sunning itself on the road as we pulled up in our canteen. Lucy ran after it, keen for the skin as a trophy.' She laughed at the memory. 'But it wasn't the wildlife that was the most dangerous.'

'The Japanese soldiers?' Olivia asked.

'Those too,' said Beatrix in a clipped tone. 'Now come on, eat up before it gets cold.'

'It's delicious, thank you,' said Olivia after swallowing another mouthful. Compared to the leftover greasy bar food and office biscuits that she'd been existing on for the past few months, it was heavenly.

'How about you?' Beatrix asked. 'What on earth made you leave such a lovely warm country to come all the way here?'

'It was easy,' Olivia said. 'I'm fascinated by the culture. The history, the sense of being at the centre of things. The art world here is bigger and more exciting to me . . . Although, I'm not so fond of the weather.' She grinned, trying not to dwell on just how much she was missing the Australian summer right now.

'God, it was stinking hot,' said Beatrix, reminiscing again. 'The sweat simply poured off us. And then during the monsoon the water wasn't safe to drink, so everything had to be boiled. Quite a few of us got sick, from sheer exhaustion more than anything else, we worked like bloody navvies. Still, somehow we always managed to keep our spirits up. It seemed like such an adventure, at least to begin with.'

'And then?'

'Then it wasn't.' Beatrix paused and Olivia waited for her to elaborate.

'We lost so many good friends; some of the best people.'

'I'm sorry.' Olivia placed a comforting hand on Beatrix's, feeling the fine bones beneath the thin skin.

'Yes, well, you can't get through this life without losing at least a few that are dear to you, can you?' Beatrix lifted up the wine bottle and peered at it to see how much was left. 'Another drop? We might as well finish it.'

Olivia nodded and Beatrix poured them both another glass. The wine and the heat from the Aga had made Olivia sleepy again, and she could feel that her cheeks were flushed. As she swallowed, she realised that her throat no longer felt like it was lined with razor blades. She hiccoughed gently as Beatrix spoke about her life during the war.

At a pause in the conversation, and emboldened by the wine, Olivia asked about the sketchbooks. 'You were an artist? I sometimes paint a little,' she surprised herself by admitting this. 'Though not much since I got here. I haven't had the time since I came to England.'

Beatrix made the same noncommittal sound she had when Olivia had asked her about the invitation. 'I dabbled; never took it seriously. Besides, very few women became artists in those days. And then not long after the war I married, had Thomas and there was no question of it after that. Women – of my class anyway – rarely worked outside of the home.'

As Beatrix cleared away the remains of their dinner, Olivia found a tea towel and began to dry the dishes. 'I'm sorry if I shouldn't have looked at them. The sketchbooks, I mean.'

'Well, they were right there on the shelf; it's not as if I'd locked them away. Besides, there's nothing too embarrassing in them – I think. I've not opened them in ages. A young girl's prattle and silly pictures mostly.'

'I think they're amazing,' said Olivia. 'Especially the ones from the war. You know, a museum – a war museum especially – might be really interested in those, in your stories. In all of your stories – the Wasbies of Number Fifty-Five canteen.'

Beatrix gave that dismissive tut again. 'We did what we had to do, no more than plenty of others. And nearly all of us survived, which is more than the men did.'

'But you were right there, alongside them.'

'We just got on with things; there wasn't a choice. And we did make a difference; I'm proud of that.'

Beatrix bent down to give Bertie, who was lurking hopefully for scraps, an absent scratch. 'I'd better go and check on the pups, and then I'm off to bed,' she said. 'Turn the lights off after you, won't you?'

Olivia nodded. 'Oh,' she said, startled into remembering. 'Would it be okay if I ring my parents? It's just that they'll worry if they don't hear from me. I can give you some money to cover the cost of the call.'

'Oh no, that's quite out of the question, I'm afraid.'

'I'm sorry?' Surely it wasn't too outlandish a request?

'The lines are down. Have been since early this morning. The snow.'

Of course. The snow.

'We're completely cut off, darling.'

~

For Olivia, Christmas truly arrived as she knelt in front of a low coffee table watching Beatrix open a large box and carefully remove a number of tissue-wrapped objects. She held her breath as each one was revealed.

First, a round wooden snail, concentrically carved, head and tentacles splayed across its shell. Through her magnifying glass, Olivia saw that the netted detail of the snail's skin was exemplary, the ripple on its side uncannily lifelike. Someone had spent many hours in observation, and then painstakingly carved it until it was almost indistinguishable from the real thing. She reluctantly put it down as Beatrix unwrapped the next one.

It was a half-eaten pear, so realistic that Olivia could imagine the juice dripping onto the wasp that had been carved nestled inside it.

Then, an ivory octopus, jet eyes peeping from behind curled-up legs, the suckers on the underside accented with ink. The ivory was worn in places, and quite yellowed. It wasn't always easy to date netsuke accurately, for they'd been made for a period spanning more than three hundred years, up until the beginning of the twentieth century when the kimono was replaced with a more Western mode of dress. Newer netsuke were often artificially aged. Though some carried a maker's mark, these had often been duplicated, making it impossible to tell for certain if it came from the workshop of a particularly celebrated netsuke craftsman.

'They're incredible,' she breathed.

'Both of my husbands were fond of animals,' Beatrix said wistfully, unwrapping two more and placing them on the table. A fat, round-eyed goldfish and a cherry-wood mouse whose paw rested on a block of what might have been cheese as its tail wrapped underneath its body. Netsuke were all carved so that nothing protruded, for they were worn against fine fabric and handled daily.

'It's a shame they're not on display. Around the house, I mean.'

'They were at one time. We had a special cabinet built, a vitrine. Backed with a mirror so that you could admire them from every angle. My husband used to let Thomas play with them on Sundays as a special treat. That was his favourite,' she said as Olivia examined an armadillo, curled in on its armoured shell. 'But then, after he died, I couldn't bear to see them. They reminded me too much of him, and I sold the cabinet a while ago.'

'Of course.' After a careful inspection, Olivia put the armadillo down and turned to a fat-cheeked squirrel with a nut between its paws, a puffed-up fugu fish fashioned from coral, and then an exquisitely carved cicada whose wooden wings appeared lacy and transparent. Each netsuke was only a few centimetres high and in the *Katabori*, or figurative style, carved in the round.

Nowadays, when so many everyday items were mass-produced and designed to be replaced, it was heartening that such things were appreciated and valued, by some people at least. 'The breadth of this collection . . .' Olivia's voice trailed away as she surveyed the more than forty creatures. 'Even without the fox-girl, they'd be worth a fair bit, if sold as a whole.'

Beatrix nodded. 'Not enough to fix the roof, though, I'd guess. I shall have to include the fox-girl.'

She looked so bereft that Olivia felt a pang of guilt, but her heart sped up when she looked at the final package left to unwrap. She wiped her palms on her trousers before Beatrix handed it to her.

NINE

✥

Shillong, 1944

Bea felt sweat trickle its way down the nape of her neck and under the collar of her new uniform. Her stomach cramped with hunger. They were sweltering in the midday sun and it had been ages since breakfast. Sergeant Williams kept them on the parade ground, which was in reality a small square in front of the house, for nearly an hour. 'How the bleedin' hell did I draw the short straw and get lumbered with the lot of you?' Bea heard him mutter.

He was attempting to school them in the basics of marching in formation, but instead of a polished unit moving as one, the women were more like a straggling caterpillar with too many legs going in several different directions at once. Bea caught Lucy's eye as they all tried to turn on his command and raised her eyebrows skywards, smothering a giggle.

'Stand up straight,' he said again, struggling to keep the exasperation from his voice. 'And only move on my command. Lift your left foot first. No – the other left!' he bawled, glaring at several of the women who were shaking with repressed laughter. 'Keep your knees high and swing your arms. No, not so high.

'All right,' he called eventually. 'That'll have to do for now.'

'I can't for the life of me understand why we need to learn to march in the first place,' Plum complained when Sergeant Williams was out of earshot. 'It's not as if we're going to need it in the jungle.'

'Do you think Lieutenant General Slim will be disappointed in us?' asked Bubbles as they broke their ragged formation and headed towards the dining area.

'He can't expect too much now, can he,' said Bea. 'We're all still pretty green.'

It turned out that she was right and the women were not expected to march past him after all. After lunch, they gathered outside again and presently a Jeep carrying the Lieutenant General pulled up. Captain Taylor stepped forward to salute him, and he shook the hand of each of the women in turn, exchanging a few words, asking them where they had come from and thanking them for their service.

'Morale is one of the most underestimated factors in winning a war,' he said as he faced them. 'Never forget that you ladies are playing a big part in that. The sight of a cheerful face from home does more to support the war effort than you might realise.'

Bea swelled with pride, conscious of her new beret tight across her forehead. She wished her family – Archie especially – could see her now; at last she was about to do something that would make a difference. She resolved to write to her mother as soon as she had the chance, and concentrated so that she would be able to repeat the Lieutenant General's words.

After the inspection, and lunch, all of the new recruits walked into town to get their pay-book photographs taken. Everyone, from the lowliest private to the commander-in-chief, had the same one, tied up with bright pink ribbon. 'I don't reckon they'll stay looking this good for long,' said Lucy, stuffing hers into a pocket.

Over the next fortnight all the women improved their shooting, and Bea did her best to teach Lucy a few words of Hindustani. Bea and Lucy passed their truck-driving test, though Plum was less successful.

'Did you see the way the examiner went white when she climbed in the cab,' said Lucy, when Plum was out of earshot.

'I thought she was going to take off down the side of the hill, never to be seen again,' giggled Bea. 'She doesn't have the faintest idea when it comes to machines, does she?'

Bea noticed Lucy's eyes swivel frantically and turned around to see Plum standing a few feet away from them. There was no doubt that she'd heard. Bea bit her lip, flooded with remorse, but before she could think of a way to apologise, Joy was standing in front of them.

'It'll be good to have a driver or two on the team, though you'll most likely be assigned a driver from the BOR – British Other Ranks,' she said. 'My last one, Rawnsley, was a terrific chap. A real gentleman. Not exactly A-one fit – trouble with his nerves, I think, and hardly surprising really – but he was very handy to have around. A useful barrier to any unwanted attention, if you know what I mean.'

~

One day, as they were returning from the town, Bea spied a small dark shape huddled up against a tree. As they drew closer, she heard a plaintive mew and stopped in her tracks. 'Oh, look at it,' said Lucy. 'It's tiny.' Two huge, sorrowful eyes peered out from among a tangle of tortoiseshell fur. Lucy cast about, looking for any sign of its mother, but the street was deserted. They were about to carry on past, when the kitten gave another meow and followed them for a few steps.

'I'm sorry, darling, but we can't look after you,' said Bea.

The kitten whimpered, a pitiful sound that ran right through her.

'I'm perfectly certain that it's against regulations to keep a pet,' warned Bea, watching the kitten pad up to Lucy and twist its way around her ankles. Lucy reached down and picked it up. 'Oh, you're so thin!' she cried, cuddling it against her shoulder and carrying on walking.

Bea began to protest, but Lucy interrupted. 'No one needs to know. What shall we call you, then?' she crooned as the grateful kitten licked her face. She stroked its matted brown and caramel coat. 'Cocoa?'

The kitten began to purr, a deep rumble that brought a smile to both their lips. It seemed it liked its new name.

~

'It's here!' cried Lucy, bursting through the door of the other women's bungalow late one afternoon. Bea looked up, her heart beginning to hammer, for she knew that the piece of paper Lucy was waving could only mean one thing. She was lanced by sadness that her new friend might be leaving her soon and that they would go their separate ways. 'We're all going together,' she said, a triumphant note in her voice. 'You, me, and you too, Plum and Bubbles.'

'Really?' asked Bea, surprised.

'Yes, ma'am.' Lucy had taken to spending time with an American officer she'd met at a dance, and had picked up some of his phrases, uttered with a convincing drawl that made Bea smile. She'd also acquired a pair of metal-framed Aviator sunglasses from who-knew-where, giving her a raffish look. 'Mrs St John asked me to give you all these—' She handed each of them a sheet of paper with their name on.

'More bumpf?' asked Plum, for they'd been showered with written instructions on everything from the length of their skirts to the number of evenings they should go out each week.

'No. Movement orders.'

'Where to?' asked Bea.

'First Chittagong, and then on to Dohazari.'

'Where's that?' asked Bea.

'Near the Burma border. Didn't you say that's closer to your brother, Bea?'

Bea shrugged. 'Honestly, he could be anywhere in Burma. There's a lot of ground to cover.' She kept her private hopes that she might encounter him to herself, for she didn't want to jinx the possibility. She hadn't written to let Archie know her news, for she didn't want him to worry, and she'd not had any letters from him forwarded to her since arriving in Shillong. It didn't stop her thinking of him, and her father, wondering where they might be, and praying for their safety.

'And when?' asked Bubbles.

'Soon.'

'Better start packing, ladies,' said Bea. The irony occurred to her that, as recently as her mother's generation, in order to survive the punishing jungles of the East, white women hadn't been expected to lift a finger, instead they were cosseted by servants who saw to their every need. Now, look at them all.

'What are you going to do with Cocoa?' Plum asked.

Cocoa, as if sensing change in the air, leaped up from her place at the foot of Lucy's bed and began to meow furiously. 'All right, don't worry. We'll take you with us somehow,' Lucy soothed, stroking the kitten's fur.

Cocoa had bonded herself to Lucy, rightly seeing her as a saviour, and curling up on the end of her bed every night. So far, no one else appeared to have noticed the kitten on the grounds, for it stuck close to the house even when the women weren't there and seemed to know not to chase the birds and attract attention. Only Plum was put out, shooing the 'bloody flea-ridden moggy' out of the room any time it ventured in.

The other women snuck titbits from their meals so that Cocoa was now sleek and lithe, a far cry from the mangy stray they first encountered. 'She's our mascot, aren't you?' said Lucy, giving the kitten a belly rub and being rewarded with a purr that would do a well-tuned engine justice. 'Why don't you mind your own business, Plum? I don't see why I can't take it with us,' Lucy replied. 'Unless we're to be airlifted in. Even then . . .' she added. 'I'll find a way.'

'Good luck with that,' huffed Plum.

'Is it just the four of us?' Bea asked.

'No,' said Lucy. 'Sergeant Hatfield is coming too. She's going to be in charge.'

'Well, at least there'll be *someone* who knows what she's doing,' said Plum.

'Suddenly I don't feel so confident,' said Bubbles. 'I mean, it's been all right being here – more than all right, actually – but out there . . . in the jungle. Surrounded by Japs. I can imagine now how Charles and Archie must feel.'

Some of the women had already left for Imphal, and stories had filtered back of their assistance to the troops on the frontline. Accompanying these stories, however, was news of heavy fighting and many casualties.

They had all been sobered by the recent news that Joy's friend Cecily Williamson had been killed while out serving the troops, caught in the middle of a skirmish. The rest of her team had been lucky to escape with minor injuries.

They fell silent as they thought about what the future might hold. One thing they all knew: there was no backing out now.

TEN

❧❦❧

Pelham House, 1999

'I can see why you love it so much. And why you'd be reluctant to sell,' Olivia said gently.

Beatrix cradled the netsuke in her palm, where its eye – made of *umimatsu* – black coral – caught the light and seemed almost to wink at them. About three centimetres high, it was exactly as Olivia remembered from the photograph: a girl with the face of a fox, clad in a hooded robe and carrying a staff.

'There have been stories of men tempted by women for centuries,' said Beatrix disparagingly. 'Harpies, mermaids, fox-girls . . . utter poppycock, the lot of it. Made up to excuse men's dreadful behaviour, if you ask me.'

The netsuke itself was not especially beautiful, indeed there were more charming pieces in Beatrix's collection, but the ivory was in almost perfect condition, pale and creamy, with ink staining the details of the carving.

Olivia had spoken briefly with Elaine before she left the office, and estimated that, whether at auction or carefully negotiated private sale, it might command anything north of one hundred thousand pounds. Now, having seen it, Olivia was even more certain of her estimate. It was the age and rarity of the piece that made it the most valuable. There were probably only a handful of people in the world who were prepared to pay such a price, but these avid collectors would compete fiercely to acquire it. It wasn't anything close to the stratospheric figures achieved in the world of painting, but it would certainly help Beatrix out of the hole she found herself in.

'People are more important than things when it comes down to it,' Beatrix said firmly. 'Besides, I can't afford to be sentimental when I need a roof over my head.'

'Quite.'

'I know he'd understand. Needs must and all that.' Her eyes were glassy, and her face had a set expression, as if she were trying hard not to break down.

'Would you mind if I write up a condition report?'

Beatrix nodded and reluctantly handed the netsuke back to Olivia.

'There is, of course, the tricky question of provenance,' Olivia said cautiously. 'It was stolen from the Ashmolean in 1976, as I understand. I imagine you have the necessary paper-work that explains how it came to be in your – or your late husband's – possession?'

Beatrix met Olivia's gaze briefly, then looked away. 'Er . . . not exactly.'

Olivia's spirits sank. There was, she realised, every chance that Bea had come across the netsuke by less than honest means. Cholmondeley's would not be able to sell the fox-girl without a watertight provenance, not on the open market at least. But Brand's would most certainly be interested. She wanted to help Beatrix, but there was also the tempting thought of the original reward – twenty thousand pounds – if indeed it still stood.

'We need to go and see someone first,' said Beatrix in a resigned tone.

'Okay. Where is this person?' If she could help straighten out the provenance, then such a sale could give Olivia's career the boost it needed.

'Actually, she's in Ireland.'

Of course she was. Olivia flicked a glance to the window and saw that it had begun to snow – lightly this time – again.

She helped Beatrix return the netsuke to their tissue shrouds, feeling much better than she had the day before, though whether it was a result of the cold medication or finally seeing the fox-girl she couldn't be sure.

~

Later, Olivia wandered into the kitchen as Beatrix was cracking walnuts at the table, using a pick to get the meat out from the shells. The old woman seemed relieved; there was a light in her eyes that had been missing before. Perhaps she'd made peace with her decision.

'There's leftover pie in the fridge if you fancy something to tide you over until dinner, darling girl, and I wonder if you might like to join me in a drink?'

'You've been very generous to have me here.'

'Well, it's not as though either of us had much choice now, did we?' Beatrix's tone was content rather than accusatory. 'There's a plum pudding for afters tonight. I made a batch for the church fundraiser and had one left over. I wasn't going to steam it just for myself, but . . .'

'That sounds lovely,' said Olivia. 'But you really shouldn't go to so much trouble.'

Beatrix fixed her with a stern look and Olivia held up her hands in surrender.

'All right, give me a shout if you need anything, anything at all.'

'A bit different from your usual Christmas celebrations, I'd wager,' Beatrix said, putting down the nutcracker and scooping the shells into the bin. 'What would you have been doing in London?'

'I'd actually planned on sleeping,' Olivia admitted. 'I was supposed to be working at the bar till close on Christmas Eve, and then was due back again on Boxing Day . . .' She hesitated. 'It sounds a bit sad, doesn't it?'

Beatrix looked at her with sympathy. 'We all have times in our lives when we're on our own. Why don't you bring those books down? If you're interested, I can explain some of the drawings. I haven't looked at them in the longest time.'

'Oh, yes please, I'd like that.'

~

They sat in the small sitting room with a glass of sherry each –
to Olivia it tasted like liquid sunshine, grapes ripened by some
long ago summer's day warming her throat as she swallowed.

Beatrix held one of the sketchbooks open on her lap. 'Pull
that chair a bit closer so you can see,' she commanded, turning
the page. 'Oh!' She pursed her lips. 'I'd forgotten all about
that.' She pointed to a pencil drawing of two men, their hair
wrapped in what looked to Olivia like turbans, carrying a giant
cylinder between them. 'One of the tea urns. Our Indian cooks
and sweepers – they organised the water – did a marvellous
job; they built ovens almost everywhere we went, out of mud
bricks they made themselves. They were jolly clever.' She shook
her head as if she still couldn't quite believe it. 'There was one
in particular, Amar. Unfailingly cheerful, despite the wretched
conditions.'

Beatrix turned the page to a drawing of a trio of soldiers,
sitting on square crates, one with a harmonica pressed to his lips,
another lighting a cigarette and the third with a book dangling
loosely from one hand. 'Ah,' Beatrix sighed. 'Jack, Fred and
Billy. American Army pilots, all three of them. Such fun.' Olivia
thought there was something familiar about one of the men, the
shape of his face and the prominent nose, as if she'd seen them
before. She leaned in for a better look but couldn't place him.

They passed an hour or so in this fashion, getting through
almost all of the first of the wartime sketchbooks, before Beatrix
sat up in alarm. 'I've forgotten all about the bird. Quick, Olivia,

you're faster than I am, would you mind going to make sure it's not burned to a cinder already, darling?'

Olivia scrambled to her feet, and when she got to the kitchen was pleased to see that the chicken in the Aga was perfectly cooked.

Conversation was stilted as they ate. Beatrix appeared distracted, setting down her cutlery and staring into space, and Olivia was forced to repeat a few questions more than once. Olivia polished off a large plate of chicken, stuffing, peas, carrots, roast potatoes and gravy, as well as two helpings of pudding with custard, all of which seemed to please Beatrix enormously. As she rose to clear the dishes, Beatrix also stood up, limping across the kitchen and out of the room. She returned with the invitation, a mixture of apprehension and resolve colouring her features.

'You'll be happy to hear that I've decided to go,' she said, holding up the card. 'To the reunion. The woman I need to speak to about the fox-girl will be there.'

Olivia had guessed as much. 'Oh good!' Another step closer to securing the fox-girl for Cholmondeley's – or Brand's.

'The forecast is for temperatures to rise and the snow to melt, so we shouldn't be cut off for too much longer.'

Olivia felt suddenly bereft at the thought of returning to her cold, empty flat.

'The thing is,' Beatrix continued, 'there's just a slight hitch. I'm not up to driving that far, not with my wretched ankle.' She looked hopefully at Olivia. 'Now, if I understand correctly, Elaine isn't reopening the office until January, and you have no pressing reason to return to town?'

'No . . .' Olivia was beginning to get an idea of exactly where this was going.

'I hope you know how to drive a manual.'

Olivia nodded slowly.

'Good. Would you come? As my driver? I couldn't pay you . . .'

'I don't know,' Olivia said, considering the offer. 'It's a long way.'

'If I can get proof of the fox-girl's provenance, then it's in your best interest to help me, isn't it?' There was a calculating expression on Beatrix's face.

Olivia hesitated; it seemed like such an odd request, to accompany an old woman to a reunion, but she would love to visit Ireland; it had always seemed to her to be such an appealing country; the accents alone were utterly beguiling. 'Elaine would probably think it a good idea,' she said.

Beatrix smiled, presuming her agreement. 'I hoped you would see it like that, darling.'

'But what about the puppies?'

'Puppies?' For a moment Beatrix seemed perplexed and Olivia wondered if her memory was failing.

'Yes, the puppies. Bette's puppies.'

Beatrix's expression cleared. 'Oh, they're all spoken for. People are prepared to pay an astonishing amount for pure breeds. Keeps me in gin and then some,' she cackled.

Olivia wondered if her good humour was because she was pleased about the gin supply, or that she'd agreed to accompany her.

'They're not ready to leave their mum yet, surely?'

'Oh, of course not. Susie, my daily lady, won't mind having them. She's due to come in tomorrow.' She stood up and inexplicably tapped Olivia on the head with a teaspoon she'd picked up from a side table, as if she were cracking a boiled egg.

'Ow! What was that for?' Olivia rubbed her head, though in truth the action had caused surprise rather than pain.

'Pleased that you can come with me, of course,' she grinned.

'Are you sure Susie won't mind having the puppies?'

'Quite. I spoke to her on the telephone. It's all organised.'

'The phone's working?' Why hadn't Beatrix mentioned it earlier?

Beatrix nodded. 'Sorry. It slipped my mind. You can call your parents. But don't be too long.'

~

Olivia managed to reach her parents just as they were getting up on Boxing Day morning, and explained why she'd not been in touch before, relieved to hear that they hadn't been too concerned. 'We thought you might be working,' said her mother, 'and not be able to call. Happy that you're okay, and we miss you.'

'Miss you too, Mum.' She wished it were less expensive to call home, or that she had a Tardis that could transport her there, even for an hour. She hung up, overwhelmed by a wave of homesickness, but then reminded herself why she was here in Winterslow: to have seen the fox-girl, to hold her, was worth the months of separation, and to be on the brink of solving the decades-old mystery was an exciting prospect.

~

Early the next morning the *plink-plink* of dripping somewhere in the vicinity of her head roused Olivia, and she opened her eyes to the sight of a growing puddle on the carpet. Beatrix hadn't been wrong about the roof. Olivia glanced about the dim room, saw a wastepaper bin next to the bookshelf and threw the bedcovers off to retrieve it.

She checked carefully, but it appeared to be the only leak in the room. There was no telling how the rest of the house was faring, though. She'd seen a few buckets in the scullery and damp in almost all of the rooms she'd so far ventured into. She dressed hurriedly, pulling on her trousers and the borrowed sweater. She reached the ground floor, seeing a number of buckets dotted along the hallway. Either Beatrix had been up in the night, or she was an even earlier riser than Olivia. As she reached the kitchen, she glanced through the window. The winter wonderland of the previous days had all but disappeared, the snow melting and leaving a stark, bleak landscape of brittle-looking trees and bare shrubs. At least the drive would now be considerably easier. She hadn't got behind the wheel since arriving in England, but the Brits drove on the same side of the road as at home, so how hard could it be?

As she reached for the kettle, she caught sight of the photograph, half-hidden behind a pile of cookbooks on the shelf above the Aga, of Beatrix's son. She'd not given it more than a cursory glance before, but now she went to look at it again. A young man with strong features and a shy smile looked out at her. She knew where she'd seen the face before: it was almost identical to one of the soldiers in Beatrix's sketchbook.

The kettle began to whistle, and she heard a loud crash from the hallway followed by some rather choice swearing.

'Are you all right?' she asked as she rushed out to see Beatrix sitting on the floor, legs akimbo and a bucket on its side. The kettle continued its shriek.

'Can you help me up, darling girl?' The voice held a barely concealed sob.

She raced over and put her hands under Beatrix's armpits, lifting her to her feet.

'Are you in pain?'

Olivia was horrified as Beatrix dissolved into tears, clinging to her. She did her best to comfort the old woman, hugging her awkwardly as they moved towards a chair in the kitchen. 'Is it your bad leg?' Olivia eased her into a sitting position and eyed her rapidly swelling ankle.

'I'll be fine,' said Beatrix, her sobs now quietened to a few sniffs. Olivia wasn't convinced – the old woman's face was drained of colour and she spoke through gritted teeth. 'Sometimes it all gets a bit much, you know?' She pulled a crumpled handkerchief from her sleeve and blew her nose loudly. 'The bills, this house . . . the blasted roof.'

'It'll be okay,' said Olivia, doing her best to reassure her, though she had no way of knowing if it actually would be. 'I'm here to help.'

'Perhaps a bit of ice? There's some in the freezer. And take that kettle off, won't you?'

Olivia moved the kettle off the hob and then found the ice, which she wrapped in a tea towel and gently applied to Beatrix's ankle.

Beatrix grimaced. 'I definitely can't drive now,' she said.

'I'm not sure we should even think about going,' said Olivia doubtfully. 'What if you've broken it? Shouldn't you see a doctor?'

'Nonsense.' Beatrix removed the ice pack. 'Look, the swelling's gone down already. No sense in making a fuss.' She stuck her chin out, as if sheer strength of will would overcome the pain.

ELEVEN

Chittagong, 1944

'It's my wedding anniversary today,' Joy whispered, inspecting the plain band on her finger.

The five women had arrived at Chittagong three hours later than scheduled, and everyone was hot, dusty, tired and hungry from the long train journey. Though it was well past sunset, the air was still heavy with humidity; sweat ran down the back of their necks and dripped from their foreheads, stinging their eyes as they wrestled with bags, trunks, numerous boxes of stores, tin hats, water bottles and handbags. Unlike nearly every other station, at Chittagong there hadn't been a single porter to help with the mountain of luggage. Eventually, long after midnight, the connecting train pulled in and once again they faced the task of transferring everything from the platform. At Joy's direction they formed a line, passing everything up to the least crowded carriage they could find, before scrambling aboard as the departure whistle sounded. Lucy had concealed Cocoa in a carpet bag, plying her with treats in an effort to keep her quiet. Luckily, her meows could scarcely be heard over the hubbub of the station and the noise of the train as it rattled along the tracks.

Most of the other women were now asleep, resting against boxes and draped over bags, but Bea and Joy remained awake, sitting alongside each other and talking quietly. The immediacy of the war had changed something; suddenly, keeping personal matters to yourself didn't seem as important, and the darkness invited confessions.

'Oh golly,' said Bea, not letting on that she'd previously overheard Joy talking about her husband in unfavourable terms. 'What a way to spend it.' She saw Joy shrug in the half-light. 'How long have you been married?' she asked.

'Three years. Most of which he's been serving. I think we've hardly had more than a few months together that whole time. He still doesn't know I've joined up.'

'What?' Bea feigned surprise. 'Why not? Haven't you written to tell him?'

'His letters – which my parents have been forwarding, bless them – have been more and more distant.' Joy hesitated. 'To be honest, I'm not sure he even thinks of me as his wife anymore.'

'Oh no, that's awful. This bloody war . . .' her voice trailed off. She hadn't much of a clue what to say next, having little experience of such things. She aimed for something positive. 'I'm sure it will be different when you see each other again.'

There was a muffled sob in the darkness and Bea's heart twisted in sympathy for the woman.

'I'm so ashamed.' Joy spoke so quietly that Bea strained to hear it.

'What on earth for?'

'Well, I've been found wanting, I suppose.' She hesitated, then confessed. 'He's mentioned divorce in his last two letters. Tells me he's met someone else and doesn't feel the same way about me anymore. Says he doesn't think he ever really loved me. That we got married too young, without really knowing each other. He hasn't even given us a chance,' she finished bitterly.

Bea was glad that Joy couldn't see her shocked reaction. Divorce was not a word ever uttered lightly. 'Maybe it's simply that you've been apart for so long.' Even as she said it, her words sounded weak.

'I should be angry – angry that he's taken away my dreams of a future once the war is over, but how can I be angry, when others have lost so much more?'

Only last month, the husband of one of the longest-serving Wasbies, Barbara Wilson, had been killed in action. The two women lapsed into silence, each thinking of the telegram that had been delivered to Cleve, and of Barbara's stoic acceptance as she read it.

'Perhaps he's temporarily taken leave of his senses?' Bea suggested. 'It could all be different when you see each other again.'

'I'm not sure I share your optimism.'

'At least you're not pining away at home,' said Bea, trying again to think of something to cheer her up.

'It's a consolation, I suppose,' Joy sniffed. 'Besides, here at least I feel appreciated: the men we serve are always so grateful for the smallest kindness. For now, keeping busy is the only thing I can do. It's good to feel useful at least.'

'And we *are* going to be useful,' Bea said, a thread of determination in her voice.

'Thank God there wasn't time for children,' Joy went on, still lost in her own troubles. 'I've no idea how I'll break the news to my parents. I can't bear to imagine the look of disappointment on their faces.'

'Why not wait until the end of the war? Let the dust settle and then see what happens.' Bea put a comforting hand on Joy's arm. 'Besides, things always seem worse in the middle of the night.'

'One way or another, we're all fated to be hurt, these days all the more so,' said Joy with a sigh.

'Still doesn't make it any easier to bear,' Bea replied gently.

'How about you?' Joy asked, putting a little more brightness in her voice. 'Got anyone special? I've noticed you're not as familiar with the officers as some of the others.'

Bea shook her head. 'I've no wish to settle down yet – I'm here for the adventure, not to find a husband like most of the others seem to be. What's that saying? "Marriage halves one's rights and doubles one's duties."'

Joy let out a snort, but none of the other occupants of the carriage stirred. 'Sensible woman.'

'Have you ever seen any?' Bea asked, changing the subject.

'Seen any what?'

'Japs?' The idea of coming face-to-face with the enemy had been playing on her mind ever since leaving Shillong.

'None that were alive at the time,' Joy replied.

Bea shuddered. 'My brother – Archie – he's out there somewhere. I've not heard from him in months. I keep wondering if I'll come across him, you know, when we're out with a canteen perhaps.' She'd thought of little else since leaving Shillong, hoping that one day it might be his face that she would spot among the crowd.

'Stranger things have happened,' said Joy.

'I just pray that he stays safe. I don't know what I'd do if . . .' She was too superstitious to even utter the words.

～

'They've not got the faintest idea about queuing, I'm afraid,' Joy said the next day as they opened up the canteen. What seemed like a whole battalion of Gurkhas in their dark green uniforms swarmed before the counter, pushing and shoving each other out of the way to get to the front of the line.

Bea felt as green as the bandeaus they all wore to keep their hair out of their faces, but she supposed everyone had to start somewhere. She took a deep breath and pointed to the man at the front of the counter.

'Crikey,' said Bubbles. 'There's hundreds of them. I don't know who to serve first.'

'This is nothing,' said Joy with a brief smile. 'Just take them one at a time; they'll wait.' The grateful expressions on the faces of the men who clamoured for food and drink were so charming, it was impossible to be annoyed, even when some of them climbed onto the roof of the truck, as they were doing now.

When the women had arrived, the temperature was easily over eighty degrees as they prepared to serve hot tea, lukewarm lemonade and slabs of cake from the side of the mobile canteen. 'Leave your hats here, chaps,' said Joy, as they handed out drinks in return. 'You'll get them back when you bring back your mugs.'

There were gallons of tea, piles of bacon butties, trays of fudge and dozens of sheet cakes baked that morning by a team of Indian cooks. The floor-to-ceiling shelves were crammed with everything from razor blades, Macleans toothpaste and shaving cream, to cigarettes and Gold Flake tobacco, greasy leather bootlaces, even tins of Bird's custard powder and Huntley & Palmers biscuits.

'How much is the hair oil again?' Bubbles wailed, a tattered rupee note pinched between her thumb and forefinger.

'The prices are all on a list over here,' Bea shouted over the noise of the men they were trying to serve and pointed to several sheets of paper tacked up on the wall.

'Right-o,' she said, handing the man his change and moving to the next soldier who caught her attention.

'Everything's in rupees, as if it wasn't already hard enough,' Plum complained.

'You'll be surprised how soon you'll get the hang of it,' Joy reassured her.

When she had the chance, Bea asked the men she served what units they were from, and if they'd come across anyone from the Signals called Archie Fitzgibbon, but the answer was nearly always no. She also kept an eye out for the unit's distinctive blue and white flash, but didn't spot it.

Hours later the light had begun to fade but there had been scarcely a lull in the stream of men, hungry and hollow-eyed with exhaustion from days spent on the battlefront. Bea was doing her best to ignore a growing soreness in her lower back from bending over the counter, and she had almost become oblivious to the curious stares of some of the soldiers, who seemed surprised to be served by a white woman.

'Two mugs of char.'

Bea looked at the soldier standing before her. He seemed familiar. She thought perhaps she had seen him at one of the dances in Shillong. She handed him his order and smiled, as she did at all the soldiers, whether they said please or not, but this man was one of the few not to return her cheery grin. A memory flooded back as she recognised the same sour expression when she'd refused a dance. She shrugged. She'd probably be in a foul mood too if she'd seen some of the things these men had.

As she continued to serve, she caught snippets of conversations, and her thoughts immediately flew to Archie when she overheard two soldiers talking about a pair of signalmen being taken prisoner by the Japanese. 'They'll be lucky to get out alive,' said one.

'You wouldn't treat a dog the way the Japs treat their POWs,' said the other, his face grim. 'Torture, starvation, beatings just for the hell of it.' He shut up when he saw the expression on Bea's face.

Joy glanced at her watch. 'Nearly time to close up,' she said, much to everyone's relief. Bea noticed that Plum in particular appeared ready to keel over with tiredness, and all of their faces were streaked with the dust that had lifted in clouds and now covered the once spotless countertop.

'Blast these boots,' said Plum, shifting from foot to foot. 'I'm sure I've got blisters on both heels.'

'You're not the only one,' said Bubbles. 'And I'd kill for a cuppa.'

'Save your complaints, ladies,' said Joy, not unkindly. 'Be thankful it's not too hot yet – there will be times when we're working in hundred-degree heat, or in the pouring rain. And think of what the men have to go through, for it is far worse than anything we will see.'

'It's really not that bad,' said Lucy, the only one of them whose pleasant expression hadn't faltered.

'Sorry Sergeant Hatfield,' added Bubbles, chastened. 'We'll all get used to it soon, I'm sure.'

Joy's expression softened. 'Plum, Bubbles, take a break and pour yourselves some tea; there's a spot in the shade over there. And when it's just us, it's Joy. Sergeant Hatfield is far too formal for my liking.'

They soon discovered that the unrelenting humidity made the canteen like a greenhouse. Bea often had to wipe the sweat from her face to stop it from dripping on the counter, but she didn't care. At long last she felt like she was making a difference – not just for getting the small comforts of life to soldiers in remote locations, but for helping to ease their worries, show them that someone cared, and raise a smile from even the grimmest faces.

For security reasons, Joy was the only one who knew where they were going each day, and kept the itinerary under lock and key in the mess. The women generally went out four at a time, leaving one of their five-person team back at headquarters in Dohazari to stocktake, process orders and check the accounts from the previous day. They had been assigned a driver – Campbell – who cheerfully navigated the rough, sandy tracks, managing to get them to the units they'd been assigned to serve. There was only really room for two in the front of the cab, leaving the others to huddle on the floor in the back of the truck, often wrenched this way and that as they navigated the pot-holes in the road. By the time they emerged into the daylight, blinking and feeling slightly seasick, they were all thankful that the ordeal of the drive was over.

Each time they went out, they had no sooner parked up in their appointed spot than all heads turned in their direction and a swarm of men surrounded the truck. Bea overheard a gunner joking that if they'd arrived during a drill there would have been nothing for it but to dismiss the men. All around them dust – in places a foot deep – swirled and they soon learned that flies settled on any item of food left uncovered for more than a second or two.

'Best char of my life,' said more than one grateful soldier as they returned their empty mugs and collected their tin hats.

The welcome the Wasbies received everywhere they went was overwhelming, and Bea soon realised that the men were as pleased to see a woman's face as to enjoy a cuppa, and that what they most wanted was the chance for a bit of chit-chat while they were being served. It more than made up for the arduous journey to get there. Most of the time the troops were polite and patiently waited their turn, sometimes for hours, uncomplaining, in the stifling heat. Some days, Bea estimated they must have served more than a thousand men. Still no one had come across Archie.

In the rare quieter moments as they packed up their canteens, some of the soldiers told her stories so harrowing that she lost all appetite, stories that she knew she would never forget. It hardened some of them, for they spoke without pity, or fear, without much emotion at all.

Some of the units hadn't been back to HQ for weeks, fighting in the jungle and supplied by air drops, so the extra comforts the women provided were especially appreciated. Bea never had to remind herself to smile when faced with the men's good humour, though it was sometimes disconcerting to be stared at by some of the Indian Army soldiers, many of whom, unlike those Bea had encountered in Calcutta, appeared never to have seen a white woman in the flesh before.

At the end of each day, their faces were streaked with dust, their hands were blistered and their feet puffy and aching from the long hours of serving, but they all felt the satisfaction of having helped.

Their sleeping quarters were in a small house – a *basha* – which they had done their best to make homely, draping scarves over their canvas stretcher beds and their trunks, the latter serving as makeshift dressing tables. Bea shared a room with Lucy, and there was a bathroom shaded by a flimsy bamboo screen next to them, with Bubbles and Plum on the other side of it. No alarms were needed here – the screeches of the local myna birds – *Shalik* they learned they were called – woke them long before dawn.

A mess tent had been set up next to a couple of mango trees, and they all watched the fruit keenly for signs of it ripening, for there were almost no fresh vegetables or fruits to be had. Rations mainly consisted of bully beef, tinned peas, Spam and corned beef, and disgusting things called soya links, a kind of ersatz sausage that was purported to 'meet all human needs'.

'Doesn't meet any of my needs,' Bubbles said glumly as they lined up for breakfast one morning.

'Have we got anything for itching?' Lucy asked, scratching her arm. 'Do you think Cocoa could have given me fleas? I swear she was free of them when we left Shillong.'

'She's probably picked them up from those monkeys she loves to chase,' said Plum, frowning at the plate of food in front of her.

'But at least she keeps them away,' said Joy.

'They're biting ants,' said Bea, tossing her a small bottle of calamine lotion. 'I found the little horrors right through my bedding last night.'

The camp at Dohazari was on the banks of the Sangu River, which, when they arrived, stank like billy-o. Thankfully, after a few days, either the smell abated or they'd simply become immune to it, and though the river remained a murky khaki colour it became a relaxing spot to spend a spare moment, watching dugout boats – *khistis* – float by. Sometimes, rafts of bamboo and teak were brought downriver, bound together and piloted by dark, wiry men who appeared to live on top of the bundles for days on end. Bea liked to snatch spare moments there, watching the antics of the snub-nosed monkeys that swarmed the trees, sketching or writing letters to Archie, and her parents.

On their second afternoon, some of the Indian sappers pulled out a couple of hand grenades and lobbed them into the river. 'Fishing trip,' said one of them to Bea in Urdu. Sure enough, after a blast that half-deafened her, the bodies of silvery fish floated to the surface and the sappers proceeded to haul them out by the bucketful, presenting some to the women. 'Come on, then,' said Lucy, ever practical. 'Let's get a knife from the kitchens and start gutting them.'

'Can you show me?' Bea asked, determined not to be squeamish, 'I wouldn't have the faintest idea how.' Until then, fish for Bea had either been served coated in breadcrumbs or filleted and garnished with parsley, presented under a silver cloche.

She had no idea what type of fish they were, but skewered and roasted over coals for dinner that evening, they proved a far more appetising alternative to the endless tinned meat. 'We used to eat fish like this – river trout mainly – at home,' said Lucy, picking over the bones. 'My cousins and I would camp out in the Snowies, walk for miles, catch our dinner every day.'

'That sounds like heaven,' Bea sighed. 'We weren't allowed any such freedom, either at boarding school or in Calcutta.'

Late one night, when they'd been in Dohazari for a little over a week, Bea was woken by the wheezing notes of a piano accordion. She'd gone to bed early, intending to catch up on her sketchbook-cum-diary by the light of Lucy's hurricane lamp, but had been too tired to write more than a few short sentences, adding to her sketch of the battle-weary troops flooding in from the jungle. She'd almost used up the three cakes of green paint in her palette, for the landscape came in every shade from acid lime to dark forest.

Bea sat up in bed, first annoyed at having been disturbed and then intrigued as to where the sound was coming from. She'd been sleeping in only a shirt, so she pulled on her uniform, thrust her feet into her boots and went outside to investigate. No more than a hundred yards away, under the moonlight, was a group of officers, sitting on camp chairs and upturned boxes from the stores. She noticed a couple of men dancing with two women who looked suspiciously like Bubbles and Plum.

As she drew closer, she saw a card table filled with bottles of varying sizes and Petromax lamps hanging from the branches of a nearby shrub like fireflies. Joy stood behind the table, a mug in one hand and a bottle of gin in the other.

'Bea!' Lucy called from where she was lighting a fire. 'Sorry, we thought you were out for the count.'

'As if I could sleep with this racket.'

Lucy put an arm around her waist and pulled her towards the small crowd. 'C'mon, don't be cranky,' she whispered in her ear before turning to the others. 'Boys, meet the final member of our team.'

The men all glanced up, a couple gave a mock salute, and Joy pressed a drink into Bea's hand. She took a sip and regarded the disarmingly fresh-faced young men in front of her. They looked no older than Bea, one dark, the other sandy-haired and freckle-faced and the other two fair, and they all had perfect teeth that gleamed against their sun-browned skin.

'They're pilots from the American base,' Lucy explained. 'This is Fred, Billy, Al, Jimmy and this is Jack.' She pointed to each of them in turn.

Bea raised an eyebrow at Lucy, who shrugged back.

The women were dressed in a motley assortment of khaki uniform and mufti, but the men looked sharp in their olive jackets and tightly knotted ties, their brass buttons gleaming in the lamplight.

As the tallest of the men stepped forward, Bea noticed he had Cocoa curled up in his arms, the cat purring contentedly. 'It seems she likes men, particularly those in uniform,' she said.

'She's got good taste then.' A slow smile spread over his face. 'Captain Jack Butler, ma'am. Say, have I seen you somewhere before? I never forget a face.' He had a brilliantly white smile, and his ink-black hair fell messily over his forehead, giving him a boyish air. But it was his voice that caused the hairs on the back of Bea's neck to stand on end, for it was low and husky and seemed to caress her without him even touching her. She could understand why Cocoa was entranced.

'If you have, I'm afraid I don't remember you,' she replied.

'Brutal! But honest, at least,' he cried, clutching a hand to his chest and making her smile.

The only place to sit was on the end of a bench, next to where Captain Butler had just sat down again. He scooted across to make more room, gently easing Cocoa out of the way, and she accepted the cigarette he offered, leaning in as he lit it for her.

'What brings you all here?' she asked.

'We met these gals—' he indicated Bubbles and Plum, who were swaying to the music a few yards away, 'this afternoon and they invited us over. Fred there plays a mean harmonica, and then of course there's Al.' He nodded to the accordionist.

'All the ingredients for a fine party,' Bea observed grudgingly. 'Good show.' It was impossible to be grumpy in the face of their cheerfulness.

Bubbles was talking to one of the men about Charles, and Lucy was grilling Jimmy about the planes they flew; asking questions about speed, aerodynamics and runway lengths. Lucy often talked about flying on the long journeys out to the troops, so it was nice to see her find someone who shared her interest.

'Afraid we don't run to ice,' Joy joked as she handed out tin mug after tin mug containing a lethal mix of spirits.

'Heck, we don't even run to glasses,' said Fred, raising his mug.

From a distance, Bea saw Lucy down her drink and reach for another in the same time that Bea had managed a single sip.

'More?' Lucy asked as Jimmy held out his hand for a refill.

Bea turned her attention back to the man sitting beside her, disconcertingly close.

He put his drink on the ground and reached into his pocket, bringing out something small and round. He held it up for her to see and it glowed palely in the moonlight. 'Say, take a look at this. Picked it up last week. Whaddya think of it?'

'I don't know; what is it exactly?' she asked.

'D'you know, I'm not sure. Someone said they reckoned the Japs used to use them to secure pouches to their kimonos.'

'May I?' Bea held out her hand. 'Why, it's a fox,' she said, delighted, 'but also a girl.' The carving, cool and smooth to her touch, depicted a robed young woman, leaning on a staff, with the delicate hands and face of a human but the snout and ears of a fox. There was a tiny scratch on her right cheek. 'Ivory, most likely,' she said, noticing the dark glint of a jewelled eye. 'How very peculiar. Look, there are two holes in it. Perhaps it was once strung on a ribbon?' She turned it over and saw a small stain. She rubbed at it before she realised what it was – blood. Dried blood. The alcohol in her stomach curdled and she felt suddenly light-headed. She handed it back. 'It's quite something.'

'Ain't it? I reckon she's my new good-luck charm,' he said, tucking it back into the top pocket of his uniform.

'How did you say you got it?' she stammered.

126

He glanced sideways, rubbing his chin thoughtfully. 'You really don't want to know that, honey.' He laughed at her shocked expression. 'I'm kidding!' he reassured her. 'I found it in a ditch – a foxhole actually, so that was appropriate. I swear I don't know what happened to the poor guy who it probably once belonged to.'

Later on, as they sat around the embers of the fire, Bea overheard Jimmy mention the word *bushido* and asked what it meant.

'A code of honour,' Jimmy said, a slight slur to his words. Bea had noticed him and Lucy matching each other drink for drink, but Lucy looked to be in better shape than him. 'The Japs choose to kill their wounded comrades rather than leave them to be captured by the enemy.'

'It sure makes for a fearless adversary,' said Jack. 'The worst dishonour is to be taken prisoner – and so they fight to the bitter end with no thought to save themselves.'

Bea shuddered. Though the women had driven deep into the jungle on many occasions now, they hadn't got close to the frontline.

Fred and Joy got to their feet and began to sway in time to the music.

'Come on,' Jack said, grinding his cigarette under the heel of his boot and giving Cocoa a fond scratch. 'We're the only ones not dancing, and that's a crime.'

Bea was grateful that she was wearing her Army-issue boots, which although ill-fitting at least protected her feet far better than the dancing shoes she'd worn when she arrived in Shillong. She took his hand and let him lead her, relaxing in his arms as he held her gently but securely. As she rested her head on his chest, the mosquito-infested jungle and the other men and women faded into the background until it was just the two of them. He was a good dancer and it was a welcome chance to forget about the sweat and the mud and the hard work for a while. She was surprised to find that they fitted together like pieces of a jigsaw, the beat of his heart a solid, comforting pulse against her ear. For the first time in months, her brother wasn't uppermost in her thoughts.

Later, Al took a break from the accordion, and a wind-up gramophone appeared. 'The Chattanooga Choo-Choo', songs from *Porgy and Bess*, 'Don't Get Around Much Anymore' and Billie Holiday's 'Trav'lin' Light' were firm favourites among the women, though Bea had noticed Joy's wistful expression whenever the latter was played. She seemed happier on this occasion, however, keeping herself occupied mixing drinks for the rest of them. Jimmy was by now leaning back against one of the trees, a glazed expression on his face, while Lucy continued to drink and dance seemingly unaffected by the booze.

Eventually, when the first fingers of dawn began to lighten the sky, the men left, weaving dangerously between the trees and gunning their Jeep along the dirt road. 'We'll clean up later,' said Joy when the dust had settled. 'I'm dead on my feet.'

'Hear, hear,' said Bea, dragging herself back to her cot, her head fuzzy from the gin and filled with thoughts of the pilot in whose arms she'd felt so safe. She was out for the count before she even had time to think of Archie, to say a prayer for him.

As she slept, she dreamed of the fox-girl, that the tiny figure was following her through the jungle, both of them stalked by soldiers with guns. She woke late, her heart racing, the dream vivid in her mind.

~

They all moved a little slower than usual the next day, and even Cocoa barely stirred from the end of Lucy's cot. After bacon butties and a gallon or two of tea, Bea began to feel more human again but was nevertheless pleased that she was rostered to stay at the base in the storeroom for the day.

Joy had put her in charge of ordering and accounts – 'With your head for numbers, it's an obvious choice,' she'd said – and Bea enjoyed making sense of the chaos, though it had taken her a while to get used to the vast quantities of everything they needed: they went through a hundred dozen bottles of lemonade each week alone, not to mention sometimes five hundred loaves of bread and two hundred large slab cakes in a day. Train-loads of troops arrived like clockwork, moving north by road or departing from the railway station, and all, without exception, were ravenously hungry and thirsty. Some days the canteen sold out of food entirely, and she hated seeing some of the men go without, especially after they'd spent hours patiently queuing.

Today, however, the columns of numbers seemed to swim in front of her eyes, and she had to struggle to keep her focus, for her thoughts kept wandering to a certain dark-haired pilot and the feeling of being held in his arms.

~

'I've been granted three days' leave!'

Bubbles waved the chit enthusiastically at Bea and Lucy one afternoon. 'And Charles is going to be there too, according to

Mummy. I can't believe it.' She jumped up and down in delight, her fair curls escaping from her turban.

Bea, on the other hand, felt her spirits sink. She knew she should be happy for her friend, but neither she nor her mother had heard from Archie in months, and it seemed unfair that Charles should have been given leave and not him.

The next day, Bubbles hopped on a flight to Calcutta, waving them goodbye with promises of gifts on her return. 'I'll be back before you even have a chance to miss me,' she joked, looking happier than Bea had ever seen her.

Later that morning, Lucy lay face-up underneath their truck, grumbling happily about crankshafts, bearings and pistons, while Plum pored over a newspaper – several weeks out of date – and Bea and Joy were busy in the kitchens.

Loud screams travelled towards them, coming from near the river.

The women ran down to the banks, where they found a group of soldiers gathered, all watching a horse thrashing in the water.

'What's going on?' Joy asked as several men waded in and tried to calm the animal.

'Some berk decided to swim his horse from one side to the other,' said a British sergeant.

'The horse fell, threw the chap and then kicked him in the head in a panic,' said another, who was waist-deep in the water.

'Oh, the poor thing,' said Bea, thinking of her beloved Domino.

'Where is he now? The man, I mean,' said Lucy, who looked as though she was ready to wade in herself.

'Somewhere in the river – we're trying to find him.'

The women watched on as several soldiers dived into the murky water, each time coming up alone. After several agonising minutes, a cry went up and Bea saw two of the men drag another to the shore. Once they had him clear of the water, they began mouth-to-mouth resuscitation, but it was to no avail.

Bea turned away, her hand to her face. Death was all around them – she wasn't so naïve as to think otherwise – but to see it up close, and one so pointless, was somehow more shocking than reading the lists of soldiers who died in battle every day.

'Come on, Bea, there's nothing we can do here,' said Joy, leading her back to the kitchens, an arm about her shoulders, the other women close behind.

'That could easily have been Archie,' she said. 'He loved to take his horse into the river at home. It's just the sort of thing he'd try here too.'

'Have you heard anything from him?' Joy asked.

'Not for ages. Mother hasn't either, not according to her last letter. All we know is that he could be anywhere in Burma.'

'First in, last out,' said Joy, echoing the motto of the Signals.

'How do you know that?' Bea asked, surprised.

'I knew someone in that unit once,' Joy replied.

Bea didn't ask what had happened, in case the answer was one Joy would rather not tell, and Bea would rather not hear. She was learning that sometimes it was best not to know the details. 'How about you? Have you heard from your husband recently?'

Joy shook her head. 'Not a dicky-bird.'

'The not-knowing is the worst part, isn't it?'

'It's hard for those at home too – we're not able to tell our parents anything very much about where we are or what exactly we're doing. No different from your brother, really,' said Joy.

'Best not to dwell on things; all we can do is keep ourselves busy and useful here,' said Lucy.

'Worrying never helps,' added Plum.

'This war has to be over eventually, doesn't it?' asked Bea, looking imploringly at each of them.

'The tide is turning in Europe, or so we're being led to believe,' said Lucy.

'Is it terrible to admit that I'm not even sure sometimes that I want it to be over?' Joy admitted. 'I've no idea what I'll do after this. I love being part of something here, not as a daughter or a wife, but as me.'

'I know what you mean,' said Lucy, putting an arm around her shoulder. 'But things will be different after the war; they have to be. We've all shown that we can do almost anything, certainly more than has ever been expected of us. There are women in factories now, engineers, ship builders, ambulance drivers, tram conductors, even pilots . . .' Her last few words held a wistful note.

'What about the men? They'll want their jobs back,' said Plum.

'Then what will we do?' Bea asked.

'One thing I know for certain,' said Joy, her mouth firmly set. 'I'm not going to go back to being just a wife.'

TWELVE

On the road, 1999

'Willy's pride and joy. Sixty-seven Jaguar S-type,' said Beatrix proudly as Olivia loaded her suitcase – a battered leather affair – in the boot.

'It's a dream to drive,' said Olivia, appreciating the car's acceleration as she put her foot down when they eventually turned on to the motorway.

Beatrix gave a bark of laughter. 'I learned to drive a Jeep and then a big old Chevy truck – the Jag's a pussy cat by comparison.'

Olivia snuck a quick look at her, eyebrows raised. The woman constantly surprised her.

'In the war, darling,' she elaborated.

'Of course.' Olivia turned her attention back to the road.

Beatrix had planned their journey with military precision and Olivia had been impressed with Beatrix's efficient manner as she made the arrangements. The car ate up the miles, there was very little traffic thanks to the holiday, and they reached Holyhead well ahead of schedule. Olivia had felt a small thrill as they crossed the border into Wales – another country that was new to her.

'Would you mind if I just pop to the shops?' Olivia asked, checking her watch. 'I need a few things.'

She managed to negotiate the snarl of traffic as Beatrix directed them and once they'd parked, she settled the old woman in a cafe, with a pot of tea and something called an Eccles cake – apparently Beatrix's favourite. She found a department store and bought the bare necessities, charging her purchases to her credit card. Beatrix had given her a small overnight bag, and Olivia was wearing her own trousers, topped by the jumper Beatrix had lent her. She added a pair of jeans, underwear, a couple of pairs of socks, and then found a chemist, looking for a toothbrush and toothpaste as well as a jar of cheap moisturiser. Luckily, she'd had a small make-up bag with her when she left London. She also found an electrical shop and purchased a new charging lead for her phone. She was about to return to collect Beatrix when a boutique caught her eye. The window mannequin modelled a plum-coloured, fine wool dress with a wraparound skirt and a deep V-neck, and although she knew it was a frivolous expense, she added it to her growing number of purchases, deciding to worry about how she would pay for it later. After all, it wasn't every day that she visited people who lived in a castle.

~

The best thing that could be said about the ferry journey was that Olivia had an unread paperback in her handbag, a page-turning thriller that took her mind off the swell of the ocean. She got up from time to time to stretch her legs, do a lap of the lounge and look out at the unchanging, choppy sea, but Beatrix, once ensconced in a tub chair in the ferry's lounge, closed her eyes and seemed to sleep for almost the entire duration.

'This is nothing compared to piggy-backing a plane-load of stores in a DC-3,' she told Olivia when she eventually stirred. 'At least there's a comfortable seat this time.'

It was late by the time they arrived in Dublin; too late to carry on to Galway, and too dark for Olivia to make out much of the city. 'I've never been to Ireland before,' she said. 'A shame we won't see the city.'

'I didn't think Plum would appreciate us turning up in the middle of the night,' said Beatrix. 'I booked us into a hotel I used to stay at with Willy. Got the last two rooms at one in Galway too. Everything seems to be so busy over the holiday.'

Olivia followed the signs to Dublin city centre, then Beatrix's directions to the hotel. Almost before she knew it they were standing in a dark-panelled reception being handed their room keys by a man with an accent as soft as mist. Olivia could have listened to him recite the phone book.

'Oh look, the bar is still open, darling, how delightful. What do you say to a chotapeg of whiskey? Keep me company.' It stopped just short of being a command, but Olivia forgave her

135

for it as she watched Beatrix anxiously twist her lips. Olivia was impressed by her stamina. They'd set off before dawn that morning, and granted Beatrix had slept on the ferry, but here she was late at night, suggesting a drink – or more likely several. Even her limp seemed less pronounced and there was a new, slightly jittery energy about her.

'Why not?' At least she'd get to find out exactly what a chotapeg was, and perhaps discover a little more about the women they were going to meet.

'Are you excited about the reunion?' she asked when they'd settled themselves in the bar, a tumbler of Irish whiskey in front of each of them.

'I'm not sure excited is exactly the word I'd use,' said Beatrix, tinkling the ice in her glass. 'It's been such a long time, though some things feel like they happened only yesterday.' She looked off into the distance. 'But memory's like that, I suppose.'

~

The next morning, after a hearty Irish breakfast – 'Plenty of iron there, you know,' Beatrix said pointing to a slice of black pudding. 'I'll stick to my sausages if it's all the same with you,' Olivia had replied – they got back in the car. Olivia wished again that they might have had time for some sightseeing, and cast a regretful glance at the rear-view mirror as they left the city, seeing creamy sandstone buildings and a cathedral spire piercing the sky.

They flew along the road, office buildings giving way to commuter towns and then to jade-green hills. After about an hour, Beatrix suggested a detour to Tullamore. 'It's quite delightful, and I could do with a cup of tea, how about you?'

Olivia pulled off the motorway and they soon found themselves on a winding road, travelling at a snail's pace behind a procession of men and women walking in the middle of the road. Olivia craned her neck and saw that up ahead at the front of the procession was a hearse.

'Yes, darling, it's tradition here,' Beatrix explained. 'Bloody nuisance if you ask me.'

Having never witnessed anything like it before, Olivia was charmed.

Once they eventually got past the mourners, who turned off in the direction of a churchyard, they arrived in Tullamore and soon found a teashop to suit Beatrix. Olivia left her, taking the opportunity to explore the town.

After a short while, she found herself standing in front of an art supplies shop, and before she knew it she was inside and had assembled a selection of good brushes, pencils, a travelling watercolour set and a couple of sketchbooks. The landscape she'd briefly glimpsed from the motorway called to her in a way that the London streets hadn't. Perhaps she might sneak a little time to paint while they were there. She had in mind a series of vignettes similar to what Beatrix had done so many years ago. Her own visual diary. She wasn't sure her life was going to be as colourful as Beatrix's had been, but she wasn't going to let that deter her.

'Oh, there you are! Thought you must have got lost.'

'Sorry, it's such a pretty place that I forgot the time,' Olivia apologised as she joined Beatrix in the cafe. 'I hope you haven't been waiting too long for me?'

'What do you think?' Beatrix's tone, formerly so friendly, was now terse, almost agitated.

'Again, I'm sorry, I shouldn't have kept you.'

'There's tea left in the pot, would you like some?' Beatrix offered, more calmly as she turned over the china cup opposite her and began to pour, not waiting for an answer.

Olivia sank gratefully into a seat.

'What's that you've got there?'

'I found an art shop.' Olivia opened the bag and showed her the contents.

'Ah, you're planning to paint while we're on our trip?'

'I'm not in the same league as you, of course, but I thought I might dabble.'

'I expect you're better than you think.'

Olivia inclined her head modestly. 'Would it be okay if I made a quick sketch of you?'

Beatrix's hands went to her hair. 'I'm sure I look a fright.' She summoned a passing waitress. 'May we have another pot of tea please, and perhaps some sandwiches. A scone or two wouldn't go amiss either.' The waitress jotted down the order and Beatrix winked at Olivia, good humour, it appeared, fully restored by the prospect of lunch.

Olivia opened her sketchbook and selected an HB pencil as Beatrix sat up and folded her hands in front of her.

'I killed a man once, you know.'

'What?' Olivia's question exploded across the room, causing several of the other cafe patrons to look up from their conversations, and her pencil to slide across the page.

'Oh don't worry, it wasn't murder. Purely self-defence.'

Olivia swallowed, her pencil stilled, and waited for Beatrix to furnish the details.

'I think I could do it again, too.'

Olivia met Beatrix's eyes, which were the guileless blue of a spring sky. What was on her mind? Was there someone in particular, or was it the kind of throwaway remark that old ladies liked to bandy about to get a reaction, to be noticed instead of ignored?

'Care to tell me about it?' she asked, going back to her sketch.

'I didn't have a lot of choice in the matter. I suppose it was a kind of automatic reaction. I'm surprised I even hit the poor beggar – I wasn't the best of shots, I don't mind telling you.'

She was about to continue, when the waitress bustled over to them with a large tray, taking her time to unload a tier of sandwiches, jam, cream, butter and scones, followed by another pot of tea. The food took up almost all of the table, and Olivia hastily moved her sketchbook out of the way as Beatrix poured more tea.

'Some more milk too, please, if you could possibly manage it?' Her hand wavered over the cup as she beamed at the waitress. 'Now then, my dear, this looks lovely, doesn't it?' Beatrix halved a scone and layered it thickly with jam and cream. 'Jam first, then cream,' she insisted.

'The shooting?' Olivia asked. 'Can you tell me any more about that?'

'Oh darling, it was such a long time ago,' Beatrix said vaguely and then took a bite of scone, leaving Olivia with the feeling that the old woman enjoyed teasing her.

She put her drawing to one side and picked up a triangle of cucumber sandwich. They ate, in companionable silence, until almost everything had disappeared.

'Let me see,' said Beatrix when she had finished eating, pointing to the sketchbook.

Olivia held it up.

'Oh I say, it's rather good. You've captured me to a tee. Aren't you clever?'

'I'm not sure I got the nose exactly right, but thank you.'

'Are you sure you really want to be an art dealer?' she asked. 'If Elaine is anything to go by, it's quite a cut-throat trade, is it not? And you seem . . . well, you seem rather gentler.'

'There's more than one way to peel an orange,' Olivia replied.

'Perhaps you're right,' Beatrix replied, returning her smile. 'I never really had a job as such,' she added with a tiny sigh. 'Apart from the Army, of course. Women in my day were expected to give up work once they married.'

'I'm very lucky to work with beautiful things nearly all of the time – like the fox-girl,' Olivia said, draining her cup and checking her watch. 'Speaking of which . . . Do you think we should be getting going again? It's another couple of hours to Galway. Besides, I think the waitress would like our table.' A steady stream of customers had come and gone in the time they'd been sitting there, and now it was lunchtime, the beginnings of a queue were forming at the front of the cafe.

'Oh all right, then.' Beatrix gathered her handbag and got awkwardly to her feet, wincing as she put weight on her ankle but shrugging off Olivia's offer of help.

'That's a lovely bag,' said Olivia.

'Lizard,' Beatrix said in an offhand tone. 'A gift from my first husband. He bought it off an arms dealer in Khartoum.' A wicked grin lit up her face.

Olivia blinked. The more of Beatrix's offhand comments and outlandish stories she heard, the less certain she was of which, if any, to believe.

'Tell me again where we are staying?' Olivia asked, taking a look at Beatrix in the rear-view mirror as they got underway. Claiming tiredness, Beatrix had decided to sit in the back seat. 'Before you have a nap and I end up circling the streets of Galway for all eternity.'

'The Park House. Forster Street.' Beatrix's eyes fluttered shut.

The reunion was scheduled for two days' time, and was to encompass several events, culminating in a party on the evening of the thirty-first, according to the invitation. Olivia found herself looking forward to meeting the women Beatrix had served with, for if they were anywhere near as spirited as her, then they would be formidable indeed. She'd also found a tourist brochure that proclaimed Galway to be one of the prettiest of Ireland's towns, situated right on a wide bay, and so she was hoping to put her new art supplies to use.

She'd charged her phone in the hotel overnight, and hadn't known whether to be relieved or depressed that there was not a single voice message or missed call. As she thought about the friendship Beatrix once had with these women, she took a mental survey of her own friends. There had been one or two at school whom her mother kept her updated on, and then a handful at university, one who wrote the occasional newsy email, full of details about life in Sydney as an art teacher. But in London, there was no one. She'd only been there three months, and most of her waking hours were spent at Cholmondeley's or the bar, but she had begun to wonder if she would ever make any friends in the country she had moved to.

The fields that rolled past had become even greener; the landscape, and the thought that they were getting closer to discovering the provenance of the fox-girl, combined to lift her out of her despondent mood.

She turned on the radio, tuning into a local station that seemed to play exclusively folk music, and hummed along to the jaunty sound of a fiddle, flute and drum. Beatrix chimed in with a gentle snore and Olivia smiled. The only person whom she could come close to calling a friend in the entire British Isles was the capricious seventy-five-year-old asleep in the back seat.

~

It was growing dark as they approached Galway. Olivia still hadn't got used to the impossibly short days, always found herself caught unawares as the light faded halfway through the afternoon. She followed the signs to the town centre but got caught in a snarl of traffic and couldn't for the life of her locate Forster Street. Beatrix still hadn't stirred, and with increasing frustration Olivia pulled over beneath Christmas decorations strung between lampposts now twinkling in the dusky light. Christmas suddenly seemed weeks ago, not days. She turned in her seat to face Beatrix.

'Time to wake up,' she said, reaching behind and gently tapping the woman's knee.

No response.

She tried again, and finally Beatrix stirred. 'Are we there, darling?' she asked, blinking and looking around. 'I really was having the most marvellous sleep.'

'Not quite.' Olivia tamped down her frustration. 'I've been driving around the town centre for half an hour now and can't find the hotel.'

Beatrix squinted out of the window. 'But it's right there.' She pointed to a long white stucco building about fifty metres further along the street.

'You're kidding?'

'No, that's definitely it. See – there's the sign.'

Olivia eased back into the traffic, cursing under her breath, and drove the short distance to the hotel.

'Don't worry,' Beatrix said, yawning and stretching luxuriously. 'There'll be a pint of Guinness for us both once we've checked in.'

'I'm not really much of a beer drinker,' Olivia admitted.

'Oh, this isn't beer,' said Beatrix. 'It's an elixir, take my word for it.'

They were shown to their rooms, next door to each other on the first floor, and agreed to meet in the bar once they'd both 'titivated' as Beatrix put it.

As they settled into their seats in the oak-panelled bar, Olivia took a tentative sip of her drink, and to her surprise found that she liked the rich, malty, slightly bitter flavour. Almost swallowed up by the ridiculously cushiony armchair, her earlier annoyance began to fade.

She turned to a slim menu on the table in front of them. Their lunch seemed a long time ago. 'How about we have a snack?' she suggested.

'What's that, darling?' Beatrix asked. 'Oh yes, yes, a terribly good idea.' She seemed to cheer up again at the prospect of food and began to regale Olivia with the story of her first visit to

Ireland. 'That was with Willy. He was a race-horse trainer; owned the Dewson Stables out at Lambourn, not that you would have heard of him, but he was rather well known in his day, had a winner in the Derby once. We used to come over all the time – they breed damn fine fillies in Ireland. It's where I got my taste for Guinness.'

'Tell me some more about the women you served with?' Olivia asked after they had ordered. 'I feel like I know Lucy, but what about the others?'

'Well, there was Bubbles Morgan-Jones – she was called that on account of how much she loved champagne. I knew her before the Wasbies, in Calcutta. Lovely woman, always looked out for everyone else.' Beatrix seemed momentarily downcast.

'What do you mean?'

'She wanted to get everything right. She tried so hard to do the right thing, and did her best to make sure we all toed the line too. We joined up together, with Plum as well. Funny thing was I couldn't stand Plum to begin with – she was such an empty-headed little thing, always chasing men. Out where she shouldn't have been on more than one occasion.' Beatrix gave her a knowing look. 'I've never met a woman before or since who could dance for hours on end like she could. But I'll say one thing for her, she was a hard worker, and she did know how to cheer a soul up. They were both good women to have on your side in a bind.'

'And Joy?'

'Ah yes, poor Joy,' said Beatrix sadly. 'She was our leader, though honestly she never made it feel like that. Married to a man who ditched her in the middle of the war, with barely a word of explanation. She took it terribly hard.'

Beatrix was interrupted by the delivery of several small plates of food, as the waiter rearranged their drinks to make room. Smoked salmon, oysters, tiny school prawns, a rectangle of pâté and thinly sliced brown bread all jostled for space on the small table.

For a while neither of them spoke, except to offer the remaining oyster, the last silky slice of salmon. 'No, you have it, darling, I think I might pop if I have another bite,' Beatrix protested.

'What time would you like me to take you to the castle tomorrow?' Olivia asked when they'd left only crumbs.

'It's not too far from here, I think. So, if we leave just before noon? We've been invited to lunch. I rang and confirmed it before we left England.'

'Me as well?'

'Yes, of course.'

'Will all the women be there?'

'I believe so.'

'I bet they've all got some incredible stories.'

'Yes, well, I'd appreciate it if you don't bring up the fox-girl. I shall need to pick my moment. It's going to be a rather delicate matter.'

'Of course.' Olivia wanted to ask why, but there was something about Beatrix's expression that stopped her from asking any more questions.

'One more for the road?' Beatrix asked, draining her glass.

'Why not?'

~

Olivia was up early the next morning, and she dressed quickly, sliding her sketchbook and paints into her handbag before taking off for the quay. She wanted to capture the soft grey light on the water and knew she would have to hurry. The streets were quiet and she breathed in the cold morning air as she walked, huddling into the waxed green jacket that Beatrix had insisted she keep, her hands buried in its pockets.

She reached an area of parkland close to the water, and at a standing stone memorial she read the story of the ships that took so many starving Irish men, women and children to America in search of a better life. They must have been heavy-hearted, to leave everything that was familiar to sail away with little hope of ever returning. Desperation made one do the unthinkable, she supposed.

For her, however, it was a very different, far more exhilarating, experience and she was so delighted by the sight of the harbourfront that she forgot she was so far from home.

Brightly coloured houses clustered along the street facing the small sandy bay. The temperature had risen a few degrees, and the sun warmed her a little as she took a seat on a low stone wall, retrieving her sketchbook and placing her bag at her feet.

The smell of salt filled Olivia's nostrils, the cold froze the tip of her nose, and the sea air tangled her hair. The stone wall bit uncomfortably into the back of her legs, but she cared little, happy in such a peaceful place. She soon lost herself in an attempt to capture a pair of fishing boats at anchor, only stopping occasionally to flex her numb fingers. She'd forgotten how much pleasure the simple act of placing marks on a page gave her, to create something out of nothing, even if no one would ever see it but her. Perhaps one day, many years from now, she might look back on this sketchbook with the same bemused expression

Beatrix had at her own drawings. Perhaps the world would be as different a place when she was an old woman as it clearly was for Beatrix now.

It was hard to imagine.

~

She made it back to the hotel just before breakfast service finished, her appetite sharpened by the early start, and found Beatrix sitting in the dining room over a pot of tea, the food in front of her barely touched.

'Are you all right?' Olivia asked, noticing the slight tremble in the woman's hand as she raised a cup to her mouth. 'It's perfectly normal to feel a bit anxious.'

'You have no idea,' Beatrix practically snapped at her. 'The concierge has booked me a hair appointment at a place down the road,' she continued, putting her cup down and rising from the table. 'Though God only knows if they'll be able to do anything with this mess.' She raked her fingers through her scalp and limped off, listing slightly to one side like a ship under sail, all the while muttering under her breath.

'I'll see you at noon,' Olivia called after her uncertainly. 'Good luck!'

The hairdresser might need it more than Beatrix.

THIRTEEN

Dohazari, 1944

The day that Bubbles was due to return came and went with no sign of her.

'Do you think she's decided not to come back?' Bea asked as the women packed up the truck that afternoon. 'Could you be court-martialled for desertion as a Wasbie?'

'I'm sure she wouldn't have deliberately left us short-handed,' said Joy, slamming the sides shut and preparing to hop into the cab.

'Perhaps she and Charles have run away to get married?' Plum suggested.

'Well, whatever it is, she's going to be in plenty of hot water when she does return,' said Bea. 'I wouldn't want to be in her shoes when Ma'am finds out.'

~

Joy was summoned to the ops tent early the next morning. On her return, she gathered the women together.

'She looks dreadful,' whispered Plum.

'She does,' agreed Bea, noting Joy's reddened eyes and grim expression.

'Regret to inform you that Miss Belinda Morgan-Jones was killed when the flight she was on crashed shortly after take-off,' Joy read from the telegram that fluttered in her wavering hands.

'No!' cried Bea before Joy had even had a chance to finish. 'That's not possible.'

'I can't believe it,' said Plum, fat tears brimming in her eyes. 'She was so full of life.'

'Gone. Just like that,' said Lucy, her voice quavering with barely suppressed fury. 'What a bloody waste.'

'What a bloody war,' added Joy, slumping down on a chair and not bothering to staunch the flow of tears now streaming down her face.

'Poor Charles,' added Bea, softly.

It turned out, they later discovered, that Bubbles, having missed her return flight, had hopped on board a later one. Engine failure was given as the reason for the crash, but no one knew for certain what had happened for it to clear the runway and then shear sideways into the jungle. Everyone on board had died.

That evening they gathered on the riverbank, not far from where they had danced with the American pilots. Bea turned to Psalm 23 in the prayer book she had borrowed from the padre, and sang, 'The Lord is my shepherd . . .' in a high, clear soprano, only stumbling when she came to the phrase about death's dark vale. Plum had picked a posy of flowers, and handed a bloom to each of the women to scatter on the water.

'Beautiful Bubbles, with your blonde hair and your bright smile, your love of dancing . . .' said Lucy.

'And champagne,' said Plum with a sniff.

'Making sure everyone was okay,' said Bea. 'Thinking of others before herself.'

'Always in good spirits,' Lucy added.

'She will be so missed,' said Joy.

'I feel hollow,' said Bea to Lucy as they reluctantly returned to their sleeping quarters later.

'Me too.'

'Will I ever feel anything else?'

'I really can't say,' said Lucy miserably.

~

Eventually, the women had no choice but to pull themselves together and do the only thing they could – get on with the work in front of them, paste on a smile, cheer the soldiers up and hope to make a tiny bit of difference in bringing the war to an end.

More troops than ever were now coming through Dohazari. Some were moved on within a matter of days, but others were held there for weeks on end and the camp was crowded with hundreds of men with too much time on their hands. The women, however, had little time to themselves, certainly none to mourn Bubbles, for they often worked double shifts, going out in the mobile canteens during the day, grabbing food for themselves when they could, and then restocking and heading out to meet troops arriving at the railway station at all hours of the night. Some of the soldiers had come straight from the front, hadn't eaten for twelve hours or more and were so grateful for the tea, sandwiches and cake on offer that Bea soon forgot her fatigue in the face of their greater need. She kept a lookout for Archie, and Jack and the other pilots now, but there was no sign of any of them.

'Sometimes I wish there were more than twenty-four hours in a day,' Lucy grumbled good-naturedly as she fed Cocoa bits of Spam that she'd saved from her meal.

'Then perhaps there might be more than a handful for sleep, you mean?' Bea asked.

'Exactly.'

They had acquired an Indian 'sweeper', Amar, who was responsible for providing the water and building the fires. He oversaw the kerosene stoves on which forty-gallon drums were boiled for tea, as well as doing a lot of the heavy lifting, but the women still found that their hands were sore and blistered from the endless cutting of sandwiches and opening of tins.

'You'll need to get that properly dressed,' Joy said, watching Bea wince one afternoon. 'In this heat it'll go septic if you're not careful. Go on, get to the medical tent while it's quieter here.'

Bea wiped the sweat from her face with the back of her arm and flashed Joy a grateful look. The hard grind had subdued even the normally vivacious Plum, and they now mostly worked in silence, conscious of the amount to be done and the limited time available.

Twice a week they went up river, loading their stores onto boats early in the morning and then hauling them off further upstream only to pack them into Jeeps for a five-mile drive into the jungle. They never seemed to have enough supplies for the men who were waiting for them, and these days were long ones – they rarely returned before dusk – but Bea enjoyed them nonetheless, for she was beginning to recognise many of the soldiers, and they nearly always had a cheerful greeting for her. Here, at least, she felt like they were really in the thick of it, rather than simply helping behind the scenes.

~

The women had been warned about the coming monsoon rains by the other soldiers, but they were still unprepared for the Biblical ferocity of the downpour when it arrived one night in early August. The river rose by what seemed like more than twenty feet in less than forty-eight hours, threatening to destroy the main bridge. Canteens were suspended as the road turned into a quagmire, and they all watched anxiously as the river crept ever higher. It was a swirling mass of debris, dead animals, even whole trees and wreckage from houses upstream, and Bea caught her breath in horror as she saw the body of a native Burmese woman carried along by the raging water.

They managed to go out with one truck, Lucy cursing as the top-heavy vehicle wallowed in the soupy conditions. 'Blasted thing isn't even four-wheel drive,' she complained.

Making it to their rendezvous, they set about serving tea laced with rum to the soaked West African sappers who had been charged with the dangerous task of clearing the bridge supports.

'They're going to try to blow up the blockage,' said Joy, who'd been chatting with some of the officers in charge.

'Bloody oath,' said Lucy. 'What if they take the bridge out?'

The women kept an eye on proceedings as they handed out hot drinks, but were taken by surprise when a huge blast rocked the canteen and almost overturned the tea urn.

Though the rain was still sheeting down, reducing visibility to a few yards, Bea could see that the part of the bridge closest to them had collapsed and even now was being pushed downstream by the weight of the water.

'They do love to blow things up, don't they,' said Lucy.

'That's kind of the point,' said Bea. 'But some of those poor chaps have been swept away.'

'I hope they can swim,' Lucy replied grimly.

~

Bea couldn't have been asleep for more than an hour that night when she found herself being shaken awake. Joy stood over her, a hurricane lamp throwing a shadow over her face, making her look ghoulish.

'Quick!' Joy shouted over the cacophony of the drumming rain. 'We've got to evacuate.'

She roused Lucy and they both scrambled into their clothes, splashing towards the mess and the storeroom to find Plum there ahead of them. The river had climbed even higher, and only moments later it burst its banks, the overspill creeping alarmingly close to the mess.

'All hands on deck,' said Joy. 'This rain's not letting up.'

Bea surveyed the huge stacks of stores. 'It's hopeless.'

'Nothing's ever hopeless,' replied Lucy sternly. 'Buck up. We'll just have to do our best. Sink or swim, huh?' She barked with laughter at her own joke.

'But we can't load them into the truck,' said Bea. They had already packed the mobile canteen until every last inch of space was taken up.

'Then we'll have to ferry them up the hill ourselves. We can't risk anything floating away. Captain Taylor will have my guts for garters if we don't at least try,' said Joy.

The women set to work, grabbing a box each and slip-sliding in the mud up the hill, their clothes soaked through and their hair plastered to their faces. Bea had to constantly stop and wipe away the water from her eyes in order to see properly where she was stepping. Several times she stumbled, and once Plum, walking a few feet in front of her, ended up flat on her back.

'You all right?' Bea called out, barely able to make herself heard over the sound of the rain.

Plum gave her a wave and struggled to her feet again.

They had been hard at it for nearly an hour when lights came bobbing along the path towards them. 'Ahoy there! Do you gals need some help?'

Bea recognised the group of American pilots who'd been at the impromptu riverbank party several weeks earlier. Fred's face loomed towards them, closely followed by those of Jimmy, Billy, Al and Jack.

'I reckon,' said Lucy. 'Grab a box and follow me.'

'Yes, ma'am.'

Joy stayed in the storeroom, nailing up crates of soya links and bully beef, and directing the three men towards the ones that were still to be moved.

Bea and Jack fell into step, walking side-by-side. Somehow his presence, as well as that of the other men, seemed to make the situation less desperate. At one point Bea's boots almost went out from under her, but Jack grabbed her elbow, juggling the box he carried as he steadied her.

'Whoops! Don't go disappearing on me now,' he shouted.

'I'll try not to,' she called back.

After what seemed an age, almost all of the stores were finally transported, while the water had risen so far that it was now lapping at the doorway.

Bea had been intent on her task and hadn't noticed the slight easing in the rain and the lightening of the sky outside. It was nearly morning. Every one of them was sopping wet, their boots soaked and their clothes spattered with mud, but as they gathered in the storeroom, a sense of elation took over.

They'd done it. Beaten the flood. For now.

'Who wants a cuppa?' Bea asked.

'Is that all you British gals think about?' asked Jack, laughing at her.

'If you ask nicely, there'll be a tot of brandy in there,' she said, smiling back at him, the sight of his face sending a warm glow through her that was completely at odds with the dreadful conditions.

They trooped over to the kitchens, where Amar and the Indian chefs were already hard at work, and Bea grabbed a handful of mugs from the shelf and began to make the tea. She saw that Jack had a leather bootlace – like the ones that were part of the supplies they sold – tied around his neck, and that the fox-girl hung from it.

'Pretty little thing isn't she?' he asked, touching his hand to his neck.

'Yes, but you . . . you've got something else there,' she said, moving closer.

He put his hand to where she was pointing and winced as he touched it. 'Goddam leeches! Got any salt?'

Bea searched the supplies in the kitchen until she found a box and handed it to him to apply.

'Better get used to it,' he said kindly, seeing her dismay.

When he'd flicked the leech outside, Bea handed him a mug of tea, feeling something like an electric shock as her fingers touched his. His eyes widened as they continued to stare at each other, neither able to tear their gaze away.

'Anyone else like a cup?' Joy asked, noticing that Bea's attention was elsewhere.

They gathered at one of the tables, wiping the mud from their faces and the women wringing out their hair as the smell of the morning's cakes wafted from the ovens.

'Nice to see you again, by the way,' Jack whispered to Bea. 'Though I'd rather it hadn't taken a drenching to do so.'

Bea noticed that the rain had separated his lashes, framing his eyes like the points of stars. She tilted her head towards him. 'I don't suppose they have rain like this in America?' she asked.

'No, but they have tornadoes, and ice storms and snow so deep it can bury your house,' he replied, not taking his eyes from hers.

The effort of moving all of their stock had been worth it for this moment, to feel Jack close by her side, his voice soft in her ear as he talked of flying over prairies and wheat fields so large that they seemed to stretch on forever, and of his home in the Midwest. Bea found herself lulled by the husky tones and deliciously drawling accent, didn't want him to stop talking.

When the Americans finally left, having extracted a promise from the women to meet them the following evening, Bea and the others paddled their way back to their sleeping quarters, which were happily on a slight rise above the mess. The rain had stopped and Bea prayed that it might let up long enough for the swollen river to subside. She didn't dare look down towards the water, fearing that there might be more bodies – animal or human – floating past. She had already seen enough.

She peeled off her damp, muddy clothes, wrapped a towel around herself and sank onto her bed. Her eyes were on the point of flickering closed when Lucy burst through the door.

'I can't find Cocoa!'

'Wh . . . ?' Bea sat up.

'I've looked everywhere. Buggered if I can find her.'

'Cats hate the rain,' Bea said, trying to soothe her. 'She'll have found somewhere nice and dry to wait out the downpour.'

'But what if—'

'Highly unlikely,' said Bea firmly. 'You know what they say, cats . . . nine lives and all that.' She wasn't sure she believed it, for she'd seen several sodden creatures the size of a cat or small dog washed along with the floodwater, but she wasn't about to tell Lucy that.

'I've got to find her,' said Lucy, looking uncharacteristically anxious.

Bea groaned, but swung her feet over the side of the bed, every muscle in her body protesting at having to get up again. 'Come on, then; I'll help you look.'

Lucy smiled her thanks. 'You're a true friend, you know that?'

'I'll never get any peace otherwise,' Bea grumbled, pulling on dry clothes.

They searched throughout the camp, calling for the cat as they peered around and up into trees and poked sticks through shrubs, but she remained stubbornly unaccounted for.

'You go to bed,' Lucy said eventually. 'There's no point in us both being exhausted.'

'I doubt we'll be able to go anywhere today,' said Bea. 'Look at the state of the road.'

They turned in the direction of the pot-holed, puddle-strewn dirt road, and knew without having to test it that the six-inch dust would have become twelve-inch mud. They were both about to go back to their sleeping quarters when Plum came towards them, picking her way fastidiously through the mud, a dark shape in her arms.

'Found her halfway to the railway station,' she said as she reached them. 'Poor thing was yowling her head off.'

'You're filthy,' said Bea, noticing that Plum's trousers looked as though they were made entirely from mud. If she'd stepped out of them, they probably would have stood up on their own.

'She was on the other side of what's pretty much now a waterfall. The road's completely cut off. Had to wade across to get her,' she said, flicking her hair out of her face.

'You could have been swept away yourself!' said Bea. 'Did you even check how deep it was before you went in?'

Plum rolled her eyes. 'I'm not as dim-witted as you think. Of course I did. Anyway, lucky for us it wasn't,' she said as she handed the cat to Lucy. 'Now, for goodness sake let's all try to get some sleep.'

'Amen, sister,' said Lucy. 'And thanks – I know you're not exactly fond of Cocoa . . .'

'We're all in this together now,' Plum smiled, her teeth shining whitely through the mud coating her face. 'Even the damn cat.'

~

Over the following days the rain continued to pour, and everyone watched the level of the river anxiously, but it remained steady, if alarmingly high, and so any plans to evacuate them were put on hold.

'For the time being at least,' said Joy.

Sorties with the mobile canteen were nigh on impossible, so the women found themselves at a loose end. Every time they went anywhere they were soaked in an instant, though, and it became impossible to get anything dry, and almost all of their clothes ended up covered in mud.

Green dye from their berets began to run down their faces, giving them a sinister appearance. 'You look like you've been dipped in paint,' Lucy told Bea as she whipped out her sketchbook to make a quick drawing of her.

'You think you're any different?' replied Bea, as they all giggled at the sight of each other, appreciating any moment of light relief from the ghastly conditions. The giggles turned to belly laughs and then to snorts as tears of mirth mixed with the dye on their faces.

Leeches were now everywhere, working their way through socks and trousers and bedclothes, and the women quickly became used to burning them off with the lit end of a cigarette, or suffocating them with salt. Any vestiges of squeamishness had long been abandoned. Dry clothes were at a premium, and before long everything had grown a layer of mould. They had to take care not to get jungle sores, because any broken skin soon became infected.

They had attempted one journey, to a unit only five miles away, but had scarcely got further than the end of their road when the truck got bogged.

'It's in up to its hocks,' said Lucy once they'd scrambled out to take a look.

'I reckon we're royally screwed,' said Plum, as Bea's eyes widened at the unaccustomed language. The weather was getting to all of them.

They weren't the only ones with little to do, and their camp became a magnet for troops positioned nearby. The women had devised a lounge of sorts, and with the help of a group of soldiers had rigged up a series of tarpaulins off the back of the mess.

One morning, during a break in the weather, a couple of trestle tables and some chairs appeared, and the women decorated the inside of the tent with parachutes and a few other bits of fabric they had with them.

'It looks almost homely,' said Plum with satisfaction.

It didn't take long for word to get out, and soon they were dishing up sandwiches, bully-beef stew and drinks until the small hours, accompanied by the loud croak of frogs and lit by fireflies.

Bea, who had brought a cribbage set and a deck of cards with her from Calcutta, set about recruiting anyone who could play, and teaching those who couldn't, using spent matches as pegs. She retrieved her books from her kitbag and set up a rudimentary lending library, with an honesty system for borrowing. Others contributed theirs too, until before long there was a large wooden box with an eclectic selection of hardback classics, pulp-fiction paperbacks and old copies of *Punch*.

Amar and the Indian chefs kept themselves amused by playing *chaupar* – a game of strategy involving a checked paper cross with cowrie shells that was a bit like ludo or parcheesi. The hooting and hollering when one of them won made Bea smile. Nevertheless, the unceasing, infernal downpour made it hard to keep spirits from flagging. Cigarettes and booze, however, flowed as generously as the rain. 'I reckon I'm at least fifty per cent gin by now,' said Lucy, flopping onto her bed late one night after they'd finally sent everyone away.

'Try ninety,' said Bea, hiccoughing.

There was time for letter-writing, though they still weren't allowed to write about where they were, which made it hard for Bea to know what to say to her mother. In the end, she wrote about the funny things that had happened – the friends she'd made, and that she'd finally learned to make a decent cup of tea. 'At least that's what the men say, anyway.' Whenever she found herself with a spare few minutes, she took out her sketchbook and made quick pencil studies of the *basha*, the other women – she found Lucy's likeness, with her high cheekbones and aquiline nose, particularly easy to capture – and the soldiers gathered there.

Jack showed up out of the blue late one afternoon as she was sitting on the verandah of the house, working on an earlier drawing.

They grinned at each other before he noticed the sketchbook on her lap. 'Mind if I take a look?' he asked, coming over to give her a kiss on the cheek.

'On one condition,' she teased.

'Oh?'

'That you let me draw a likeness of you.'

'As long as you promise to get my best side,' he replied with a wink. 'Where would you like me?'

Bea felt herself go red as her imagination drifted to something she couldn't possibly say out loud. She cleared her throat, dismissing her inappropriate thoughts. 'How about the seat opposite? And perhaps you could look over towards the river?'

Cocoa slunk out from the house and jumped onto his lap, and she laughed, the tension of the moment eased. 'I told you she liked you.'

He arched one eyebrow. 'The feeling's mutual.'

Bea had a sudden intuition that he wasn't just talking about the cat.

She felt nothing but admiration as she studied him, taking in the sun-browned skin and the new lines of tiredness around his eyes. This man faced death almost every day, and yet he seemed as laidback as if he hadn't a care in the world. She was sorry when the light began to fade – she could have watched him for hours.

FOURTEEN

✻

Galway, 1999

'It's awful, isn't it?'

Olivia cocked her head to one side and pretended to consider the woman in front of her, putting a hand to her chin and pursing her lips. 'Actually, I think you look wonderful.'

Beatrix's hair had been washed and blow-dried so that soft waves surrounded her head before being caught up into a loose knot at the nape of her neck. She'd applied a light dusting of powder to her cheeks and a touch of pink highlighted her lips. A cluster of tiny seed pearls glowed at each earlobe.

'It shows off your wonderful bone structure. And those earrings are lovely.' Olivia saw that Beatrix had applied polish, that the nails of her left hand were slightly smudged, and felt a rush of unexpected affection.

163

'It was certainly a process. I'm not sure I even recognise myself,' Beatrix huffed. 'And the frock? I think it's too young for me.'

She had abandoned her usual dog-hair-covered baggy tweed skirt and buttoned-to-the-neck blouse in favour of an emerald dress in a floaty fabric that was gathered at her waist and wrists. Low-heeled court shoes replaced her sensible Oxfords, and she carried a small matching handbag.

'Very elegant.' It was the first time Olivia had seen Beatrix display the slightest bit of vanity, and told her just how nervous she must be. 'You look lovely.'

'Battle dress.'

'I'm sorry?'

'If one is going into battle, then one must be appropriately attired.'

'Please tell me there's not a gun in your handbag,' Olivia joked.

Beatrix didn't deny it, barely cracked a smile.

Olivia felt distinctly underdressed, in the same borrowed sweater she'd been wearing for nearly a week, but she supposed it made little difference, for she was simply the driver, the assistant on this trip.

'Come on then, we don't want to be late.' Beatrix gripped her handbag.

'I'll bring the car round, ma'am,' said Olivia, doing her best to lighten the mood.

'I don't think I've been called that since the war,' Beatrix finally laughed.

The drive was a pretty one, along a winding road with lush green pastures, low hedges and occasional clumps of trees.

'According to Plum's directions, we go five miles past Athenry and then take a left. It should be signposted.' Bea read from a sheet of paper that had been included with the invitation, glasses perched on the end of her nose.

'Got it.'

'We were twins, you know,' Beatrix said out of the blue.

'What?'

'Archie and I. He was the creative one – right-brained I think you call it now. I was better at maths. He was much better at drawing.'

'Well, he must have been exceptional, because from what I've seen, you're pretty good yourself.' Olivia saw the turn-off up ahead and flicked on the indicator.

'He should have been an artist,' she said wistfully.

'We're almost there,' said Olivia, concentrating as a truck barrelled towards them on the narrow road. Then, once they were clear, she looked across at Beatrix and asked quietly, 'What happened to him?'

Beatrix hesitated, her features slackening, making her look suddenly much older. 'Archie died far too young.'

Olivia felt Beatrix's sadness radiate from her. 'I'm so sorry.'

Beatrix shrugged. 'I still miss him, and it's been years. Decades, in fact.'

Olivia was forced to concentrate as she squeezed past a truck to turn into a long, tree-lined driveway. She gave a low whistle and slowed down as the house came into view. Two lichen-covered lions stood as sentries, there was an ornate verdigris bandstand to their left, and then, sitting among sweeping emerald-green lawns, was the house, its pale stone lit by the winter sun. A large square portico with fluted columns was flanked by four sets of windows, two storeys high, and a cluster of chimney pots sat at each corner of the roof. Dark green ivy crawled up one side of the building. The house wasn't precisely a castle, but it was certainly grand.

Olivia remembered the question that had been nagging at her since Beatrix had told her of her frequent visits to Ireland over the years. 'Did you ever come to see Plum when you were here with your husband?'

Beatrix gripped her handbag, and in that one movement Olivia knew that there was more to her relationship with Plum than she had let on. 'The timing was never right.'

It sounded like an excuse rather than the truth. Was it, Olivia wondered, something to do with the fox-girl? Had they perhaps fallen out over it?

She pulled up to the left of the house, where there was provision for parking, and turned off the engine. She went around to the passenger door and opened it for Beatrix, who climbed out and then stopped in front of the house, looking it up and down, as if taking its measure.

As they walked the few steps to the front door, it opened ahead of them and a slim silver-haired woman in narrow-cut tweed trousers, a dark sweater and bright ballet flats flew out.

'Bea! It *is* you!' she cried, arms out wide in welcome. 'I swear you don't look a bit different.'

Beatrix put a hand to her hair. 'I doubt that,' she said ruefully.

'Well, we're all greyer or even whiter now, of course. But honestly, you look wonderful. I'm so pleased you could make it.' She stepped forward and embraced Beatrix. 'We'll have nearly a full complement – Lucy's come all the way from Australia, can you believe that?'

Olivia noticed Beatrix's shoulders relax a little and saw a genuine smile curve her lips.

'And who's this? Your granddaughter?'

'No, no, a friend who's been staying with me. She offered to drive; I had a little problem with a dicky ankle.' She turned to Olivia. 'Olivia, this is Plum.'

'Well, I'm so pleased you came. And very nice to meet you, Olivia. We must get inside and find you a seat.' Plum hooked her arm through Beatrix's and ushered them inside.

They stepped into a vast hall, their footsteps echoing on the floor. Olivia gazed around her at the gilt-framed, dim oils of hunting scenes and, rather alarmingly, an enormous one of a tiger, its teeth bared, that lined the walls, the out-of-season flowers massed in silver vases on an antique table, and inhaled the smell of lemon furniture polish. Everything gleamed, not a speck of dust to be seen. The contrast with Beatrix's house could not have been more stark.

'We're in the dining room,' Plum said, directing them to a door further along the hall on their right. 'Make yourself at home. The others should be here soon.'

'Will your husband be joining us?'

Olivia heard a note of apprehension in Beatrix's voice and turned to check that she was all right. Nothing had been said, but a noticeable awkwardness suddenly stretched between the two.

Plum's mouth turned down. 'Unfortunately not.' She turned to Olivia. 'He's a judge,' she said by way of explanation. 'Frightfully busy. About to be elected to the Supreme Court of Ireland, but you didn't hear that from me.'

'No good deed,' said Beatrix wryly and Olivia could have sworn that she seemed relieved.

'Anyway, it's just us girls today. I figured we would have so much to catch up on that any men would be *de trop*.' Plum gave a trill of slightly brittle laughter. 'Oh, I think that must be the door again,' she said as a bell chimed. 'Back in a tick.'

Beatrix and Olivia entered the dining room, a square room with tall windows and soaring ceilings. There was a large marble fireplace at one end, with, rather incongruously, two stuffed peacocks either side of a tarnished, gilt-edged mirror. The room was also furnished with a long white-clothed table set for lunch. Crystal glasses at each place sparkled, and the silver, old and well-polished, reflected the light. Small posies of flowers gathered around several elaborate candelabra had been placed as centrepieces.

'I always knew she'd land on her feet,' said Beatrix, picking up a knife and inspecting it.

'Would you like a seat?' Olivia went to pull out a chair, but Beatrix waved her away.

'No thank you. It sounds as though we won't have to wait long, in any case,' she said as the noise of footsteps and the chatter of light, high voices carried towards them.

Plum appeared at the door with two women following close behind her. Olivia watched as each enthusiastically exclaimed over the other, embracing and laughing. One of the women had a distinct Australian accent, with features that were more weathered than the others, a fan of fine lines radiating across her face, though her tan gave her the appearance of robust good health. Tall and broad-shouldered, she had cropped silver hair and eyes that twinkled with intelligence and good humour. She was dressed far less conservatively than the other women, in loose trousers, flat boots and a silky jacket with a Mandarin collar.

'Olivia, this is Lucy,' said Beatrix, introducing her, and Olivia heard the note of pride in Beatrix's voice as she spoke of her friend. 'A fellow countrywoman.'

Lucy gave her a wide smile, which Olivia returned, warmed by the familiar accent. 'We're a long way from home, aren't we?'

The second woman – Joy – sounded faintly American, and wore cat's-eye glasses perched on a beaky nose. She was rather more rounded than the others, and wore a well-cut black wool dress, a slash of bright pink colouring her lips.

'How's Fred?' Plum asked.

'Making the most of Ireland's wonderful golf courses,' she replied. 'He'll be here for New Year.'

As they all spoke at once, Olivia looked from one to the other, matching them up with what Beatrix had told her. She saw a shadow of the good-time girl in Plum, as she gesticulated and practically danced around them with unbridled excitement, whereas Lucy, with her tall stature and imposing presence, effortlessly commanded attention. Joy appeared more reserved, though no less warm. Beatrix looked happier than Olivia had ever seen her, especially when she was talking to Lucy.

None of them seemed to notice as she retreated to a corner, content to observe, watching as the years unspooled around them. She dearly wanted to get her sketchbook out of her bag, for they were all so lively and vibrant that each would have made a fascinating subject for a portrait.

The door opened and a young woman about the same age as Olivia brought in an ice bucket and a bottle of champagne.

'Oh, lovely,' said Plum, accepting a glass. 'Isn't this all rather jolly?'

When the others all had a drink, Beatrix raised her glass and they fell silent. 'Absent friends,' she said, taking a slug.

'Absent friends.'

'Cin cin,' added Plum, and they all grinned at each other in recognition.

'Would you like a glass?'

Olivia had been so intent on the older women that she hadn't noticed the other young woman beside her.

'Oh, thank you.' She accepted the drink that was held out to her and took a sip, enjoying the feeling of the bubbles fizzing on her tongue.

'They're quite something, aren't they?' the woman said.

'There's certainly a lot of love in the room,' Olivia replied. 'It's wonderful to see. Such old friends. They must have been through so much together.'

'Granny's been at fever pitch for weeks. I don't think I've ever seen her so excited. She told me that these women were once some of her closest friends.'

'Oh,' said Olivia, startled. 'Plum is your grandmother?'

'Yes, why did you, er . . .'

Olivia reddened.

'Perfectly normal to mistake me for the help,' she reassured Olivia with a wink. 'Especially when you consider the surroundings.' She raised her eyes to the coffered ceiling.

'Sorry.'

'I'm Alex. I'm visiting for the Christmas holidays. Mum and Dad have gone back to England, but I wanted to stay on for a while. I've got a ton of study to do and thought it might be quieter here than at home.' She set the bucket on a sideboard and poured herself a glass, flicking her long blonde hair over one shoulder.

'Oh?'

'I'm researching my doctorate at SOAS. The School of Oriental and African Studies. It's part of London University.'

'Actually, I've heard of it,' said Olivia. As she explained a little of her own background in Asian art, Alex's eyes lit up and they soon discovered that they knew some of the same people in the Australian art world. It was an unexpected pleasure to talk about mutual friends, even if they were on the other side of the globe, and Olivia began to feel somewhat less of an outsider.

'I can't believe you haven't met up with anyone at SOAS since you've been in London,' Alex said.

Olivia shrugged. 'I know that "I've been too busy" sounds pretty lame, but in this case it's the truth.'

When Olivia mentioned where she'd been working, Alex made a sympathetic face. 'Elaine does have a reputation for being rather tough.'

Olivia nodded.

'Then you must know Jeffrey Martinson as well?' Alex continued brightly. 'Lovely chap; been a family friend for years.'

Olivia nodded, but before she could delve any further they were interrupted by Plum tapping on her glass and calling for quiet. 'I can't quite believe we all made it,' she said once the women had stopped talking. 'I'm appalled that we've left it so long for a reunion. We should have done this ages ago.'

'Bloody lucky we're all still alive,' said Lucy with a throaty cough.

There was a beat of silence and then Beatrix spoke, 'Yes, well, we all did drink like fish and smoke like demons, didn't we?' she said with a rueful grimace. 'Speaking of which . . .' She held out her glass for a refill.

'This is my granddaughter Alex,' said Plum to the other women.

'I'll just fetch another bottle, shall I, Granny?' Alex asked.

'Thank you, darling, there should be plenty more in the fridge.'

'Would you like a hand?' Olivia asked.

'That would be great, thanks. I'm serving lunch too – the caterers delivered it this morning; I just have to bring it out.'

'No problem, I can help with that.'

Olivia followed Alex to the kitchen and then returned to the room carrying a platter of chicken as Plum began to direct the women to their seats. 'Now, why don't you sit here, Joy . . .'

She placed the chicken on the sideboard and then returned down the corridor to the kitchen, passing Alex with a smile on the way. They had brought the last of the food in, and Olivia was on the point of stepping out of the room, when Plum stopped her. 'There's a place here for you too, Olivia, and one for Alex – we've put you at the end.'

'That's very kind, thank you.'

Olivia didn't hesitate to accept, for she wanted to make the most of the opportunity to hear the women's stories. Listening in fascination at Lucy's description of running a wildlife refuge in the Hunter Valley, of nursing baby wombats and orphaned joeys, made her slightly homesick; Plum's talk of fly-fishing in Kashmir made her feel woefully unadventurous; and Beatrix's recollections of running a racing stables left her wondering if she would ever have a legacy as impressive as theirs. She discovered that Lucy had trained as a pilot after the war. 'And then I became a parachutist, now the wildlife sanctuary keeps me out of trouble.'

Then, as Plum began to talk about her husband again, Olivia noticed Beatrix sit up a little straighter, her arms frozen in the act of cutting her chicken. The wary look she'd worn during the car journey was back. Olivia had begun to suspect that Plum and her husband were the people Beatrix needed to confront about the fox-girl, and that it was not going to be an easy conversation.

None of the other women seemed to have noticed any shift and the talk moved on to other subjects. Olivia and Alex chatted quietly at their end of the table, with Alex recommending a few places in Galway that she should try and visit while she was there.

After they'd finished eating – and emptied several bottles of chablis – the women began to reminisce about the war and their part in it.

Plum went to a sideboard and came back to the table with an envelope. 'When I knew you were all coming, I looked out these old photos.' She slid out a handful of small black-and-white squares and began to pass them around.

'Oh, there's Cocoa,' said Beatrix as she picked up the first one.

'Cocoa?' Olivia asked.

'Lucy adopted a cat, if you can believe that. She came everywhere with us,' said Beatrix. 'Whatever happened to her?'

'Used up her nine lives eventually,' Lucy replied sadly.

'Do you remember when I rescued her from the monsoon?' Plum laughed. 'God, that was a nightmare.'

'And this is us serving out the back of the truck.'

Olivia examined the photos as they were passed to her, recognising each of the women's younger selves. 'You all look wonderful. Who's this?' she asked, seeing a picture of some of the women partnered by men.

Beatrix leaned over towards her. 'That's Jimmy, and Fred. American pilots. And that's Jack.'

Olivia peered at the photo and was startled to see that one of the men – Jack – wore a dark string necklace, on the end of which appeared to be the fox-girl. The photo was blurred, but she was almost sure of it. She glanced quickly at Beatrix, who flashed her a warning look.

'Alex, dear, would you mind clearing?' Plum asked.

'Of course.'

After Olivia helped Alex take the plates away, she sensed that the moment was right to bring out the sketchbooks from India and Burma.

'Oh darling, that *was* thoughtful of you,' Beatrix said as Olivia placed them in front of her. 'Look, do you remember this?' she asked the assembled women, opening to a page showing a gracious bungalow surrounded by brightly flowering shrubs. 'Cleve.'

There was an answering chorus of sighs, as they all crowded around to get a better look. 'It was a damn sight better than most of the other places we bunked,' said Joy.

'We certainly slummed it on occasion,' Plum shuddered. 'Remember the rats?'

They all groaned as Alex and Olivia swapped a smile.

'The filthy houses we stayed in?'

'Camping under parachute tents in the monsoon – that was definitely the worst. Whose bloody idea was that?'

'They weren't exactly waterproof,' Lucy explained to Olivia.

Beatrix opened a folded sheet of newspaper. 'Oh Lord, remember this?'

'Christ, we were babies,' said Lucy as she examined the picture it showed.

Olivia bent over to have a look, seeing the four women standing proudly in front of an Army truck.

'There's me,' said Beatrix, 'and you Lucy, and Plum and Joy. All of us.'

'Well, not quite all of us,' Joy reminded them.

'Do you mean Bubbles?' Olivia asked. She'd been wondering what had happened to the fifth member of their team.

'She was killed in a plane crash,' said Lucy bluntly. 'When she was on leave to see her fiancé. So cruel.'

'She was very kind,' said Plum. 'And generous. I remember her lending me her coat once when I'd forgotten mine. Even though it was freezing and she only had a blouse on underneath.'

'She had such a sense of fun,' Beatrix added.

'Though she was almost always late. But golly did she make us laugh,' said Lucy. 'Even at her own expense sometimes.'

'The sun seemed to shine a bit brighter when she was in the room,' said Joy.

'I think we need another photo,' said Alex, breaking the silence that had fallen. She brought out a small camera. 'Come on, huddle together.'

Olivia saw that Beatrix and Plum placed themselves the furthest away from each other, though it was so subtly done that she couldn't tell if it was deliberate or not.

As Alex took the photos, Olivia glanced out the window; the light was already growing dim.

'Fancy a coffee?' Alex asked when she'd taken half-a-dozen snaps.

'Actually, I wouldn't mind some fresh air.'

'Good idea. Anyone need anything before we head outside?' she asked.

'No, no dear,' said Plum. 'We can certainly manage if we do. Thank you.'

The two young women walked companionably along a gravel path that led towards a large walled garden. 'There are orchards, and over that way a tennis court.'

'It must have been a wonderful place to come as a child.'

'Pretty idyllic, really. Though my grandfather can be a bit much sometimes; thankfully he was in Dublin more often than not. Everyone's a little afraid of him, even Granny sometimes, though he can be perfectly charming when he chooses. You'll meet him at the party tomorrow night.'

Olivia took a punt on an idea that had begun to form in her mind. 'Is he an art lover?'

'Oh, yes. Well, you've seen the house, obviously. He's also got a particularly fine *Japonaiserie* collection. If you'd like, I can ask him to give you a viewing. There's a whole gallery here devoted to it. When I was little he would walk me through, tell me about each piece and where it came from, why he liked it. It was largely because of him that I first became interested in Asian art.'

'And did he and your grandmother meet during the war too?'

Alex paused. 'I think so. In Burma, actually; although they got to know each other much better afterwards, I believe.'

The information was useful, but Olivia was still no closer to figuring out precisely how all the pieces of the puzzle fitted together. As Alex chatted away, Olivia struggled to pay attention to the conversation, for her mind was whirling with the possibilities. It was looking increasingly likely that Beatrix had known Plum's husband in Burma as well. Was she once involved with him, and was that why she jumped like a scalded cat every time he was mentioned? Could she and Plum have fallen out over him and was that why they hadn't been in touch for years?

'Come on, then,' Alex said eventually. 'Should we head back and see how much trouble they've got themselves into?'

The dark was well and truly drawing in as they turned back, and a light drizzle had begun to fall, beading on their hair and jackets.

'Ireland,' said Alex, glancing skywards. 'Thirty different kinds of damp.'

As they got closer to the house, Olivia spied several rectangles of light coming from within. Outside, she spotted two shadows, moving occasionally, a tiny fiery glow bobbing around in the centre of each of them. Then she heard a rasping cough, followed by low, urgent voices. Smelled smoke.

'Joy? Lucy?' she asked, surprised to see the old women outside.

'Having a fag for old times' sake,' said Lucy as Joy, standing next to her, collapsed with what sounded like giggles.

'Aren't you cold?' Olivia asked, surprised that they had neglected to put on coats, hats or even a scarf.

'Oh we've been through a lot worse than this,' said Lucy.

'Did you know Lucy was expelled from school for setting fire to it?' Joy said, her eyes alight with mischief and her mind clearly on other misdemeanours.

'Why am I not surprised to hear that?' replied Alex dryly.

'Come on, we'd better get back,' said Lucy, stubbing her cigarette out on the wall in a shower of sparks.

They went inside to find Beatrix and Plum in a cosy sitting room, warmed by a log fire and furnished with soft, flowered sofas and thick velvet curtains. They seemed mid-conversation but stopped short as the others entered. Might Beatrix have used the time to bring up the fox-girl?

'There you are, darlings,' Plum said. 'I was wondering what had happened to you all.'

'We really must be off,' said Beatrix, gathering her things. 'It's been quite the day.'

The other women agreed that it had.

'We've got all morning tomorrow,' said Plum as they made their way towards the front door. 'I thought we could meet for elevenses?' She named a cafe in Galway.

'Splendid,' said Lucy.

They left in a flurry of affectionate *à bientôt*s and *au revoir*s, Beatrix leaning heavily on Olivia's arm. 'I really shouldn't drink during the day; I do sometimes forget how old I am.'

'You've the energy of a far younger woman,' Olivia reassured her. 'How's your ankle holding up?'

'Never better,' she said, but gave a slight groan as Olivia helped her into the back seat of the car.

As they drove away, Olivia worked up the courage to ask Beatrix if she'd had a chance to mention the fox-girl, but a glance in the rear-view mirror told her that the woman was already fast asleep.

FIFTEEN

Dohazari, 1944

Almost as suddenly as they began, the monsoon rains ceased and work started again in earnest. The week before, with little to keep them busy, Plum had been granted a few days' leave, hitching a ride on a US Air Force DC-3 Dakota to Shillong. It was hard for them all to say goodbye; what had happened to Bubbles was never far from their minds.

Plum wasn't due back for another few days, and in the interim both Joy and Lucy came down with a fever. They couldn't stomach solid food, but when she wasn't out at the canteen Bea brought them cups of black tea and cooled boiled water.

'I wish I had more for you,' she told Lucy. 'If we were at home I'd get Lucozade. That's what they gave you in the San at school when you had a temperature.' She dipped a piece of linen into a basin of water and gently wiped Lucy's hair from her forehead. 'You're burning up.'

'I don't think anyone's taken care of me like this since I was a little tacker,' said Lucy, her voice uncharacteristically feeble.

Bea crossed her fingers that it wasn't malaria. 'If you haven't improved in the next twenty-four hours, I'm going to get a medic to take a look at you both.'

That day, she was the only one available to work the static canteen and singlehandedly served several hundred men. For the first time since she'd signed up, she had to remind herself to smile as she dished up dozens of sausage rolls and opened endless tins of fruit cocktail. She hadn't seen Jack or the other pilots for days, which only added to her worry.

Later, when the men had dispersed and she had almost finished clearing up, she was overcome with a wave of exhaustion so violent that she nearly collapsed on the counter, tears pricking her eyelids. She missed her brother so much, and had gone months without hearing from him. Her earlier thoughts of running into him seemed laughably naïve now. All she wanted was to know that he, and her father, were safe and well, to have some word from them.

'You're doing a great job.'

The voice took her by surprise. She had thought all the men had gone.

'I'm terribly sorry but we're closed. There's nothing left, in any case.'

'Oh, I don't need anything to eat.'

Bea became suddenly aware that she and the mystery man were alone. Even the Indian cooks had returned to their quarters.

She quelled a shiver, though she didn't know if it was from apprehension or sheer tiredness – or worse: the beginnings of the fever the other women had.

'Who are you?' she shielded her eyes with her hand, trying to get a better look at the man who stood in the shadows. The accent was an American one, but that wasn't so unusual, there were plenty of US soldiers in the area.

'Lyle Cotton, ma'am. *Chicago Daily News*.' She blinked as a tall, rangy man with a shock of red hair and wearing tropical uniform emerged out of the darkness. For a heart-stopping moment Bea thought she was looking at Archie, but of course her brother didn't have an American accent. She saw the dark green US Army War Correspondent cuff on his arm, which was inexplicably reassuring. 'I'd like to talk to you if I may?'

'What on earth for? You can't want to report on us Wasbies,' she said. 'Surely your readers are more interested in hearing about the thick of battle? Wins and losses? Triumphs of the Allies and so on?'

'You may be right. But many of our readers are women, you know. They'd like to hear what drives a gal such as yourself to want to stick it out in this place. Whether you're incredibly brave or considerably foolish.'

His tone was curious, but Bea wasn't sure at first how to answer. 'I'm afraid I don't agree,' she said, after a pause. 'I've never thought myself a fool, but nor am I brave. My brother Archie's the brave one – not me. Archie – Archibald Fitzgibbon.' She suddenly felt the need to talk about him, as if her words would somehow bring him closer to her. 'He's in the Signals. Probably somewhere out there,' she pointed a knife towards the doorway. 'Behind enemy lines, I would bet.'

Lyle Cotton's face lit up with a broad grin. 'At least it's not your sweetheart.'

'No, it's not,' she said crossly. 'I don't have time for one of those. Now if you'll excuse me, I've had one hell of a day and all I can think about is finding my bed and crawling into it.' The last thing she wanted was to flirt with him.

He raised his eyebrows.

'Alone.' She shook out the tea towel she'd been drying up with, and spread it over the counter. Unlike Plum who seemed able to effortlessly charm men, Bea had discovered that the only way to deal with them, particularly the flirtatious ones, was to be pleasant but firm, often calling to mind her indomitable headmistress, who had never suffered fools gladly. It seemed to work. Most of the time.

'Apologies, ma'am. Perhaps you might have a few minutes tomorrow? I genuinely am interested. My photographer's here with me – I'd love to get a few pictures of you all. There *are* more of you here, aren't there?'

He seemed so sincere that she relented. 'We are down in numbers at the moment, some are on leave and the others under the weather, but if Lucy and Joy are feeling up to it in the morning, I'll let you know.'

'Much obliged now,' he drawled.

'I can't promise anything. And you'll have to be quick, we've got to get out to the gunners tomorrow.'

He turned and raised a hand in farewell. 'I'll let you get some rest.' He left the canteen, whistling as he went.

≈

Though her feet were swollen and tender and she was beyond exhausted, Bea struggled to fall asleep that night. She was covered in ant bites and tossed and turned, unable to find a comfortable position at which to rest. There was also something about the way Lyle Cotton had spoken to her that intrigued her. Perhaps it was because his laconic drawl reminded her of some of the other American soldiers and pilots she had got to know – Jack in particular. She hadn't seen him for weeks now, and found herself missing his slow smile and the way he looked at her as though she were the only other person in the room.

It was well into the early hours before she finally dropped off.

The next morning, she woke late to find Lucy already up and happily tinkering under the bonnet of the canteen truck. Joy, too, appeared to be feeling much better, and Bea sent up a silent prayer of thanks that they had both recovered.

Plum came back from leave, much to their relief, bringing with her generous amounts of chocolates and lipsticks for each of them. Bea was so pleased by the renewal of her normally buoyant spirits that she wasn't even irritated by Plum's silly talk of parties and handsome soldiers.

True to his word, Lyle Cotton returned as they were loading up the mobile canteen, and he spoke to each of them about their work.

'We've all lived rather strange lives, I suppose,' said Joy. 'Many of us come from India; one girl's father is the Governor of Assam. We've all got here in different ways. Some of us have husbands or brothers fighting in Burma, quite a few of us speak passable

Urdu, which helps of course.' She paused in her chat as she hefted a box of cigarette cartons into the truck. 'We're all anxious to help in any way we can.'

'It's a bit of an adventure, isn't it?' Plum added, batting her eyelashes at him. 'And we're not afraid of hard work.'

'I can see that,' he said.

'I hope we're making a real difference,' said Bea earnestly. 'The morale of a fighting force should not be underestimated. Wars have been won or lost based on it.'

'I absolutely agree with you there, Miss . . . ?'

'Private Fitzgibbon,' Bea replied.

After that, he carefully noted all of their names, along with their ranks.

When they'd loaded up, they waited for a few brief moments for his photographer to take pictures of them all as they stood to attention alongside the truck.

Bea tried not to squint into the sun and had to nudge Lucy to smile. 'Come on, it's not that bad,' she whispered.

'Ooh, look at us,' said Plum. 'We'll be famous, won't we?'

'Last thing I'm interested in,' Lucy muttered.

'Shake the stardust out of your eyes, Private Vellacourt,' said Joy with a good-natured grin.

As they were about to leave, Bea caught sight of a soldier walking towards the mess tent. She thought she recognised him and smiled, but he simply scowled back at her, and she couldn't shake the feeling that he was angry – whether with her or Lyle Cotton, or the fact that they were all being photographed, she wasn't sure. She put the notion out of her mind, and concentrated on locking up the truck. There was too much to do to waste time and energy worrying about the occasional odd look.

'I'll try to make sure you get a copy of the article,' Lyle said as they got ready to leave. 'Been a real pleasure talking to you.'

'You too, Mr Cotton,' said Bea warmly, remorseful for her rudeness the previous day. 'It was nice to talk about what we are here to achieve, and for someone to take notice.'

~

They had no sooner pulled up at their first stop and climbed out of the truck than a crowd descended. Joy and Bea served at the counter, while Lucy lit the kerosene stove and put the water on to boil.

'Hello Joy.'

Bea immediately recognised the man, for she'd seen him in a photograph Joy had shown her, taken at a far happier time.

Joy's face had taken on a chalky pallor and she almost dropped the mugs she was carrying. 'Good Lord, Peter. I didn't expect to see you here.'

'I'm as surprised to see you.' He blinked at her as if he didn't believe what he was seeing. 'This is no place for a woman.'

'I can't really talk right now,' Joy replied, a strained expression on her face.

'It's all right,' said Bea gently. 'I can manage here.'

'If you're sure?' Joy didn't look like she wanted to go anywhere, not with her husband anyway.

'Unless you'd prefer not to?'

'No it's fine.'

'I'll give you a shout when it's time to leave.'

Bea watched as they walked off together towards a stand of trees. She couldn't help but notice the distance between them, the awkward way Joy held herself apart from her husband.

She put her head down and busied herself with the trays of cake; she was sure she would hear all about it later, if Joy wanted to talk. Though Joy was her immediate superior, it never really seemed that way, and ever since their conversation on the long, dark train journey the two women had become close, working easily alongside each other.

When Joy returned to the truck only a few minutes later, her mouth was set in a firm line and only a slight wobble of her chin betrayed how difficult a conversation it must have been.

Bea paused in her pouring of tea, setting the large pot down on the counter and giving Joy a reassuring squeeze, but they couldn't stop for long, as the line of men wanting refreshments seemed to grow in front of their eyes. Joy blinked rapidly and then pulled her shoulders back and pasted on a beaming smile. 'Right, who's next?'

Later that evening, as she was on her way to bed, Bea knocked softly on the door of Joy's room, which was set a little further along the corridor from the others. 'Mind if I come in?' she asked.

'Not a bit.' Joy was perched on the end of her bed, her head down and her arms wrapped around her knees, looking like a forlorn bird sheltering from the rain.

Bea sat down on a box opposite. 'Are you all right?' she asked.

Joy gave a loud sniff but nodded. 'It was the shock of it, really. I had no time to prepare, though I suppose I had imagined it was likely I would one day run into him out here.'

'Was it awful?'

'Ghastly. No cross words, though, which actually made me even sadder. It's like all the emotion had run out of him. He's definite about a divorce. As soon as the war's over.'

As soon as the war's over. So much was waiting on the war to be over.

'I suppose we rushed into things. Getting married, I mean. We didn't know each other very well, but then, what with the war . . .'

Just as Bea was silently reminding herself never to be carried away like that, an image of Jack Butler swam before her.

'Don't blame yourself,' she said, pushing thoughts of Jack away. 'It's not your fault.' She paused for a moment, and then an idea came to her. 'You know what?' she continued. 'You could say that your husband was killed in battle. Died a hero. If you wanted, that is. No one need ever know any different.'

'Oh, I don't care what other people think,' Joy sighed.

'Good for you.'

'Well, not much anyway, apart from my parents, and I couldn't lie to them. But I can't help feeling like such a failure, wondering what on earth I should have done differently. It feels like my fault that he doesn't want to be married to me anymore, as if I've done something wrong. That's why he's found someone else.'

Her shoulders shook and she pressed a handkerchief to her mouth. Bea got up and sat down beside her, placing an arm about her friend. 'Don't put the blame on yourself, there's absolutely no point. It takes two people to make something work.'

'Thanks,' Joy said after a while. 'I really shouldn't be feeling so sorry for myself. Plenty of people have it worse than I do.'

'Now stop that,' said Bea sternly. 'You've got a lot on your plate without giving yourself a beating over it. Why not try to get some rest? It might not seem as bad in a few days' time.'

~

'Post!'

Joy appeared bearing an armful of parcels and letters as the other women returned from a trip into the jungle.

'There's one for you, Plum.' She handed over the topmost parcel. 'And a couple for Lucy. And a parcel for you, Bea.'

News from home and loved ones always helped to lift their spirits.

When the women had finished their chores, they each retreated to a quiet corner of the *basha* to read. Bea's contained a tin of toffees and a four-page letter from her mother. She forced herself to read slowly, to draw out the pleasure of hearing her mother's voice in her head for as long as she could. She read of cocktail parties and lunches, that the orchid trees along their street were now in bloom, 'a pleasing sight that, for whatever reason, always fills me with hope', and that Bea's father was back in Calcutta on leave 'having damaged a tendon in his foot, though God knows it's making him frightfully grumpy'. Bea smiled at this, could well imagine how frustrated he must be, and then, as she turned the page, her eye was caught by a final PS, written in a rushed hand, the ink somewhat smudged. 'Terrible news. Archie reported captured. POW. Waiting to hear where he's been sent. More as soon as I have it. Try not to worry.'

Bea's breath caught in her throat and she felt a burning mist behind her eyes. All of her prayers had failed to keep him safe.

189

She put the letter down next to her, unable to stop her hands from shaking. She tried her best to calm herself and think things through in a logical manner, but all she felt was numb. Numb and sick to her stomach.

'Not bad news, I hope?' Lucy, who had been sitting across from her, had noticed Bea's changed demeanour. She put down the letter she'd been reading and searched Bea's face. 'Oh God. Who?'

'It's Archie,' Bea said. 'POW. Whereabouts unknown.' A sudden image surfaced. It would have been one of the last times they were in Calcutta together. Archie in his smart new uniform, his hair brutally short, freckles like scattershot across the crooked bridge of his nose (broken in a school rugby game), a look of sublime confidence on his face. Strong, healthy, ready to take on any challenge.

Would anything be left of that carefree young man on the brink of what might have been, but for the war, the brightest of futures?

SIXTEEN

Galway, 1999

The next morning, the only sign that Beatrix might have consumed a considerable amount of champagne and chablis the previous day was the waywardness of her hair and a slight puffiness around the eyes. She seemed in high spirits at breakfast, polishing off a huge plate of bacon and eggs and several rounds of toast.

'Cast-iron constitution,' she said when she had finished, signalling to the waitress for more tea.

Eventually, when the two of them had thoroughly dissected the previous day's meeting – 'I had no idea how much fun it would be to see them all again,' Bea said. 'It was like it was only yesterday. Funny how time has the ability to concertina like that.' – Olivia decided to take advantage of her good mood and broached the question uppermost on her mind.

'So, did you get a chance to talk to the person you needed to?' she asked, putting her knife and fork together and wiping a speck of egg yolk from her lips with her napkin. 'About the fox-girl, I mean?'

Bea hesitated. 'Not exactly.'

Olivia withheld a groan of frustration at Beatrix's evasiveness.

'It's something of a confidential matter, and as you saw, there were too many of the others there to have a proper *tête à tête*. I shall try again this morning, I promise.'

'Would you like me to come with you?' Olivia asked. 'I saw the cafe earlier – it's across the road. Is your ankle up to it?'

'I don't need you to babysit me, darling,' said Beatrix with a touch of annoyance.

'Are you able to tell me anything else about who you need to speak to about the netsuke?' Olivia pressed. 'Is it Plum?' she asked, frustration leading her to voice her suspicions. 'Did it once belong to her?'

'Actually, no,' Beatrix said, draining her cup and not looking the slightest bit surprised at Olivia's guess. 'Her husband believes it belongs to him.'

'The judge?'

Beatrix nodded.

'The one who's about to be elected to the Supreme Court of Ireland?'

'The very same.'

'But why would he think that?'

'Well, now that's a story for another day,' she said, sighing heavily. 'Perhaps when I'm feeling stronger; or when this wretched matter is resolved. It was never actually his in the first place, though he may take some convincing of that. I really don't wish to discuss it any further, my dear. I promise you, however, I will do my utmost to get you the provenance we both so badly need.'

Beatrix's tone brooked no argument, and Olivia didn't miss the change from 'darling' to merely 'dear'.

'Of course,' Olivia said, reminding herself that Beatrix was the client in this odd relationship, never mind that she had imagined they might be becoming friends.

∼

The women weren't in the cafe when Olivia went to check later that morning, but as she was about to return to the hotel, she ran into Alex, who suggested they try the pub instead.

O'Connell's Bar, a few yards from the hotel in a quaint cobblestoned laneway, was jammed with people and Christmas tinsel and noise and a fug of warmth. They quickly shed their jackets and scarves, and Olivia listened, entranced, as the lilting Irish accents swirled around her.

'There they are!' Alex called out over the hubbub of conversation. 'By the fire.'

Sure enough, the four women were sitting at a table, each with a pint glass of Guinness in front of them. The women were animated, smiling and gesticulating as they spoke. The century had only a day left to run, and from the look of the women they were all ready to sail enthusiastically into the next one.

'If you can't beat them . . .' Alex made a drinking motion.

Olivia nodded her thanks and as Alex shouldered her way to the bar, Olivia went over to where Beatrix was sitting, perching next to her.

'Hello darling, nice walk?'

Olivia smiled. She was back to darling again.

'Blew all the cobwebs away. And it's just beautiful out there.'

'Excellent.'

Alex arrived with drinks and a plate of bread and cheese then passed a pint to Olivia. 'I think half the population of Galway is in here today,' she said, surveying the room.

'That's because it's too bloody cold to be anywhere else,' said Lucy.

'We've been catching up on the past fifty-odd years,' said Beatrix.

'I imagine there's a lot of ground to cover,' said Alex, sipping her beer and winking at Olivia.

'We need to remind each other of our stories,' said Beatrix as she and Lucy exchanged a knowing look. 'Of surviving the worst of times.'

'And the best,' said Plum. She was either oblivious to the undercurrents that swirled between the other women, or a rather accomplished actress.

About half an hour later the crowd in the pub had thinned considerably and Olivia looked up as the door jangled once more, bringing with it a rush of cold air and a tall, square-jawed, grey-haired man in a dark, expensive-looking coat. A real silver fox.

'Harold! Over here,' Plum cried, an expectant look on her face.

Olivia turned to see Beatrix's face blanched of all colour, her knuckles white as they gripped her glass.

SEVENTEEN

Dohazari, 1944

A suffocating humidity had descended upon the camp and each day became much like the next – long, hot and busy.

'At least it stops us worrying,' said Bea to Lucy as they sat in a rare moment of solitude, sipping gin by the river and swatting away the ravenous mosquitoes that swarmed in thick clouds as the sun went down. They'd all taken to wearing trousers most of the time, to keep the worst of the insects from biting them, but still the itching nearly drove Bea mad. Lucy called it the 'Aussie wave' as they continually batted away the blasted creatures: some so large they seemed capable of carrying off an infant.

Plum and Joy had gone off to a drinks party with some British soldiers. It had got to the point where they took it in turns to accept invitations, for they often needed a night off after the long and exhausting days. According to one of the many rules that governed them, they were only supposed to have three late nights a week: one until 2 am, and two until midnight, but of course little heed was paid to this, as well as some of the other more archaic instructions, such as always carrying a pencil while on duty.

'What office-bound idiot thought that one up?' Bea had wondered aloud when she first read the rule book.

She'd received another letter from her mother only that morning, with news that Archie was definitely in a prison camp in Burma, though his exact location was unknown. Sometimes, when she thought she couldn't bear it anymore, she turned to her sketchbook for solace, adding notes about her activities, from the things that had infuriated her – the cooks not turning up for work every day for a week, which meant the women all had to pitch in and bake in addition to their other duties – as well as those that had made her laugh. She was careful to hide her sketchbook beneath her mattress, for strictly speaking they were not allowed to record anything about their time there, though Joy always turned a blind eye. Bea did her best to notice fleeting moments of humour, lest she slide into a ditch too deep to climb out of. She told herself that one day, when she saw her brother again, she would give the sketchbook to him, and they could share their stories.

Jack had been deployed further south, and although he couldn't tell her exactly where he was, he had written several times, dryly amusing letters that made her laugh out loud as she read them. The letters made Bea even fonder of him than she was already, and she had begun to wonder – daydream even – what might happen after the war was over.

'Luce?'

'Mmm?'

'I don't think I want to go back to my old life. After all this. I can't imagine doing nothing but going to luncheons and tennis parties.'

'I know what you mean,' Lucy replied, 'I want to do something more.' She leaned forward, confiding. 'I want to train as a pilot.'

Bea blinked. 'I don't doubt you will.' There was a determined quality about Lucy, and a self-belief that Bea admired. She could easily imagine Lucy at the controls of a plane, guiding it through the sky as effortlessly as she navigated dirt roads in a Jeep. 'I'm not *that* ambitious,' Bea continued, 'but I'd like to do something to make a difference. It seems wrong somehow to go back to such a frivolous life, especially when others have given up theirs.'

'Amen, sister,' said Lucy, grinding out a cigarette butt. 'And every day gone is another day closer to the end.'

'I'll drink to that,' Bea replied, holding out her glass for a top-up. 'And to absent friends,' she added, thinking of Bubbles, missing her cheerful good nature.

'Absent friends.'

~

The next morning, Bea was startled to see Joy hurrying towards her, a newspaper flapping in one hand.

'Come and see,' she cried. 'We're in print – the *Chicago Daily News!*'

She reached Bea and held it up. There they stood, in black and white, smiling in front of their Jeep. 'Golly, we all look rather carefree, don't we?' she said, taking a closer look.

'Oh, Joy, it's a great likeness of you,' said Lucy, who'd come out to see what the noise was about. 'Christ, I look like a well-fed wombat.' She grimaced. 'Anyone would think that working in this heat would make the weight drop off.'

'Hush now,' said Joy. 'You look lovely. We all do. Well, as lovely as you can in Army greens and a bandeau.'

'Imagine Americans reading about the four of us all those thousands of miles away. That's crazy,' said Bea.

'We're on page two; that's pretty good, isn't it?' Joy said, going on to read in her best American accent. '"A taste of home," it says. "When this three-ton truck pulls up in a remote clearing in the Burmese jungle, a cheer goes up, and the men stop what they're doing and rush to meet them. The Women's Auxiliary Service (Burma), or the Wasbies as they are more fondly known, do more than just hand out cups of hot tea and slices of homemade cake. Their work is vital, boosting morale and supplying those essential sundries that make the life of a soldier on the move so much more comfortable. From shoelaces to hair cream, razor blades to chewing gum, they're a commissary on wheels, serving officers and other ranks without fear or favour. Approved by the highest-ranking commanders in this theatre of war, they work under the same conditions as our boys, sometimes within the sound of enemy fire, and do it all with a charm and warmth."' She gave them a happy grin, the first Bea had seen from her in weeks.

'Look, our names are all there,' said Lucy. 'In the caption under the photograph. Oh, that's just wonderful.' She put an arm around Bea's waist. 'Why don't you keep it safe for all of us, once Plum's seen it?'

~

'I've had a message,' said Joy, as the women gathered at the end of the day. 'From Wasbie HQ.'

'Oh yes?'

They all stopped what they were doing – messages from Shillong, apart from the regular movement schedules, were rare.

'Apparently Captain Taylor says that we should have sought permission before doing that newspaper interview.'

'But he was only here for one day,' Bea protested. 'How were we supposed to do that?'

Joy held up a hand, 'No harm done, she says. In fact, she said to pass on how proud she is of all of us. And we're being moved closer to the front, as of tomorrow.'

~

Cox's Bazar was on the coast, just shy of the Burmese border, and if anything it was even hotter and more humid than Dohazari. Eggs went rotten, butter rancid and any fresh stores that they could get perished even before they could be used. Thousands of troops poured in from Arakan after heavy gun battles, tired and hungry, many of them airsick, and the women were rushed off their feet serving meals, cakes and endless cups of tea.

This was as close to the front as they were allowed without an escort – and there were warnings of dead Japanese soldiers buried not far from the canteen, with advice not to dig holes for any reason.

Bea stayed mostly at the static canteen, helping Amar, who had come with them, to supervise the cooks, and trying but failing to balance the books. She learned, after a week or two, that a perfect set of accounts was almost impossible, and achieving an approximate result was the best she could expect.

One morning, a few weeks before Christmas, they were told to expect an air drop of supplies. The four women, plus Amar, went out to the drop zone in a Jeep and waited on the edge of the clearing, listening out for the drone of an approaching plane.

'How long are we going to have to wait?' Plum moaned, as they all wiped the sweat from their foreheads and craned their necks to see the aircraft.

'As long as it takes,' replied Joy, taking out her bottle and forcing down a sip of brackish water.

'There it is!' said Lucy, pointing to a tiny speck, no bigger than a flea, in the distance.

Within moments, the planes were sweeping low overhead, and the women's ears were filled with the noise of the engines. One by one, crates attached to parachutes began to float earthwards, as the planes made several passes to deliver their cargo. 'I hope it's something tastier than Spam,' said Plum.

When the aircraft had disappeared into the sky, the women approached the crates.

'Can you hear that?' Joy asked.

A loud, indignant cacophony of squawks came from several of the crates.

'"Poultry?"' Bea read the large letters heavily inked on the plywood. 'Oh Christ, they've sent us live ones,' she said. 'What berk thought that up?'

'Look,' Plum called. 'They're escaping!'

A couple of the crates had split open on landing, and several turkeys and a pair of geese had squeezed out of their confinement and made a bid for freedom.

The women did their best to chase them, but the birds were faster and flapped off, disappearing into the surrounding jungle. 'It's impossible,' puffed Joy as they all reassembled and admitted defeat.

'They were literally running for their lives,' said Lucy, before breaking into gales of laughter.

'I suppose it'll have to be that wretched bully beef instead,' said Bea with a grin. She looked around. 'Where's Amar?'

Lucy began to yell for him, and the other women joined in. Eventually, he emerged from the jungle, holding a goose upside down by its webbed feet.

'Priceless!' said Plum with a giggle.

'Oh, well done!' Bea called out.

Amar's grin was so wide it almost split his face in two.

They returned to camp with the goose, which continued to honk mournfully for days on end, calling for its missing friends, as Amar resisted the entreaties of the women who tried their best to persuade him to roast it for Christmas dinner.

One of the crates contained decorations, and the women dressed the mess with tinsel and coloured parachutes. Tins of mincemeat had been included in the air drop, and the women and some of the soldiers in the unit donated their brandy rations, 'to make sure the mince pies have the proper taste', according to Joy.

There was also a crate of mail, among which was a parcel from Bea's mother. She tore off the tape and found a new sketchbook, the cover snowy-white and clean compared to her now tattered one.

'Oh my goodness!' she cried, her face lighting up in delight.

'Good news?' Lucy asked hopefully.

'Look!' she held up a small rectangle. 'It's a postcard. From Archie.'

She sat down abruptly, feeling her knees give way as she saw the familiar handwriting, the curled 's' and sharp downstrokes so like her own. It had been sent from an unidentified POW camp.

'"Dear Mother and Bea,"' she read out loud. '"Am fit and well. Have seen David Hamley. He is well. Love to all at home, hoping they are well. Love A."'

Underneath was a tiny self-portrait.

How typical of him to be worried about everyone else. 'David Hamley is an old school friend of his,' she explained. 'I'm sure it will be good to have a chum out there.'

'Oh, what a wonderful present!' said Lucy, giving her friend a hug.

'The best,' said Bea, her eyes shining with happiness. 'Well, almost.'

On Christmas Eve, one of the padres conducted a candlelit service at midnight, and Bea was forced to swallow the lump that rose in her throat as they sang 'Away in a Manger'. She caught Lucy's eye and noticed that her normally unemotional friend was also blinking away tears. Bea had spent Christmas apart from her father and brother before; the previous year it had been just her and her mother, but this time they were all scattered to the four winds. She prayed that perhaps next year they'd be together again.

Christmas Day passed in a blur of serving food and alcohol, and Bea barely had time to think about her family. The days that followed were just as busy. On New Year's Eve the women put on another special evening, with music and food and, as always, plenty of booze.

'Here's to the future,' said Bea, raising her mug and feeling lighter than she had in all her time serving in the Wasbies.

'Whatever it may bring,' said Lucy.

'To the future,' echoed Plum. 'Nineteen forty-five and beyond.'

'Cin cin,' said Joy, clinking her tin mug to Bea's.

Not for the first time Bea hoped she and her friends would stay as close as this always. These women offered unconditional loyalty and earned her trust in a way that she had never experienced outside her family.

In the early hours, before falling into bed, she made a brief note of that night's celebrations in her sketchbook before sending out a fervent wish that she – along with so many others – might be reunited with their loved ones before the year was out.

～

Not long after New Year, they received orders to move out again, and they soon climbed aboard a US Army plane leaving for Shillong.

'Now there's a sight for sore eyes.'

Bea turned her head at the familiar voice. 'Fred!' she stumbled to her feet in the confined space and gave the pilot a hug. 'What are you doing here?'

203

'I could ask you the same thing,' he said, squeezing her tight and almost lifting her off her feet, before turning to the others and greeting them in a similar way.

'And how about the others? Jimmy and Al? Billy? And Jack?' Plum asked.

The smile left his face, sudden as a tropical rain shower. 'Jimmy and Al didn't make it.'

'Oh,' said Bea. 'God, I'm so sorry.'

He shrugged. 'This is the war, baby.'

'And Jack?' She swallowed the lump in her throat, afraid of the answer.

'Took a bullet in the shoulder. Last I heard he was at one of the casualty clearing stations, in Shillong as it happens. I'm gonna try to track him down when we get there.'

'Can I come too?' she asked, relief that he was still alive flooding through her.

He smiled, 'I'm sure he'd like that.'

They found perches among the boxes and bedrolls, and Bea settled herself near a window so she could look out once they'd taken off. The women were silenced by the buzz of the engines as the plane revved up and began to taxi along the runway. A moment of weightlessness as the plane lifted off the ground, and then they were sailing high above the land, and as Bea looked down she could see the river curling through the dense green jungle. How serene and peaceful it seemed from the air.

~

As soon as they arrived in Shillong, Bea and Lucy went to the military hospital.

'Clipped my wing,' said Jack when they found him, sitting up in bed, his left arm in a sling. He looked so much more vulnerable in a pair of rumpled pyjamas, with his hair, longer than it had been when she last saw him, falling over his forehead. 'But I'll be out of here in a day or two; they've done a pretty good job patching me up and I'll be good as new before you know it.' He smiled at both of them, but his gaze lingered on Bea. She found she couldn't look away.

'I'll leave you to it,' said Lucy diplomatically. 'Good to see you Jack. Stay out of trouble, you hear?'

'You too, Luce.'

As her friend departed, Bea saw that the fox-girl was still around Jack's neck.

'She kept me safe,' he said. 'Well, as safe as it's possible to be out there.' Bea wasn't certain how something made by the enemy, even in a time of peace, could offer any kind of protection, but she'd seen first-hand how many of the men were superstitious about all manner of things. 'Light me a ciggie, won't you?' he asked.

Bea reached for the packet at his bedside, offering him one, briefly aware of the warmth of his fingers against hers, feeling a spark run through her at the touch. It was still there; she hadn't imagined the connection between them when they first danced together all those months ago.

Flicking his metal lighter, she placed it in front of the cigarette resting lightly between his lips and waited as he inhaled.

They stayed as long as they could afford to, chatting about this and that, everything and nothing, determinedly ignoring the elephant in the room: his two fallen comrades. After a while,

Bea brought out her sketchbook. 'Do you mind?' she asked. 'The fox-girl? Might I make a quick drawing of her?'

'Be my guest, honey. But you'll have to remove it first.'

He sat up and Bea leaned towards him, her fingers fumbling as she undid the knots of the shoelace, suddenly aware of how close she was to him, feeling his breath warm on her cheek, the male smell of him. After a moment she was able to remove it, and she placed it in the palm of his hand and began to draw. She concentrated on her task, acutely aware that his eyes remained firmly fixed on her, an amused expression on his face.

Eventually, she left him with a stack of well-thumbed *Punch* magazines and her copy of *The Hobbit*. 'I'll expect it back at some point,' she said lightly. She'd done her best to ignore the flutter she'd felt when she retied the necklace for him, and now she resisted the urge to tell him that she would miss him. Getting too fond of someone like him – anyone, actually – was a bad idea while so much about the world was uncertain.

'Absolutely, Second Lieutenant Fitzgibbon,' he said, saluting her with his good arm while glancing at the extra stripe on her sleeve, a recent promotion.

Bea grinned. 'Apparently I'm not terrible at balancing the books.'

'I'm not surprised in the slightest.'

'Have you heard?' Plum asked when they returned to Cleve. 'We're being attached to the thirty-sixth.' She danced around Bea and Lucy in excitement. 'We're off to the frontline.'

'What? You're kidding,' said Lucy.

'We're going into Burma,' said Joy. 'Things have gone from defence to attack.'

'That has to be good, yes?' Bea asked.

'Everyone says the Japs are running scared now. And they're particularly wary of coming up against Lieutenant General Festing.'

'Frontline Frankie,' said Plum. 'One of the best.'

'I'm afraid we've got to get a move on,' said Joy. 'We've only got two days to organise our equipment and stores.'

'What in heaven's name are these?' Lucy asked, pulling a swathe of brightly coloured silk from a box on the floor.

'Lunghis,' Plum explained. 'I thought it would be good to have a few gifts for the local Burmese women; some of them might be able to help us.'

~

'There's a message from Captain Taylor,' said Mrs St John, the Wasbies' Assistant Commandant, later that day. 'She's extremely impressed by all that you've done so far and wants you to know what a distinction it is for a women's unit such as the Wasbies to be attached to a division. She says she's sure you'll be a credit to us all.'

'It's practically unheard of,' said Lucy, and Bea swelled with pride to learn that their team had been the only one specially selected for this honour.

'You'll be closer to the fighting than any of us, and living under the same conditions as the men, but you've all demonstrated grace under pressure and a calm efficiency in going above and beyond to get the job done. We know you'll cope admirably.' She beamed at them like a proud mother hen, but Bea couldn't help feeling a twinge of apprehension at her words.

'Careful what you wish for, hey,' Lucy murmured.

EIGHTEEN

❧❀❧

Galway, 1999

'Hello! You made it.' Plum sounded jaunty, but there was an unmistakeable apprehension in her eyes.

The man walked towards them, his silver-flecked hair lending a distinguished air, although a faint twist of his mouth lightened his serious expression. He looked good for an old guy, Olivia thought. His shoulders were broad and his sweater flat against his stomach; he took care of himself. As he bent down to kiss Plum's cheek, Olivia saw that Beatrix was sitting absolutely still, her face frozen.

'Everyone, this is my husband,' Plum said. 'Harold Byrne.'

He acknowledged each of the women in turn as Plum made the introductions, but he didn't appear to recognise any of them. Beatrix's eyes were blank as she nodded at him but her lips were now pinched tightly together, as if she were afraid of saying somthing she shouldn't.

'The traffic from Dublin wasn't too bad; I made good time,' he said. 'How wonderful that you have all found each other again, and that some of you came from so far afield.'

'Did it all go well?' Plum asked.

'I believe so,' he said, giving little away.

'Very nice to meet you, Mr Byrne,' Olivia said, keeping her eyes on Beatrix. 'But I think I should probably take Mrs Pelham back to the hotel.'

Beatrix shot her a look of pure relief and Olivia fetched their coats, saying goodbye to the other women and helping Beatrix out of the pub. The older woman's limp seemed more pronounced than in previous days and she appeared suddenly very tired.

'Why don't you get some rest, before tonight?' Olivia suggested when they reached the hotel.

'Yes, yes, don't fuss over me,' Beatrix snapped.

Olivia held her tongue, the question she'd been about to ask about Harold Byrne stilled on her lips.

'If you could collect me at seven sharp.' It was a statement more than a question.

'Of course.'

Something about the way Beatrix had reacted to Harold Byrne confirmed to Olivia that the mystery of the fox-girl was linked to the women's time in India and Burma. When she reached her hotel room, she opened Beatrix's sketchbooks again, searching for clues. Near the end of the book, she turned a page to find a watercolour of the fox-girl, pale and ethereal, its dark eyes like beads of jet. Beatrix had painted it nestled in the palm of a man's hand – Olivia knew it was a man's by the callouses and dark wiry hairs on the back of the fingers – as if it were an offering.

After that, there weren't many more drawings – a few simple sketches of a village scene, with scrawny chickens scratching in the dust – but then, tucked away in an envelope at the back of the book, she found a handful of drawings she hadn't seen before.

These showed scenes rather different from Beatrix's other ones.

For a moment she wasn't sure exactly what she was looking at. Then as she realised what it was, she inhaled sharply.

Splayed hands of bamboo leaves filled the foreground and skeletal, emaciated bodies, their ribs and backbones visible, with wasted limbs and swollen joints, naked but for a loose kind of loincloth, reclined on low platforms. A leg of one of the men was severed at the knee.

How had Beatrix got hold of these? They didn't look like her other drawings. Had she got them from someone else who'd been out there? Olivia realised that she really didn't know Beatrix at all. It looked increasingly as though the mystery of the fox-girl wasn't as simple as she'd first anticipated, and that it was likely to be a painful unravelling.

~

Olivia woke with a start. The room was in darkness save for Christmas lights flashing red and white outside the window. Glancing at her watch, she saw that it was quarter past six. She flew into the shower, quickly washing and then drying her hair before stepping into the purple dress she'd bought in Holyhead.

She arrived in the lobby at six fifty-eight to find Beatrix waiting for her.

'That's a pretty dress, darling. It goes perfectly with the shoes.'

When Beatrix had realised Olivia didn't have any footwear other than her boots, she had pulled out a pair of vintage pumps. 'I brought spares and we're about the same size, I think.'

'Thank you. You look very nice too.'

Beatrix glanced down at the simple black floor-length frock she was wearing. A rust-coloured fur capelet was topped by a silver brooch in the shape of a lion that glittered below her throat. 'I know it's terribly poor form to wear fur nowadays, but I don't often get the chance. Besides, it's always freezing in those draughty old houses.'

'Are you feeling better?'

'I think so.' She brandished her handbag like a weapon. 'Once more unto the breach, dear friends . . . Stiffen the sinews, summon up the blood . . .'

'It won't be that bad, will it?' Olivia looked at her with curiosity.

'When the blast of war blows in our ears, then imitate the action of the tiger.'

'Okaay . . .' Had Beatrix been at the gin already?

'Shakespeare, darling,' she explained, seeing Olivia's puzzled expression.

When they were in the car and underway, Olivia turned to Beatrix. 'You've met Plum's husband before, haven't you?' she asked.

'Harold?' Beatrix pretended to be very interested in something out the window.

'But he didn't appear to remember you, did he?'

'I hardly expected him to. Anyway, it was an awfully long time ago.'

Not to you, Olivia thought, the drawings she'd found earlier appearing in her mind's eye.

'There were some other sketches in the back of your book. In an envelope . . .'

'Oh, yes. Those.' Beatrix's hands fluttered in front of her face and her eyes misted over.

'I'm sorry, I didn't mean to upset you.'

'No, it's all right. I'd forgotten they were there, that's all.'

'From someone who was on the railway?'

Beatrix nodded, her mouth wobbling slightly. 'It was . . .' She lapsed into silence and Olivia had no desire to open up old wounds any further, not right now. Maybe later when Beatrix was in a more forthcoming mood, perhaps over a whiskey or two.

They drove on in silence for a while.

'Any New Year's resolutions?' she asked, hoping to cheer Beatrix up.

'Not to be so afraid,' she replied, and Olivia heard a new note of resolve in her voice.

She turned to Beatrix in surprise. 'But you're one of the bravest women I know.'

They reached the long driveway, which, now that it was evening, was illuminated by a series of lanterns looped through the trees, joining a line of cars approaching the house and stopping to disgorge passengers in front of the entrance.

'Not really, darling,' said Beatrix. 'I've avoided facing up to things for far too long; but that's all about to change.'

NINETEEN

Burma, 1945

After a hot and dusty drive from Shillong to Moran, the women, together with Amar and three Indian cooks, and accompanied by boxes and boxes of their camp kit and supplies, were due to continue their journey on board a US DC-3 Dakota at dawn the following day. They weren't cleared for take-off until late in the afternoon, by which time they were all thoroughly sick of waiting around with nothing to do but drink tea and play cards. Lucy was teaching Joy basic Japanese – 'My father was a silk trader and we had a Japanese maid when we lived in Kobe for a few years, before we went back to Australia. I was only young, but I remember a few phrases,' she explained when Plum gave her a curious look – and Bea listened in as she sketched her friends in various stages of frustration as they griped about the unnecessarily early start.

Finally, they were given the green light. It was Amar's first time on a DC-3, and though Plum laughed ungenerously at his alarm, the whites of his eyes showing in the dim light, Bea did her best to reassure him, chatting away to him as they took off hoping to take his mind off the experience. Cocoa was none too impressed either, and she screeched and spat at the noise of the propellers for the entire journey, Lucy was hard pressed to keep a firm hold of her, crooning softly in her ear to calm her.

The cargo area of the plane was hot, sticky, loud and uncomfortable, and they had to sit among the boxes and bedding rolls, but Bea was able to ignore all of it as she peered through the window, fascinated by the thick forests and mountain ranges below. Her heart seemed to thud louder as they descended, for she could see the scattered wreckage of gliders, looking like toy planes from such a height, the remnants of recent battles. The plane circled and even though she did her best to keep her eyes on the horizon, she started to feel desperately nauseous. She turned to look at the others, who were also white-faced but doing their best not to show it.

When the plane began its descent towards the shortest airstrip Bea had ever seen, she shut her eyes and held her breath. They landed heavily and engines were thrust into reverse to slow them down. She only opened her eyes once the plane had come to a halt. Amar had folded his hands together in prayer. They were at the very edge of the clearing.

An American soldier threw open the doors of the plane. 'What cargo do you have on board?' he asked.

'Wasbies,' they called out in unison and then fell about with relief at having landed and on seeing his astonished expression.

'A plane-load of women? You've gotta be kidding me,' he said, scratching his head. 'That's a first.'

They clambered out from among the sea of tin hats and haversacks, and piled into a waiting Jeep. 'We'll get all your gear loaded, don't you worry,' said the soldier, pointing to a truck that was waiting alongside the airstrip. As they sped away, Bea looked back at their stores, hoping he would keep his promise.

~

'Is this it?' Plum asked in a subdued voice as they stood in front of a dilapidated-looking bungalow, its low-slung verandah bowed like the rictus of a dead man.

'At least it's still standing,' said Bea, 'Unlike Indaw.' They'd passed through that town, or all that was left of it, seeing a flattened mess of bombed-out buildings and ramshackle wooden houses.

'It might not be so bad inside,' said Joy optimistically just moments before a large rodent scurried across the front verandah. 'Come on, we've faced worse than this.'

'Just as well we've got Cocoa,' said Plum.

Bea looked at the cat, who was nestled in Lucy's arms and had paid not the slightest bit of attention to the creature. 'I'm not sure she'll be much use as a ratter.'

'I'm sleeping with the doors and windows firmly shut,' said Plum as they walked gingerly towards the entrance.

There were three small rooms – a kitchen and two bedrooms – and a complete absence of furniture. Between them, though, the four women soon had the floors swept of debris and sleeping mats set up. They were all covered in red dust from the drive, and took it in turns to freshen up in what passed for a kitchen, ferrying water from a well in the scrubby back garden.

'At least we don't have to think about feeding ourselves tonight,' said Bea when they'd washed and brushed up.

They had been invited to the nearby mess, but when they arrived they were somewhat taken aback by the size and formality of the set-up.

'So, this is what it means to be attached to a unit,' said Lucy as they stood on the threshold of a tent filled with long tables at which sat row after row of uniformed officers.

Bea might have once been intimidated at walking into such a large group of men, but now she barely gave it a second thought. As the women looked around for a spot to sit, some of the men noticed them standing there and shuffled along a bench to make room for them.

'We'd heard about you,' said one of them.

'Not sure it's the place for a woman,' said another.

Bea felt Lucy, who was standing next to her, stiffen and saw her fists clench at her sides. 'We're not here for a bloody picnic, you know,' she said.

The soldier looked chastened and went back to his food.

~

After an uncomfortable night, the women packed up and moved on to Katha, a settlement on the banks of the Irrawaddy, which they were to make their base. It was another long, dusty journey but a pretty one, surrounded by beautiful forests, thick with paddle-leaved teak trees and yellow-flowering rosewoods.

When they finally reached the river, they let out a collective breath at the sheer size of it.

'Golly, it's a mile or more across, I'd say,' said Plum.

Less impressive were the buildings they had been assigned.

'I hadn't expected a palace, but this?' said Bea. 'Honestly?'

The shell-pitted wooden structures had apparently once been a school. As the women wandered through the filthy, rubbish-strewn rooms, assessing their purpose, their spirits sank.

'Buck up,' said Joy. 'We'll get this place shipshape in no time. But before then, we'll be catering for at least five hundred for supper tonight,' she added, reading from a briefing sheet.

Bea stifled a groan. It was already noon.

Odds and ends of furniture had been left behind, and they salvaged what they could, collecting a motley assortment from the houses that surrounded the school while Amar and the cooks sourced firewood and water.

'At least one of the field regiments has built us some ovens,' said Bea, inspecting the structures made from empty ammo boxes and mud bricks.

They began the task of unpacking hundreds of mugs and plates, knives and forks, before starting on tins of sausages, bacon, peas and baked beans. For pudding, there were canned peaches and evaporated milk, and cocoa after that. Inevitably, after opening tin after tin, several of them ended up with blistered and cut hands. There was a medical station not far from their makeshift mess, and Joy dispatched those with injuries – including a couple of the cooks – to find someone to dress their wounds.

Despite being exhausted from a non-stop day's work, Bea felt some of her tiredness lift when she saw the line of men as they prepared to open up.

The evening fast became a blur of serving endless plates of food, while Lucy and Joy helped in the kitchen and heated up gallons of cocoa.

'You sure do get around.'

Bea looked up to see Jack standing in front of her, no sign of his injury evident, a gleaming-white grin lighting up his still-tanned face.

'It seems like you turn up like a lucky penny yourself,' she said, delighted by his surprise appearance among the sea of uniforms. 'Are you sure you're recovered?'

'Never better,' he said with a wink as he took the plate she was holding out, though Bea noticed that it rattled before he steadied it with his other hand. 'I'd heard you ladies had already got here.'

'This morning, if you can believe it,' said Bea. She turned to serve the next man in line.

'I'll try and come back later, when you're less busy, though we've an early start tomorrow, so I can't promise,' he said. 'Mighty good to see you, Bea.'

She felt herself flush at his words.

When the rush had tapered off and nearly all the food had disappeared, the women finally paused for breath and regarded the piles of greasy plates and mugs that had been stacked on nearby tables.

'I'm done in,' said Joy, wincing as she inspected the dressings on her hands.

'Looks like you could use some help.'

A couple of orderlies from the dressing station had begun to ferry the dirty dishes to the washing-up area.

'I'll say.'

'We'd be ever so grateful,' said Plum, fluttering her eyelashes.

Bea groaned inwardly but acknowledged that there were times when a bit of feminine charm came in handy.

It was nearly midnight before they finished, but Jack hadn't reappeared, and Bea ignored the stab of disappointment. She reminded herself that it wasn't worth getting attached to anyone, especially not an American pilot, no matter how handsome he was.

'Oh Luce, you're an angel,' she said as they reached their room to find beds waiting for them.

'I stole a moment this afternoon to come and set up,' Lucy replied. 'Figured we'd all be too tired to do it later.'

'You really are an absolute gem,' said Bea, falling on her cot fully clothed.

It took them three days, working from sunup to sundown, clearing and sweeping and scrubbing and then unloading and sorting through the stores before they were properly organised. Plum washed several pairs of curtains and strung them across the window openings, where they added some brightness to the dingy rooms.

'Make do and mend, hey?' she said as she balanced on a chair and tacked them up with a hammer and nails.

'Where's the Raj princess of Calcutta now?' Bea teased, then ducked as Plum lobbed a length of fabric at her.

They quickly established a shop, as well as a canteen that served up char and wads throughout the day, and they were roped in to help prepare the food for the officers' mess.

'A damn sight better than K-rations,' said Plum.

'Bea, can you go and collect some chops from the supply point?' asked Joy, as they got ready to open up.

When Bea arrived at the stores, she was surprised to hear a loud squealing coming from behind the building.

'It was a live pig!' she told Lucy later, collapsing with mirth and indignation. 'They were going to give me a ruddy live pig. Oh, you might well laugh about it, but let me tell you it certainly wasn't funny at the time.'

'What did you do?'

'I told them I'd be back in an hour to collect the chops – I wasn't going to kill the poor thing.'

'And?'

'I duly went back and they presented me with the entire sodding carcass. "I was told to collect chops," I said. "Sorry, ma'am, but we're not butchers," was the reply. I said in that case they had to at least give me a decent knife, and they produced one with a twelve-inch blade – practically a sword, sharp as a razor it was – and I went at it.' She shuddered. 'I had to hack the bloody thing apart myself. Can't say I enjoyed the sound of metal grating against the bones, but they didn't leave me with much choice.'

'See what you're capable of when you try?'

Bea grinned. 'Did a pretty good job of it in the end.'

~

Early one evening, the women borrowed a Jeep and drove out to a few of the nearby villages, dodging ox carts and the occasional local on a bicycle. They stopped when they came across a group of young boys in ragged shorts playing an energetic game with a hollow wicker ball, passing it from player to player using only their feet and heads.

'Not much different from boys everywhere,' said Joy.

They joined a small crowd of onlookers as toddlers with almond-shaped eyes peered at them shyly from behind their mothers' skirts.

Burma had been ravaged by the occupation. The ornate, ancient temples and stupas that dotted the country and gave it such a distinctive skyline had been stripped of their statues and bells by the Japanese Army, just as the jungle had been stripped of its foliage by the bombing on both sides.

The women came across a temple a little further along the road, its surface carved with elephants and Buddhas and surrounded by brilliant magenta bougainvillea. They took off their shoes and entered the soaring space and Bea was immediately struck by a sense of peace. She stood in the cool interior, hands clasped in front of her and began to pray – the same prayer that ran through her head and her heart almost every night – that the war might soon be over and her brother would come home safe.

Later, as they returned to the banks of the river, they saw ships from the Irrawaddy Steam Ship Company lying neglected, already beginning to rust, weeds sprouting from their decks and portholes.

In 1942, when the Japanese invasion began, many Burmese had fled their homes, but most only got as far as Katha on the railway before being forced into the jungle on foot. Only the day before, a man had come to the camp. 'Have you seen these children?' he asked in broken English, producing a faded photograph of two dark-eyed girls and a boy. 'My daughters and son. Three years ago we lost them. We search everywhere.'

The women could only shake their heads sadly, offering him cigarettes, which he would only accept if they joined him in a smoke.

'Would you like me to see if I can repair those?' Lucy asked, pointing to the man's spectacles, which were held together by a piece of string.

He handed them over, blinking owlishly, and Lucy went to fetch the small repair kit that she carried almost everywhere.

Bea asked him about his children, their names and how old they were, as Lucy tinkered away with a pair of tiny pliers.

'That should do it,' she said, handing back the spectacles, now secured with a piece of wire that she had neatly wound around one arm of the frame.

He was profusely grateful, bowing and shaking their hands.

It was nice to have helped the man, even if in only a very small way, but Bea was struck again by how much the war had damaged not only the ancient buildings of this once-beautiful country but also the local people, most of whom were poor villagers and fishermen who wanted nothing more than to get on with their lives. The country had been changed forever; its peaceful people caught in the middle of a war started such a long way from here, in the name of avarice and the pursuit of power. It all seemed so senseless.

~

When Bea woke on the morning of her birthday, someone – Lucy, she suspected – had left a bottle of gin on her trunk next to a mug of tea. As on every birthday, she immediately thought of Archie, and her mood flattened. She sent him a quiet message. Though she'd never set much store by twin telepathy, she allowed herself to believe that he might have heard her, might also be thinking of her this morning.

She wasn't given time to be glum, though, because the other women soon arrived with a stream of good wishes.

Joy promised to make a chocolate cake. 'There might even be candles, though I'm not sure I'll manage to find twenty-one of them!' she laughed, reaching forward to embrace Bea.

They brought parcels and letters too, for the mail plane had landed the day before and Lucy had gone early to collect the mail bag. A letter from Bea's mother held not a word of complaint that her twins were not with her on their twenty-first birthdays. She'd included a note from Bea's father, which although it was brief, told her how proud he was of her. There was no further news of Archie. 'I'll keep your present safe,' she wrote. 'For it is the string of pearls of mine you have so long admired.'

Bea had fond memories of playing with it when she was little; how her mother would place the pearls around her neck as she admired herself in the mirror, entranced by the soft glow against her skin, the warm feel of them. That girl didn't exist anymore; such things as pearls and jewels meant little when the world was at war, when men were giving their lives every day and her brother was still missing. She hoped that one day there would be a happy occasion on which to wear them.

They still had plenty of work to do, but Joy let Bea finish early. 'Go and freshen up and we'll have a celebration for you later,' she said.

Bea took advantage of the rare time to herself and went for a walk down towards the landing strip. She loved to watch the little 'Jeep planes' – Stinson L5 Sentinels – take off and land. They were tiny aircraft that carried only a couple of passengers, but they could set down on a postage stamp and were well suited to the rough landing strips that had been hacked out from the jungle as the troops moved forward. There was a slight chance she might see Jack there, for he was based in the area.

She had finally stopped fighting her feelings for him, admitting she had grown fond of his lopsided smile and missed the sound of his voice, low in her ear. He and a few of the others, Fred (who always seemed to have a musical instrument of one kind or another in his hand) included, had taken to dropping by the canteen at the end of their shifts, exhausted by having spent all of the daylight hours in the cockpit, but still with the energy for a chat and a drink or two. She often found Jack by her side, quick with a funny tale to cheer her up, a joke that made her groan, or a sleight-of-hand trick that left her confounded.

Shielding her face with her hand, she gazed up into the cloudless sky, but there was no sign of the khaki-green aircraft. She was about to turn and leave the runway when she heard the buzz of a returning plane, and she waited and watched as it came in to land. As it taxied to a halt and the pilot climbed down, she recognised the man she'd been most hoping to see.

'Bea!' he called out, his face lighting up with pleasure. 'A little bird tells me it's your birthday today.'

Bea smiled back, feeling a thrill of excitement at the mere sight of him.

'Well, I'd say that calls for a joy ride.' He turned back to the plane. 'Come on then, we'd better be quick before we lose the light.'

She wasted no time in following him.

As she climbed in next to Jack, she flashed him a nervous glance and he began to taxi along the runway. She'd never been in such a small plane, but she wasn't about to admit that to him. They gathered speed and she grabbed the nearest handhold, her stomach dropping to the soles of her boots as they became airborne.

She soon forgot her nerves as they gained altitude, and began to revel in the soaring feeling. Then Jack brought the plane in low, pointing out the temples and pagodas that popped up above the thick jungle canopy. She caught her breath as she saw more of the splintered gliders resting at unnatural angles in the treetops, like so many discarded playthings.

All too soon, they returned to the airstrip, which as they approached looked little bigger than a matchbox from the air.

'Hang on,' Jack said cheerfully when they hit the ground with a bump, the wheels squealing in protest.

She would never forget such serene beauty, nor the delight in being airborne with Jack by her side.

'That was the most perfect birthday present, thank you,' she said as the plane came to a stop and silence enveloped them.

'We aim to please, ma'am.' Jack gave her a mock salute and helped her down. She took his hand, and felt her heart begin to beat faster. When she'd found her feet, he pulled her gently towards him, a question in his eyes. She nodded imperceptibly and he lowered his head to hers. Oblivious to her surroundings, Bea gave herself up to the feeling of his lips warm against her own, something she'd been thinking about every time she saw him, had dreamed about more than once.

He kissed her with exquisite tenderness, teasing her, making her want more from him, more than she'd ever dared want from a man. It was every bit as heart-stopping as the flight, and just as wonderful. She wished the moment would go on forever and was lost when he reluctantly pulled away.

'Don't . . .' she said, her voice husky with desire.

'Don't what?'

'Don't stop,' she gasped and he bent to kiss her once more.

Bea left Jack to finish his flight report and returned to the camp feeling as though she was walking on air. Her mind was replaying her first proper kiss over and over, so it took her a moment to realise the trouble the others had taken to decorate the mess with streamers. There was cake and singing, and the gift of a delicate hand-sewn yellow parachute-silk scarf. She immediately tied it around her neck, brightening up the dull khaki of her uniform shirt.

Some of the other American pilots were there too and had mixed up a cocktail that Fred called a 'Tom and Jerry'. It seemed to have used half of their egg rations, but she didn't care because it was delicious. She had to blink to stop the tears, for she was overcome with a sudden rush of emotion. She'd once imagined her twenty-first might be celebrated with a lavish dance, but somehow this was perfect. Well, it would have been if Archie had been there too.

'Happy birthday, honey.' Bea was encircled in a pair of arms and lifted clean off the ground.

'Jack! Put me down!' she protested loudly, but he took no notice and swung her around until she was dizzy. He set her on her feet again and planted a kiss right on her lips, paying no attention to the crowd of onlookers. Bea felt herself blush at being embraced in such a way in front of her friends and workmates, but in her happiness she decided that she didn't care a jot.

Later, Jack pulled her to a quiet corner. He reached into his pocket and pulled out an object on a leather bootlace, then fastened it around her neck. The fox-girl.

'But I can't, it's your good-luck charm,' she protested.

'A fox-girl for my fox-girl,' he said, twisting a lock of her dark red hair around his finger. 'I wanted to give you something special, and this is pretty much it right now. Besides, I've plenty of luck to spare,' he said, tucking the trinket under her collar and kissing her again. She melted into his arms, returning his embrace more forcefully, bolder even than she had been before.

Later that evening they all piled over to the officers' mess, where a weekly dance was held. There were joined by some of the nurses stationed in Katha but there were still only a dozen of them compared to the hundred or so men, so Bea was practically swept off her feet. For once she didn't mind the energetic swing, jive and jitterbug, for she felt as if she could have danced all night.

Towards the end of the night, Jack caught her up in a slower number and she had to struggle to control the fierce thud of her heart against her ribs.

It had been an almost perfect birthday.

TWENTY

❧✦❧

Galway, 1999

The sounds of a string quartet floated towards them on the cold night air as Olivia helped Beatrix out of the car, and she caught a glimpse of waiters standing just inside the house, holding trays crowded with champagne flutes.

'All right?' she asked.

'Fine, thank you.' Beatrix was curt, her jaw set in a firm line as they walked through the house, past the musicians and towards a large marquee on the lawn. Heaters blew warm air into the space, ruffling tablecloths and the skirts of chairs and causing the petals of the flower arrangements to flutter. Coloured lights swooped around a dance floor at one end as a band set up.

'The great and the good of the entire country are here,' said Lucy, coming towards them, wearing a long, bottle-green velvet dress, her silver hair sleek. Olivia felt Beatrix relax slightly at the sight of her old friend. 'Word is that Harold is up for some big appointment; they're planning on announcing it tonight. Plum couldn't help boasting to me.' She sounded unimpressed. 'Doesn't make him any less of a bully, if you ask me. Smart, charming, but still a bully.'

'So I hear.' Beatrix gave a weak smile then turned as a waiter offered them champagne. They each took a glass, and Olivia stood back to survey the crowd. There were a good deal of jewels on display, a smattering of military dress uniforms, swarms of silvertails in black tie, and plenty of off-the-shoulder taffeta and plunging cleavage. She felt distinctly underdressed but was grateful for her foresight in actually having a dress to wear, and was pleased when she saw Alex giving instructions to one of the waiters – together they would at least be lowering the average age by a few years.

'Hello Bea. Olivia.' Joy swept up to them, looking regal in magenta taffeta, a medal pinned below her left shoulder instead of jewellery. She kissed them on both cheeks. 'Plum suggested we wear them,' she said, noticing Olivia looking at it. 'More interesting than diamonds. Did you bring yours, Bea?'

'It's in my bag. I was waiting to see if she really meant it.'

'Come on, Bea,' said Lucy. 'If the others have theirs . . .'

'Oh, do,' said Joy as a man in tails wearing a bar of four medals across his chest appeared beside her. 'Oh, there you are, honey,' she said with a smile. 'Fred, you remember Lucy and Bea, and this is Olivia, Bea's assistant.'

'Pleased to meet you.' He took Olivia's hand and gave a small bow. 'Bea! Lucy, you haven't changed a bit.' He leaned in and kissed them before enveloping each of them in a hug in turn. 'How wonderful to see you both looking so well.'

'I could say exactly the same about you,' Beatrix laughed, and Olivia was pleased to see that she appeared to be relaxing in the company of her friends.

'His family's in food,' Lucy whispered to Olivia. 'Snap-frozen peas. Worth a fortune, apparently. And we all thought he was destined to be a penniless musician!'

Olivia excused herself and went to search for Alex.

'There you are!' Alex, wearing a striking blood-red dress that accentuated her fair skin, embraced her at the entrance to the marquee. 'So pleased there's someone here my own age to play with,' she whispered in Olivia's ear. 'I've put you across from me at dinner and away from the most boring old farts. Granny let me invite a couple of lads I know, so we'll have some amusing company at least.' She paused, appearing to remember something. 'I've been telling Grandad all about you.'

'Telling him what, exactly?' asked a voice behind them.

Olivia turned to see Harold Byrne, in his Army dress uniform, with a bar of medals affixed to his chest and a loop of gold braid on one shoulder.

'It's all good, Grandad,' Alex reassured him.

He smiled, but seemed distracted. 'Alex, darling, have you seen your grandmother?'

'Afraid not, but this is Olivia. You remember I was telling you about her – she works at Cholmondeley's, with Elaine. Olivia, this is my grandfather, Harold Byrne.'

'We met briefly the other day,' said Olivia, taking his outstretched hand. 'And I'm more of an unpaid intern actually,' she added.

'Nonsense. She's being far too modest. I told her you'd show her the *Japonaiserie*.'

'Did you now? I'd be happy to, but perhaps not right now, darling. I still have to welcome our guests. Granny seems to have invited half of Dublin.'

He gave Olivia a charming smile, but she couldn't shake the feeling that under the soft accent and urbane exterior, he was as unyielding as rock.

'Of course,' she replied. 'Some other time. This is quite a party. Thank you so much for inviting me.'

'Thank my wife for that. Now, if I could work out where she was . . .' And he was off, stopping every few metres to greet guests, exchanging a few words and then moving on again.

'I warned you he was bad-tempered, but I forgot to add rude,' Alex apologised.

'Not at all,' said Olivia. 'He is hosting a party, after all. And these are his friends.'

'I'm not so sure about that – acquaintances and hangers-on, more like. Come on, let's find Fergal and Donny.'

'Who?'

'The lads I mentioned.'

There must have been several hundred people invited to the party, and most of them seemed to be milling about at the entrance to the marquee, causing a bottleneck. When everyone was seated, a process that seemed to take an inordinately long time as they searched for place names and inevitably ran into friends and stopped to greet each other, Olivia caught sight of Harold and Plum at the head of the largest table at the far end. He tapped a glass for quiet and, when the chatter had subsided, he began to speak, welcoming friends and family, 'and friends who've come from the other side of the world', who had joined them 'to celebrate the dawn of a new century, including some very old and dear friends of my wife's from our time serving in Burma'. There was a murmur of interest at this last remark.

Olivia followed Plum's gaze as she inclined her head towards the edge of the room. Ah, there they were: Joy, Lucy and Beatrix, her fur removed now and sporting a similar medal to the one that the other women wore. Olivia was too far away to be certain of her expression, but she was pleased to see that Beatrix seemed to be okay.

As Harold sat down, the man to his right stood up and called for quiet again. 'I shan't keep you from your dinner for much longer, but Harold is a modest man . . .' He paused as a round of laughter swept through the marquee. Clearly he wasn't especially modest to those who knew him. 'And I am extremely proud of his tireless work in our judiciary. I am therefore delighted to announce he is soon to be appointed Chief Justice of Ireland. Please join me in a toast.' He raised his glass and there was a squealing of chairs as the party guests stood up. 'To Harold.'

'To Harold,' came the thunderous reply, followed by a chink of glasses that sounded to Olivia like a thousand icicles chiming and then a moment of silence as everyone drank. She watched Plum hesitate for a fraction of a second before downing her glass in one long draught.

Eventually, as everyone resumed their seats, a team of waitstaff began to serve the first course, bowls of vibrant green soup.

'Watercress,' said Alex's friend Fergal, who was sitting to her right. 'The county is known for it – all that rain.'

'Were you born and brought up here?' she asked.

'Aye, I was. I work in Dublin now though, came back from London when things started to boom here. The "Celtic Tiger" is on the rise, don't you know.' Olivia half-listened as he spoke about Ireland's economic policy, her eyes scanning the room, returning to Beatrix from time to time, noticing that although she was talking with her old friends, she seemed to be eating very little of her soup, which, Olivia now knew, was most unlike her.

The first course was cleared away, more wine poured, and a main course – escalopes of salmon in a cream sauce with asparagus – was served. Fergal was now waxing lyrical about the superiority of Irish produce, and though she could understand his fierce nationalistic pride she was growing a little weary of it, for there was not much she was able to contribute beyond the occasional impressed 'You don't say' and 'Mm-hmm'. It didn't help that everyone else at their table was knocking back the wine as if they were at the last party on earth, rather than the last one of the century. Because she was driving later on, Olivia had limited herself to one champagne and a glass of wine with dinner and she was starting to feel even more like an onlooker.

She smiled as Alex, who was sitting across from her, rolled her eyes as she caught something Fergal was saying, and told herself to stop worrying and just enjoy the evening. Given that she had expected to be serving increasingly drunk revellers in a bar on New Year's Eve, being a guest at a glamorous party in what was practically a castle in Ireland was not exactly a hardship. Olivia reminded herself not to be ungrateful, that it was an experience she would probably one day boast about with as much pride as Fergal was now carrying on about his superior country.

As the guests finished their salmon and began to get up from their seats, Olivia seized the opportunity to excuse herself. She threaded her way through the tables and the throng of guests towards Beatrix and perched on an empty seat next to her.

'Everything all right?' she asked.

'Well, I doubt I'll be on the dance floor later, but I'm fine, thank you, darling. Are you having a nice time?'

'Oh yes, Alex put me at her table,' she replied, touched that Beatrix had bothered to ask. 'So, who's going to tell me the story of how you came to be awarded these?' she asked, seeing that Lucy was wearing an identical medal to the one on Beatrix's chest.

'Well,' said Joy, a look of anticipation on her face. 'It all started when they disobeyed orders—'

'With damned good reason,' Lucy interrupted.

'I can still see the expression on his face,' said Bea, thoughtfully. 'I don't think he expected to see a white woman.'

They were suddenly all sombre and Olivia kicked herself for bringing up the subject. It stood to reason that it would have involved something unpleasant as well as brave.

She was saved from further embarrassment at her gaffe by the arrival of dessert – a circular chocolate mousse – and the sound of a trumpet warming up. The swing band was getting underway.

'Remember the Palais Glide, Bea?' Lucy asked, her shoulders lifting in time to the music.

'And the jitterbug,' said Joy, with a rueful expression. 'I doubt my knees could cope with that these days.'

'Come on, honey, you're never too old,' said Fred, getting to his feet and extending a hand to his wife.

Olivia watched in impressed amusement as the two of them, the first couple on the dance floor, began to twirl and twist, rolling their hips and kicking up their heels in perfect rhythm. As Fred whirled Joy around, her long skirts flaring, they seemed suddenly ageless, and Olivia caught a glimpse of what their younger selves must have been like.

'She always was a good dancer,' Beatrix said to Olivia. 'We all were. We had to be – there were always far more men than women and we were never off the floor for long.'

Fergal came over to ask Olivia to dance – he asked Beatrix first, but she declined due to her injured ankle; 'But I do appreciate your manners, young man.' – and Olivia followed him onto the floor, relieved to discover that he was a better dancer than conversationalist.

She danced for several more numbers and then, pleading sore feet, took a break for a drink, gulping down a glass of water. She found a seat at the edge of the marquee, surreptitiously easing off one of her shoes where a blister was threatening and watched the dancers for a while. No one matched Joy and Fred for style, but they had long since retired from the floor and younger feet than theirs tapped out the syncopated beat with varying degrees of skill.

She glanced at her watch: less than an hour until midnight and the end of the century. Beatrix had disappeared, but then so had most of the rest of her table, possibly driven to find a quieter spot in the house. Olivia eased her shoe back on, wincing as she stood up (she and Beatrix weren't quite the same size, so it turned out), and went to find her.

She peered into what seemed to be a library, with shelves lined with books, but it was thick with smoke and occupied solely by men puffing on cigars, so she walked on, along a wide corridor punctuated at regular intervals by doors. She tried the handle of each, finding a sitting room, the dining room where they had all had lunch two days earlier, and a morning room furnished with a writing desk and two armchairs, but in none of them was there any sign of Beatrix or her friends.

She found a small powder room and went inside, checking for any signs of occupation, but it was empty. Olivia caught a glimpse of herself in the mirror and thought for a moment that the sallow reflection was that of a stranger. It had been a long time since she'd felt the sun warm her skin. She was about to leave when she bumped into Alex.

'Just the person I was looking for,' she cried, tossing her hair over her shoulders. 'I've managed to drag Grandad away from his boring friends for a few minutes to show you the Long Room.'

'The Long Room?'

'It's where the majority of his art – the Oriental collection – is hung. Come on, quick, before he gets cornered by someone else.' She grabbed Olivia's hand and pulled her along the corridor, coming to a door at the very end. She pulled a key from her clutch purse and inserted it into the lock. 'Grandad promised he'd come right away; we can wait for him inside.'

Olivia could hear the band music only faintly now, and as they entered the room and closed the door behind them, it disappeared completely. The room was much colder than the rest of the house and she shivered involuntarily, goose bumps rising under the fabric of her sleeves. It was dim, too, with pencil lights illuminating a number of tall plinths scattered the length of the room. The walls were hung with a number of varying sized canvases, each one lit from above and below. It was set up exactly like a museum gallery. Olivia was about to take a step towards the closest painting when the door opened again and, with a blast of cigar and brandy fumes, Harold arrived.

'Ah splendid,' he said, slurring slightly. 'Olivia, how lovely to see you again.' He glanced down, as if puzzled by the empty balloon glass in his hand. 'Alex, darling, I don't suppose you would be a love and fetch me another?' he asked.

'Of course Grandad,' she said, taking the glass from him. 'I'll be back in a second,' she added to Olivia, disappearing into the corridor.

'Now, where would you like to start? With the lacquerware, the netsuke or the portraits?'

'The netsuke are a particular interest, and it would be a privilege to see them, sir.'

'Very well, but let me show you a couple of the portraits first.'

He came to stand behind her as they looked at the first painting and Olivia felt suddenly very uncomfortable. His breath was warm on her shoulder and he leaned even closer towards her, brushing a hand, ever so casually, against her arm as he spoke. She tried not to squirm. She'd experienced her fair share of inappropriately familiar men, but never someone as old as Harold Byrne. Suppressing a shiver of revulsion, she stepped away from him, saying brightly, 'Alex tells me you started collecting after the war.'

'I did indeed.' He looked at her as if he were assessing her like a piece of art, and Olivia felt her skin crawl. 'Came across my first netsuke in Burma. Lovely little thing, it was. The fox-girl. You'd probably know all about it – stolen in a robbery from the Ashmolean more than twenty years ago, along with a number of other, lesser carvings.' His voice was tight, and Olivia could see that the loss still angered him. 'I offered a not-inconsiderable reward, but I doubt it will ever come to light.'

She didn't say a word. Possession of the fox-girl was Beatrix's secret to reveal, not hers, but she couldn't help but feel a thrill as the mystery began to unravel before her. So, *he* had been the anonymous owner and the one to offer a reward. In which case, why did Beatrix so firmly believe it was hers? Olivia inched further along the room, torn between wanting to see the rest of the collection and thinking it might be more prudent to return to the party. She decided to opt for the former, reasoning that Harold was an old man and he would hardly try anything in his own home, in the middle of a party. She was being foolish to even imagine such a thing. Still, what was taking Alex so long? She glanced at the door, but before she had a chance to speak, Harold came up uncomfortably close behind her once again, sending a beat of alarm pulsing through her.

Olivia had paused in front of a woodblock print of a kimono-clad woman looking back seductively over her shoulder.

'Ah, *The Courtesan*,' Harold said. 'One of my favourites.' This time he rested a hand on her shoulder, stroking the fabric of her dress with his thumb in a slow, deliberate motion. She couldn't bear it any longer and ducked away, heading for the door, but he moved more quickly and blocked her way.

'I like to flatter myself that my word counts for a great deal, Olivia,' he said slowly. 'I could make your life a very great deal more agreeable . . .'

His voice was as soft as a caress but his meaning was crystal clear.

He seemed so at ease, so unhurried, she knew with a flash of insight that he'd done exactly this kind of thing before. And likely got away with it. The soon-to-be Chief Justice of Ireland.

She edged towards the door, thinking that if she wasn't quite so worried by what he might be capable of, she would find this awkward dance ridiculous. She wasn't concerned that he might physically overpower her, for she was younger and fitter and in possession of sufficient self-defence skills to put him out of action if she had to, but she knew he wielded a different kind of power.

She hesitated, torn between not wanting to offend him and a desire to tell him exactly what she thought of his behaviour. In the moment, saving his pride seemed the smartest course of action. 'That's very kind of you, sir. Someone with your connections in the art world would be an ally indeed, but you must have other, far more important, demands on your time to bother with someone as lowly as me.'

He leaned closer to her and she could see the spittle that had dried in the corners of his mouth, was almost overwhelmed by the sour smell of brandy on his breath. 'Oh, I think you're definitely worth bothering with, sweetheart.'

TWENTY-ONE

Katha, 1945

Bea was one of the last left at the mess, staying to help clear up the debris after Jack and the other pilots had gone to get some sleep.

'It's the least I can do,' she insisted, waving Lucy and Joy away. 'I shan't be long.'

Selfishly, she wanted a few moments alone, and soon lost herself in thoughts of Jack and what kissing him might mean for the future, then in memories of other birthdays spent with Archie, wondering how he might be celebrating this day and wishing they were together.

She was about to head back to her room when an officer came into the mess. She thought she'd seen him around the camp, perhaps even at the dance that evening.

'Locking up,' he said.

There was something about the intensity of his stare that made the hair on the back of her neck prickle, and she rubbed at it tiredly. She looked around, realising that everyone else had disappeared. 'Oh, right yes, sorry. I'm just about finished now.'

'I'll escort you back,' he said.

'Oh, I'm sure I'll be fine; it's really not far.'

'I insist,' he said, softly but firmly.

A faint unease began to curdle in her stomach, but Bea couldn't think of a way to refuse without seeming foolish, so she gathered the last of the glasses and walked over to the door.

They'd not gone far when she felt his hand grip her elbow, the smell of whiskey floating towards her.

'How about a goodnight kiss for me, then?' he asked. 'I saw you giving out plenty earlier this evening.'

Bea tried to wriggle out of his grasp. 'No!' she hissed. 'Thank you,' she added, hoping to put him off. 'I've got a sweetheart.'

He hustled her along, still gripping her elbow tightly. 'I've seen you girls, teasing us with your smiles, pretending to be friendly, then turning us down like we aren't fit to shine your shoes. Little vixens, the lot of you. Different story when it comes to the Yanks, though, isn't it? Those lazy accents work a treat on you girls, don't they? They so much as crack their gum and you come running. You're shameless, like bees to bloody honeypots.' His breath was warm in her ear and Bea froze, stunned by the vicious tone as much as his words.

Everyone in Katha had been so friendly that she'd let her guard down, forgetting the warnings the women had been given to stick together, especially after dark.

He yanked her forward and Bea realised that he was leading
her in the opposite direction from their building, towards the
path to the airstrip. She wanted to scream, but no sound came
from her throat when she tried. She was paralysed with fear.

'You think you're untouchable. Won't associate with the likes
of us. No, we're not good enough for you, are we?'

Her pulse pounded in her ears and her breath came in short
gasps that echoed in the air around her. She struggled against
his grip, but it was as though an iron band had been placed
around her arm.

'Don't even think about calling for help. You're too far away
for anyone to hear,' he said, his voice ominously quiet.

She lowered her eyes, saw the glint of a curved knife in his
belt and recognised it as one that the Gurkhas carried. A *kukri*,
she remembered being told, and that it was usually sheathed with
two other, smaller knives. Bea's whole body began to tremble.

'Don't . . .' she said, finding her voice at last.

'Don't what?' he said.

'Please don't hurt me,' she begged.

'Oh, I'm not going to hurt you, sweetheart. I promise you'll
enjoy it too.' Another gust of sour breath turned her stomach.

Bea's blood seemed to freeze in her veins as she registered the
meaning of his words. *Think*, she told herself. *Think, for God's
sake.* But her mind felt scrambled, a confusion of thoughts making
it impossible to decide on the best course of action.

'Don't you have a sister? A mother?' she asked eventually.
'Imagine if someone scared them like you're scaring me. How
would that make you feel?'

She saw him shake his head, the underside of his chin blocking the faint light from the moon. 'Stop talking,' he growled and pulled her roughly towards the airstrip. 'Or you'll really be sorry.'

Bea struggled to stay upright, tripping over her feet. She gave a small gasp when she stumbled, but he merely yanked her up again.

After what seemed an age, he stopped abruptly and the next thing she knew was the feeling of dirt grinding into her back as he pushed her to the ground with one hand.

'Pretty little thing,' he said, bending down and taking the fox-girl Jack had given her between his finger and thumb. He tugged sharply on the bootlace, snapping it, and her scream of protest was cut short as he covered her mouth. She struggled against him, desperate to escape, but he was too strong and she could scarcely breathe. Then she heard the clink of metal on metal as he unbuckled his belt. Before she could wriggle away, he was upon her, pinning her underneath him.

She knew what was coming next. She shut her eyes.

He grasped her head with both hands, holding it still while he mashed his lips against hers. She tried to scream, to bite him, but the weight of him crushed the air from her lungs and it was all she could do to try to catch a shallow breath, silenced by the force of the man on top of her.

She felt him fumble at her skirt, a tearing sound as he ripped the cotton of her knickers. She screwed her eyes tight, and for a moment the world went black.

~

When Bea came to, she didn't know where she was for a second, but then the sour smell of whiskey reached her and her stomach heaved as she remembered. She struggled against the man on top of her and it took a moment to realise that her arms were free. She tried scratching his face, but he swatted her hand away as if she were no more than a fly buzzing about his head, grabbing her arm and yanking it to the ground with his other hand. It caught her hair and made her scream out in pain. He covered her face with his hand and she tasted grit and dirt. She could hardly breathe, and tried again and again to move out from underneath him, but she was helpless against his brute strength as he forced his way into her.

She screwed her eyes tightly, as if that would make it all go away, but it didn't.

Moments later, she remembered the *kukri*. She reached lower, feeling revulsion as she encountered bare flesh. Then, something small, hard, unyielding.

One of the handles she'd been searching for. She let out an involuntary groan.

'Oh, you like it now, do you?' he growled, reaching for her breast, pinching the skin, hard.

Without a second thought, she grasped the handle and slid the small knife out of its leather sheath, bringing it down into his side as hard as she could. A sudden memory of butchering the pig came to her as she pressed the knife between his ribs, and she pushed it with every bit of strength she had.

The blade was sharp and easily cut through the man's shirt.

She buried it up to its hilt.

He stilled for a moment and then let out a howl of pain, rolling off her and onto his back, the knife stuck at an obscene angle in his torso.

'What the hell!' he shouted.

As soon as she felt his weight lift off her and without thinking, she reached forward and grabbed the handle of the knife and pulled it out. Then, scrambling to her feet, she took off back along the path, sobbing with fear and horror at what had just happened. What she had done.

Her knees and palms were skinned and the way was dark and uneven, but she ran faster than she'd ever run in her life, hoping she wouldn't trip and not daring to look behind her.

It wasn't far, but the ten or so minutes it took to reach camp seemed to take forever. As she approached their sleeping quarters she forced herself to slow down, not wanting to wake anyone, to draw attention to herself. Before she got to the house, she bent double, retching the contents of her stomach onto the ground. Wiping her mouth with one hand, she finally crept into the room she shared with Lucy and began to peel off her uniform, doing her best to quiet her ragged breath and still her shaking body.

'Have a nice night?' Lucy murmured sleepily from her cot.

'Y–y . . .' Bea couldn't bring herself to answer. She was too confused by the rush of events to reckon with what had happened to her. Here in the safety of her room, it didn't seem quite real.

'What is it?' Lucy sat bolt upright. 'Was it Jack? Did he get fresh?'

Bea shook her head, knowing that if she tried to speak she would break down. Her chest heaved with the effort of keeping it to herself.

'What's that in your hand?' Lucy asked, seeing a glint of metal in the moonlight coming through the window.

Bea looked at the *kukri* – its blade no longer than a fruit knife – as if she'd never seen it before. Noticing that it was dark with blood, she dropped it on the sheet. 'Oh God,' she cried, burying her face in her hands.

Lucy leaped from her cot and went to her. 'What's wrong? What is it? What happened?'

In halting sentences, Bea gave Lucy the briefest outline. 'He . . .' She hitched a breath as she relived the terrifying few minutes. 'He . . . you know.' Shame coursed through her. She couldn't bear to say the thing that had been done.

'We have to report this,' said Lucy, rubbing Bea's back and handing her a mug into which she'd sloshed several inches of rum.

Bea refused the rum – the sickly sweet smell of the alcohol reminded her of the man and made her want to heave again. 'It's my own stupid fault.' Bea's hands shook and she shuddered involuntarily. Someone walking on your grave, her mother had always said. 'I shouldn't have stayed behind.'

'Nonsense,' Lucy said firmly. 'You didn't ask for that to happen.'

'We've all been warned enough times to stick together, you know we have.'

'That's still no excuse for what happened to you. It's a *crime*, for goodness sake. We'll go to Joy in the morning; she'll know what to do. We *must* report this.'

'No. I can't do that. They'll ship us – all of us – out of here faster than you can say boo. And it'll be over, for everyone.' She didn't add that there was also no way she wanted Jack to find out.

'But this man – whoever he is – should be found. Punished. Locked up and the key thrown away.'

Bea made a grim noise that was somewhere between laughter and alarm. 'He squealed like a stuck pig.'

'Are you sure you're not hurt?'

Bea shook her head defiantly.

'What did he look like? Do we know him? You'd recognise him again, surely?'

Bea couldn't begin to think about it, shook her head.

'We can decide what to do in the morning,' Lucy suggested gently.

'No.' Bea shook her head once more. 'I'm not going to tell Joy about it, nor anyone else,' she insisted. 'Swear you won't either. You know how talk gets around: I'll be the one who comes out of it looking like the guilty party, like it was my own stupid fault.'

Lucy didn't answer.

'Swear you won't tell a soul!'

'If that's what you really want,' she replied finally in a quiet voice.

'It is. I don't want to go home, nor do any of us. I won't be the cause of the entire Wasbies shutting down. That won't help anyone.' Bea slumped back on her bed and Lucy lay down next to her. 'I didn't think I was capable of stabbing someone,' she admitted, doing her best to focus on what she had been able to do, that after minutes of sheer helplessness she had fought back. If she thought too much about what had been done to her, she'd never get through it.

'None of us knows what we're capable of until we're forced into a corner,' said Lucy. 'If nothing else, this war's shown us that.'

Bea lay on her cot, feeling the ache where the man had wrenched her arm, a soreness between her legs, and a tenderness at the back of her head where he had ground it in the dirt. It was quite some time before she realised that she was shaking, not only with fear, but also, under that, with rage. It was an entirely new feeling, but it only served to scare her even more.

'Shh . . .' Lucy soothed her, stroking her hair. 'You're safe now.'

TWENTY-TWO

Galway, 1999

O livia was milliseconds away from driving an elbow into Harold Byrne's solar plexus when the door opened and Alex came in, bearing a refilled glass.

'Has he given you the full run-down yet?' she asked, giving her grandfather an odd look.

Olivia nodded, surreptitiously lowering her elbow. 'Fascinating,' she managed to say, surprised at how calm she sounded.

'Anyway, it's nearly midnight, we should probably return to the marquee. Granny's got a surprise waiting for everyone.' She linked her arm through Olivia's. 'Shall we?'

'Thank you Mr Byrne, it was a real treat to view your collection,' Olivia said, breathing an inner sigh of relief.

'The pleasure was all mine, Olivia. Perhaps we might continue our exploration of Japanese art some other time. Do send my regards to Elaine when you return to work.' His words were cordial but his expression was glacial.

Olivia heard the veiled threat, but she smiled sweetly back at him while thinking she would be happy to never lay eyes on him again.

'Aren't you coming, Grandad?' Alex asked as they turned to leave.

'No, you girls go on; I'll be there in a minute,' he said, waving them off.

When Alex and Olivia reached the marquee again, flaps at the end of the tent had been opened, letting in a sharp breeze. Waiters offered tots of Irish whiskey, while others cleared the tables, now covered in abandoned napkins, half-empty glasses and partly eaten desserts.

Most of the guests had now gathered on the lawn, heels sinking into the soft grass, with the rest making their way there, though a few couples still shuffled on the dance floor.

The band stopped playing and Plum began to hustle the stragglers outside. Then, from the microphone, a countdown began. Olivia caught sight of Beatrix and hurried to catch up with her.

'Ten . . . nine . . . eight . . .'

'Everything all right, darling?' Beatrix asked in between the chanting.

'Seven . . . six . . . five . . .'

'Absolutely,' said Olivia.

'You're sure?'

'Really, everything's fine.'

'Four . . . three . . . two . . . one!'

The skies erupted in a cacophony of whizzing Catherine wheels, Roman candles and exploding rockets as the crowd rushed to embrace each other, greeting the new century with gusto. Olivia turned to Beatrix and hugged the old woman. 'Happy New Year.'

'And to you, darling girl.'

Together they watched the bright colours light up the sky.

Later, after the glow from the fireworks had faded, the band struck up again and the singing began. Strangers joined hands and swung them as they sang 'Auld Lang Syne', creating circles within circles, coming together and then stretching almost apart. Olivia found herself caught up in the moment, her sore feet forgotten, hands linked with those of Beatrix and Joy. In the distance, she saw Harold and Plum, standing slightly apart from each other. She looked away, not wanting to rest her eyes on him a second longer than necessary.

～

Olivia and Beatrix slept late the next morning, arriving for breakfast in time for the last service.

Beatrix had drunk three cups of tea before she was even capable of more than the rudiments of speech, and their conversation was subdued. As they finished, she mentioned that she had arranged to return to Plum's in the afternoon.

'There's something I need to tell you,' Olivia began. 'Last night, just before midnight, I went with Harold – Mr Byrne – to the picture gallery. Alex had suggested that he show me his art collection, and I was very interested to see it.' Olivia stopped, unsure, now she'd begun, if repeating the man's actions the

253

night before was the wisest course of action. After all, they'd been alone, so it was only her word against his, and he'd had plenty to drink. She took a deep breath and decided to continue. 'Alex went to fetch him a drink and he . . . well, he made me feel extremely uncomfortable.'

Beatrix sat suddenly very still, the piece of toast frozen on its journey to her mouth. 'Did he hurt you?' she asked sharply.

'No, nothing like that, not really. But he implied that unless I cooperated with him, he would make life very difficult for me. Professionally, that is.'

'Oh Christ.' Beatrix swore under her breath. 'A leopard never changes its bloody spots, does it.'

'What?'

'I'll tell you in a minute. What happened after that?'

'Alex returned, thank goodness, and I was able to leave with her.'

'Good.' She looked relieved.

'Please don't tell Plum; I really don't want to cause any trouble.'

'I understand. But that man—' she almost spat the word, 'has been getting away with this kind of thing, and worse, for years.'

'How do you know?' Even as she asked the question, something clicked in Olivia's brain. Harold's behaviour almost certainly had something to do with the mystery surrounding the fox-girl.

The dining room had emptied now, and in a low voice that shook with anger, Beatrix began to explain what had happened on the night of her twenty-first birthday; the whole long, painful story. 'I thought afterwards that perhaps I was somehow responsible – I shouldn't have been there on my own, and that maybe it wasn't as bad as I remembered, that things had simply got a little out of hand. But Lucy found me afterwards; she knew I hadn't made any of it up.'

Olivia sat, open-mouthed with shock, as she listened to the story. She had new admiration for Beatrix, for the courage she had shown at the time of the assault, and also for the strength she found to be able to sit in the same room as the man who did that to her.

'I've spent a lifetime trying to put the whole ghastly incident behind me, but I've not been able to let it go. I've carried it around like a stone in my shoe for years. I doubt he'd even remember, but for the scar he doubtless still carries,' Beatrix finished.

'But . . .' Olivia was practically speechless. 'I don't understand why you didn't report it at the time.'

'Don't you?' Beatrix asked, looking at her sadly. 'I always thought times were different then, but now I'm not so sure that anything's changed very much at all.'

Olivia thought for a moment. 'No, I suppose they haven't,' she said quietly.

'Nevertheless, I'm sorry that happened to you. I feel responsible.'

'Don't be,' said Olivia. 'Anyway, there was no damage done.' *Not like to you.*

'Harold took the fox-girl from me that night,' she said bitterly. 'Jack had given it to me as a present, you see, and Harold pulled it from around my neck in the struggle.'

Suddenly the remaining pieces clicked into place. She could hardly believe the truth. '*You* were the one who stole it from the Ashmolean?' she asked, with a mixture of shock and awe.

Beatrix nodded and took another sip of her tea, a hint of satisfaction on her face. 'I hadn't intended to. But when I saw it . . . They reported that the case was broken, but actually it had been left unlocked.' She gave a dry bark of laughter and finished her tea. 'Men such as Harold like to possess things – art, real estate, women . . .'

Olivia remembered Elaine saying something similar.

Beatrix put the cup down on its saucer with a firm chink. 'Now, I've asked Lucy to come with us this afternoon. She's prepared to back me up.'

'Why are you going to tell Plum? Do you think she knows what he's like? Anyway, wouldn't it be better to confront Harold directly?'

'His ego wouldn't allow it. Besides, just like you, I never want to be in a room with that man again unless absolutely necessary.'

'What will you say to Plum?'

'I'm still not exactly sure. I do know, however, that it will probably be the end of our rekindled friendship. More's the pity.'

⁓

That afternoon Beatrix, Lucy and Olivia made the return drive to the castle.

'Thank you for a wonderful evening; it really was spectacular,' said Beatrix to a rather dishevelled-looking Plum when she opened the door.

'It was good fun, wasn't it?' She brightened. 'Anyway, come on in out of the cold. There's a fire in the small sitting room and we can have a cup of tea.' She ushered them into the house and along the corridor. 'Alex,' she called. 'Alex, would you mind putting the kettle on?'

Her granddaughter appeared. 'Hello there, ladies. Is Joy not with you?'

'No, I think she and Fred are still sleeping off their late night,' Beatrix replied, her hands gripping her handbag.

'Oh, that's a shame, but never mind. She *was* still going at four this morning,' Alex said in an amazed tone. 'And yes, Granny, I'll organise some tea for you all.'

They sat down: Olivia, Beatrix and Lucy on one sofa, and Plum on a chair opposite. 'Oh dear, I feel as though I'm about to be grilled by a panel,' she said with a light laugh.

The other three women remained straight-faced.

'I'm afraid we have come here today to talk about something rather serious,' said Beatrix.

'What in heaven's name could it be? Has something happened? Are you ill?'

'No, nothing like that,' said Lucy.

'Oh well, that's a relief. I couldn't bear the thought of losing any of you now that we've only just found each other again.'

'It's about this—' Beatrix reached into her handbag and withdrew a small wooden box. She opened it and unwrapped the contents.

'The fox-girl!' Plum gasped. '*Harold's* fox-girl? What . . . Where did you get her?' She reached out to touch it, but Beatrix kept hold of it. 'I don't understand . . .' Her eyes darted between the three of them.

Alex came into the room carrying a tray laden with tea things and a plate of biscuits. She placed them on a side table and began to pour, offering a cup to each of the women. As she drew closer, she caught sight of what was in Beatrix's hand and her eyes grew wide with astonishment. 'Is that what I think it is?' she asked, nearly spilling the tea.

'Bea was just about to explain how it comes to be in her possession,' said Plum, a bemused expression on her face.

'This I need to hear,' said Alex. She finished pouring tea for everyone and then perched on the chair next to her grandmother. 'Do you mind?' She held out her hand to Beatrix, who reluctantly handed the little carving over. 'It's quite something, isn't it? How amazing to finally see it, after hearing about it for so long. It was Grandad's favourite, wasn't it? Just wait till he sees it again.'

There was a heavy silence as the women all watched Alex examine the netsuke, then Beatrix began to speak. 'A long time ago, in Burma, there was a man who found the fox-girl in a ditch, probably dropped by a Japanese soldier. He wore it on a bootlace around his neck, convinced that it was a good-luck charm. Then . . .' Beatrix faltered, swallowing. 'Then, he gave it to a young woman. As a present at a party for her twenty-first birthday. That young woman was me.'

'I remember that party,' said Plum, sounding puzzled. 'But I don't recall the fox-girl.'

'I think you might have been dancing at the time,' said Lucy, not unkindly.

'If that is true, then how did Harold come by it?'

'I lost the fox-girl that night,' said Beatrix. She paused, swallowing hard before beginning to speak again. 'I stayed behind at the officers' mess to clear up. A man who had been watching me, watching all of us, came in when I was on my own and insisted on walking me back to our room. Instead, he attacked me.' Her voice choked up and Olivia reached for her hand. 'He tore the fox-girl from around my neck, and though Lucy helped me look for it, I never saw it again. At least not until it appeared in the exhibition in Oxford.'

Realisation began to dawn on Plum. 'You can't mean . . .'

'It's the only thing I have ever stolen.'

Plum gasped. 'But how could you even be sure it was the same one? There are probably dozens of fox-girls. It's not an uncommon carving, I understand.'

'Not this one.' She took it from Alex and turned it over. 'See – it has a small nick on the side. Exactly the same as the one Jack gave me.'

'You can't prove that.' Plum sounded defensive now.

Olivia, who had anticipated such an eventuality, reached into her handbag and brought out Beatrix's sketchbook. 'There's a drawing of it,' she said, searching for the page. 'Look, here. See, there's a caption. *Jack and the Fox-Girl, Shillong, 1944.* And if you look carefully, Beatrix has drawn the tiny scratch on it, here.'

Plum thought for a moment, examining the sketch. 'Perhaps someone – the man who attacked you even – found it and then sold it to him? Harold's out on the golf course at the moment, but all we have to do is ask him when he gets back.' She smiled but her expression was hesitant, as if she wasn't convinced of her words.

Beatrix shook her head sadly at Plum's refusal to acknowledge the truth. 'I discovered the name of the man who attacked me. I can appreciate that you might not believe me, which is why Lucy is here. She remembers the incident and can confirm what I have said.'

Plum's eyes narrowed. 'She wasn't actually there, though, was she?'

'No,' said Lucy. 'I wasn't, but I saw Bea afterwards, and she told me what had happened. I wanted to go to Joy, but she wouldn't let me. Didn't want it to jeopardise the work of the other Wasbies.'

Plum flushed. 'You're making this up. I don't know why, but you are. You did this to me once before, don't think I don't remember. You can't seriously be accusing Harold? He just wouldn't . . . he didn't . . . he's not that kind of man.'

'Dearest Plum, we have no reason to lie about this,' said Lucy gently.

'Plum, listen to me,' said Beatrix. 'Harold Byrne offered to walk me home after a party and then he raped me. It happened more than fifty years ago, and some of the time it feels like it was *yesterday*.' Her voice broke on the final word.

Plum looked at all of them, aghast, her face frozen for a moment, then crumpling like a discarded tissue. 'Why do you have to come here and make such horrible accusations? I believed you were my friends. But you've never liked me, have you, Bea? Always thought I was pointless.'

Plum folded her hands in her lap, on the surface perfectly composed, but Olivia could see the white of her knuckles.

'I'm sorry, Plum, really I am,' Beatrix said. 'But I didn't make this up. I wouldn't. Couldn't. He also has a scar,' she added. 'Probably about two inches long. On the left-hand side of his torso.'

Plum was silent.

'Does he, Granny?' asked Alex quietly.

'How could you possibly know about that?' Plum spluttered.

'Because I stabbed him. With his own knife.'

Everyone fell silent.

Beatrix and Lucy exchanged a glance as Lucy placed a comforting hand on Beatrix's shoulder.

'Why now?' Plum spluttered. 'Why rake over long-dead coals and bring this up, after so many years? What exactly do you hope to achieve?'

'I'm afraid I find myself in rather straitened circumstances.' Beatrix looked uncomfortable for the first time in the conversation. 'The roof on Pelham House needs replacing, and it is a rather eye-watering sum that I simply do not have. Some weeks ago I regrettably came to the conclusion that I shall have to sell the netsuke; there is nothing else of sufficient value.'

'There is the issue of provenance, however,' said Olivia, bringing the subject around to the matter at hand. 'We need Harold to sign a declaration that he relinquishes ownership of the netsuke, that it belongs to Beatrix.' She held out an envelope. 'I have a document here. All he need do is sign it.'

'And you expect *me* to persuade him?' Plum was incredulous, a vein pulsing beneath the fine skin of her temple, her jaw clenched.

'We think it would be best,' said Lucy.

Plum refused to acknowledge the envelope, averting her gaze, and Olivia placed it on the table next to them. 'Why don't we leave this with you, give you some time to think it over?'

'This feels rather like an ambush,' said Alex, putting a protective hand over her grandmother's.

'It's not really about the roof, is it?' asked Plum, looking Beatrix square in the eye.

'I'm sorry, really I am,' said Beatrix. 'And yes, I'm afraid my home is in dire need of a new roof. But you're right, it's also about justice. He stole something from me and I've spent too long pretending that it never really happened; trying to forget it. Blaming myself.'

'Blaming yourself?'

'For being out late at night on my own, for not seeing it coming.'

Olivia remembered her first encounter with Beatrix, the barrel of the shotgun in her face. She'd thought Beatrix fearless at first but had come to realise the pain that stoic exterior was really hiding.

'Fifty-five years is a long time to be scared,' Beatrix added. 'And quite frankly, I'm sick of it.'

~

'Will she be able to get him to sign the letter?' Olivia asked when they arrived back at the hotel after leaving the house. They were sitting in the bar, Olivia with a pint of Guinness and Lucy and Beatrix each with a double whiskey.

'If I know Plum, she'll manage it,' said Lucy. 'She's a lot smarter than she seems.'

Olivia startled as a ringing sound came from her handbag. Her phone. It had been silent the entire time she'd been away. Who could be calling her now, on New Year's Day? She retrieved it and stepped away to a quiet corner of the bar.

'Olivia Goddard?' She couldn't immediately place the voice.

TWENTY-THREE

Katha, 1945

'How are you doing?' Lucy appeared in the doorway, carrying two mugs.

Bea sat up, wincing at the pain in her arm from where the man had grabbed her. 'I'll survive. Thanks for the tea – that'll help.' Her whole body felt as though it were one enormous bruise, but although the bruises would eventually heal, she knew she would never be the same again. Never so trusting, always glancing over her shoulder, jumping at shadows.

'No worries,' said Lucy. 'Have you had time to think any further about your decision?'

'There's nothing to think about,' Bea replied. 'I'm not jeopardising the entire Wasbie operation because of my foolishness. We can't give them a single reason to think of us as a liability.' Bea had decided to lock the attack away in her mind, telling herself that it had happened to someone else. Things like that didn't happen to women like her. She also refused to let it ruin any chance of happiness she might have with Jack.

'All right.' Lucy squeezed her hand gently. 'I understand. But I *am* going to try to find out if anyone went to the dressing station with a stab wound this morning.'

'That's if he made it there,' said Bea, suddenly even more worried. She didn't think the knife was big enough to have caused serious damage, but she had no way of knowing for certain. Would he come after her again? Accuse *her* of a crime? Oh God, what would she do then?

'We'll find out soon enough.'

'I don't want anyone to confront him,' said Bea. 'I think he was very drunk, not that that excuses him in the slightest.'

'It was *he* who attacked *you*, Bea,' said Lucy, exasperated.

'And how will I prove that? I know what will happen. They'll say I led him on.' Her voice dropped to a whisper. 'That I wanted it.'

Lucy sighed and dropped the subject. 'I'll tell Joy that you're feeling crook. That you're staying in bed.'

'Absolutely not. It'll take more than a scuffle in the dirt to keep me down. I'm fine, really. I just want to forget all about it.' She gave Lucy what she hoped was a convincing smile.

'If you're sure?' Lucy asked.

Bea nodded.

'Best get up soon then. We're burning daylight here. Joy will only give you so much latitude before she starts asking questions.'

Bea stretched, feeling for the sorest places of her body, and thinking of the wonderful day she'd had leading up to the moment in the dark. She remembered dancing with Jack, the feel of his breath against her hair, the low rumble of his laugh. Her hand went to her neck. The fox-girl.

She felt a stab of loss in the pit of her stomach.

~

That afternoon, Lucy brought her a name.

'Major Harold Byrne.'

Harold Byrne. It was a name she would never forget.

'Apparently, he slipped and fell on his knife.' She arched an eyebrow. 'A knife he wasn't even supposed to have. I don't think he wants to make a big hoo-ha about it either. From what the orderly said, he was rather embarrassed by the whole thing.'

Bea still wasn't convinced the man wouldn't come after her again, catch her unawares, take his revenge. She shuddered at what that might entail. She would have to make sure she was never on her own, whatever the time of day, wherever the place. She dreaded the thought of bumping into him again.

'Lucy, do you mind if we take a walk to the airstrip when we've finished up here?' she asked. The less they talked about the incident, the better as far as she was concerned.

'Are you sure you really want to go back there?'

'I've got to. Last night, before . . . before all that *business*, Jack gave me a necklace – the fox-girl. The man . . .' She couldn't bring herself to say his name. 'He tore it off me.'

'And you think there's a chance it ended up on the ground there?'

Bea nodded.

Lucy placed a hand on her shoulder. 'I'm not letting you go back there, even in daylight. I'll have a look for it.'

'Thank you. I'd be ever so grateful.'

Lucy was gone for more than an hour and Bea, who had gone back to their room, could do nothing but stare at the ceiling above her bed.

'I searched for ages,' she said breathlessly on her return. 'I'm so sorry Bea; I couldn't find it.'

⁓

Bea didn't get the chance to confess the loss to Jack. Two days after her birthday, Joy stumbled into the mess, her eyes brimming with unshed tears.

'What? What is it?' Lucy demanded.

'What's happened?' asked Bea.

Joy looked at Bea. 'It's Jack. Captain Butler.'

In spite of the heat, a thread of ice snaked its way down Bea's spine. She sat completely still, not believing that Joy was talking about Jack, *her* Jack as she now thought of him.

'His plane's gone missing. He and his navigator are presumed dead. I heard it from one of the other Army pilots. I'm so sorry, Bea, I know how fond you were of him.'

Bea slumped against the counter, the accounts she'd been working on fluttering to the floor. 'It's my fault,' she murmured. 'It's all my fault.'

Lucy moved to comfort her. 'Now, don't you talk like that,' she said sternly.

'But the fox-girl – she was his good-luck charm. He should never have given it to me. Especially as . . .' Her voice cracked and she laid her head on her arms in despair.

'Come on, now,' said Lucy. 'You know that's just superstitious nonsense.'

'It's *not*,' Bea said stubbornly. 'It's all my fault.'

Joy went to the storeroom and returned with a bottle. 'Have some of this; it's good for shock.' She nudged a beaker containing a couple of fingers of brandy towards Bea. 'Apparently he went out on a sortie this morning, dropped a couple of bods off at a camp west of Indaw Lake, but never made it back.'

Bea took a swig of the drink, saying nothing.

'It might not be that bad,' said Lucy. 'He could have had to set down somewhere, have run out of fuel or something.'

They all knew that was the least likely course of events.

'Well, I'm very sorry to say this,' Joy said, 'especially under the circumstances, but we've been given our marching orders. We need to pack up and move on to Bahe. We've got the rest of today and tomorrow to get ourselves organised.'

For once, Bea resented Joy's pragmatic approach. She didn't think she had the energy to pack up again. But then, a move would take her further away from *that man*, as she thought of him, and her flagging spirits lifted a touch.

'That's on the way to Mandalay, isn't it?' Lucy asked.

'It certainly is.' There was a moment of silence before Joy continued. 'Orders are to travel light, so we'll need to decide what to take and what to leave behind. I've been promised that anything we don't take on the plane will be transported to us by river, but that it could take a while.'

Bea knocked back the rest of her brandy, and banged the glass down on the counter. 'Well, there's no time to waste, then, is there?' she replied coldly.

They were finally going to the front.

～

Joy was to fly on ahead with the cooks and Amar the sweeper, leaving Bea, Lucy, Plum and Cocoa to take the two-day journey through thick jungle in a mobile canteen.

'Being this close to the front, you'll have a military escort,' Joy informed them as she prepared to leave. 'Take care, and we'll see you soon.' She embraced them all, giving Bea an especially long hug. 'It'll get easier,' she whispered in her ear.

The first day of their journey was uneventful, if uncomfortable, as the truck jounced along an increasingly rough, dusty road. An hour or so before sunset, they called a halt near a clearing and began to make camp for the night. 'What I wouldn't do for a swag right about now,' said Lucy.

'A what?' Bea asked.

'We have them at home – stockmen use them when they're out in the bush for days at a time. It's basically a small tent and a bed rolled into one. The good ones have thick wadding in them. Best night's sleep you'll ever have in one of those.'

Plum looked at their thin sleeping mats and hotchpotch arrangement of sheets. 'Beggars . . .'

'I know. It's only for one night, at least.'

Snowy, one of the soldiers escorting them, and who had earned the nickname when his hair reportedly turned white overnight after a particularly fierce battle, went foraging for wood and built a fire, while Bea and Lucy opened a tin of hot dogs to roast over the coals.

As they settled down for the night, Bea drew her sleeping mat closer to Lucy's. 'I hope there's no Japs out there,' she whispered.

'Why do you think I've got this?' Lucy whispered back, showing her the butt of a revolver, the same one they had all been issued before leaving Katha. 'Though it feels like another lifetime ago that we last practised shooting.'

'Is it loaded?'

'What do you think?'

'I shan't sleep a wink,' she said, but there was no further talk from Lucy, and as Bea looked across to her friend she heard gentle snores coming from her bedclothes.

The next morning, Lucy turned the key in the Chevy's ignition and the engine spluttered, coughed and then died. She turned it off, waited a moment and then tried again. This time the engine didn't even cough, instead it sounded more like an old man in the end stages of lung disease.

'Bugger!' Lucy hit the dashboard with the flat of her hand and then climbed down from the cab. 'I'll take a shufti at it,' she said. Seemingly unconcerned that her clothes would get even filthier than they already were, she crawled under the chassis.

'What's up?' Snowy came over as Lucy scooted back out.

'Well, the suspension's shot, but I already knew that. That's not what's causing the problem.'

Together Lucy and Snowy lifted the bonnet and peered inside.

'There's a few things it could be, but unless I spend a bit of time investigating, I'm not going to know exactly what's causing it,' said Lucy. 'One thing's for sure, we're not going anywhere in a hurry.' Snowy walked over to the Jeep and conferred with the other soldier who was escorting them.

'What do you think we should do?' asked Bea.

'There's no sense us all waiting here,' said Snowy coming back to them. 'It could take hours to fix. Tommy and I are going to push on to Bahe and pick up a mechanic. You ladies will wait here until we get back. Do not . . . I repeat *do not* leave this camp. It's not safe on the road.'

Bea nodded, but Lucy already had her tools out and her head in the belly of the truck.

The men's Jeep disappeared in a cloud of dust and Bea found herself with nothing much to do. As Plum lay back against a tree and closed her eyes, Bea rummaged through her things and pulled out her sketchbook and a stub of a pencil, beginning to draw Lucy and the truck, cross-hatching the trees and sketching the remains of the campfire in the foreground. It was early morning and not too hot, so it was rather pleasant to sit in the shade, lost in her task, Cocoa snoozing at her feet.

After half an hour of listening to the clang of wrenches and the occasional curse, Plum decided to get the portable kerosene stove going.

'Cuppa?' she asked, holding out a mug to a now oil-stained Lucy.

'Oh, ta.' She straightened up and beamed. 'I think I might have worked out what's wrong with the old girl.'

'And?'

'It's either a dirty fuel filter or clogged lines.'

'Do you think you can fix it?'

'Hope so.'

It took Lucy nearly two more hours, and plenty of swearing, but eventually she gave a triumphant shout.

'Hop in the driver's seat and see if you can start her up,' she said to Plum.

Doing as she was asked, Plum turned the key and whooped with joy as the engine spluttered into life.

Lucy gave her a satisfied grin and a thumbs up and began to pack up her tools – but then stopped as Plum turned the truck off and opened the door.

'What do you think you're doing?' Lucy asked.

'Waiting for our escort.'

Lucy shook her head. 'Uh-uh. We're getting out of here. Haven't you been listening?'

Bea cocked her head to one side and registered the low hum of noise that had been growing in intensity over the past hour or so. She had been so absorbed in her drawing that she hadn't paid it much attention until Lucy pointed it out.

Gunfire. Getting closer.

'But Snowy said not to move,' said Plum.

Lucy arched an eyebrow. 'I'd say things have changed since he gave that order, wouldn't you? For goodness sake, there's no point in hanging around.'

'I reckon we should scarper while we still have a chance to,' Bea agreed. She knew that the frontline was roughly to the east and that they needed to head almost directly south, following the course of the Shweli River, to reach Bahe. 'I hope to God we don't get cut off.'

'You and me both, sister.'

Bea collected her sketchbook and bag, stamped out the fire and they squeezed into the cab of the truck.

'All we have to do is follow this road south – Snowy told me it goes all the way to Bahe. I reckon we've got about another five hours of driving to go. And with any luck, we'll meet them on their way back to us.'

'With any luck,' Bea echoed, doubtfully.

TWENTY-FOUR

The road to Bahe, 1945

Tight-roping a fine line between speed and safety, the women drove as fast as they could without putting themselves in unnecessary danger. The gunfire could still be heard over the rattle of the engine and they all involuntarily ducked each time a shell went off.

After a few hours of hurtling along, their bones feeling as though they had been shaken loose in their sockets, Bea slowed and they agreed to take a break and have some food, as they hadn't stopped for lunch.

'There's some tins of beans and some of ham as well,' said Plum. 'They'll be lukewarm but that's the least of our worries.'

As Bea pulled over to the side of the road, and turned the engine off, they became aware that another battle – or was it part of the same one? They had no way of knowing – was raging in the distance. The three of them looked at each other, uncertain what to do next. Towering trees and dark, dense jungle made seeing anything beyond either side of the road almost impossible.

'I'm starving,' said Plum. 'Another five minutes won't make any difference.'

'I'm not so sure,' said Bea, going to the back of the truck. She returned with her gun but not the food.

'What?' Plum asked, her expression making clear her annoyance.

'I'm pulling rank, Private Vellacourt,' said Bea. 'That—' she indicated the gunfire, 'is way too close for comfort.'

Plum sighed heavily, and sulkily climbed back in the truck, leaving the door open for Bea to join her. Lucy went to the driver's side and started up the engine.

They continued on but had only gone another mile or so when Bea pointed to something up ahead of them, where the track intersected with another. 'Dust.'

Sure enough, the air was thicker there. Something – or someone – had recently disturbed it.

Lucy slowed and eased the truck off the road, driving through a gap in the wall of jungle foliage until eventually they came to a halt between two enormous teak trees, each with a trunk so wide that the three of them could not have joined their arms around it.

'What do we do now?' asked Plum, her eyes searching the undergrowth.

'I don't think we can be seen,' said Lucy, opening the door quietly and peering out.

'Good,' said Bea. 'I think we should wait here until we get a better idea of what's going on.'

'Can I at least get some food?' asked Plum.

Bea shook her head. 'We can't afford to make a sound,' she whispered. 'There could be snipers anywhere.'

Plum finally seemed to grasp the seriousness of the situation and slumped back against the seat.

Sweat trickled down Bea's collarbones and into her shirt, but she barely noticed it, all of her focus on any unusual sounds – sounds that might indicate that the women weren't alone in this part of the jungle.

They waited for several minutes, but beyond the rustle of the breeze in the trees, they heard nothing. No birdsong, or animal chirrups. Even the gunfire had stopped. It was eerily quiet.

Then, the distinctive rattle of a motor vehicle. Bea prayed that any dust they might have stirred up would have, by now, dispersed. The sound was on their right initially and for a moment grew louder but then passed them somewhere up ahead and then faded away to the left.

'That didn't sound like one of ours.' Plum's eyes were wide with fear.

'No, it did not,' said Lucy.

They waited again, but no further vehicles followed.

'I think it was only one,' said Bea.

'Let's hope so.' Lucy eased open the door and went to the back of the truck. 'I'm inclined to agree with Plum. We really should eat something.'

Bea glanced at her wristwatch. It was four in the afternoon and they'd had nothing since breakfast. 'Right you are, then.'

'Imagine the stories we'll tell our daughters,' said Plum with a tremulous smile as she swallowed a spoonful of cold beans. 'And our granddaughters.'

'That's if we make it out alive,' said Bea, still on high alert.

After they'd eaten, and shared the last of some very warm, brackish water, Plum retreated behind some trees for a loo break.

'Take this,' said Lucy, handing her a revolver.

'Really?'

'Definitely.'

A few minutes later, Bea was on the point of following Plum to answer the call of nature, when she heard the snap of a twig. She stilled, hoping that it was only Plum returning or an animal somewhere in the dense trees, but she heard nothing more and so went off, making sure to take her own weapon.

She had placed the gun on the ground and was on the point of unbuckling her belt when she heard the slightest movement behind her, no more than a breath. She whirled around and found herself staring into a pair of dark eyes that were as astonished as her own.

For a moment neither of them moved, then the Japanese soldier, who appeared to be no more than a teenager, not old enough even to shave, spoke a few words – none of which she understood – and indicated with a flick of his rifle that she should raise her arms above her head.

He seemed as bewildered as she was, but he was the one with a gun; her own lay only a few feet away in the undergrowth. Bea willed herself not to look at it, lest the soldier follow her line of sight.

He continued to speak, and Bea stammered back the only Japanese words she knew: *kon'nichiwa, genki desu ka* (Hello, how

276

are you?) – woefully inadequate at a time like this, but it was the best she could do. *Keep him talking*, she told herself, *just keep him talking. Maybe he won't shoot you.*

Was he here on his own, she wondered desperately, or part of a group? And where were Lucy and Plum? She hoped, for the others' sake, that there was only him, but she didn't like their chances either way: he had a gun, and it was pointed directly at her.

She racked her brain for any other Japanese phrases but had to just blurt the same one over and over, hoping it might somehow help. She could have easily been talking complete gibberish, but the words held his attention and his grip on his weapon slackened a fraction. She stopped speaking and raised her hands slowly in the air, the universal sign of surrender, and he seemed uncertain, as though trying to make up his mind what to do. Bea swallowed, held her breath as seconds ticked by, the only sound that of distant gunfire once more.

Then, from the corner of her eye, she saw Plum creep towards her, one finger to her lips, the other hand holding her revolver. Bea could see how much Plum's hand was shaking and her spirits sank. They were all going to be killed. She stood up straighter and swallowed the fear that was making her palms sweat and her stomach clutch at itself.

Then, out of nowhere, the loud crack of a gunshot. Bea staggered backwards, momentarily deafened by the noise, one that would cause her to flinch every time a car backfired for years afterwards.

She expected pain, but couldn't feel a thing. It was as though she were numb from the top of her head down to her toes. Was this what it was like to be shot?

She watched, as if in slow motion, as the soldier crumpled at the knees and fell forward.

He lay, face down on the ground, blood trickling from the base of his neck.

'Oh God, I hit him,' said Plum, rushing towards her. 'I actually hit him. Bea?' she asked. 'Bea, are you all right?'

Bea nodded slowly, stunned by what had taken place in the space of less than a minute. 'You saved my life, Plum. He could have killed me.'

Lucy came running towards them but stopped dead in her tracks as she saw the soldier. She moved again, more slowly this time, and bent down when she reached him.

'You managed to shoot him right in the gap between his helmet and his shoulders,' she said. 'Severed his spinal cord. Amazing.'

'I was aiming lower,' said Plum shakily.

Bea picked up her abandoned gun and shoved it in the front of her belt. 'What do we do now?'

'We need to search him,' said Lucy firmly.

'What?' Bea replied, horrified at the idea.

'He might have maps, other intel.'

As they waited for someone to make the first move, only Bea noticed the slightest waver of the undergrowth in the distance. Catching the movement, she spun around, revolver in her outstretched hand.

'Who's there?' she shouted as they all ducked down.

Bea had no time to feel afraid, instead fury coursed through her like hot metal. She wasn't going to let anyone kill her or her friends. She fired towards the tall grass. She fired again, and again, until she was out of bullets. Then, a silence so loud it seemed to roar in her ears.

Coming to her senses, she hid behind the nearest tree.

'There was another one?' Plum whispered.

Bea shrugged her shoulders. 'Maybe.'

They all waited.

And waited.

'We have to get out of here,' said Plum.

'I'm going to make sure,' said Bea, creeping forward.

'You're *what*?' Lucy was incredulous. She cursed but then followed Bea, Plum not far behind.

'He's dead,' said Bea flatly as Lucy and Plum found her crouched over a slight, uniformed body several yards away. 'I suppose we should search him.' She no longer felt anything. Not guilt, not anger, not regret; certainly not victory. Just an all-encompassing numbness.

'I'll do it,' said Lucy, bending down and beginning to talk softly to the dead soldier.

'I'd forgotten you spoke Japanese,' Plum said in surprise.

'I understand it better than I can speak it, but I'm telling him that we are sorry, that he died a noble death and that his parents would have been proud of him.' Lucy shrugged. She checked his pockets, and found a small scrap of linen on which a number of lines and symbols were drawn. 'I was right,' she said, a note of triumph in her voice. Then she began to feel under the collar of his shirt.

'What now?' asked Plum.

'I'm looking for his ID tags – Fred once told me that they wear them around their neck and under their arms. We should take one with us as proof. Ah, yes, here it is.' She showed them the two brass oval discs that featured three vertical lines of characters and were threaded on a length of cotton tape.

'Use the bayonet on the end of his rifle,' Bea suggested.

Lucy located his weapon and severed the tape, wrapping up one of the tags and pushing it into her pocket together with the fabric map. Dispassionately, she located his weapon. Almost as an afterthought, she checked the chamber of the rifle.

She let out a loud groan.

'What?' hissed Bea.

Lucy showed her the empty chamber.

'Oh God.'

'Poor bugger was out of ammo.'

They all looked at each other. No one spoke.

'Well we weren't to know that,' said Plum eventually.

'You're right, of course,' said Lucy. 'But that doesn't make it any easier to bear.'

They returned to the first soldier's body.

'They must have been on their own,' Lucy said as she searched his pockets while the others kept watch. 'But I don't think we should hang around.'

Bea took his weapon, almost didn't want to check for ammo, was almost ashamed of the relief she felt when she found it was loaded.

'Shouldn't we bury them?' Plum asked.

'No time,' said Lucy bluntly. They all knew that the noise of the gunshots would have carried for miles, that other enemy soldiers wouldn't be far away. She stood up from where she'd been kneeling and hastily brushed dirt off her trousers.

For the remainder of the journey to Bahe, Lucy drove like a woman possessed, launching the truck in the air several times as they bounced over the pot-holes in the uneven road. The cab was silent as each of them became lost in their own thoughts, replaying the event in their minds. Bea had to clasp her hands together to stop them from trembling, praying that they wouldn't burst a tyre or break down again.

They were two hours further down the road – two hours that felt like a lifetime – when they met up with their escorts. Lucy pulled up in front of them and the women climbed out.

'Your orders were to wait with your vehicle,' said Snowy, clearly unhappy to come across them on the road.

'The battle sounded like it was drawing closer. I'd managed to fix the vehicle and so it seemed wiser to continue on,' Lucy replied, her voice terse.

'Well, you're here now, I suppose. But it will have to be reported.'

Lucy lit a cigarette and Bea noticed the slight tremor of her hands as she put it to her lips. 'Very well,' she replied, taking a long drag and turning to get back behind the wheel.

As soon as they arrived at the camp, they all marched in to see the commander-in-chief.

'Sir,' said Snowy after they had all saluted. 'Second Lieutenant Fitzgibbon, together with Privates Robertson and Vellacourt, expressly disobeyed orders not to leave their location.'

'I see,' said Lieutenant General Festing, regarding them coolly. 'And what do you have to say for yourselves, ladies?'

Bea spoke up. 'Private Robertson had managed to clear the fuel lines of the Chevy, sir, and we observed the sound of a gun battle drawing closer to our position. We were of the opinion that the situation had changed since being issued with our original orders, and to obey them would have meant almost certainly being caught in the middle of a skirmish, something we were not equipped to deal with.'

'Very well. Sergeant, do you have anything to add?'

Snowy was red in the face and looked as though he were desperate to add something, but apparently thought better of it. 'Nothing sir.' It occurred to Bea that the two soldiers probably shouldn't have left them in the first place.

'There is one more thing, sir,' Plum spoke. 'At approximately sixteen hundred hours, we pulled off the road, having observed dust, likely from a vehicle, in the distance. In light of the battle somewhere up ahead of us, we made for a position where we could not be seen from the track.'

'And? Get to the point, if you please; I haven't got all day.'

Lucy pulled the two identity tags and the map from her pocket and placed them carefully on the desk in front of him.

'I had been further into the jungle answering . . . ahem . . . answering a call of nature,' Plum continued. 'As I returned, I came upon a soldier of the Imperial Japanese Army. He had his gun aimed at Bea . . . at Second Lieutenant Fitzgibbon.'

The general's eyes betrayed a flicker of surprise at her words.

'I drew my revolver and fired at him. A bullet lodged in his neck and he was killed instantly. Then Second Lieutenant

Fitzgibbon saw a movement in the grass. With no thought for her own safety, she fired into the area. She shot and killed a soldier hiding there.'

Bea held out the rifles. 'We also seized their weapons.'

'Unfortunately,' said Lucy, with a slight break in her voice. She cleared her throat and began again. 'Unfortunately, that soldier's gun was not loaded.'

'I see,' he said, picking up the dog tags and turning them over in his hands. 'You were not to know that.'

'Yes, sir.' Lucy clamped her lips together and Bea could see that she was trying valiantly not to break into a sob.

'See that I receive a written report of the incident. On my desk by tomorrow.'

With that, they were dismissed.

~

News that the women had killed two Japanese soldiers spread through the camp faster than a gun shot, causing some of the American soldiers to give them the nickname of the 'Pistol-packing Mommas'. No one seemed to care that one of the soldiers had been out of ammunition, but none of the women could take a jot of pride in the matter. Bea, especially, found it hard to shake off the events of that afternoon.

'Can you tell me again?' Joy asked, her mouth gaping with astonishment when she heard the story.

'Plum saved my life,' said Bea.

'She's certainly improved her aim,' said Lucy wryly.

Bea found that she simply couldn't stop herself shaking, not just her hands, but her whole body. She kept repeating to herself that she could have been killed; but she couldn't get away from the fact that she herself had killed a defenceless man. Guilt twisted her insides into knots and she found she couldn't eat, could only manage sips of water.

As soon as she was able, she collapsed back on her cot, dry-eyed but shaking uncontrollably. All she wanted was the comfort of Jack's arms around her, soothing her, shielding her from everything that was broken in the world. She had tried to be strong, to get on with her job and put him out of her mind, but it was proving all too hard. She felt as though she had tipped over the edge.

'Delayed shock,' said Lucy, coming over to her. 'Try to take some slow breaths. Joy's gone to the medic to see if she can get something to help you sleep. You've done really well. It's all over,' she soothed. 'Nothing bad can happen now.'

'I'm afraid I don't believe you anymore,' said Bea, unable to muster a smile.

TWENTY-FIVE

Bahe, 1945

'The men will have to sharpen burnt sticks soon,' said Joy.

'You could be right – there's no ink, or pencils,' Joy looked up from the boxes in front of her.

'Plenty of notepads, though,' said Lucy, holding up a pile from the box she was unpacking. Inexplicable shortages and surpluses were a frequent occurrence at the canteen bulk stores.

Bea was doing her best to pretend that she had recovered from her ordeal, but she still startled every time an aircraft flew overhead, and at night the sound of gunfire woke her often. She no longer found solace in her sketchbook, for she could not calm the faint tremor in her fingers to hold the brush still enough to paint. So, she buried herself in the accounts, and for once there was a small comfort in the orderly rows of figures.

Whereas previously Plum had been the first to get up and dance or joke around with the soldiers in their hours off, she was now often found in the company of the padre – an incongruous-looking man with a tattoo of Christ's face on his well-muscled forearm – walking the perimeter of the camp and engaged in earnest conversation.

Lucy appeared to be the least bothered by their encounter with the Japanese soldiers, though Bea had heard her cry out in her sleep on more than one occasion, so perhaps she was only better at hiding it during waking hours.

Bea could scarcely bear to write about any of it, noting the loss of Jack briefly in her diary before moving on to other, less personal topics, and preferring to sit with Cocoa curled up on her lap, or with a drink at the end of the day. Even her favourite books, now tattered and worn, offered little respite, for she found she couldn't concentrate on the words as they swam in front of her eyes, and reminded her too much of Archie, for he had loved them too, sometimes reading them out loud to her when they were younger, if she pleaded for long enough.

'I know I've got to pull myself together,' she said to Lucy on a rare day off, 'but I just can't seem to.'

'You killed a man,' Lucy replied. 'Not to mention we've all been under the most terrific amount of stress. And you were attacked, Bea, in the most horrible way. Are you still sure you don't want to report it? It's never too late. I'll come with you; back you up all the way.'

Bea shook her head. 'I've just got to keep on going.'

'Morning prayer?' said Lucy the next day, wrinkling her nose. 'Are we really expected to attend?'

'It's not what you think,' said Joy.

Indeed it wasn't. Instead of reciting the catechism, 'morning prayer' was a euphemism for an intelligence briefing. After breakfast, the IO – Intelligence Officer – updated the entire camp on the current state of play. He brought maps that showed the area of operation, and where gains and losses had been made, sometimes overnight. It was the first time the women had been included in such a briefing and they all found it fascinating, and a welcome distraction from their own woes. It also brought home how close they were to the thick of the fighting.

Later that day, they drove the canteen out to the battery, where the gunners operated the big twenty-five pounders.

'God, it's loud,' said Lucy, covering her ears.

'I heard that you ladies aren't afraid to shoot. Want to try firing one of these?' one of the soldiers asked.

Lucy didn't need to be asked twice. She slid into position and the gunner stood behind her, giving instructions.

'Can you put your fingers in my ears while I fire?' she asked him. 'Or else I might go completely deaf.'

By the time they returned, there was a summons to Lieutenant General Festing's office waiting for them.

'What have we done now?' asked Plum.

The camp was in a state of chaos, with soldiers running everywhere, and Bea noticed that the number of guards around the perimeter had doubled in the time they'd been gone.

'Not a clue, but we'd better get there quick-sharp; I've heard he doesn't like to be kept waiting,' said Joy.

They entered the general's office and saluted him.

'I'm afraid you'll have to pack up,' he said. 'The intelligence is that an enemy unit has broken through the lines and is rumoured to be circling around behind us. There's no time to waste. Prepare for an evacuation at oh-six-hundred hours tomorrow. It's no longer safe for you to be here.'

Bea stifled a groan.

'All hands to the pump,' said Joy as she divvied up the responsibilities.

Very little sleep was had in the camp that night, as everyone was involved in the process of dismantling and packing up the entire place.

'I'll never move house again once I get settled after the war,' said Bea. 'I've seen enough packing crates to last a lifetime.'

Finally, about half an hour before they were due to fly out, the last crate was nailed up, and the women, Amar and the cooks, waited for transport to the airstrip.

They left aboard the now-familiar US DC-3 Dakota, a stomach-churning but scenic trip, for the plane had no door on it and offered a bird's-eye view of the heavily forested country.

'Looks hellish,' said Joy, peering tentatively out and seeing the thick jungle below.

As they landed, and the engines quietened, they heard the sound of a battle raging somewhere in the distance.

'According to the pilot, it's only about six miles away,' shouted Joy.

Hustled into Jeeps, they continued their journey by road as part of a large convoy of soldiers. The track wound alongside the Shweli River and they were forced to cover their mouths with scarves to keep out the dust. The suspension on the vehicles didn't cope with the heavily rutted road and Bea had a splitting headache within minutes of setting off.

There was devastation at every turn. What had once likely been a lush, green landscape was now pitted with craters and the broken limbs of trees. The area had been torn apart from the shelling and bombing.

'It looks like a bulldozer's been on a crazed rampage,' said Lucy.

About four hours after they had set off, the road became so steep and narrow that the larger trucks travelling with them were forced to edge back and forth in order to navigate the hairpin bends. The women had drunk all their water and Bea began to feel increasingly dizzy.

'Look,' said Lucy, pointing up to the treetops, where parachutes dangled, some with their loads still attached.

The air was filled with an acrid reek from the burnt-out vegetation and they pulled their scarves over their mouths and noses again to avoid the worst of it. Wooden crosses lined the road, some with tin hats hanging from them, and the smell of death hung in the air. Bea could taste the sourness of bile, though it felt more like fear.

'It's no place for women,' said the driver, as they sped on.

'It's no place for anyone, man or woman,' Bea muttered. It felt like the end of the world; an apocalypse manifested before their eyes.

'Why are we stopping?' asked Plum as they came to a halt once more.

Lucy offered to hike up to the front of the convoy to find out, and returned several minutes later. 'Lieutenant Generals Festing and Browning received word that there's a battle going on in the hills. It's too dangerous to continue at the moment.'

There wasn't a single inch of shade and everyone groaned as they prepared to wait it out in the boiling sun.

Hours later, they arrived in Myitson, joining the divisional HQ, to find that a large parachute tent had been strung between a stand of wide-leaved teak trees for them, and they quickly established their camp, setting up narrow folding canvas beds and basins.

'It's like being on safari,' said Plum, wrestling with a large, patched canvas that would afford them some privacy while they washed.

'You think so?' Bea was far from convinced.

The heat was unrelenting and the dust so thick that they were filthy almost immediately, their faces streaked with sweat and red dirt. Bea had tied a scarf over her jungle hat to keep the worst of the dirt off, but Plum's platinum blonde hair had now turned an unusual shade of henna. The local Kachin tribespeople – 'I don't think they've ever seen a white woman before,' Plum said, self-conscious under the scrutiny – stood and stared at them.

Bea and Lucy unpacked the stores, though there was nowhere safe to keep them and they had to make do with a tarpaulin and the promise of two soldiers to guard them at night.

'Why don't we all do a bit of a recce?' Joy suggested when they'd got everything as shipshape as they were able.

'Right-o,' said Plum.

The women, including Bea who now made sure she was never without the company of at least one of her friends, marched off to familiarise themselves with the camp. Bea kept her head down, still aware of the prospect of running into Major Byrne. The likelihood of him being in Myitson was only a slim possibility, according to Lucy, who had done her best to keep tabs on the whereabouts of his regiment.

They had gone no further than a few yards towards the mess tent when Plum pointed to a large metal cylinder lying on the ground.

'Don't touch it!' Lucy cried as Plum moved closer.

Bea jumped at the note of alarm in Lucy's voice. She'd never known her friend to sound so rattled.

'What?' Plum asked.

'It looks like a phosphorus bomb, wouldn't you say?' Lucy asked.

Joy nodded. 'We'd better get someone to come and move it. And perhaps we'll postpone our walk?'

As the women backed away from the bomb, Bea felt her legs shaking as it dawned on her how close they had come to being blown to a million pieces. She looked at the others – they didn't seem to be as bothered by it as she was. Even Lucy, despite her initial concern, was sharing a joke.

They returned with a couple of soldiers from the bomb-disposal team, who checked it over and then carried it very gingerly to the river. Sure enough, as it hit the water it exploded with a thunderous bang, sparks and clouds of spray and smoke flying into the air.

'I don't think I'll ever be able to watch fireworks again,' Bea grimaced.

~

The next morning, the cooks got the field ovens up and running and Amar organised a relatively clean water supply. In no time they were churning out sausage rolls and hundreds of rounds of sandwiches from a very basic set-up – the poor cooks had no tables, nor proper kitchen utensils, and they'd made cake pans from the beaten-out metal of old cigarette tins.

Bea knew that the accounts were in a mess, with some stores left behind, some brought with them and some still in transit God only knew where. They'd lost more than a few items to petty pilfering as well. The dust had invaded her account books and the sheets she was supposed to send to head office were just as bad.

'Any idea how to cook the books? I've checked and re-checked the stocktaking but it still won't add up,' she wailed to Lucy one afternoon. 'I reckon we're about seven hundred rupees in the hole. Captain Taylor is going to think I can't cope.' Bea herself was beginning to think she couldn't cope. Little irritations, which she would have shrugged off in earlier days, now kept her awake at night, tossing and turning in the early hours, and her mood rested on a knife edge. It was all she could do to keep from snapping at poor, good-natured Amar.

'I'm sure she'll understand,' Lucy soothed.

'How can you say that?' she snapped. 'Stop trying to make me feel better.'

Lucy, who rarely lost her cool, turned and walked out of the tent, and Bea immediately felt remorseful. The truth was, the heat had sapped all of their energy, making tempers flare. Added to that, there had been no letters for weeks, which had sent all of them into a funk.

'I'm sorry I'm so ratty,' she apologised to Lucy later. 'It's not fair to take it out on anyone else, especially you.'

'I've forgotten it already,' Lucy replied. 'Anyway, you've had to deal with a hell of a lot more than the rest of us. I'm proud of how you've come through it.'

It was comforting to hear, though Bea didn't think she'd dealt with the dreadful thing done to her at all – she'd simply refused to let the memory surface, burying it deep within her.

That evening, a visit from Fred, who somehow always seemed to know where to find them, cheered them all, especially when he brought out a penny whistle and proceeded to play any tune they could think of. He also brought some photos taken in Katha and Bahe. Bea had to look away when she saw one of Jack, laughing uproariously at something, a glass in his hand. He looked so young and carefree.

'I don't suppose you've had any news?' she asked.

Fred shook his head.

Bea brushed away sudden, hot tears and could barely stop herself from collapsing in despair. She'd been so hoping Fred might have heard something, for she'd been clinging to the faint possibility that Jack might, by an improbable stroke of fortune, have survived the crash and, like Archie, be in a POW camp somewhere in the jungle. She had been a fool to believe that he might have been so lucky.

They were only in Myitson for a few weeks, had no time to settle into a rhythm before orders came to move again.

'I suppose this is what you get when you're attached to a unit,' said Plum as they rolled up their bedding and took apart their cots. 'Constant upheaval.'

'You'd better believe it,' replied Lucy.

The next stop was to be Mongmit.

'At least there'll be stores,' said Joy.

'Here's hoping,' said Bea.

It was a bone-shaking, day-long journey in a convoy of more than a hundred vehicles, meaning they had to stop often along the road as the larger trucks inched their way around the tightly curved bends that took them into the valley below. Finally, as they were approaching the town, news filtered back that the causeway bridge had collapsed under the weight of one of the larger trucks and would need to be repaired before they could go any further.

The women climbed out of their canteen and went to investigate. Up ahead, past the dozens of trucks in the convoy, they saw the chaps of the Royal Engineers, stripped to the waist and sweltering in the heat, moving tons of stone by hand to shore up the damaged section.

'Honestly, it feels like a travelling circus,' Lucy whispered to Bea.

They eventually crossed the bridge, holding their collective breath as the trucks rumbled over the mid-point, and travelled the remaining miles without incident, arriving in Mongmit late in the afternoon. It had likely once been a pleasant and flourishing town, but as the women drove through it, all they could see was devastation: there was little sign of the local people, instead, there were empty, bombed-out buildings, gaping holes in walls, missing roofs, and the splintered remains of furniture.

They were allocated a wooden house, a shell of a building with no windows or doors, and once again they began to unpack and get everything as shipshape as they could manage.

Lucy rustled up a supper of cheese on toast and they brewed up a drum of water for tea.

'None of those "God Wots" in there, please,' said Plum, checking her mug for unidentified objects. 'God, what's this?' had become the catchcry whenever someone found an insect, or worse, floating in their tea.

Bea found a few moments to open her sketchbook and make a quick pencil drawing of the women, sitting on packing cases, mugs in their hands. She had found her way back to art; it helped her to stop thinking too much, for it required nothing but to focus on the scene before her.

They weren't to stay in Mongmit for long, however, and no sooner had they got themselves set up, than orders came through to be on the move again in two days' time, to Mogok and then on to Namsaw and then Meiktila as the Army surged ever southwards. Despite the spectacular scenery – the tulip trees were in full bloom, as were the white-flowered, sweet-smelling almond trees – the journey was another white-knuckle ride along steep mountain inclines and around bends sharper than a hairpin.

Mogok, known for its nearby ruby mines, had been evacuated by the Japanese Army only days before, leaving a splintered mess. Packs of mangy dogs hung around the women's house, and despite Cocoa hissing at them to keep away, they crept ever closer. After less than a week, orders had them on the move once more, and they made a halting journey to Namsaw.

No sooner had they arrived, however, than the monsoon rains began. Water poured through their parachute tents, which offered them no more protection than muslin, soaking everything, and the women spent their first night huddled miserably on their tin boxes, protected from the elements only by their monsoon capes. When dawn broke, they discovered that the camp had been all but destroyed, tents pulled down and the stores ruined. Flour had turned to paste, sugar was like treacle and raisins swollen like stewed fruit. Joy was only a breath away from tears at the mess of it all.

None of them had been able to find Cocoa in the downpour, and Bea traipsed the sodden campsite the next morning, alternately cursing and calling out the cat's name, much to the bemusement of some of the men, who thought she was offering them a hot drink.

While the women got themselves organised and cleared up the stores as best they could, orders were given to dig slit trenches around the camp, to give the water somewhere to run off. Before long, a loud shout brought everyone running. It turned out that the camp was on the site of an old burial ground, and the soldiers had dug up a number of green-tinged bones. The women were too busy to be horrified.

Lucy searched for Cocoa the entire morning, and Joy had to reprimand her for not getting on with her work, but the scrappy little cat was nowhere to be found.

'I almost don't want to find her,' Lucy said to Bea in between handing out mugs of tea. 'Not if she's . . .'

'Reckon she's used up her nine lives now?' Bea asked.

Lucy could only nod.

Despite days of searching, Lucy had to resign herself to the fact that Cocoa must have met with misfortune. Bea could tell she was putting on a brave face, but saw how much it distressed her animal-loving friend. They'd all lost someone or something during this godforsaken time, but every loss seemed to pile onto the last, making it even harder to bear. The only thing that kept them going was the news, more frequent now, that the tide of the war in Europe was turning and victory was within the Allies' grasp.

~

Meiktila, their next stop, was a far from pleasant town. A communications snafu, as the Yanks loved to call it, meant that the women were shuffled from one place to the next, with no one having made plans for where they should rightly be. They had arrived not long after a battle, as bodies were being carried into the lake, sunk like so much unwanted rubbish. It was a miserable job for the soldiers and after that the water had to be thoroughly boiled and chlorinated before it could be used.

'It still smells hideous,' said Bea.

'Doesn't taste much better,' replied Lucy, draining her mug nevertheless.

Later, as Bea and Plum went looking for a site for a new canteen they came across the bodies of three Japanese soldiers. They'd been moved to the side of the road, placed on their backs next to each other as if they were sleeping.

'They were covered in flies and stinking to high heaven,' Bea told Lucy matter-of-factly when they returned. 'We had to leave them there. I expect they'll be buried eventually.' She didn't add that they'd also walked past piles of unexploded ammunition and the ruins of a tennis court littered with skulls. Neither she nor Plum had given them a second glance.

The torrential monsoon downpours uncovered more bodies. Getting up early one morning, Bea nearly tripped over a pair of booted legs that had become exposed during the night. She stepped around them without so much as a shriek and went to find someone to re-bury the poor man.

One day, she and Joy came across the tiny body of a native toddler propped up against a wall, chubby cheeked with dark, glossy hair. For a moment, Bea thought the child was resting, but when she came closer she saw that he was far too still to be alive, and a sob rose in her throat as she forced herself to turn her steps in the other direction. That a tiny, innocent child had been caught up in the destruction was too much to bear. They'd all become rather hardened to death, but that small, perfect face began to haunt Bea's dreams and she often found her cheeks were wet with tears when she woke in the morning.

Some of the time they were stationed near the airstrip, where they had to boil water in tin baths and Bea calculated that they often sold more than four hundred gallons of tea a day. The hours were long and the work was hard, but they had all become almost oblivious to sore feet, blistered hands and weary muscles. They did their best to keep clean, sponging themselves down with water collected in their canvas camping basins, but they all sported a semi-permanent ring of dirt at the back of their necks, and hair-washing was an almost-forgotten luxury.

Happily, mail was more frequent, and letters from loved ones helped boost their flagging spirits. Bea's mother wrote regularly, and although her father was safe, there was no further communication from Archie. Then, finally, news of Victory in Europe came through, though it made little difference to those embroiled in the war raging in the East. Everyone received an extra drink ration, and that was about the size of it.

One morning, when they'd been in Meiktila for several weeks and become used to making regular visits to troops in the area, they were in the process of setting up their canteen when Bea looked up, alerted by a movement in the trees. She nearly dropped the mugs she was holding, startled to see several Gurkhas in full battle kit, only partly camouflaged by the trees. She noticed others creeping through the long grass.

'They're the lookouts,' said a sergeant coming to meet them. 'You're right on the edge of the combat zone here, ladies.'

Joy heard from one of the Spitfire pilots that there were troops marooned north of Rangoon, completely cut off by the Japanese, stuck in paddy fields and utterly miserable. 'I thought we'd make up some parcels for them,' she suggested. 'Something small; apparently they're completely out of ciggies.'

'Why don't we add a note too?' Plum asked. 'Let them know someone is thinking of them.'

Joy arranged for a pilot to drop these along with other supplies, and they were rewarded a few weeks later with a thank-you note from Brigadier Vickers on behalf of the stranded men.

'Another one for the scrapbook,' said Joy, handing it to Bea for safekeeping.

⁓

Bea returned to Calcutta for a few much-needed days' leave, her first in months, hitching a ride on a transport that flew regularly to the city. As she walked down her old street, she couldn't shake the surreal feeling that so much had happened since she was last home, while life appeared to have gone on unchanged there. She glanced ruefully at her crumpled, muddy uniform, but brushed herself down, tucking her hair behind her ears and adjusting her cap to a jaunty angle. She was nothing like the naïve, enthusiastic girl who had left the city the year before, but thankfully her mother was exactly the same as she had always been.

'Darling!' Her mother dropped the stitching she'd been doing and scrambled to her feet as Bea burst through the door. 'I had no idea you were coming!' She embraced her, squeezing her tight. 'Oh heavens, you've gotten so thin.'

Bea was comforted by the warmth of her welcome. 'It's been too hot to have much of an appetite,' she shrugged as her mother released her. 'Besides, you should see what they give us to eat.' She made a face.

'We'll soon sort that out. Jeet!' her mother called. 'Food! How've you been?' she added.

'Oh, you know, best as can be expected. Tired, that's all.' Bea couldn't bring herself to tell her mother everything that had happened while she had been in Burma, for she didn't want to cause her any more distress than she was already suffering. 'Any news from Archie?' she asked, her heart thumping in her chest.

Her mother shook her head, and Bea swallowed a stab of disappointment.

'And Daddy?'

Her mother smiled. 'Safe and well. Come now, let's get you washed and fed.'

After nearly a year of camp beds and sponge baths and mosquitoes, it was bliss to enjoy hot running water and to eat fresh vegetables and fruit that didn't come from a can laden with syrup. That night, lying on her own bed, on soft, clean white sheets, she felt a small, broken part of herself begin to mend.

The next morning, she came down late to breakfast to find her mother listening intently to the radio, waving her to be quiet.

'The Allies have bombed Hiroshima.' Her mother looked up at her when the radio report had finished. 'That *has* to be the end of it.'

The news, horrific as it was, gave Bea a slender thread of hope. 'Then perhaps Archie will be home soon.'

'Let's pray for that, and for all the other poor boys.'

They went to lunch at the Calcutta Club, Bea wearing one of her old dresses, although it was now much too large for her. There was an air of celebration in the streets and at the club, but it was muted by the enormity of the bombing.

It was difficult for Bea to farewell her mother a few precious days later, but she left with a promise and the knowledge that she would be home again soon, and that perhaps Archie would be as well. She was halfway back to Meiktila, aboard *Chinthe*, the Twelfth Army Commander's Dakota, when she heard the longed-for news.

The war in the East – their war – was finally over.

A note was passed back from the flight deck, stating that the Japanese had surrendered. A cheer went up among the few passengers on board, but all Bea could feel was numb. The moment that they had all been waiting for, for so long, had finally come, but it didn't feel real at all. After so much time spent wishing it would all be over, it was almost an anti-climax. Not having her friends with her to share the news also added to the sense of unreality: it simply wouldn't sink in.

Besides, she and the other Wasbies would likely have plenty to do in the coming months, as prisoners of war were released and troops relocated. They had already been told that, in the event of the end of hostilities, Rangoon would be a staging post for those coming from Siam and Indo China before they were sent on to Singapore for repatriation. Her work was far from over.

TWENTY-SIX

Galway, 2000

'Martinson here.'

'Jeffrey, how are you?' Olivia masked her surprise as she wondered what on earth he could be calling her about, and where he had got her number.

'I'll get straight to the point. I heard a very interesting rumour over the Christmas holidays, and I didn't want to wait until the office opened again before finding out more.'

'Oh yes?'

'Tell me, is it true you're on the trail of the fox-girl? The one stolen from the Ashmolean?'

Olivia nearly choked. 'Where on earth did you hear that?' she asked, doing her best to keep the surprise out of her voice.

'Never mind where I heard it, is it true?' he asked impatiently.

'It's possible,' she admitted, glancing across the room at Beatrix. 'Why?'

'I also heard that you're not officially a paid employee of Cholmondeley's. Is that correct?'

The art world leaked like a sieve and nothing was a secret for long, but nevertheless, who could he have been speaking to? Had Alex had been the one to spill the beans? She'd mentioned that she knew him well.

'I expect to be taken on permanently very soon,' she said, rattled. 'Elaine asked that I serve a three-month internship first.' If he knew that, did he also know about the retainer she collected in return for passing on information about stolen artworks? If he did, and if he told Elaine, she'd be out of a job faster than you could say *Mona Lisa*.

There was a bark of laughter from the other end of the phone. 'You poor thing. Didn't you know that she does that to all her so-called "staff"? Believe me, she has no intention of paying you a cent, not when there is a queue of eager art-history graduates ready and willing to take your place.'

'I'm not sure that's exactly the case,' she said carefully. Jeffrey's words hit a nerve, however, and she resolved to ask Elaine directly on her return to work.

'I'd like us to meet. No need to mention it to Elaine.'

She hesitated. 'I'm afraid that's not possible, not at the moment anyway.'

'I know it's still the New Year's holiday, but I can promise you, it will be worth your while.'

'I'm afraid I'm not in London.'

'Oh. I see.' He sounded momentarily less sure of himself. 'When do you expect to be back in town?'

Olivia looked over at Beatrix again. 'I'm not exactly sure. I'm sorry to be so vague, but I'm travelling at the moment, with someone else, and I'm afraid I'm rather constrained by their plans. I can't just up and leave.'

'But you'll be back at Cholmondeley's on the fifth? Wednesday?'

That was only four days away, but she and Beatrix were booked on the afternoon ferry on the third. 'That's certainly the plan.'

'Meet me for a drink on the fourth?' He named a small wine bar in Kensington, not far from where Elaine lived.

'How about somewhere slightly more discreet?'

'Oh yes, of course, good call. I have to confess I'm not very good at this cloak-and-dagger stuff. How about you suggest the venue?'

Olivia mentioned a place two streets away from her Brixton bedsit, and they agreed on a time to meet.

She hung up, shaking her head. What on earth was that all about? Rather more worrying was his assertion that Elaine had no intention of taking her on as a paid member of staff. She remembered the handwriting of her predecessors on dusty slips of paper, but she'd never heard their names used. Perhaps that was because they'd never stayed for long.

'It's decided,' said Beatrix as Olivia returned to the table in the hotel bar, where Joy and Fred had joined them.

'What's that?'

'We're all going to Arizona next year – for Christmas. Joy says it's the most perfect place to get out of the cold and the wet.' Beatrix beamed.

'How lovely,' Olivia said absently, her mind still on the phone call.

'You're more than welcome to come too, honey,' said Fred generously. 'There's plenty of space.'

'It's a ranch,' said Beatrix, her eyes alight. 'With horses. I haven't ridden in years. Do you remember that time when that Australian officer lent us his horses, in Shillong? Wasn't that glorious?'

Lucy nodded.

Olivia listened to their excited plans, thinking that she hadn't the faintest idea where she would be in a year's time, especially now it seemed that she had been chasing a job that didn't exist.

'Everything okay, darling? You seem rather glum.'

'Oh I'm fine, really. A little tired perhaps. It's been quite a day.' Olivia finished her drink and smiled at them with a false brightness. 'If it's all right with you, I might have an early night.'

'Of course, off you go. I'll see you in the morning.'

She walked up the stairs to her hotel room, feeling suddenly exhausted, and very alone.

She took out Beatrix's sketchbooks and lay back on her bed. She flipped through the drawings until she reached the fox-girl. Who had laboured over this artwork, spending months painstakingly carving it? What had their dreams been? Who had first worn it? Had they once treasured it as Bea had? Such things were lost in time. Jack . . . Beatrix said someone called Jack had given it to her. What could have happened to him?

~

'We've been summoned back,' Beatrix said as soon as Olivia sat down opposite her for breakfast the next morning. 'Plum left a message with the concierge for me to call in this morning. Lucy and Joy are going to join us. We've told Joy everything.' She looked hopeful. 'That's a good sign, yes? That Plum wants to see me again?'

'I think so,' said Olivia. 'If she's had a chance to talk to Harold, then perhaps we can wrap things up.'

'We'll find out as soon as we get there.'

'What time are we expected?'

'Ten-thirty.'

When they were in the car, the three older women kept up a steady stream of conversation, and Olivia had to strain to hear them in the back seat over the drumming of the rain on the roof. A heavy shower was making the roads slick and visibility tricky. Beatrix, Lucy and Joy were talking about a time when they used to drive their trucks onto a ferry – 'You had to go at it hell for leather and then slam on the brakes at the last minute lest you overshoot and end up in the drink,' said Lucy. 'Bea, do you remember the trip to Dohazari?'

'The bloody lorries kept breaking down. Took us hours longer than it should have. The roads were dreadful, of course.'

'Speaking of lorries breaking down . . .' Olivia said, indicating a white van that had come to an inexplicable halt two cars in front of them.

'Looks like we might be here for a while.'

Lucy was right. The road was narrow, with overgrown hedgerows on either side, and there was no room for the other cars to pass, nor for the van to pull over.

'Come on,' said Joy, opening the door.

'But it's pouring!' said Olivia.

'Only water,' came the reply.

'Beatrix, your ankle,' Olivia said.

'Oh, it's much better,' Beatrix said over her shoulder as she climbed out. 'Good as new, in fact.'

Olivia watched with a mixture of concern and disbelief as the three women splashed up the road towards the van, the windscreen wipers sloshing away the rain pouring from above. After a few moments she realised she couldn't let them continue on their own. Turning on her hazard lights and putting on the handbrake, she waded after them.

'There's a passing place a few yards further along, apparently,' Beatrix called as Olivia reached them, and two men from the van. 'You're the lightest – you hop in and steer,' she said.

'But—'

'No time to argue; we'll only get wetter,' said Lucy.

Olivia wasn't at all sure that Beatrix, Joy and Lucy, together with the men, were going to be able to push the van anywhere, but Lucy's tone was commanding and so she did as she was told.

The women grunted as they pushed. Slowly the van began to move and Olivia looked in the rear-view mirror to see that another driver had also emerged from his nice, dry car to help.

A couple of minutes later, the van was safely off the road and the women left, words of thanks from the driver ringing in their ears.

'I can't believe you just did that,' said Olivia when they were back in the car, wiping the water out of their eyes. 'And we're soaked.' They passed the van with a beep and a wave, and continued on their way.

'We're not completely useless,' said Beatrix tartly. 'Not yet, anyway.'

'That's not what I meant.'

'I didn't exactly appreciate getting quite so wet,' said Lucy. 'Not to mention that I've got mud right up to my hocks.'

'Nothing we haven't done before,' said Joy.

The women laughed at the state of themselves, Beatrix ineffectually blotting her face with a tissue that quickly disintegrated, and Olivia couldn't help but join in.

As she drove, Olivia remembered something that had been niggling at her. 'The medals that you were wearing on New Year's Eve; what were they for?' she asked once the laughter had subsided.

The older women looked at each other.

'That's for Beatrix and Lucy to tell,' said Joy.

'Well . . .' Lucy began, as between them, they told the story of their encounter with two Japanese soldiers, as Olivia listened, entranced, almost missing the turning to Plum's house.

'You mean you drove into the jungle with nothing more than a couple of revolvers for protection?' she asked.

'We knew the Japs were close, but not quite that close,' said Beatrix.

'Besides, we didn't have a great deal of choice.'

'She saved my life,' said Lucy.

'And Plum saved mine,' Beatrix countered. 'I can't forget that.'

Olivia glanced in the rear-view mirror and saw Beatrix, Lucy and Joy grasp each other's hands, blinking rather rapidly, the warmth of their affection for each other palpable in the close confines of the car.

'You would have done the same had the situation been reversed. We all looked out for each other then.'

'What a shame we can't say the same thing now,' said Beatrix sadly.

These were tough-as-nails women. Olivia had no doubt they would be more than a match for a sleazy judge, no matter how powerful he might be.

~

The four of them arrived at the house, their hair ruined and clothes damp, but with their heads held high.

Alex greeted them at the door, but she didn't meet Olivia's eye. She showed them into the living room, where Plum sat, perfectly coiffed and outwardly composed, on the sofa. There were no kisses of greeting this time.

'I would offer tea,' Plum said bluntly, 'but I doubt this will take very long.'

As Alex sat down next to her grandmother and the women opposite, Olivia searched the room but could see no evidence of the paperwork assigning provenance that she'd left the day before.

'He says it's utter nonsense.'

'Well, of course he would—' Beatrix began.

'That you must have come by the netsuke some other way. Beatrix, I do remember your first husband was a collector of treasures such as these, as Harold is. Perhaps it reminded them both of their war service.'

'That is not what happened,' Beatrix insisted. 'In fact, I eventually told him how I came to have it in my possession again, and indeed how it had been stolen from me.'

As Beatrix opened her mouth to continue, the door opened and Harold Byrne walked in. He stood behind the sofa, his hand on his wife's shoulder and coolly regarded them.

'Now then, ladies.' He addressed them all, but focused his gaze on Beatrix. 'I understand you have something that belongs to me. Something that I value very highly.'

Olivia was astonished. Did he really think he could intimidate them into handing over the netsuke? Was he really that arrogant?

'Actually no, that is not the case. Plum mustn't have made things clear. We came here expecting you to sign the letter of provenance for the fox-girl.'

Olivia heard the determination in Beatrix's voice.

Harold chuckled dismissively, as if she were joking with him. 'I don't know what you think you remember, but I assure you I played no part whatsoever in it. I acquired the netsuke from a fellow officer in a game of cards. I admit, I did not ask him the circumstances of how it came to be in his possession, but I received it fair and square for a winning hand.'

'How interesting that you have a completely different recollection of events,' Beatrix replied as she reached into her bag and pulled out a silk scarf wrapped around a rectangular object. She let the scarf fall open to reveal a small wooden-handled blade. 'It's part of a set of traditional Gurkha weapons. No doubt you recognise it.'

Harold was silent, a flush rising up his cheeks, his eyes hardening. He began to bluster. 'They are a common artefact, and I can't say I've seen this particular knife before.'

It was obvious to Olivia, as it must have been to everyone in the room, that he had.

'Your story is a false one,' Beatrix continued, staring him down.

Olivia noticed that Alex had taken her grandmother's hand and that Plum had shaken off Harold's grip. 'I would wager that you know exactly what happened on that particular night in February nineteen forty-five.'

'More than fifty years ago? At a time when I was knee-deep in the jungle, in the middle of a war? You can't possibly expect me to remember one night in the midst of all the others.'

'But you remember the night you were stabbed, don't you? Stabbed with your own knife?'

There was a pause before Harold spoke again, as if he was wrestling with his own anger. 'We were *at war*. I sustained an injury at the hands of the enemy,' he said, sudden fury turning his face so beet-red that Olivia worried he might be at risk of a stroke. 'Now really, I was hoping you might have brought the netsuke with you and we could stop all this nonsense. You've upset my wife, and I won't have that.'

Beatrix looked as though she was going to be sick. 'Do I really have to spell it out?' she asked. 'In front of your wife and your granddaughter again?'

Harold rocked back on his heels and folded his arms. 'This is preposterous. Do you know who you are dealing with? I have welcomed you into my home, and you have done nothing but abuse my hospitality and intimidate my wife.' He raised his voice, so that he was nearly shouting. 'According to her, you did nothing but tease her when you served together.' He returned a hand to Plum's shoulder briefly and Olivia saw her flinch at his touch. 'Shame on you.'

'We were never cruel,' Joy murmured.

'This is absolute horseshit,' said Lucy, rising from her seat.

'The shame is on you,' said Beatrix, glaring at him. 'You've got away with such appalling behaviour for so many years, protected by your privilege and power.'

'It seems there is nothing to be gained from this exchange. It's time you left,' he said icily.

'It was a crime,' Beatrix continued, undaunted. 'One of the worst things a man can do to a woman, and as a judge I'd expect you to know that.'

'Who would believe a frail old woman, someone who's done nothing in her life, over a judge in the highest court in the land?' he scoffed. 'Come on, really. You have no proof whatsoever. What exactly is it that you are alleging?'

Olivia could see that he was counting on Beatrix being unable to say out loud what he had done, but he had underestimated her.

'You assaulted me. Raped me.' Bea's hands gripped the knife in her lap and her voice quavered on the word, but she refused to look away.

Harold made a choking sound and Olivia began to wonder if he really was going to be taken ill, while Plum looked straight ahead, as if she were wishing she was somewhere else.

'Utterly egregious,' he spluttered eventually. 'Ridiculous allegations.'

'There are enough details to go to the papers with,' said Lucy evenly. 'And I believe your appointment has not been officially confirmed yet.' The thinly veiled threat in her words was evident.

Harold started to reply, but Plum stopped him. 'No. Harold.

313

I cannot sit by and listen to you tell more lies.' She gripped Alex's hand for support.

'Olivia,' she said, her voice shaking. 'Alex came to me after you left yesterday and told me what happened in the Long Room on New Year's Eve. I am so very sorry, my dear.'

Olivia looked at Alex, puzzled.

'I overheard him threatening you. I'm very sorry too,' Alex said. 'I didn't believe what I'd heard at first.'

'You weren't to know,' said Olivia softly.

'*I* was, though,' said Plum. 'I turned a deaf ear to the rumours over the years, and there were a few . . .' Her voice trailed off. 'You tried to warn me yourself, Bea. Before we left Burma.'

'I've always regretted that I didn't try harder,' said Beatrix sadly.

'I only wish I'd listened.'

'Plum?' Harold gripped her arm tightly enough for Olivia to see her wince.

'I'm sorry, Harold, but this has gone on too long.' Plum shifted away from him, moving closer to Alex, who placed a protective arm around her grandmother's shoulders. 'I choose to believe my granddaughter; these women too.'

'This is absurd,' Harold blustered. 'You're all in cahoots against me. You're complete fantasists, the lot of you. Do you know who I am? What I represent?'

He was starting to sound like a petulant child.

'All we want is the signed letter of provenance,' Beatrix reminded him calmly. 'And the other matter will be laid to rest.'

'I brought another one,' said Olivia, withdrawing an envelope from her bag. 'In the event that you had misplaced it.' She stood and carried it the short distance to him, holding out a pen as well, doing her best not to show her revulsion for the man. 'I'm sure Lucy would be happy to witness your signature, wouldn't you, Lucy?'

Lucy nodded.

Harold looked from his wife to the women and back to his wife again, an expression of disbelief on his face. Olivia continued to hold out the pen and the envelope. Stalemate.

'Believe me, I am not afraid to take this further,' said Beatrix, her expression resolute.

There was a beat of silence, and Olivia could hear her own thudding heart as everyone seemed to hold their breath.

'You're absolutely mad, the lot of you,' he said eventually. 'But if it will make you happy, Plum darling . . .' He gave a mock sigh, as if he were indulging his wife in a frivolity, but took the pen and signed the letter, then passed it to Lucy and went to hold open the door. 'I think you should leave now. I do not expect you to return.'

'Oh, don't worry,' said Beatrix. 'We have no such intention. Come along, ladies, we really don't need to take up any more of our time here.'

'I'm the one who should be sorry,' said Plum as she saw the women out of the house. 'I spent too long trying not to rock the boat, to keep everyone happy. Told myself the accusations were probably made by people jealous of him, of us and everything we had.' She made a dry, mirthless sound. 'You know what the worst thing is? He probably doesn't even remember it.'

'No,' said Beatrix sadly. 'He probably doesn't.'

As they drove away, Beatrix lay back against the back of the seat and closed her eyes. Olivia could see how much the confrontation had taken out of her, saw her hands clasped tightly around the handle of her bag.

'You did brilliantly,' said Lucy.

'You certainly did,' added Joy. 'Bravest woman I know.'

Beatrix opened her eyes and the women shared a smile, but instead of elation at having achieved their goal, Olivia felt only sadness – sadness that one person's actions could have had such a damaging effect on another for so many years. It hurt her to think how long Beatrix had lived with such pain.

'I still can't believe Plum backed us up,' said Lucy.

'And that she stood up to him. That took a hell of a lot of guts,' said Joy.

'She always did surprise us,' said Beatrix. 'I think we underestimated her. Then and now.'

'Alex too,' said Olivia. 'It can't have been easy. To accuse your grandfather of harassment, especially when he's as powerful a man as that.'

'I think that's what made the difference,' said Lucy. 'Plum chose to believe her granddaughter and not her husband.'

'I hope I never have to lay eyes on him again,' Beatrix said. 'But by God, revenge is a satisfying dish, even when it's served more than half a century cold.'

～

'You can go ahead and put her up for sale,' said Beatrix later as they sat in the hotel bar, Jameson for the older women, Guinness for Olivia. She brought the fox-girl out of her bag, unwrapped it and placed it on the table in front of them. 'Such a delicate little thing,' she said wistfully. 'Jack loved it so much.'

'Strong, too,' said Olivia.

'She does exert a strange fascination, doesn't she,' said Lucy, picking it up. 'A most unusual creature, neither woman nor beast.'

'Er, I wanted to talk to you about that, Beatrix,' said Olivia, twisting her fingers around each other. 'Officially, I'm not *actually* employed by Cholmondeley's.'

'What?' Beatrix was astonished.

'I'm an intern – an unpaid intern. "Work experience", Elaine calls it, though I am well qualified – over-qualified actually.'

'Oh.' Beatrix sat back in surprise. 'But I don't understand.'

'I know that Cholmondeley's has represented you for years,' Olivia said carefully, 'but I wondered if you might be willing to take another approach, to sell the fox-girl via slightly different means.'

'Honestly, darling, I'm happy for you to oversee the sale in whatever way you see fit. I owe you a very great deal; you've been a complete star this past week, and I really couldn't have done all of this without your support. Yours too, Lucy, and Joy.' She reached for her friends' hands. 'Just make sure we get the best price possible – I need that damned roof fixed, and pronto.'

'Got it. As soon as we're back in London I'll get things moving.' Olivia hadn't put the finishing touches to her plan as yet, but she had a fairly good idea of what she might be able to achieve.

'Now, who would like some dinner?' Bea asked with relish. 'I don't mind admitting that today has given me quite an appetite.'

TWENTY-SEVEN

Rangoon, 1945

There was little time to celebrate the war's end once Bea landed, for all of the women were summoned to a briefing on their latest responsibility – serving the POWs returning from captivity, where they had been put to work on the construction of the Burma Railway by the Japanese. Bea hoped with everything she had that Archie would be among them.

'I cannot stress how important it is that you remain calm and dignified,' they were instructed. 'Do not under any circumstances show your horror at the state of these men, for they will likely be in very poor physical condition. Compassion is the order of the day, and just try to be as normal as possible. And for goodness sake, try not to stare at them.'

Somehow, this felt like the most important work of their war.

They did their best to make the canteen as inviting as possible. Plum collected flowers and found some fabric for tablecloths and curtains. She persuaded the sergeant in charge of the stores to give them the most recent English newspapers and magazines, and some of the soldiers stationed nearby brought copies of their own papers, 'in case there are some local lads who want news from home'.

As soon as the camps were located, aircraft were sent in to evacuate the men. 'It's the quickest way to get them out, and we expect some of them to be very ill indeed,' the women were told.

When the first plane landed, and the men – more like walking skeletons than living beings – arrived, they walked haltingly across the airstrip. The women did their best not to show their shock, but Bea had to continually remind herself not to stare. The men's eyes were dark and sunken in their sockets, and she could have counted their ribs, the knobbly bones of each spine.

Some wore ragged shorts and shirts with their regimental badges stitched proudly to the front, but others had nothing except nappy-like rags tied around their waists with string. What nearly brought Bea undone was the fact that few of them had shoes – they were either barefoot or wore strips of bark tied together with string on their feet. Others had lost legs, she saw, and lurched on crude artificial limbs or makeshift crutches.

'Pull yourself together, Second Lieutenant Fitzgibbon,' Lucy whispered, seeing Bea's face crumple in sympathy, tears springing to her eyes. 'Let's go and escort them inside, shall we?'

'Sorry,' she sniffed. 'Leakier than a bloody tent roof.'

The women went to greet the men, linking arms through theirs and introducing themselves, chatting brightly as if it were the most normal thing in the world. The soldiers looked dazed, overcome with exhaustion and weak from malnutrition. 'Where are we?' one of them asked. Some could barely walk. Bea noticed several great gouges of muscle missing from their legs, and remembered the warnings they'd been given about tropical ulcers.

For a while, the men seemed to barely take in their surroundings and had to be gently guided to the tables, where Joy, Lucy, Plum and Bea served them Scotch broth, plates of stew and mash, tea and buns, fruit salad and custard. Cigarettes were also given out freely.

A few of the men cried to see them, at everything waiting for them, and it was all Bea could do not to break down in tears alongside them. She noticed Lucy turn away at one point, busying herself with a tea urn, her shoulders shaking silently.

They learned that many had been held prisoner for more than three years, had done the backbreaking work of hacking through the jungle to build the Burma Railway, and Bea could scarcely imagine what they must have gone through. What Archie must have also endured.

Everyone was very quiet, until one soldier piped up, 'Watch out for the silver, miss, the padre is here.' This broke the ice, and everyone laughed and started to talk, wanting to know the news from home, to be reassured that the war was really over, showing tattered, treasured photos of their wives and girlfriends, bemused by talk of DDT and penicillin, even by the Jeeps, aircraft and the amphibious tanks around them. Most of the men hadn't seen women for the entire time they'd been POWs. 'My head's nearly spinning off my neck,' said one of them. 'So much has changed.'

Plates were scraped clean, but Bea noticed several of the men go around the back of the hut afterwards, their stomachs not used to the rich food.

The monsoon rains poured down and the women handed out hundreds of waterproof capes and canvas shoes, for the men had nothing but the scant, frayed clothing they were wearing, and the rain gear was all the women had been provided with. Bea cursed the Army's lack of foresight, but the men were grateful for everything, some staring in delight at the capes as if they were the finest Jermyn Street tailoring. As Bea inspected the line of half-rotted footwear that the men left behind she was pierced with sadness at the sheer bloody waste of the war.

That evening, she struggled to find the words to write about it in her notebook. Some things were simply too horrific to express. Working from memory, she made a quick sketch of some of the men as they had walked across the runway. That would have to suffice.

Hundreds of POWs poured in daily, and each time Bea scanned their faces, searching for Archie among the hollow eyes and shaved heads, though she doubted she would recognise him – these men probably bore little resemblance to their pre-war selves, in looks or in spirit. She tried to find out more information on the released prisoners, but there were no specific names until the men arrived at the airport.

Then, one afternoon, as they waited for the last flight of the day, Bea had a sense that Archie was near. She couldn't have explained it logically, but something in her heart told her that he was on the approaching flight. She scolded herself for being so foolish; that it was madness to get her hopes up.

But, as Bea saw the first figures disembark and begin to walk towards them, she felt as though the breath had been knocked from her lungs. Without thinking about what she was doing, she threw down the tea towel she'd been using and ran across the runway. There was one man, so gaunt that his head looked more like a skull than a face, but who was as familiar to her as the back of her own hand.

She stopped a few yards short of him and let him come towards her, saw the expression of recognition, then disbelief, flood his face. Tears ran freely down her cheeks and her whole body began to shake.

'Archie?'

'Beebee? Is that you?'

She nodded, smiling through the tears, and then he reached her and they clung to each other as they hadn't done since they were little. She tried her best to hide her shock at his emaciated frame, the withered muscles of a once young, strong and healthy man. 'We thought you might be dead. We didn't hear anything for so long . . .'

'I wasn't bloody well going to die in a place like that, not as a slave in the jungle. There was this Aussie doctor – he saved my life, saved the lives of so many of us. Without him . . .'

Archie, who seemed to have used all of his remaining strength with those words, began to shake and Bea wrapped her arm around him as he leaned on her shoulder. They began to walk slowly towards the canteen.

'Hush now,' she soothed him. 'It's all right now, everything is all right.' But Bea didn't know if her brother would be all right; he looked as bad as any of the men she'd seen so far.

He began to mutter about being in the valley of the shadow of death, of fearing no evil, and his words chilled her more than any she'd heard. He – along with all the men forced to work on the Burma Railway – had been in a place worse than hell and only some had made it through. She was selfishly grateful that Archie was one of them.

Bea found him a spot at a table in the corner, and brought him a cup of broth and a cigarette. 'There's food, too; I'll bring that in a moment, but I thought this would be a good start.'

He gave her a grateful smile and brought the mug shakily to his lips, drinking it down in one.

'Another?' she asked.

He nodded, holding out the mug towards her.

Bea hadn't needed to explain who she was looking after, for the other women all knew she'd been watching out for her twin for weeks. She went back to serve some of the other men, but Joy shooed her away. 'We've got it covered here. Go and sit with your brother.'

After downing another mug of broth, Archie looked up at Bea as if he were only properly seeing her for the first time. 'You're the last person I expected to come across here; what . . .'

Bea saw him take note of her stripes and shrugged. 'I wasn't able to say anything in my letters to you, but I've been in India and Burma for more than a year,' she said, a note of pride creeping into her voice. 'We take our trucks out and serve the men on the frontline, or those coming back for some R and R; anywhere we're needed, really. I couldn't just sit around and do nothing, not with you out there. Besides, secretarial college was the *worst*.' She wrinkled her nose at him and grinned.

He smiled back but it didn't reach his eyes, and Bea could tell that her brother's once mischievous spark had been doused.

'How many of you are there?' he asked.

'In total? I'm not exactly sure – several hundred, at least.'

'Well, I never,' he said, his eyes widening. 'Though I'm not surprised – my little sister's got as much get up and go as anyone.'

'Little by ten minutes,' she reminded him with a gentle punch to his shoulder. 'And not nearly as courageous as you.'

He flinched as she touched him, and she immediately felt remorseful.

'Just a bit jumpy, you know?' he said, attempting to smile again.

Bea had heard stories from some of the other men who had returned about the conditions they had to endure, stories of backbreaking work with poor tools, a diet of rice infested with rat excrement and maggots, constant illness – malaria, dysentery, dengue fever and cholera – wiping out men day after day, the clothes rotting off their backs, and even worse, the punishments inflicted by their sadistic captors.

'Of course, sorry. Would you like some proper food now?'

'I thought you'd never ask.'

Bea brushed away fresh tears and choked back a sob as she went to fetch him a plate of stew.

She returned to the table with Lucy and Plum, for most of the men had been fed and they could be spared.

'Archie, these are my friends. You remember Plum, from home, and this is Lucy, from Australia.'

The women shook his hand and pulled out chairs next to him.

'The three of you are a sight for sore eyes,' he said, taking them all in. 'What does a chap have to do to warrant such delightful attention?' His words were flirtatious but his tone was still subdued.

'Have a sister who's one of the bravest women I've ever met,' said Lucy.

Bea blushed. 'There are a lot of things to tell you.'

'She saved my life,' said Lucy. 'No word of a lie.'

'Only after Plum saved mine,' Bea protested.

'I can well believe it,' said Archie. 'Now, tell me exactly how . . .'

All too soon, it was time for the planeload of men to move on, the sickest to special POW hospitals that had been set up, the others to begin the long journey home.

Bea hugged Archie as tightly as she dared. 'Mother will be so happy to see you when you eventually get home; she'll spoil you rotten, I know it.'

'I'll be back to my old self before you can say boo,' he reassured her.

Bea didn't believe he ever would. The war had changed them all, but some so much more than others.

Weeks passed as the women of No. 55 WAS(B) canteen served the returning POWs. The most urgent cases had been evacuated first, and then those not in need of medical treatment arrived at a new canteen at Insein, spending their time catching up on several years' worth of news and putting as much food back into their starved bodies as possible, until their passage back to England could be arranged.

Not everyone who came through was a soldier, and the women served many civilians who had been interned in Thailand and Singapore, among them children who had been born in captivity and had never seen food in such abundance. It was all Bea could do to stop them stuffing themselves, but they were so sweet that there was no way she could be cross with them when they grabbed an extra bun or a third piece of cake.

Another canteen operated at the docks, and Plum and another couple of Wasbies were sent to help there, serving those heading home with a final cup of tea and offering them the chance to stock up on any essentials before they set sail.

Whenever she could, Bea visited her brother, who was in one of the hospitals in Rangoon, and slowly looking more like his former self. They talked, and talked, and talked some more, for they had nearly three years to catch up on.

'I got your postcards,' Archie said. 'Your drawings were the best – especially the ones of the horses.'

'I'm not sure if they helped, really, but I wanted you to know we were always thinking of you, even if I couldn't tell you much of what I was up to.'

'Tell me now, Bea.'

And so she recounted stories of times when the monsoon rains saturated all of their gear, about the time she was caught in the altogether as the privy tent blew away and forced to clutch a towel to herself to maintain her dignity, of serving over a thousand men in a day and then going dancing afterwards. She didn't speak of the awful times. But Archie did, a little, and she was happy to let him ramble, though it was heartbreaking to hear of the torture and deprivation. He gave her a few drawings he'd been able to keep hidden from the prison guards. As she examined the charcoal sketches, many of desperately thin men lying on low bamboo platforms, her heart broke again for the conditions he and so many others had suffered.

Sometimes when she arrived, Archie was asleep, once in the throes of a nightmare, calling out about lizards. She asked him about it later, when he was feeling stronger.

'Oh yes,' he said, frowning. 'The Lizard, that was what we called him. His job was to round us up for the engineers working on the railway. If there weren't enough of the fit men to make up a crew, he went to the medical huts, jabbed you in the back with a rifle and didn't stop until you moved. One poor chap must've said or done something wrong and ended up with a ruddy great piece of bamboo up his jacksy.'

She shuddered. 'How did you get through it all? And you never said what happened to David.'

Archie's face crumpled, and he shook his head, unable to speak.

'Sorry,' she said, overcome with remorse. 'I shouldn't have asked.'

'After . . . after he went, I stuck together with two other chaps – one of them was a medic, and he kicked up a stink if he thought you were really ill. But honestly, if you didn't have a chum or two, you wouldn't have survived. We kept each other going, looked after each other.' He stopped, nearly breaking down again. 'I owe those men my life.'

∼

One afternoon, as they took a quick break from serving, Bea wondered out loud what they might all do after their work with the Wasbies was done.

'Fred writes to me fairly regularly,' said Joy. 'I thought you knew.'

'Why would I?' Bea asked.

Joy reddened. 'Wasn't it obvious that, well . . .'

Her friend's meaning suddenly dawned on Bea. 'God, I must have been walking about with my eyes shut. Really? You and Fred? Golly.'

Joy nodded, going slightly pink. 'Under the circumstances . . . Fred knows everything, and despite it all has asked me to be with him, to meet him in Illinois. He's going to join the family business.'

'I thought he wanted to be a musician.'

'I thought so too, but he seems keen to go back and help his father out. Peter's already filed for divorce, so as soon as the paperwork's done, that's where I'm going.'

Bea beamed at her. 'Oh, I'm so pleased for you. America. Heavens. Another adventure.'

'I hope so,' Joy said. 'Though I'll miss all of you so much. Promise you'll write, and send me the occasional drawing.'

'Of course I will,' said Bea, feeling deflated at the prospect of going back to her old life before the war. Returning to her unfinished secretarial diploma and a pampered expatriate existence of tea dances and tennis tournaments held limited appeal, but at least, she supposed, she would be safe, and there would be Archie to look after, her parents to be with.

Lucy desired little more than to return to her family farm in Australia. 'I never want to see another uniform again, nor a monsoon,' she frequently said.

And Plum, much to everyone's surprise, told them that she had decided to study nursing in London – 'What? Don't you think I've a strong enough stomach for it?'

'Is there a man involved?' Lucy asked suspiciously.

Plum blushed.

'I knew it!' she cried. 'Come on, spill. It must be serious.'

'We-ell, I actually think it might be. He's ever so good to me, gives me little gifts, tells me how pretty I am. He's so thoughtful, and anyway, I like being around him.'

'So, why haven't we met him?' Bea asked.

'He was only here for a short while; he's back in England now.'

'What's his name?'

'Harold Byrne.'

Bea felt sudden nausea overwhelm her and she thought she might have to excuse herself.

She and Lucy exchanged horrified glances.

'Major Harold Byrne?' Lucy asked.

'Why? Do you know him?'

Lucy opened her mouth to speak, but Bea jumped in first. 'Are you sure? It's just that . . .' She couldn't bring herself to finish the sentence.

'He's not who you think he is,' Lucy finished when her friend didn't. 'He doesn't exactly have the best reputation.'

Plum's mouth had set in an unhappy line. 'I don't want to hear a word said against him. Just because you've got no one special,' she spat at them, 'doesn't mean you should try to destroy someone else's happiness. I thought you'd be pleased for me.' She stormed off.

Bea hesitated for a moment, but then chased after her, kicking up dust as she went. 'Plum,' she gasped, 'wait, please!'

They were a few hundred yards away from the other women when Plum stopped and turned. 'What? What is it? Or do you just want to warn me off again?'

'Please,' begged Bea. 'Listen to me. Harold is not a decent man. I wish for your sake that he was, but he isn't.'

'And how do you know that? I think you're just jealous.'

Bea was suddenly lost for words. She wasn't sure she could bring herself to say what Harold had done. 'Believe me, I'm not jealous. He . . .' She halted, trying to decide how to proceed. 'He has . . . hurt other women.'

'Who? Name them if you're so sure.'

Bea bit her lip, afraid to voice what had really happened to her.

'See, you can't prove anything, can you?' added Plum, scornfully. 'I don't believe a damn word you're saying. Harold's *not* that kind of man. I just know it. Leave me alone, will you?'

Bea was left to watch her friend march off again. She could only hope that once Plum had a chance to calm down, the meaning of her words might sink in.

~

'Last one,' said Bea to Lucy, making sure the urn was hot and the sandwiches were ready. It was two days before they were due to pack up their canteen and move on, and they were waiting for the final POW evacuation flight to land. 'I'm almost sad about it.'

'I know what you mean. It seemed as though this war would never be over, and now here we are.'

Their little team, which had been together for more than a year, was breaking up. Plum hadn't spoken to Bea since their conversation about Harold, and Bea found herself unable to breach the silence. Their once strong group of five was now diminished and fractured.

Before returning to Australia, Lucy was going to Japan, where she would be attached to the 2nd Dorsets not far from Hiroshima, and Joy was off to the Dutch East Indies – to Java first – to assist with the repatriation of POWs there while waiting for her divorce to be finalised. Bea had been given compassionate leave, on account of her brother, and was going first to Calcutta and then on to London, for her mother had decided that it was time for them all to return home. They would stay with her grandparents at their house in Wiltshire, at least to begin with.

Try as she might, Bea could not forget Jack – the way her heart thudded uncomfortably in her chest when he looked at her, the lazy drawl that sent shivers through her whole body. She would never meet anyone like him again. Though her pillow was sometimes damp with tears in the mornings, she told herself she was grieving not only for him, but for all the lost soldiers. Lost but never forgotten.

'Let's make it the best, then,' Bea said, standing straighter as the aircraft taxied along the runway.

Later, they thought they had served almost everyone who'd come in on the flight. 'There's only the pilot, co-pilot and navigator left I think,' said Lucy. 'Here they are now.' She caught her breath. 'Oh, there's one more.'

'I'll be with you in a moment,' Bea said, sensing someone waiting in front of her but not looking up from the jug she was carefully pouring.

'Oh, I've got all day, especially when it means lookin' at you, honey.'

Bea let out a strangled yelp and nearly spilled scalding tea all over the table. 'Jack? Oh my goodness, Jack! Is it really you?' She blinked in disbelief.

It *was* him. A little less exuberant and a lot thinner, but definitely, unmistakeably him.

'Last time I checked, honey,' he said, winking at her. 'Say, you look like you just saw a ghost.'

'I thought you were dead.' Bea knew she was grinning idiotically, but she couldn't have cared less. She put down the pot, fumbling to untie her apron before ignoring it and racing around the canteen counter to envelop him in the biggest hug she had to give. 'I thought you were gone forever,' she said, her voice thick as the tears she'd held back for so long flowed down her cheeks, dampening his ragged shirt.

'Didn't you once call me a lucky penny – always showing up when you least expect it?' His words were light-hearted but his voice, too, was gruff with emotion and he embraced Bea just as tightly, not letting her go.

At that moment, Bea thought she had never been so happy in her life.

'You look . . .' She stopped, for Jack's face was gaunt, his cheekbones sharp. 'Quite different.'

He laughed. 'Not exactly K rations where I've been.'

'No, I suppose not.'

They stood, foolishly gazing at each other, before Lucy ushered them to a corner table. She brought each of them a cup of tea, with a plate of sandwiches and cake for Jack. 'Good to see you back, Captain Butler,' she said, greeting him with a kiss on the cheek and a warm hug.

'Very good to be back, ma'am.'

Lucy disappeared, tactfully leaving them alone.

'How . . .' Bea stopped.

'How long am I here for?'

She nodded.

'Why, looking to get rid of me already?'

'No, Jack . . . Oh.' She stopped, realising he was teasing her.

He reached across the table and entwined his fingers in hers, clearly not caring who might be looking. 'Sometimes the thought of you was all that kept me going.'

She met his eyes, telling him without words that she felt the same. The rest of the canteen, the hum of soldiers talking and eating, faded away. They could have been marooned on an island all by themselves for the notice they took of anyone else.

'I still can't believe you're here,' she said. 'On the last flight in.'

'Better late than never,' he teased again.

Her face fell. 'But I'm leaving in two days' time. My brother, Archie . . . oh, there's so much to tell you.'

'Think you can get away tonight?' he asked.

Bea grinned. 'Wild horses wouldn't stop me.' She named a hotel, The Strand, one of the few in Rangoon that had not been requisitioned by the Army. 'I'll be in the bar at six; meet me there?'

'I won't keep you waiting.'

~

Bea arrived early, Joy having shooed her away from the canteen in plenty of time for her to return to their living quarters and attempt to tidy herself up. She had put on her favourite silk dress, which she had to belt to make fit, and examined herself in the sliver of mirror in the bathroom, taking in the sun-weathered skin, the unkempt hair. 'Wild as a brumby's,' Lucy often teased her. She brushed it out then pinned it up behind her ears with a pair of combs. It would have to do.

As she walked through the hotel's giant teak doors, her nerves jangled at the prospect of seeing Jack again, but she needn't have worried. As soon as she spotted him, sitting on his own at a table at the far end of the bar, relief flooded through her.

He was dressed in a borrowed uniform, for it hung on him much like her dress did on her, and he'd found a barber, his shaven skin pale. His face was shadowed, but to her he looked even more wonderful than he had the night they'd first kissed. As soon as she saw his smile, the pain and the hardship of the previous months receded to nothing.

He stood, and they embraced again, meeting like lovers, and she could hardly bear to let him go.

'You're so beautiful,' he said. 'I nearly forgot what you look like. I'm afraid I can't stop staring.'

'Then don't,' Bea replied as happiness – such an unfamiliar feeling – surged through her. 'Stop, I mean.'

'I took the liberty of ordering you the sour; it's very good,' he said as they sat down, his voice sounding uncharacteristically shaky.

'Cin cin.' They raised their glasses. 'This will be interesting,' he added. 'The first alcohol I've had in nearly a year.'

'You'll be tiddly before you know it,' she said with a carefree laugh.

'Tiddly?'

'Buzzed.' She laughed and took a sip of her drink. 'This hotel was occupied by the Japanese until recently,' she said, casting about for conversation in an effort to hide her sudden shyness.

'Well, they've done a miraculous job getting it up and running again. Just in time for us.' He reached towards her and traced a line along the plane of her cheek. 'Are you real or am I dreaming this?' he asked.

'Quite real,' she reassured him. 'Flesh and blood, right here before you.'

They sat for a while, each drinking in the sight of the other, their hands intertwined, oblivious to the crowd growing around them.

Jack drained his glass. 'You were right. I think another will finish me off.'

'I'm already light-headed,' Bea admitted.

'Then you won't mind if we call it a night?'

She felt a stab of disappointment. They'd been there less than an hour.

'What, too early for you?'

'It's just that . . .' she began, watching a slow smile spread over his face.

'I've booked a room. Will you join me?'

All she had to do was nod, but something, the feeling she'd had when she was attacked perhaps, stopped her. Then, she dismissed the memory and took his hand. 'I thought you'd never ask.'

As they left the bar Jack wobbled for a moment and Bea placed a steadying arm around his waist. 'See what a guy has to do to get some attention,' he joked.

That night, as they undressed each other carefully, Bea did her best not to let her shock at his painfully thin frame show. Jack hadn't been held prisoner for as long as some, but even a few months of near-starvation had taken their toll.

She confessed to losing the fox-girl. 'The lace around my neck broke without me realising it. It was right before you went missing. Lucy and I looked everywhere for it but we couldn't find it . . . I'm so sorry.'

'We found each other again, that's what's important,' he said, tracing a line of kisses across her collarbone.

She giggled.

'Oh, that's too corny for you, is it?'

'Never,' she said, kissing him back.

'The thought of you, of this . . . is what kept me going,' he said, nuzzling her neck and sending shockwaves of pleasure up and down her spine.

He led her towards the bed, but Bea hesitated. 'Something happened, out there in the jungle,' she stammered. 'I don't know if . . .'

'What is it?' he asked, his eyes searching hers.

She collected herself. 'It doesn't matter, not now at least.' She pulled him closer, steadied by the feel of his skin underneath her hands.

'Dreadful things happened to us all,' he said gently. 'We can tell each other when we're ready.' He hesitated. 'But we don't have to, you know . . .'

'Oh I think we do,' said Bea.

With hands and mouths they began to erase the bad memories, replacing them with those that were joyous.

Afterwards, they lay in each other's arms, talking softly for a while, before Jack fell asleep mid-sentence. Bea lay awake for longer, unwilling to close her eyes lest she wake up and find him gone.

~

'So, what's next?' he asked as the sun lightened the room the following morning.

'Breakfast?' she replied, nestling against him, her head on his shoulder.

He stroked her hair, winding a curl around his finger. 'And after that?'

Bea told him of her plans to return to England, of Archie's reappearance.

'Just as well I don't mind the rain, then.'

'What?'

'I should be able to apply for a transfer – there's a couple of bases in Wiltshire. I'll march all the way there if I have to.'

'But that's where my people are from. My grandparents have a house, near Salisbury.'

'Do you think that I don't know that,' he grinned, and bent to kiss her again.

TWENTY-EIGHT

Rangoon, 1945

'No sorrowful farewells,' Lucy scolded.

Plum, who had already dissolved in a puddle of tears and gin, sniffed loudly. It was the women's last night together before they were to go their separate ways. She was still frosty with Bea, only speaking to her when it was absolutely necessary, but according to Lucy, she had cooled things off with Harold Byrne.

'For God's sake, someone give that woman a hanky,' Lucy said, but her tone was indulgent rather than frustrated.

They'd pooled their remaining bottles of alcohol, with Joy mixing up a lethal cocktail she called a Mickey Finn. 'Fred taught me, though I'm not sure I paid enough attention to the proportions,' she said, squinting as she handed a drink to Bea. For once, there were no hangers-on in attendance. 'Women of the Wasbie number fifty-five only,' Joy had insisted.

'To absent friends,' Lucy toasted, raising her mug.

'Absent friends,' the rest of them murmured, thinking of Bubbles, and all the others who hadn't made it.

'Hey, d'you remember that time . . .' began Plum after a moment's silence. And then they were off, laughing and joking and ribbing each other, though Plum avoided speaking to Bea directly.

Lucy, in particular, seemed to have an uncanny recall of even the smallest details. 'How about when we were learning to drive?'

'I thought the poor instructor was going to put his foot through the floor when it was my turn,' said Bea. 'Don't forget our first target practice,' she added. They all sobered for a moment, remembering how Plum and Bea had put those skills to use.

'The look on the commander-in-chief's face when we told him what we'd done,' Lucy reminded them.

'We're better at so many things than when we first arrived,' said Plum. 'Slicing up Spam.'

They all groaned.

'My poor hands,' Joy said. 'They were so badly cut up from all those bloody tins.'

'You were lucky they didn't go septic,' said Lucy.

'Dancing the jitterbug.'

'And don't forget the Palais Glide.'

'Whipping up dinner for five hundred at a moment's notice.'

'Navigating our way through the jungle.'

'Coping with rats and dead bodies and . . .'

'Sleeping through a gun battle.'

'Not me, though,' said Bea ruefully. 'I never did get the hang of that.'

'Packing up and setting up and then doing it all again the next day, and the next and the next,' said Joy.

'I'll drink to all of that,' said Lucy, draining her mug. 'Though I never want to see another crate again, nor another wretched soya link.'

'More?' asked Joy, seeing Bea's mug almost empty.

'Why not?' she replied, draining it and then hiccoughing gently. She leaned her head against the back of her chair and looked at Joy and Lucy, knowing that she was unlikely to have such close friends again. She was so grateful for them, for the end of the war, for the jungle, for Jack and Archie making it through, for the whole bloody thing. She closed her eyes for a second; she was more than a little drunk and she didn't give a damn.

TWENTY-NINE

London, 2000

Contrary to all predictions, the chaos of Y2K failed to eventuate, and Olivia and Bea took the ferry back to England on a calm winter's day. They arrived at Pelham House very late at night.

'It's been a pleasure to drive,' she said, handing the keys to the Jaguar back to Beatrix.

'Yes, Willy thought so too. I'm going to sell it, though. Find something smaller and more practical. And cheaper.'

As Beatrix put the key in the lock, the dogs came rushing to the door, several of the puppies trailing behind them.

'Oh, they've grown already,' said Olivia as she bent down to greet them.

'Thank goodness there's been no rain since we've been away,' said Beatrix, going to check the various buckets in the hallway.

Beatrix's daily lady had left a pot of soup for them in the kitchen. 'Don't know what I'd do without her,' said Beatrix, taking two bowls out of the cupboard.

'I've so enjoyed the last week – most of it, anyway. It's been quite an adventure,' said Olivia as they sat down to eat. 'I'll miss you.'

'Me too,' Beatrix's eyes softened. 'But I fully expect you to visit – consider it an open invitation to come down any time, for we're firm friends now. You know all my secrets – well, most of them.' She stopped, as if a thought had just occurred to her. 'We can go sketching together.'

Olivia nodded, suddenly choked up by Beatrix's words. 'I'd like that.'

'And of course we'll be in touch about the netsuke.'

'Absolutely,' Olivia said, swallowing the lump in her throat along with the soup. 'My train's at eleven tomorrow,' she added. It would get her back to London in plenty of time for her meeting with Jeffrey Martinson in the evening.

'Jolly good. I'll run you to the station, and then I'd better get in the garden.'

'Well, be careful; you don't want to wreck your ankle again.'

Beatrix made a face at her. 'It's fine now.'

'It probably wouldn't hurt for you to slow down a bit,' Olivia teased.

'Pfft,' Beatrix dismissed her. 'Don't be ridiculous.'

~

The Brixton wine bar Olivia had suggested was one she often walked past on her way to and from the Tube, and it was quiet

343

when she went in and took a seat at a table towards the back of the room, ordering a glass of pinot noir. She didn't have to wait long for Jeffrey, as he soon bowled through the door in a fluster of cold air and nervous energy, his hair ruffled and his cheeks pinked by the wind.

'I don't usually come this far south,' he said, leaning over to kiss her on both cheeks. 'Happy New Year,' he added.

Olivia passed him the menu and waited while he gave his order to the waitress.

'I'm glad you found it all right,' she said after taking another sip of her wine. She couldn't help but feel underhand at meeting with him, but then she reminded herself of his assertion that – according to him, anyway – Elaine never had any intention of employing her. She still wasn't entirely sure this was true, and had resolved to raise it with her boss on her return to Cholmondeley's the following morning.

'Now, about the fox-girl,' he said, not wasting any time.

'The owner has agreed to sell. We have the provenance.'

'Oh splendid, splendid,' he said. She could almost see him rubbing his hands together with glee at the prospect. 'And exactly how did you manage that?'

'It's a very long story,' she replied, 'and not really mine to tell. But she has informed me that she would like me to handle the sale. Obviously I will need to work in conjunction with an established auction house.'

It was gratifying to be the one with the power for a change.

'Yes, of course. That is why I asked for this meeting. Martinson's is, as you know, one of the most highly regarded auctioneers in the country. We pride ourselves on our expertise, and of course, our relationships with our clients. Our business is increasing, and as a result, I'm looking to bring in another dealer to work with me.'

Olivia blinked. A dealer?

'A friend of mine, a professor at your old university I believe, stayed with us over Christmas. He mentioned you were in London, couldn't speak highly enough of you. "Best student of her year," he said. "Quite the rising star." I should like to make you an offer for the position.'

Olivia was shocked. 'That's certainly very flattering.'

He named a generous salary and she did her best to appear as though she often received such offers, nodding solemnly.

'And of course there would be all the usual perks,' he added. 'Paid holidays, and so on. Another glass?'

'Thank you, that would be nice.'

'Why don't you come to the office? You can meet the rest of the team, get an idea of what you'd be in for.' He looked at her encouragingly.

'Tell me,' she asked, 'would you have offered me the job if I hadn't secured the fox-girl?'

He smiled. 'Of course.'

She wasn't sure she believed him. 'May I have until the end of the week to think about it?' she asked, still trying her best to play it cool.

'Take all the time you need,' he said. 'Tell you what, why don't you pop in tomorrow after work?'

He really did want her – or more likely the fox-girl. Not that there was such a problem with that, if it opened the door to the job she needed. She took a sip of the fresh glass that had been placed in front of her. 'All right, then.'

'So, tell me about the owner,' he said. 'Is she as fearsome as everyone says she is?'

'You know who it is?' Olivia asked.

'Not much gets past me.'

'Actually,' said Olivia, 'she's a complete sweetheart.'

Jeffrey's eyebrows shot towards the ceiling. 'You must have a skill with difficult women.'

'Oh, she can be tricky,' said Olivia. 'No doubt about that. But she's an incredibly loyal friend, and really very kind underneath it all. She's survived more than either of us will ever know.'

Olivia arrived at Cholmondeley's at ten minutes to nine the following morning. Elaine was already at her desk, and on the phone. Olivia took off her coat and put it on the hook, then popped her head around the door to Elaine's office.

'Happy New Year,' said Elaine as she put down the phone. 'Did you have a good break?'

Olivia nodded. 'Very nice, thank you.'

'Are you feeling better? Beatrix said you collapsed on her doorstep.' She tutted. 'Not a very good look, I must say.'

'I am, thank you.' Olivia ignored the barb.

'So, how did you get on? Is everything in order? Is she going to sell?' Elaine's eyes gleamed at the prospect of a large commission.

Olivia sidestepped the question. 'I wonder if we might talk about my employment?'

'Your employment?' Elaine sounded bemused.

'Yes, my employment. I've been here more than three months now, and the agreement was for an internship, which, all being well, would result in, if not a permanent position, then a paid one at least,' Olivia reminded her.

'Oh my dear, has it been three months already? Heavens!' Elaine took off her glasses and rubbed the bridge of her nose. 'Well, of course we should offer you something. Let me talk to Reg and we'll see what we can do.'

It was something, Olivia supposed, but not exactly as appealing an offer as Jeffrey Martinson had made. 'Thank you.'

'Now. The fox-girl, and the other netsuke. Tell me all about them.'

'They're all rather lovely, and the fox-girl is the real thing.' Olivia hesitated, savouring the moment of telling Elaine. 'We got the provenance.'

Elaine rocked back on her chair. 'Oh, splendid, splendid. Now we'll need to market the sale. Make a bit of a splash, I think. How soon can we get it photographed?'

'Any time, I think.'

'Excellent. Can you get onto arranging that right away?' Elaine began to hum contentedly to herself, waving Olivia away. 'Oh, and a cup of coffee wouldn't go amiss, either.'

Olivia went to put the kettle on, passing the untouched, overflowing filing tray on her desk and thinking that if she left, she wouldn't have to worry about it. She scolded herself; making a decision on which job to take should not come down to a filing tray. It was, however, symptomatic of the type of work she would still be expected to do if she stayed on at Cholmondeley's. Martinson's on the other hand . . . a position as a dealer . . .

She was interrupted from her musing by the ringing of her mobile phone. It was Alex, apologising for calling out of the blue. 'Could we meet – this evening perhaps?' she asked, and much to Olivia's surprise, she found herself agreeing to catch up.

On the dot of five-thirty she reached for her coat, slipping out of the office while Elaine was on the phone.

It was a short walk to Martinson's and she arrived, somewhat breathless, for she had hurried, fifteen minutes later.

'Oh, there you are!' Jeffrey beamed to see her as she was shown into his office, coming out from behind his desk. 'I'm so pleased you could come. Let me introduce you to the team.'

Olivia shook hands with the rest of the staff members of the office, six in total, all of whom seemed friendly, and a couple who were close to her age. She blushed as Jeffrey sang her praises; it felt surprisingly good to have her qualifications taken seriously for a change.

After she'd been there for nearly half an hour, she made her excuses and left, still not quite believing that she had been offered what could turn out to be exactly what she had been dreaming of ever since leaving Australia. Alex had suggested they catch up at a pub in Soho later that evening, and so she caught the Tube to Tottenham Court Road.

Olivia was surprised to see Alex with another woman when she arrived at The Dog and Duck, and she greeted Alex, feeling somewhat awkward given the nature of their last meeting. 'How's your grandmother?' she asked politely.

'Fine I think,' Alex replied, clearly not wanting to go into detail. 'This is Juliet,' she said, introducing them. 'She used to work for Elaine.'

Juliet shook her hand, the corners of her mouth turning down at the mention of Cholmondeley's.

'Oh really?' Olivia replied. 'Then I definitely have some questions for you.'

'I thought you might have,' said Alex. 'That's why I suggested she come along.'

'Let me get a drink and we can talk. You okay?'

The women indicated their nearly full pints and so Olivia went to the bar, noticing the curved glass overhead, the chandeliers that cast shadows on the dark timber panelling.

She ordered a beer, and the barman smiled when he heard her accent. 'G'day,' he said, placing a glass on the bar. 'Aussie?'

She nodded, and then smiled back. 'Olivia. From Sydney.' She didn't know why she'd just introduced herself, but the words were out of her mouth before she even had time to think about them.

'Ben. Also from Sydney.' He made a comical face at the coincidence.

'Nice to meet you, Ben.' She lingered for a moment, drawn in by his warmth, until a man behind her cleared his throat politely.

'Oh, well, I'd better get back to my friends.'

'Catch you later, Olivia,' he said, his smile widening even further.

'So,' she said, joining Alex and Juliet at the table, and putting Ben the disarmingly attractive barman out of her mind. 'When did you work for Elaine?'

'About two years ago. I was her assistant.'

'Was there a pile of filing there then?' she joked, taking a sip of her drink.

'Only about three feet high,' said Juliet. 'I'm not even kidding.'

'I don't think it's been touched since.' Olivia laughed. 'Do you mind me asking why you left?'

'Honestly? She kept stringing me along with promises to make me a permanent member of staff, that she'd hire another assistant for both of us and that I would be allowed to build a client list of my own. I was there for nine months, and she only paid me for five of them. I gave up fighting for any holiday pay; and I couldn't afford to be sick, even for a day.'

Olivia's spirits sank. She'd had an inkling that this might be the case, but it was still depressing to hear it said out loud. 'I feel so stupid,' she said. 'I believed all of it.'

'You're not stupid – just keen. It's such a small industry and there are so few jobs.'

'And a glut of art-history graduates out there,' said Alex.

'I'm sorry,' Juliet added, 'but I thought you might want to know the truth.'

'Absolutely. And thank you. You've done me the biggest favour.'

Their conversation moved on to other things, and as Olivia got up to leave nearly an hour later, the barman caught her eye and beckoned her over.

'I'm not working tomorrow . . . that is . . . if you felt like going somewhere – perhaps a movie, or a pizza?' He looked a little awkward. 'I haven't been here long and don't really know many people. It's good to hear a familiar accent, you know?'

Olivia smiled. She did know. 'That would be nice. Do you have a pen?'

He scrabbled beneath the bar and came up with one. Olivia grabbed a beer coaster and wrote her name and number.

'Have a nice evening,' he said as she handed it to him. 'See you tomorrow?'

'Sure,' she replied, leaving the pub with a lighter step, skipping over puddles and hardly noticing the rain as it began to soak her coat. When she arrived home, and even though it was late, she rang Jeffrey Martinson.

'I'd be delighted to accept your offer,' she said.

'Then I'll bike a contract over to you first thing tomorrow.'

Olivia guessed he was counting on Elaine seeing the letterhead, but she didn't object.

～

Elaine did not take the news of Olivia's defection at all well.

Olivia arrived at work the morning after accepting Martinson's offer to find an envelope waiting on her desk with the auction house's stamp on it and addressed to her.

'Olivia!' Elaine bellowed from her office. 'Is that you?'

Olivia set down her bag before greeting her boss. 'Yes Elaine, good morning.' Her voice sounded far calmer than she felt.

'What the bloody hell has Jeffrey sent you? Hmm?' She narrowed her eyes suspiciously at Olivia.

'I believe it's a contract,' said Olivia blandly.

'A contract?'

It gave Olivia the greatest pleasure to tell Elaine that she had been offered a paid position at her biggest rival, and a much more senior one at that. 'I'm afraid I will not be staying on. And as I am not an employee,' she added, 'I don't believe I owe a notice period. If it's all right with you I should like to wrap up my internship this morning.'

351

'Ungrateful little madam,' Elaine spluttered as Olivia's words sunk in.

'I have no wish to leave on bad terms,' said Olivia, pretending she hadn't heard Elaine's remarks. 'No doubt we'll see each other in the future. Jeffrey simply made me a very fair offer.'

'But I had offered you a position here,' she replied. 'Only yesterday. Or have you forgotten that?'

'I met Juliet Ashby last night.'

'Juliet who?'

'Juliet Ashby. She worked for you two years ago. She told me that you made her very similar promises, but that you never followed them through. I'm sure she's not the only starry-eyed graduate you've taken advantage of in this way.'

'I have a living to make, a business to run,' said Elaine, her voice rising. 'Do you think this place pays for itself?' She looked skywards at the chandelier that hung, glittering, above her, gestured to the expensive furniture.

'With all respect, I too have a living to make. I am of course thankful for the internship, but I know that you got as much out of it as I did. I'm sure we will see each other in the future, but for now I'll say goodbye, Elaine.'

Olivia calmly collected the few personal items from her desk, took a last glance at the tower of filing and only just refrained from skipping out of the office.

THIRTY

London, 2000

I t was one of the most anticipated sales of the year. Olivia had spent the days leading up to it fending off enquiries from newspapers and radio stations, as well as ensuring that as many potential buyers as possible were aware that the fox-girl, unseen for more than twenty years, was to be offered.

Beatrix had come up from the country specially for it, and Olivia met her at Paddington station. She was wearing her fur and had styled her hair underneath a neat felt trilby, a look of keen excitement shining from her face.

'You look lovely,' said Olivia after she and Beatrix had embraced each other. 'Let's find a cab and we can go to the office. Jeffrey's dying to meet you, and we're all so excited for this.'

'Oh, so am I,' said Beatrix, taking Olivia's arm as they walked towards the taxi rank.

'Now, darling, how are you getting on?' Beatrix asked after they had settled themselves in the taxi. 'You look a good sight happier than when I first met you, I have to say. Is that due to working at Martinson's, or something else?' She regarded Olivia shrewdly.

'Martinson's is wonderful,' said Olivia with a wide smile. 'We've got some very interesting pieces coming through. Some in tonight's auction, actually. It's our biggest Asian art sale of the year.' She pulled a glossy catalogue out of her bag and handed it to Beatrix. 'I've marked the page for you.'

Beatrix opened the booklet and turned to the back.

'There are the others, and then the fox-girl is the final item – we've got at least six interested parties, at my last count, so we should have a very competitive auction and get you the result you're hoping for.'

'Oh, look at her,' said Beatrix wistfully.

'It's hard to give up something so precious to you,' said Olivia, placing a hand on Beatrix's arm.

'A little sad, that's all.' She squared her shoulders. 'But I know Jack would understand. We met at a time when I didn't think I would ever fall in love, didn't really even want to. But then he came along and everything changed. This was the first gift he ever gave me and I didn't manage to hold onto it for five minutes before I lost it for another thirty years. Got it back in the end, though,' she winked at Olivia.

'I've never asked how long you and Jack were married.' Olivia said.

Beatrix shook her head. 'We got engaged as soon as he came to England, and married a month later – there was no sense in waiting in those days. We had five wonderful years together, though it was not nearly long enough, by anyone's standards. The POW camps left so many men in poor health, including Jack and Archie – but at least they were lucky enough to survive.'

'Oh, I assumed Archie died in the war?' Olivia asked, confused by Beatrix's words.

'He might as well have done. He came back, but he was a different man. Never recovered from the beatings, nor the illness. Many lost husbands, sweethearts, fathers, friends . . . to all intents and purposes I lost my brother. War is a frightful thing, darling, absolutely frightful.' She paused, a faraway look in her eyes. 'I was a widow for a long time, until I met Willy, and by then I was tired of being on my own. He was a good man, but I'm afraid to say I never felt about him the way I did about Jack.'

'First love?' Olivia asked, remembering an experience of her own.

'Much more than that. Still, I counted myself fortunate to have Thomas. Spitting image of his father. Though he's so far away now.'

Olivia remembered the photograph on the mantlepiece in the bedroom at Pelham House, the young man so like the drawing in Beatrix's sketchbook.

They lapsed into silence for the rest of the journey.

Beatrix brightened considerably when they arrived at the office and Jeffrey presented her with a glass of champagne.

'I thought we could go to Bibendum for lunch,' he suggested. 'You like oysters, I hope?'

'Certainly. How splendid.'

After lunch, Olivia took Beatrix to her hotel, promising to return for her later.

'The auction starts at six sharp,' Olivia said, leaving Beatrix in the lobby. 'You can sit at the back and watch the proceedings. It's probably better that no one in the room knows you're there,' she added.

'Don't worry,' said Beatrix. 'I love a good blood sport. And I've got a huge pair of sunglasses.'

～

That afternoon, Olivia and some of the other Martinson's staff made sure everything had been triple-checked, and that all the last-minute jobs had been completed. The artworks had been transferred from Martinson's secure storage facility to the saleroom and each one thoroughly examined and crossed off against the catalogue as they were assembled in the order of the auction. All the phone lines were tested, and the extra staff and security needed for the sale were carefully briefed. Jeffrey was to act as auctioneer, and Olivia checked that his gavel was in place at the lectern at the front of the room, together with a copy of the catalogue and his notes. Finally, she ran a sound-check on the microphone. She wasn't leaving anything to chance.

Just before five, Olivia left to collect Beatrix and found her waiting in the hotel lobby.

'I tried to rest, but I'm far too nervous,' she said, greeting Olivia with a kiss to both cheeks.

'Me too,' Olivia admitted. 'But it's a good kind of nervous, yes?'

'I think so. Come on then, Liv, or we'll be late.'

'Liv?' She raised her eyebrows at Beatrix.

'And it's about time you called me Bea. My friends always do.'

~

The saleroom was abuzz with men in dark suits and women in fluttering dresses and velvet blazers or tweeds and felt hats, gossiping as they flipped through the auction catalogue. Bea and Olivia slipped through the door unnoticed and although it was standing room only, Olivia found Bea a reserved seat towards the rear.

'Are you sure you'll be okay? I can sit with you if you like,' Olivia reassured her.

'Nonsense. I've survived far worse than this, my dear. Off you go.' Bea waved her away.

Olivia went to the front of the saleroom, smiling distractedly at the assembled staff, and then to where Jeffrey was waiting.

'All set?' she asked.

He checked his watch, nodded and walked over to the lectern to take up his position. He called for silence, and gradually the noise diminished and everyone found a seat.

Olivia stood to one side, observing the crowd as Jeffrey introduced the proceedings. There was a ripple of applause as he announced the first lot. She glanced towards the back of the room, searching for Bea, her smile widening in surprise as she saw the smartly dressed woman sitting next to her.

Lucy.

She'd come to be with her friend.

Bidding was initially cautious, but as the pace picked up, Olivia was pleased to see that almost all the items listed surpassed their reserve prices, some going for far greater sums than Jeffrey had predicted. After each lot, he banged his gavel and the applause grew in volume. The atmosphere in the room became tense as the final few – and most expensive – pieces came up.

At around seven o'clock, Jeffrey announced: 'And now we have one of the rarest and finest examples of eighteenth-century netsuke ever seen. Missing for many years, we are delighted to offer this highly collectable little treasure for sale.' A scattershot of flash bulbs went off and there were audible intakes of breath as the fox-girl was brought forward, magnified on a screen behind him. 'May I have an opening bid?'

Olivia held her breath as the room fell silent.

'Shall we start at eighty thousand pounds?'

Silence. No one wanted to be the first to make a move. Then, out of the corner of her eye, she saw a man in the third row raise his hand.

'Eighty thousand pounds,' said Jeffrey. 'I'll take an offer of ninety? Will anyone give me ninety?'

One of the staff manning the phones raised her hand, and suddenly the bidding was off and away and Olivia found she could barely keep up with the avalanche of bids that came from around the room and via the phones.

Offers stalled at a hundred and thirty-five thousand pounds, but then the woman on the phone indicated an offer of a hundred and forty. All of the bidders except two – both phone bidders – were eliminated, and the room watched on, fascinated, as the battle continued.

'Two hundred thousand pounds,' Jeffrey said eventually as one of the phone bidders raised her hand again. 'Any further bids?'

The other continued to whisper into the handset, but shook her head.

'Sold!' he cried, banging his gavel for a final time. 'The fox-girl netsuke sold to bidder number forty-five, for two hundred thousand pounds.'

A wave of excited chatter and clapping swept the room as Jeffrey thanked everyone for coming and closed the auction.

Olivia glanced at her watch, working out the time in Australia. She had told her father the story of coming across the fox-girl not long after she returned from Ireland, and she couldn't wait to tell him the result of the sale.

'It's a record price,' she whispered to Bea after almost everyone had left the room. 'Certainly enough to fix a leaky roof.'

~

Champagne flowed again that night, as Olivia, Bea, Lucy, Jeffrey and several other Martinson's staff piled into a wine bar across the road from the auction rooms.

'To Beatrix,' Jeffrey toasted.

'To the fox-girl,' replied Bea, raising her glass.

'Are you allowed to say who placed the winning bid?' Olivia asked quietly, seeing Bea caught up in conversation with Lucy.

'I'll wager you'll be as interested in the underbidder as well,' Jeffrey said cryptically.

'Who?'

Her eyes stood out on stalks as he whispered two names.

'Can I tell her?'

He shrugged. 'I don't see why not.'

Later, after emptying several bottles of Clicquot and seeing that some of the members of the party were flagging, Olivia offered to escort Bea and Lucy back to their hotel.

'Nonsense, darling, you've done quite enough already,' said Bea, draining her glass and getting unsteadily to her feet.

'It's really no trouble.' Olivia finally convinced Bea to let her call a cab. 'It's practically on my way home,' she argued as she opened the door for them. She was waiting for the right moment to broach the subject of the winning bidder, not to mention the name of the underbidder, and when they arrived at the hotel she still hadn't managed to break into Bea's and Lucy's ceaseless, back-and-forth conversation.

'Join us for a nightcap?' Bea asked as Olivia paid for the taxi. 'We're simply not ready to go to bed yet.'

'I've got to work in the morning,' Olivia protested.

'I think Jeffrey might allow a little leeway, don't you?' she asked, a smile playing about her lips.

'Okay,' Olivia found herself agreeing. 'Just one.' She had been on a high from the success of the sale but could feel all the nervous energy now seeping out of her like air from a balloon. 'Besides, there's something you might – actually you both might – be interested to know.'

The three women found a cosy banquette in the hotel bar and Lucy ordered a double scotch for everyone. 'Plenty of ice, please.'

They were about to toast the result again, when Olivia seized the moment.

'So, would you like to know who bought the fox-girl?'

Bea looked suddenly uncertain. 'Would I? I'm not sure, actually.'

'Oh, yes,' cried Lucy. 'Do tell us.'

Olivia looked from one to the other, and Bea slowly nodded.

'Well, the underbidder was Harold Byrne.'

'What?' gasped Bea.

'The bloody nerve!' said Lucy.

'Of course,' said Bea as the news sank in. 'He wanted it at any price. The only thing that man is – has always been – interested in is owning things, having them for himself.'

'Well, as I said, he was the underbidder,' Olivia said gleefully.

'So, who did make the winning bid?'

'Plum.'

'Plum?' Bea echoed.

'What on earth!'

'According to Jeffrey, she had a pretty good idea that Harold would be likely to bid for it, and she wanted to make sure he wouldn't succeed, even if it meant having to bid against him.'

'Bloody hell,' said Bea.

'I always said we underestimated her,' added Lucy.

~

Six weeks later, Olivia stepped off the train at Pewsey, seeing the fuzz of green on bare branches, the silky buds of pussy willow, and everywhere bursts of cheerful daffodils peeping from beneath the trees. The light was gentler, a breath of spring in the air, and she felt the anticipation of it everywhere. The countryside looked entirely different than it had on her first encounter.

She stood outside the station, casting about for Bea, and as she turned to her right she saw Bea's car thundering along the road before screeching to a halt. She picked up her bag with one hand, her other going to the netsuke around her neck. Bea had invited her for the weekend – 'Bring your sketchbook, we can paint *en plein air*; everything is looking quite beautiful.' – and Olivia couldn't wait to see her.

'Darling!' Bea greeted her with enthusiasm, her hair wild and a wide grin lighting up her face.

Stowing her luggage in the boot, Olivia climbed into the passenger seat and they set off. 'How are you?'

'Never better. And you?' Bea flashed her an enquiring look, nearly veering off the narrow road.

Olivia wondered briefly if they would get to Pelham House in one piece, and let out a sigh of relief as they turned through the back gates. The gardens were transformed from the former bleak and wintry landscape to a sea of yellow and white.

'Did you plant all of these yourself?' Olivia asked.

'Most of them,' said Bea, gunning the car along the drive. 'They're perennials; come up again year after year. Some people are the same,' she added wryly. 'Can't keep them down for long.'

They drew up at the house, and Olivia just had time to notice the framework of scaffolding on the roof before several dogs raced out to greet them.

'It's been quite a job!' Bea shouted over the cacophony of barking. 'But they're nearly done. To be honest,' she confided, 'it's been rather nice to have the workmen's company. Lovely chaps.'

Olivia bent down to greet the dogs, recognising Bertie and Bette.

Later, Olivia took her bags up to the nursery – 'It's still the warmest room in the house.' – and returned with a bottle of Jameson in one hand and a small box in the other. There was no sign of Bea, so she placed both on the kitchen table, before going to the window. There, in the garden, the old woman kneeled, furiously pulling up weeds from an overgrown bed. She looked up, as if sensing Olivia, and waved.

'Thought I'd attack this before I forgot to,' she said as Olivia went out to see her.

The woman never seemed to stop; she had the energy of someone half her age.

'Shall I put the kettle on?' Olivia suggested.

'Oh Liv, that would be terrific. I shan't be long,' said Bea, pushing her hair out of her eyes and inadvertently smearing herself with mud.

'Good, because I've got something for you,' said Olivia before turning back to the house.

'Oh darling, really you didn't need to bring anything,' said Bea coming into the kitchen a few minutes later and seeing the bottle on the table. 'But I do love a good drop.'

'I know, and I wanted to. Besides, there's something else, but it's not from me.'

'Oh? Shall I go and clean up first? Shan't be long.'

Olivia spooned leaves into the teapot and poured the hot water over them, trying to quell her impatience. She'd had the box in her possession for nearly a week, and was practically busting to see Bea's reaction when she opened it.

Finally, Bea bustled back into the room.

'What's this?' she asked, picking up the box.

'Why don't you open it?'

'All right, but I'm parched. Has that tea brewed yet?'

Olivia nodded and poured it into two china cups, setting them on the table before standing back and looking pointedly at Bea. 'Go on, then.'

'The tea or the box?' Bea asked, a mischievous light in her pale blue eyes.

'Bea!'

'All right, all right,' she grumbled good-naturedly.

Olivia held her breath as Bea opened the box.

'But I don't understand . . .' She looked at Olivia and then the contents of the box again.

'Plum wanted you to have it. A last reunion, of sorts, she said. She told me she knew that it meant far more to you than to her. That it had been yours all along.'

For once, Bea was lost for words.

Acknowledgements

I first came across netsuke – the small, intricately carved Japanese toggles – several decades ago while briefly temping as a secretary at a London art dealer's in its Asian and Far East department. I was immediately fascinated by the craftsmanship, by their variety and beauty. I began to think about a story that might centre around the theft of a rare netsuke.

As I began to research, I read of the Women's Auxiliary Service (Burma): a group of around 250 English, Australian and Canadian women who were originally recruited as cipherettes (encoders) in Burma in the Second World War, but later re-formed to run mobile and static canteens for troops on the frontline, fighting what became known as 'The Forgotten War'.

The Wasbies, as they were called, worked closer to the frontline than any other women's service, for anything up to sixteen hours a day, battling mosquitoes and mud, often under machine-gun fire and the threat of bombing. They offered tea and cake – 'char and wads' – and all manner of other small luxuries and necessities that helped ease the life of a soldier fighting far from home in the dense jungle. More than that, these formidable women proved invaluable in boosting the morale of the troops. They were mentioned in dispatches for their courage, and several were awarded the OBE and MBE after the war.

Unfortunately, very little information about them exists, and I am very grateful to two books in particular, *Front Line and Fortitude* by EJ Lockhart-Mure (do seek it out if you would like to read a first-hand account of the experiences of Jeanne Elspeth (Maria) Pilbrow MBE, who served in the Wasbies), and *Chinthe Women* by Sally and Lucy Jaffé. I am also extremely grateful to have had the chance to speak to Elsa Hatfield, who is still alive and thriving in Melbourne, and who has such clear and proud memories of her time as a Wasbie.

The Imperial War Museum's oral histories, especially those of Elaine Cheverton, Fleurette Pelly, Jean Patricia Wythe and Michael Anthony Demetriadi were also invaluable, as were many harrowing first-hand accounts of soldiers who survived as prisoners of war building the Thai–Burma railway.

In the course of my research, I read a short paragraph describing one woman's terror at being left alone with an American soldier, noting that she had to do some fast thinking and swift talking to get out of the situation with her virtue intact and was extremely shaken by the encounter. I began to wonder what might have happened had the situation had a different outcome.

As I discovered these intrepid, adaptable and purposefully cheerful women who simply rolled up their sleeves and got on with it, supporting each other through the worst of times, I saw how important their friendship was, and I endeavoured to imbue this novel with that spirit.

Fiction is about what is possible, not what is actual; my imagining of the events is exactly that – an imagining and not based on an actual event. All incidents and dialogue and all characters, with the exception of a few, are products of my imagination and are not to be construed as real. Where real-life people do appear, the situations, incidents and dialogue concerning them are entirely fictional and are not intended to depict actual events. In all other respects, any resemblance to persons living or dead is entirely coincidental.

hachette
AUSTRALIA

If you would like to find out more about Hachette Australia,
our authors, upcoming events and new releases you can visit
our website or our social media channels:

hachette.com.au

 HachetteAustralia

 HachetteAus